The Stars Would Curse Us

Book One

Stephanie Combs
& Valerie Rivers

Midnight Tide
PUBLISHING

Copyright © 2024 by Silverflame Books LLC

All rights reserved.

No part of this book may be reproduced in any form or by any electronic or mechanical means, including information storage and retrieval systems, without written permission from the authors, except for the use of brief quotations in a book review.

The story, all names, characters, and incidents portrayed in this book are fictitious. No identification with actual persons (living or deceased), places, buildings, and products is intended or should be inferred.

Published by Midnight Tide Publishing

www.midnighttidepublishing.com

Cover illustrations and design by Valerie Rivers

Character art by Valerie Rivers

Map by Gustavo L. Schmitt

Developmental/Copy/Line Editor - Rachel Bunner
Email: rachels.top.edits@gmail.com
Instagram: @rachels.top.edits

1st edition 2024

Paperback ISBN: 978-1-958673-60-7

Hardcover ISBN: 978-1-958673-61-4

Content Note

This story contains content that could be sensitive for some readers. The main characters are faced with death, violence, and attempted assault. Please note that there are also references to children dying (off page), minor domestic abuse to side characters, and victim blaming. There is also mild (non-graphic) sexual content.

Courts of Esterra

Court of Water - Argenti
Court of Fire - Aurum
Court of Earth - Aereus
Court of Air (abandoned) - Adamas (extinct)

Pronunciation Guide

Characters

Aella - AY-luh
Arianwen - Ah-ree-AHN-wen
Viera - Vee-AIR-ah
Kaleidos - Kal-eye-dos
Wynn - WIN

Elemental Fae Races

Argenti - Ar-JEN-tee - water elementals/silver skin
Aurum - OR-um - fire elementals/gold skin
Aereus - AIR-ee-us - earth elementals/bronze skin
Adamas - Uh-DOM-us - air elementals/opalescent ivory skin

Places

Esterra - Eh-STAIR-uh
Iveria - Eye-VEER-ee-uh
Prisma - PRIZ-muh
Zephyria - Zeh-FEAR-ee-uh
Ilithania - IL-ih-THEY-nee-uh
Easthen Forest - EAS-then Forest

Esterra

Dedication

For the ones who went their whole lives waiting for permission to chase their dreams, this is it.

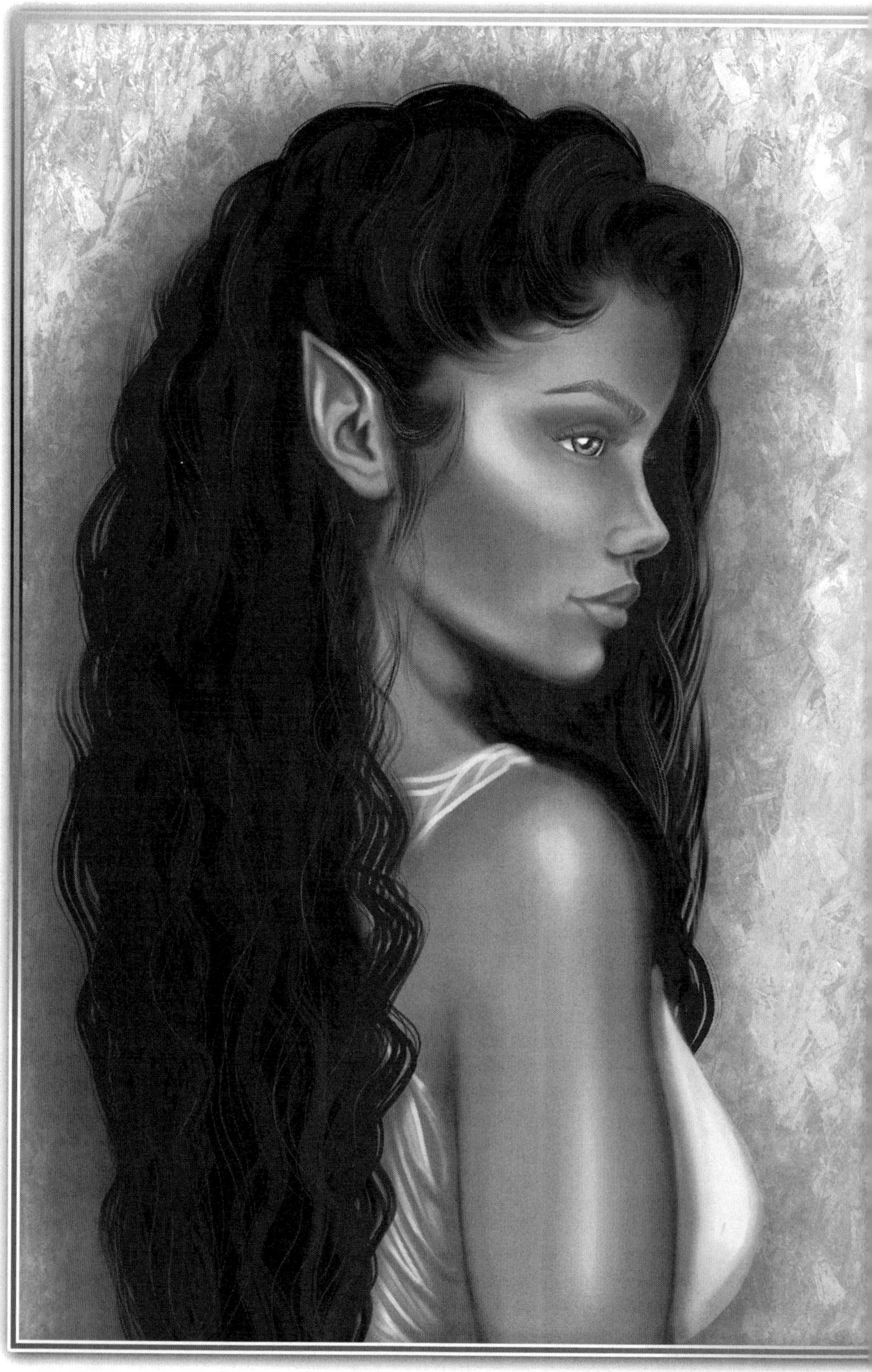

The Prophecy

Born of great defiance
Marked by the stars
Truth no longer silenced
The choice will be hers

Born of courts united
Illusions will crumble
One will rise to power
A mighty kingdom tumbled

Born with powers
Past wrongs to be righted
Stars grant their blessing
Once separate, now united

Born under cloak of night
A glimmer of hope shines
End of a kingdom's might
When the stars align

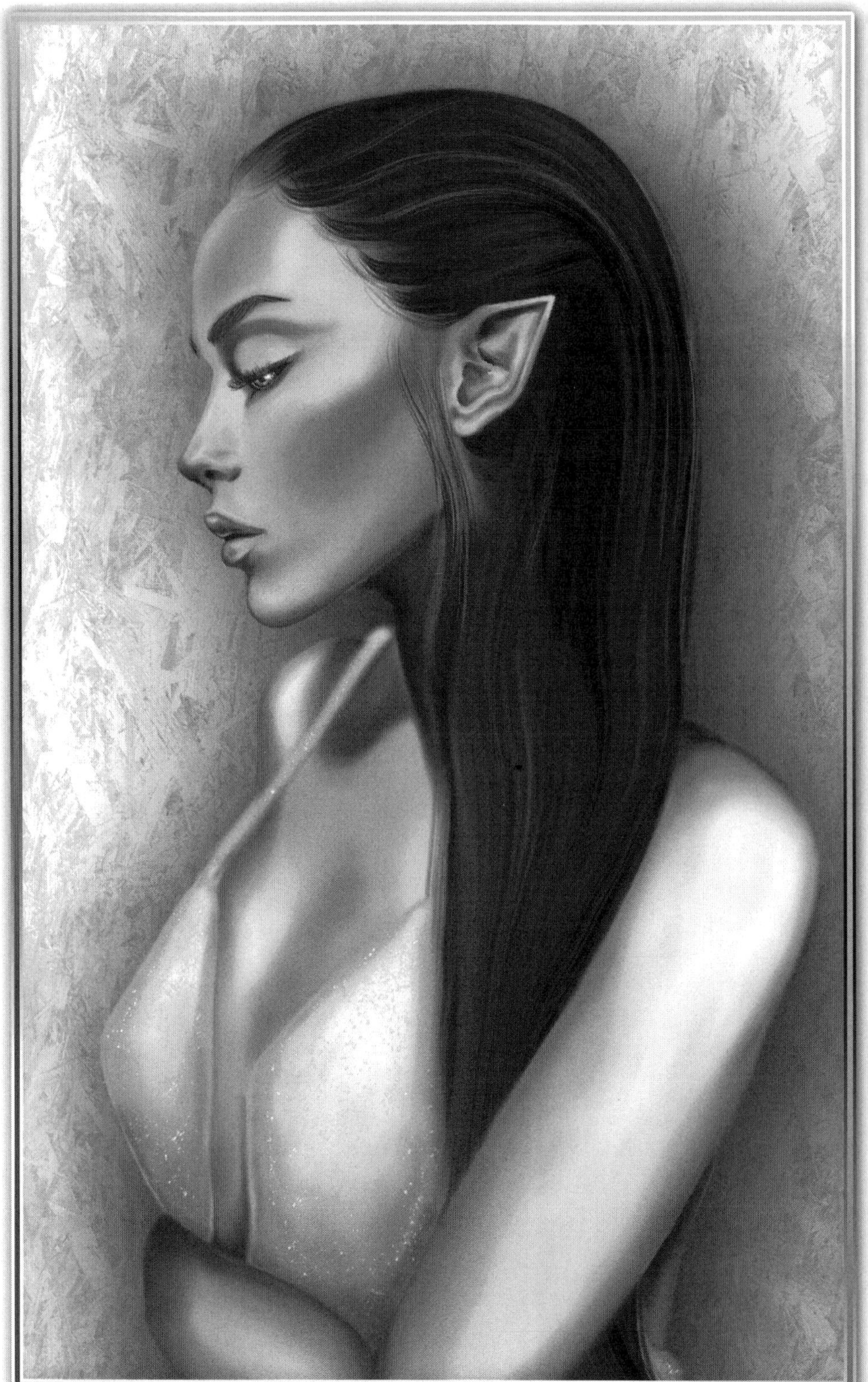

PROLOGUE

They thrived on chaos, death, and destruction. Reveling in our demise.

The roar of the crowd reverberated through the air, thousands of feet thundering against the stands. Their jeers and rallying cries rained down upon us like fuel for hounds in a race. But rather than ignite my spirit, they left me downtrodden and demoralized.

The faces of my friends and family flashed before my eyes, their presence anchoring me to hope. Memories of them, like a lifeline, were all I had left. I had no other options. I had to fight, I had to survive, for them. Driven by love and determination, I battled on.

All I could do was cling to the knowledge that the Iris would not kill us all, and to the unlikely chance that we might make it through this final event. But perhaps death would be a small mercy.

My throat tightened and my eyes burned with tears as I clung to the side of the rock, my hands coated in blood and sweat. If my muscles gave out, I would not survive the fall.

The cloudless sky stretched above me, and in the darkness, I could not see any stars. They had abandoned us.

Chapter 1
Iveria by the Sea

Aella

"Don't you want to be chosen?" my fifteen-year-old sister, Mila, asked me, excitement in her voice. "You might have a real chance to go to Prisma and marry not just any Iris noble... but the prince! Oh, Aella, I heard he's lovelier than a sunset!" She preened in front of the mirror, her voice sweet and dreamlike. "Radiant like a pearl! I heard he even carries Adamas blood and can harness the power of air."

"Unlikely," I said, rolling my eyes.

Mila continued, ignoring my comment. "If only I were old enough for the draft this year. I'd give anything for the chance to gaze upon his shimmering face every day. What a life I would live as a princess, riding around town in one of those crystal boxes, dressed in the finest clothing with sparkling jewels in my hair." She carefully threaded seashells into her hair, weaving it into one of those elaborate meshwork of braids she was so good at.

During a typical draft, they only drew ten names from all of Esterra. The City of Iveria—where I lived—had an immense population, so the odds of me being chosen were relatively slim, and most of us made it through our mating seasons without being selected.

"I would live in the Palatium Crystalis. I bet just my bathroom would be bigger than our entire house." Mila giggled. "And the best part? I sure as mud would never have to share a bed with your fishy feet in my face again!"

I grimaced looking down at my toes.

"You're so lucky you get to be in the drawing this year." She sighed. "There probably won't be another one like this for . . . oh, I don't know, maybe a hundred years!"

I couldn't help zoning out as Mila continued fantasizing about life in the Palatium Crystalis. I didn't feel like talking about the draft or romanticizing the people who controlled our lives. And even though being a part of the prince's draft was likely a once-in-a-lifetime opportunity, I did not feel lucky. The last thing I wanted was to be anywhere near an Iris, let alone the royal family. I began pacing in the cramped room, squatting to pick up my scalloped seashell off the floor. I rubbed my fingers over its contour, the rugged outer texture smooth from years of handling. I sighed as I sat on the edge of the bed and stared at it.

Tonight would be my dawning ceremony, held to mark my transition into adulthood. It was an event few females looked forward to. Sure, the party would be plenty of fun, but it was what came after that I dreaded. By the break of dawn, I would be twenty-five, officially of age, and that meant either being drafted into marriage with an Iris noble or accepting an arranged marriage to another Argenti fae from the Court of Water like myself. Neither option was great because I had no choice in the matter either way. Whether I liked it or not, at the end of the year, I would become someone's wife, and then a mother, and my life would no longer be my own. The idea made me shiver.

I tucked the seashell safely under my pillow and stepped behind Mila to check that my hair was secure. I needed to get started on my chores soon so that I could finish in time for my dawning. My mother had assigned me an extensive set of new tasks to master in order to prepare me to run my own household after marriage. It felt overwhelming to have so much added responsibility, but as a wife, I would be expected to do all the cooking and cleaning until I had children of my own to assist with the labor.

My first task of the day was to practice haggling skills above the surface, and since the markets were about to open, I couldn't delay.

"Have you even heard a word I've been saying?" Mila accused with an incredulous look as she noticed my far-off gaze.

"Oh, yes, Mila, you're right. You're absolutely right! I should be so lucky!" I kissed her knitted brow. "Gotta swim! And don't worry, I'll make sure my toes are extra fishy just for you when I get back!" I teased.

Scoffing, she threw her slipper at me. Her near-perfect aim at my head suddenly angled to the left, as if a strong current had blown it off-course. In dead silence, Mila and I shared a knowing glance before I darted out of the room.

△

The fastest way to the surface was a swim, so I exited through the mudroom where our family's magic kept the water from entering the open door. It was like stepping through a bubble into a wall of water. The water was icy cold, so I didn't mind using my powers to help me reach the more temperate surface faster.

The closer I got to the top, the warmer the waters became, and they grew more crowded with Argenti fae hustling and bustling about. After climbing the stairs out of the water, I used my magic to will the moisture to leave my clothes and hair. My thin garments normally dried quickly in the sun, but it was not yet high enough in the sky. Water snaked down my arms and legs into a puddle on the ground, and within moments, I was dry.

As I made my way to the markets, I watched a large vessel approach one of the docks to the south. It was an envoy from Prisma by the looks of it. Its pristine sails and gold-plated figurehead were a dead giveaway. The prow of the ship was adorned with a female; her magnificent, feathered wings framed the ship's bow, and her eyes were set with two sizable gemstones. In her raised hands was a silver circlet with a triangle-shaped crystal set in the center acting as a prism.

The whole ship was awe-inspiring, but what should have been a symbol of unity and life seemed to lose its significance while being wielded by the Iris. Despite how much they'd claimed to do for us, it had never actually felt that way. If anything, Iveria—really, all of Esterra—felt more divided by the ruling class than unified. Many in our city fought starvation and homelessness. The Iris turned a blind eye to our needs, only focusing on what they could get out of us. I wondered if it was like that in the great city of Prisma.

A bell rang to signal the opening of the markets, so I hurried along, eager to get my chores out of the way. Once in the markets, I was elated to see Viera. She was a month older than me and preparing for marriage just like myself.

Viera had a magnetism that drew people in. Heads turned as she strolled along the outskirts of the market, her hair rippling in the wind. It cascaded down her back in luscious waves, blending to a light silver as it caught the sunlight. She was lovely to look at, with delicate features, silver skin with a bluish-green tint, and freckles scattering her nose like stardust. It was not just her physical appearance, even the way she moved evoked an ethereal fluid grace. She was water made female.

Viera lived in a grand mansion, half above and half below the sea. It was practically a castle in comparison to where I'd grown up. Her family was a part of the small percentage of well-off Argenti who worked closely with the Iris Guardians who governed our city. It was silly that she was even in the markets since her family had a full staff in their household who would normally perform those duties. But tradition was important to our people, and even the wealthier among us understood the value of maintaining it. Viera ran toward me, the ends of her macrame dress fluttering behind her.

"Did you see the ship?" she asked, her voice animated. "My parents are meeting with them today."

"Do you think it's about the draft?" I asked.

"No doubt!" She leaned in close, whispering, "I overheard my parents speaking last night about Prince Kaleidos. They said the number of candidates in his marriage draft is going to be tripled! That means *ten* females from *each* element! And this might sound a little bit crazy, but they may be choosing the names with more discrimination this time."

"I thought it was supposed to be random!" I blurted out a bit louder than I should have. Quickly hushing myself, I asked, "Do you know what they're looking for?"

"You know how the Iris are known for being vain. My parents have seen it first-hand. They're probably only going to choose the most attractive females."

Fear hit me like a ton of sand.

"Oh, Viera, I can't bear to lose you. You're my truest friend!"

"I'm not going anywhere," she said with confidence. "I doubt they would draw my name anyway, considering my parents' close ties to the Iris. It's actually *you* I'm worried about."

"Me?" I almost laughed.

"Don't think I haven't noticed the way males stumble when they walk by you," she said with a smirk. She wrapped her arm around my shoulder and squeezed me from the side as we began to cross the boardwalk.

"I'm sure it's only because I'm standing next to you," I replied with a sidelong glance, brows raised. "But how would they even know who to select when drawing the names? It's not like they keep a list of all of Iveria's citizens with beauty rankings next to them."

"I'm not sure, but I'll let you know if I learn anything else. I promise," she said.

Viera and I had known each other from a young age, as my mother performed healing work for her family over the years. Even as a baby strapped to her bosom, I'd accompanied my mother on most of her house calls, since she had never trusted anyone else to watch over me. I was thankful for that, because if it weren't for her style of parenting, I never would have met my best friend.

As we made our stops around the market, Viera's haggling skills were on proud display. She had a way with people, possibly due to her confidence or the command in her voice. Growing up the way she had, she'd seen her mother order enough people around. People didn't play games when they knew you meant business. While I tried my best to emulate her bargaining methods, I hadn't quite mastered the "*I don't really need this*" attitude as well as Viera. But although my deals weren't as favorable as hers, I was content enough with my trades. As I was about to head back home, Viera stopped me.

"Before I forget, stop by my house tonight before your dawning. I have a surprise for you!" she crooned with a sparkle in her bright turquoise eyes.

△

Wealthier Argenti like Viera would be permitted to rest most of the day in preparation for their dawning ceremonies. I did not have that luxury. After returning from the market, I had to forage for edible crustaceans in the seagrass, which required quite a swim from home. Anything closer had been completely picked clean by the locals. I spent a good couple of hours after that scraping barnacles and tubeworms off the exterior of our home.

My parents had a modest dawning ceremony planned for me. Beginning at dusk, we would be celebrating until dawn. Typically, I would have been excited about an event such as that, but I found myself somewhat rushed and underprepared. It also didn't help that I was exhausted from all the day's chores.

"Aella," my mother called out from the hallway as she rushed around our home making last-minute preparations for the night ahead. "You might want to hurry up if you're going to be on time for your celebration. Dusk is in less than an hour, and it's a twenty-minute swim from here."

"Yes, Mother! I'm about ready!"

I looked at myself in the mirror one last time before heading out. I wondered if I'd feel differently tomorrow. My body had changed a lot in only a year's time, and I couldn't help noticing the difference in the way others gazed at me. I'd been used to people staring, but this was different. They had gone from examining me like a rare specimen to looking at me with hunger in their eyes.

There had always been something unique about my appearance. Nothing I could quite put a finger on, but people couldn't seem to help themselves from noticing me. I'd learned to keep my eyes down—a skill I'd practiced from an early age to avoid attracting too much unwanted attention. *"Better to blend in,"* my mother had always said.

As far as I was concerned, I was attractive enough but not a great beauty like Viera. My skin was a light silver with a slightly blue hue to it. Many Argenti had blue, green, or lavender tints in their silver coloring, making for a decent camouflage underwater. My eyes stood out, a deep blue with tiny flecks of silver, and I had long dark hair which I usually wore in a wide fishtail braid that graced the length of my back. My hair gave me a sense of security, acting as a sort of armor.

For the dawning, I wore a long, seafoam green dress made from seaweed linen that hugged my curves and then pooled on the ground around my feet. It was slightly off the shoulders with a scalloped neckline and long, elegantly angled sleeves that covered my hands. The dress was embellished with tiny seashells and pieces of coral. It was sophisticated, if not maybe a little mature for my taste, but it was nicer than anything I'd ever tried on. We could never have afforded something like that. One of my mother's clients had given it to her as a hand-me-down when she'd heard about my dawning ceremony. The only problem was that I had no idea how I would swim in it, let alone dance in it, because it was way too long for my petite stature.

My mother walked in, and upon seeing me, she stopped, tears beading her eyes. She took a deep breath, blinking rapidly.

"It's a little long. I'm sorry I didn't have time to alter it."

"It's more than I could have asked for. Thank you, Mother." I fingered the back of my neck in a soothing way to calm my nerves.

She got to work pulling the sleeves back on themselves—until my hands peeked out of the shorter ends of the belled sleeves—and made a few quick stitches.

"There. Much better. You'll just have to hold the skirts while dancing."

I kissed her on the cheek. "I'm going to meet up with Viera first, and then I'll head to the lagoon."

"Don't be late, Aella!" Her head tilted and she raised an eyebrow. I didn't have the best track record with punctuality, as I often underestimated how long things would take. As I ran out, I heard my mother rounding up my six younger brothers and sisters—the youngest of them was five—making sure they were all dressed appropriately.

Being the eldest, I was expected to set a good example and gracefully accept my fate with enthusiasm. It didn't feel like something to celebrate though. I was just starting to figure out who I was and what I liked, and suddenly, because I was of age, I had to give it all up for a mate? My mother couldn't possibly understand. She'd embraced her role as wife and mother and expected the same from me.

△

I needed help getting to Viera's since I couldn't very well swim in the dress, so my mother said I could use Stella. Stella was a pretty, light pink seahorse with a tiny coronet. She eyed me with suspicion when I brought the saddle and harness over to her. Stella only really liked my mother and tended to buck me and my siblings off during riding practice. It wasn't her fault though. She had been abused before my mother rescued her, so it was only natural for her to be skittish with other riders. Besides, not all Argenti were made equally when it came to our affinity toward sea creatures. I was determined to win her over regardless.

"I brought you something special from the market," I told her as I held out a big, juicy shrimp. Sheepishly, she sniffed toward my hand before quickly gobbling it up. She whinnied then nuzzled her snout against my palm, allowing me to pet her and apply her harness.

Please don't buck me off.

I hiked up my skirts a bit before climbing into the saddle, and within an instant, she bolted. My hair and my dress whipped behind me as I hung on for dear life.

Before long, we made it to Viera's. After securing Stella, I stepped out from the underwater stables. As I emerged, my friend ran down from her house, her eyes swollen as though she'd just been crying.

"What's wrong?" I asked.

"Come, we have to hurry. It's almost dusk!" she said with a forced smile plastered to her face.

"Viera!"

"I'll tell you about it later," she whispered. "Come, come!"

I urged the water on me to return to the sea and followed her inside. We entered Viera's massive bed chambers, and she took me over to her vanity. Although I was now dry, my hair was a complete mess from the wild ride.

"For your dawning." Viera presented me with a gorgeous tiara made from starfish and tiny pearls.

My eyes widened in disbelief. "I couldn't possibly accept this."

"Please, I want you to have it."

"V, this is way too much."

"What do you think I did with all the extra coin I had left after haggling today? It's really no big deal! Here, let me help you." She started to undo my braid for me, and I quickly spun out of her reach.

"I've got it!" I said.

She gave me a slightly offended look, then turned toward the doors.

While I unbraided and untangled my hair, I asked her, "What happened earlier, V? Are you okay?"

"I'll tell you about it tomorrow," she said. "I don't want to spoil your night."

"You are not going to spoil my night." I took her hand and looked her directly in the eyes. "Viera, it's all right, really. I can't go the whole night not knowing what upset you like this. Please, just tell me."

She inhaled deeply then lowered her voice. "Some of the officials from Prisma were here this afternoon." Her voice cracked. "They took my brother. He's going to the capital to join the royal forces. I might never see him again, A. You know they never come back from Prisma." Her eyes locked onto mine as though she were looking for answers.

"But what about your parents' status? Can't they stop this?" I asked.

"My father is proud. And having his son involved in the royal forces improves his status with the Iris even more, so he won't fight it," she said, her voice going flat. Tears welled up in her eyes again. "I heard my mother screaming. They never come back, Aella. They never come back," she sobbed.

"Oh, Viera. I'm so sorry." At that moment I felt powerless. I didn't know what to say. I didn't know what to do. All I could manage was to hold her while she cried, repeating, "I'm so sorry, V."

She sniffed, quickly pulling herself back together the way she'd been trained to do.

"It's fine. I'm fine," she tried to convince me. "I'll see him again. I'll go to Prisma to marry the prince, and I'll be near him."

"I thought you said you wouldn't be selected." My heart sank.

"That's the other thing. My mother fought with them on this too, but they said no one is above the draft, and every eligible female will be required to attend the drafting in person in a fortnight. Failure to do so is considered treason and is punishable by death."

I stared at her blankly as I considered everything she'd just said. If the draft was rigged to select the most attractive contestants as Viera had gleaned, then the odds of her being selected were much higher, and I was facing losing my best friend.

"Now, will you let me put this tiara on you?" she asked, taking another deep breath.

I had a feeling there was more she wasn't sharing, but I did not want to press. I nodded my head, and then she proceeded to place the diadem atop my—now loose—mane of hair. She smiled genuinely, and I instantly felt lighter.

"You look like a goddess."

I squeezed her hand and smiled demurely. The light in the room turned a rich gold.

"The sun is setting! We need to go, quickly!"

△

Once we'd made it back to the stables, Viera eyed Stella up and down briefly before turning to face me. "You are not riding on that thing to the party. I'm sorry, Aella, but the way you two washed up had you looking like a wet cat!" She teased.

I shrugged, giving Stella an apologetic look, but I knew Viera was right. She hooked a small, floating carriage to the saddles of two of her parents' well-trained sea horses, and we climbed inside.

Chapter 2

Dawning

AELLA

We arrived at the lagoon just in time to watch the final moments of the sun's descent. Its last light glittered upon the sea. The lagoon was one of several holy places for the Argenti and therefore protected against anyone trying to build on or around it. While our people mostly used lagoons for celebrating traditions, I'd come regularly to rejuvenate my soul. There was something magical about the lagoons, a closeness with the planet and the sea that I could only feel there. I didn't need to use magic because the place was full of it.

My immediate family, extended relatives, and friends were all there. One by one, the females began layering me with traditional beaded necklaces, bracelets, and anklets. They put rings on my fingers and threaded bits of coral into my hair. The smell of smoke tinged the air as bonfires were being lit.

The musicians among the group began to pick up their drums, marching across the beach as they formed a loose circle. Their footsteps synchronized to the beat, and with each step, a percussive thud sparked a glow in the sand. Their collective stomping and drumming infected the beach with a pulsating rhythm. I could feel it in the sand, I could feel it in the air, I could feel it penetrating deep into the fabric of my soul. My friends began dancing to the beat of drums, and my hips swayed compulsively to the rhythm.

I was in complete awe that my parents had planned such an elaborate event for me. I couldn't help feeling guilty when I thought about how long it must have taken them to save up or about the amount of time my mother must have put into planning such an extravagance. Everyone was watching me, and I felt a little awkward being the center of attention. My favorite aunt noticed my discomfort and poured me some wine into a nautilus shell.

"You're of age now, enjoy!" She raised her own shell, so I took a small sip from mine and cringed slightly, not expecting the sharp taste. I closed my eyes and gulped it down quickly, then returned the shell to her.

My aunt laughed. "Well, that's one way to do it."

I looked to Viera who was slowly sipping her wine in—what I now realized was—the proper way.

Before long, it started to get dark, and I began feeling the effects of the wine. The music called to me, compelling me to spin around and around. I felt light as a feather, like I could float away, subject to nothing but the whims of the wind. Carefree, I danced with the others, a glowing trail following our footsteps before slowly fading away. The beach was colonized with bioluminescent algae which glowed in response to friction. It was one of nature's magical ways of worshiping the stars. Even the algae in the ocean lit up—the gentle waves creating a soft glow at their crest with tiny fish leaving dashes of blue and green light beneath. It was mesmerizing.

For hours I danced under the stars, the sand glowing beneath me, my heart in tune with the drums. My dress clung to my skin, slick with sweat. When the water called to me, I ran to it. The waves greeted me like I'd been gone too long and they missed me already. I fully submerged myself then floated weightlessly in the shallows of the beach, staring up at the night sky as the surrounding algae created a light green aura around me. My body ebbed and flowed with the current. I felt so blissful, so at peace.

I had been drifting for a while when Viera came to join me. In silent agreement, we floated, hand in hand. Everything was about to change. Viera would very likely be drafted, but even if she wasn't, within a year, the two of us would be married off and bonded to our wifely duties. I couldn't imagine my life without her in it. Thinking about those things made my heart feel like it was being crushed. I didn't want to let the thoughts and sad emotions ruin our limited time together, but a tear escaped my faithless eyes. As if reading my mind, V squeezed my hand. I took a deep, cleansing breath and pushed those thoughts far, far away.

As the night went on, we ate, drank, and danced without inhibition. The little ones retired to tents while the rest of us huddled around the fires. Dawn would soon approach, and this would all be over. My parents sat lovingly in each other's arms across the fire, whispering to each other and grinning.

"Your parents are so lucky to have chemistry like that," Viera said. "Your father treats your mother with so much respect. They make it look so easy."

My eyes met my mother's through the flames, and she gave me a smile. I tried to return it, but a wave of concern washed over her face, and she got up to make her way over to me.

"What's wrong, my dear?" my mother asked while settling down next to us.

"I guess I just thought that when this day came, I would feel ready. But that couldn't be further from the truth. And if I can be honest, I'm scared. I'm not ready to start my own family yet. I hardly feel like an adult myself. How am I expected to take care of a husband and children all on my own? And what if I end up with some horrible male?"

"Don't you know that your father and I will do everything in our power to find you the most suitable match?"

"You should see some of the people my parents have brought home." Viera laughed bitterly. "They all seem much more concerned with how the marriage will benefit them than how it will affect me."

"How so?" my mother asked.

"Well, the last one spent the entire dinner speaking with my father about me as if I weren't even at the table. He didn't bother to ask me a single question about myself. The one before that went on and on with an exhaustive list of requirements and expectations he'd have for me if I were to be his bride."

"Stars above, who do these males think they are?" my mother snorted.

"It sounds like they've picked up some distorted sense of entitlement from working so closely with the Iris," I retorted.

"Aella! I won't have you speaking about the Iris in such a way!" my mother admonished me quietly, looking around to make sure no one was paying attention to our conversation.

"It's okay, Mother. Viera doesn't care."

"Girls, you never know who is listening," she said in a more serious tone. "People have been imprisoned for less."

I gave my mother an apologetic look. She had never liked speaking of the Iris. Any time I had asked questions, she'd quickly shot them down. It was almost as if she thought merely mentioning them would bring us bad luck. There were so many other topics that were off the table for discussion as well. It felt like every question I tried bringing up was immediately shut down.

"We'll discuss it when you're older."
"This isn't the right time or place."
"We can talk about it later."

But it was never the right time. I'd eventually stopped asking, and in a way, our relationship had grown more and more distant as a result.

"It's crazy to think that, one day, we could be sitting here with our own daughters having the same conversations," I said to Viera to which she nodded silently.

The stars disappeared as the night sky gradually brightened to a pale blue. Friends and family slowly packed up and said their goodbyes. Dawn had come, but instead of hope, I was left with a sad, empty feeling in the pit of my stomach. My family was the last to leave, making sure to clean up and restore the lagoon to its pre-celebratory state. When we were finished, I kissed my parents goodbye before riding back with Viera to pick up Stella.

"You're really counting on getting picked for the draft, aren't you?" I asked.

Viera looked away from me when she answered, "It's the best option for me. Even if I'm not chosen by the prince, I'll at least be in the capital. I just can't imagine being stuck here, married off to one of those detestable creatures my parents keep bringing home for me. I don't want to end up like my mother."

I understood her reasoning, but I couldn't help but feel saddened at the thought that she wanted to leave so badly. The odds of both our names being chosen during the draft were extremely low. But if it really was based on appearance, her name would certainly be drawn. If that's what she truly wanted, then I needed to be supportive.

"Well, then," I sighed, picking a small piece of seaweed out of Viera's hair, "how do we get you ready for the prince?"

Chapter 3
Ten Names

Aella

My family gathered at the town center near the docks for the draft. The packed crowd of Argenti fae was charged with a nervous energy. Ten names would be drawn in Iveria today. Ten Argenti females would say goodbye to their families forever. It was an honor, they said.

An intimidating number of guards surrounded the perimeter of the square in their gleaming armor—a combination of gold, silver, and bronze metals worked together in a beautiful but terrifying display of power.

The Iris Guardians had spent the previous two weeks updating their census and recruiting males and females for work in the great city of Prisma. For some recruits, it was an opportunity to improve their family's social ranking, as it came with a few perks. For the vast majority, it was the only way to escape poverty—and that was only if they were lucky enough to be selected.

Working in Prisma came at a cost. Although their families were paid a large sum in exchange—enough to keep their families fed, clothed, and housed for the rest of their lives—those enlisted had to cut all ties to their home courts, and they could never marry nor have children. Most families had at least one child who would enlist, their sacrifice needed to put food on the table back home. Elemental fae from the three courts who moved to the capital never returned.

Esterra was home to three elemental races of fae: the Aereus, who lived in the Court of Earth; the Aurum, who lived in the Court of Fire; and the Argenti, who lived in the Court of Water. In the past, there had been four elemental races, but the Adamas from the Court of Air died off long before I was born. The Iris, our ruling class who had come to us from the stars, could wield multiple elements alongside their aether which gave them powers of their own. The only place in Esterra where the stars allowed the gathering of more than one race of elemental fae was Prisma.

Lord Caelum, our highest ranking Iris Guardian in Iveria, approached the podium with at least a dozen Iris guards around him. They were not as high-ranking as Lord Caelum—anyone could tell because their skin tones weren't nearly as marbled or iridescent as his—but regardless, they outranked every member of our society and looked down on us with disdain. They were also stronger, faster, and more powerful than any of us, making them nearly impossible to resist.

Although he was centuries old, Lord Caelum appeared to be a middle-aged male. He was handsome in a cruel way with a sharp jaw and long, straight nose. His brows converged as he cast his gaze upon us. Every family with a daughter my age was required to attend, making the space tight as we stood shoulder to shoulder.

My heart thundered in anticipation. My only hope was that I'd have a chance to say goodbye to Viera if her name was called. The process usually went quickly, and she was closer to the podium with her family.

The crowd was so silent, I would have been able to hear a raindrop land as Lord Caelum began calling out names. My mother squeezed my hand tightly, as if her hold could keep them from taking me away. My other hand gripped the seashell in my pocket, its scalloped shape threatening to leave a mark in my palm even with its smoothed out ridges.

The first few names were girls I didn't know.

Each time a name was called, we became more hopeful, and our grips loosened a bit with relief.

When he called out Viera's name, her mother wailed before her father slapped her into a stunned silence. She gripped her daughter tightly, tears streaming down her slowly reddening face. Viera stood there, emotionless and staring straight ahead.

My heart felt heavy, and my eyes burned with tears. Although we'd discussed the possibility of it happening, nothing could have prepared me. My legs began shaking, and continuing to stand there felt nearly impossible. I wanted to crumple to the floor.

The Guardian continued down the list until the last name was called. I could hardly hear anything anymore, my mind so loud with grief for my friendship with Viera. Until someone from the crowd shouted, "She was wed just last night."

It wasn't uncommon for people to have last-minute weddings right before a draft, but Lord Caelum, with an irritated expression on his face, looked back down at the list for a moment that stretched on like an eternity.

"In that case, the final contestant will be Miss Aella Kalani."

"Aella, they called your name!" Mila gasped, and I looked at my sister, mirroring her shocked expression.

I turned to my mother, eyes wide and my mouth agape. She opened her mouth as though she had something to say, then closed her eyes, shaking her head. She took me into her arms, one hand around my shoulders, one hand on the back of my neck.

"Trust in your heart. Trust your instincts," she choked out. The rest of her words were drowned out in all the commotion, all except, "Star-blessed."

I wanted to press for clarification, but the guards were coming, and I was running out of time.

"I don't *really* want you to go, Aella," Mila whimpered.

I swallowed the lump in my throat and turned to her, pressing my seashell into her hand. "Here, I want you to have this," I said before pulling her in for a big hug.

She withdrew, her big round eyes growing impossibly wider as she realized what I had placed into her hand. "But what if you feel scared or alone without it?"

"Knowing that you have it is all I'll need to feel connected to you, no matter how far we are from each other," I said, brushing a stray hair back behind her delicate, pointed ear. "You're the big sister now, I'm passing the baton to you. Keep them safe."

I embraced my other brothers and sisters, my hands shaking as a wave of numbness took over my body and mind. They began crying.

"Please don't cry, little ones. It's okay," I found myself saying, trying to comfort them. "Everything will be okay."

I kissed their heads, smelling them one last time. A memory to take with me.

My father took me into his big arms with a kiss to the top of my head. "No matter what happens, Aella, always remember that I am proud of you and that being your father has been one of the greatest honors of my life."

My parents took my shaky hands. I inhaled deeply and nodded to them with a sad smile saying more than words ever could.

The guards were there to take me away. As I was ushered out, my littlest brother, Dean, began chasing after me, crying, "Aella! Aella!"

Mila grabbed him, holding him tightly to her chest. Dean's cries followed me through the crowd, threatening to crumble my indifferent facade. It took everything in me not to fall apart, but I was determined to stay strong for my family and not make it harder on them.

The guards led me to the great ship with the golden figurehead. As I boarded, I ran straight to Viera. She stared at me with a look of bewilderment on her face.

"I thought I'd lost you!" I shouted over all the noise. And in the midst of all of the shock, numbness, and tears I should have been shedding, to my surprise, I found myself laughing. "I can't believe we're both here."

Laughing together, we stood at the side of the ship, staring back at Iveria as we began to set sail. Our laughter subsided with the shock and was finally replaced with tears. We stood, holding each other as reality sank in, as we mourned the loss of our families and our lives in Iveria. Eight other females stood around us portside as we watched Iveria shrink away into the distance. We would never see our hometown again.

△

Two other ships had set sail with us, filled with guards and new recruits for Prisma's forces. Soon after we began sailing, an Iris female—who introduced herself as "Himmel" in a high-pitched, proper-sounding accent—led us back to our cabins. The cabins were small, with only enough space to fit two slender bunks in each and a tiny window to let in a dot of light—too high up to see out of.

Viera and I made sure to claim a room together. Himmel eyed us suspiciously, then continued on with the others.

Sitting on opposite bunks, we took in our new, temporary home.

"If the prince chooses you, will you at least make me your handmaid?" I asked.

"Only if you agree to do the same," she replied.

"What do you think he's like?"

"Spoiled like the rest of them," she said, not hiding the bite in her tone.

"Well, if our upbringing has anything to do with it, I'm sure you'll fit in much better than me," I teased.

"Are you calling me spoiled?" she accused with a laugh.

"Maybe just a little bit." I winced jokingly while massaging a sore spot on the back of my neck.

Viera whacked me with her pillow which exploded into a plume of feathers that floated about the cabin, fluffy white and gray bits of plumage lodging themselves into our clothes and hair.

"I deserved that." We both laughed at the mess.

"What do you think about the others?" Viera asked, sweeping feathers off the side of her bed. "It really does seem like they went for looks, doesn't it?"

"Stars, I can just picture our pretty prince, ordering them to choose the fairest fae in all the land," I said dramatically, trying to mimic Himmel's accent. "Picture his face when he sees the two of us plucked hens." I picked a feather out from the top of my dress before blowing it toward Viera.

She rolled her eyes.

"It is kind of creepy, though, to think that they have that sort of information about us," I added.

Viera huffed then settled her head onto her now-less-fluffy pillow. She reached her hand across the gap between our beds, and we lay there listening to the other females' sobs through the wooden walls. Their cries slowly died off as the sound of waves and the sway of the ship rocked us all into a deep, dreamless sleep.

Chapter 4
A Different Path

Arianwen

I was to be married in three months. My name had not been called in the draft, so my parents had arranged a betrothal for me. Verus came from a hardworking family who lived in an underwater section of Iveria, while my family lived in one of the homes up above. I had never met the male, but stars willing, my parents loved me enough not to arrange a marriage with a complete psychopath. I guess my time for some romantic love story had run out.

"Arianwen!" my mother called from the kitchen. "Are you ready to go? Your matri-ritus needs to start before nightfall!"

"Almost ready!" I yelled back as I packed my bag with the supplies I would need.

I would be gone for a few weeks and wanted to make sure I didn't forget anything. As it was my first time leaving the safety of home, my anxiety was higher than usual. The journey also marked the official end of my life as I knew it. When I returned, I would be locked into a marriage with Verus and all that it entailed.

My hair was a mess after all of my chores—the unruly waves did not like to be tamed—so I decided to re-braid the thick, onyx strands. Once

I was done, I changed into more sensible hiking clothes and out of the loose, flowy dress I had been wearing. Being in and out of the water so often, I typically liked to dress in the lightest things possible to minimize the drying time, but these materials were the opposite. They felt stiff and wrong, especially because they were new. Glancing down at my loose blue tunic and light-gray fitted pants, I frowned a little.

Not the most attractive look . . . but it's not like I'm going on my matri-ritus to meet handsome fae males.

My pack was heavy on my shoulders, and I started rethinking some of my packing choices as I made my way into the kitchen. My mouth watered as I smelled the food my mother was wrapping up for the road. Folding my arms around her in a gentle hug, I kissed her silvery cheek. "Thanks for taking such great care of me."

"You'll need this for the trip. You won't get to an inn until sometime tomorrow!" she said in her motherly way.

"Yes, Mother. I'll make sure to stretch these provisions as long as I need to."

"I'll tell your father that you headed off. He'll be sad to have missed you, but he couldn't get away from the shipyard. Lord Caelum has been pressuring him with strict deadlines and quotas to meet."

My full lips turned into a slight pout. I knew it wasn't his fault, but it still hurt that he hadn't made more of an effort to see me off. His work was more important than his family, it seemed. His sense of duty was one of the only things I had in common with him. Well, that, and we shared the same dark silver eyes.

Trying to be the loving, supportive daughter my mother expected me to be, I replied, "Please give him a hug from me. I'll be back before you know it!"

My siblings bounded into the room, wrapping their arms around me and showering me with kisses and well wishes. My face broke into a smile as they instantly lifted my mood.

"Don't worry about me! Nothing exciting happens on these rites of passage anyway, right?" I blew them all a kiss, rolled back my shoulders, and walked out the door.

My trek would take me north toward the alps of the abandoned Court of Air, the thought of the cool nights making me shiver. On my journey, I'd visit villages at the edge of the Court of Water. My entire life had been spent in or near the Iverian Sea, and being away from the salt water made me feel nervous but also excited. I was strongest near my element and would need to rely on the streams melting off the glaciers or nearby lakes to recharge my power.

The matri-ritus was supposed to bring enlightenment and prepare me for marriage, but I didn't see how hiking in the mountains and meditating would prepare me for anything other than how to survive in the wilderness. Tradition was tradition though. I supposed I should be grateful that we were even allowed our traditions.

Ever since the stars had sent the Iris to rule Esterra millennia ago, so much of what we had been allowed to do and how we'd lived had been altered, all in service to their greatness.

Back when the Iris had first come and subjugated the elemental courts, we'd all been required to pay a yearly tribute to them. To strengthen and continue their family lines, each Iris had been wed to an elemental fae. For reasons unknown to us, the Iris could no longer reproduce with each other. Over time, the yearly tributes had evolved into the marriage drafts.

As a healer in training, I'd hoped that I could put off marriage indefinitely—or at least until I found a male *I* would have liked to wed—but Lord Caelum had mandated marriage by the age of twenty-five so that there would always be enough of us available to maintain their way of life. I rolled my eyes at the thought of the pompous Lord Caelum. The Iris thought they were so much better than us with their godlike appearances and enhanced abilities.

Sometimes I wondered what our world had been like before the Iris came. Our history books were vague when it came to anything before their reign. Asking questions about the time before was discouraged, and people who were too vocal about their dislike of the Iris' rule often disappeared and were never heard from or seen again.

As a child, I had always been incredibly inquisitive, my hunger for reading and learning unquenchable. Once, in school, I'd asked too many questions about our history and was rewarded with lashes from the Iris. I still had scars on my hands to prove it. What was meant to beat me into submission had only watered seeds of hatred toward our oppressors.

My family had done their best not to make any more waves after that, and we were mostly left alone. I was the cautionary tale my siblings were warned with. A part of me yearned to break from the mold they wanted to keep us in, but I didn't dare speak of that desire—I seethed in silence.

We lived by so many rules and regulations set by the Iris that it would be a breath of fresh air to be out on my own for a short while.

Since elemental fae were contained to our respective courts, I felt a bit rebellious knowing my trek would take me so close to the border. It was a petty rebellion, considering the Adamas fae of the Court of Air had been annihilated long before my lifetime. I had once questioned why the laws kept us separate from the other courts, but when I remembered the tragedy of Concordia, I banished those thoughts.

Centuries ago, fae from the various courts had created a settlement in the heart of Esterra. As the settlement grew, the stars took notice and decimated it, sparing not even a single male, female, or child. The destruction of Concordia served as a deterrent to any elemental fae who would dare defy the Iris' rule and the laws they had written in service to the stars.

I tried to quiet my mind as I walked up the unfamiliar path toward my first destination, a small village named Lakehaven. Quite a few villages skirted the Iverian Sea with small settlements of Argenti, but the majority of the Court of Water resided in Iveria. Most of the villages practiced the old ways and kept to themselves. I was hoping I could meet some healers and learn from them before I resigned myself to taking care of my soon-to-be husband and bearing him children.

I got completely lost in thought as the sun started to set, and my legs burned from the constant change in elevation as I hiked further up the mountain. My body was lithe and strong from all the swimming I did, but I was not used to being so far away from my element. No currents were present to help push me along and speed up my journey. Stars knew why our ancestors had thought a hike was a good idea to prepare water elementals for marriage. I would need to find some kind of shelter soon, as Lakehaven was another day's hike away.

A flock of birds suddenly shot into the air above some trees ahead of me, and I nearly jumped out of my skin. The sound of something crashing through branches followed by a pained groan reached my ears as I stood momentarily frozen in fear.

Was someone up ahead?

I had to make a choice: investigate, or be smart and head the other way. Although, if I was being honest with myself, there was only one choice to make.

Chapter 5
Healer

Arianwen

My healer instincts kicked in, and I rushed toward the sound, not giving a second thought to the potential danger. I spied something—no, some*one*—in a crumpled, red and white heap at the bottom of a cluster of trees.

"Hello?" I called out as I rushed toward the still figure. "Do you need help? I'm a healer!"

Blood was everywhere, and he appeared unconscious. I saw a large bolt protruding from his shoulder that seemed to be the source of the damage. Without stopping to think, I knelt next to him and ripped his shirt away from his shoulder to appraise his injury.

My stars, where did he come from?

Based on the trees, it looked like he had fallen from the sky, but was that even possible?

"Are you all right, sir? I'm not here to hurt you, I just want to see if there is anything I can do." I reached out a hand to touch his shoulder, my healing magic probing at the wound, and he groaned, his eyes fluttering open. They were a startling shade of icy blue and were tinged with pain. I held back a gasp at how strikingly attractive he was despite his condition but tried to remain focused and keep him at ease. "We need to remove this bolt, and it's going to hurt. I'm sorry, but I don't have anything with me for the pain . . ." I trailed off.

He groaned again, and his voice came out gravelly as he said, "Just do it."

I cringed at the thought of doing it on my own so far from help, but he was losing blood, and I wasn't going to walk away without trying to do everything in my power to save him. I placed one hand on top of the bolt and tried to gently push it through. He winced, then placed his hand over mine and helped put more pressure on it. My pulse quickened, and my eyes flicked over to his at the unexpected sensation of his hand over mine.

Not the time to get all fluttery! Stay professional!

With another strong push, the bolt was out, and more blood started gushing out of the wound. Immediately covering it with my hands, I used all my strength to put pressure on it while calling on my healing power to slow the blood flow. Once the blood finally started to clot, I reached out to my element, relieved when I sensed a stream nearby. I sent up a quick thank you to the stars as I summoned some water to gently clean the puncture wound. Fumbling through my pack for something to bind it, I pulled out a clean tunic. I caught him watching me, barely flinching as I wrapped and tightened it around his shoulder.

I blew out a slow breath. "That will have to do for now."

"Thank you," he said quietly, closing his eyes, looking like he might pass out.

With his gaze no longer on me, I took the time to peruse the rest of him, making sure there was nothing I'd missed. I held in a gasp as I saw cuts and abrasions all over his torso and grayish-blue bruises beginning to form. His opalescent, alabaster skin was unlike any I had seen before, his muscular form riddled with scars. A warrior's body, his skin the tapestry telling tales of previous battles and injuries. Without realizing it, I found myself tracing them lightly. He shuddered under my touch, and I startled, looking up and meeting his gaze, his face framed with snowy white hair.

"Shouldn't I know your name before I let you put your hands all over me?" he rasped with a hint of humor.

"Stars, I'm sorry. I have never seen anyone like you before." I blushed, pulling my hands back.

"You're lovelier than the stars themselves, or maybe you're a star in disguise . . ." He trailed off, his eyelids fluttering shut.

I observed his chest's slow rise and fall as he lost consciousness.

A star in disguise. Ha! My cheeks warmed. I sat back and quietly sighed. His reaction wasn't really surprising, but it was my first time experiencing something like it. The healers I'd trained with in Iveria told me many tales of male patients developing feelings for the healers who cared for them. That was surely all it was.

Hopefully he makes it through the night.

I looked around to see if there was any way to make him more comfortable because, until he regained some strength, he wasn't going anywhere. Pulling a blanket out of my pack, I covered him with it, trying not to disturb his rest.

Do I just leave him here? I've done all I can for now . . .
He could be dangerous.

Glancing over at him, I knew there was no way I could leave him on his own. I felt inexplicably drawn to the stranger and had to know more about him and how he'd come crashing down in front of me.

It was getting dark, and the healing had taken more out of me than I realized. I pulled another blanket from my pack and rolled it up to use as a pillow, then I lay down on the hard ground, facing the handsome stranger, and drifted off to sleep.

※

"Good morning, my star," a deep voice rumbled next to me.

Icy blue eyes met mine as I was startled awake. Somehow, during the night, I had migrated closer to his warmth and had wrapped my arm around him, nestled into the side of his body. My face flushed as I quickly sat up and moved away from him.

Trying to compose myself, I asked, "Feeling any better, sir?"

He groaned and tried to stretch. "Faex, that hurts, but I don't think I'd be feeling anything if you hadn't come running to my rescue."

"Really, it was no trouble at all," I replied, a hint of a smile on my face. "I would hope that if I ever needed saving, someone would stop and help me."

"Does my rescuer have a name?" he asked, his voice tinged with pain.

"Arianwen, but you can call me Ari. And I promise, I am not some star in disguise," I said, teasing him slightly.

He groaned, sounding mildly embarrassed. "My memories from yesterday are a little hazy, to say the least, but I wish I'd been a little smoother in the presence of such a beautiful female."

Stars, he couldn't be smoother if he tried.

Ignoring his compliment, I asked, "Do you mind if I take a look at how things are healing?"

"Please, go ahead."

I carefully unwrapped his shoulder, and he hissed a little as the fabric peeled away. The wound looked angry and inflamed, which made me wonder if the bolt had been laced with some poison.

"I'm sorry, this needs to be cleaned out again." I placed the back of my hand against his forehead, alarmed at the warmth. "You feel a little feverish, I'm worried this has become infected, and I don't have the necessary herbs on me."

"Do you think you could get me some water, please?" he asked weakly.

"Of course!" I exclaimed and summoned my element from a nearby stream. I let it pool in my hands, then held it up to his full lips. I watched him as he took small sips of the water and muttered a quiet thank you, so softly I had to lean closer to hear him. I used the rest of the water to rinse out his wound and then placed my hand over it to push some healing power in. He shivered a little and leaned his head back against a tree.

"I would offer you something to wear, but nothing I have will fit you, and I kind of destroyed your shirt yesterday," I confessed, avoiding his gaze.

"Never apologize for taking me out of my clothes," he said, the hint of a smirk on his face.

Stars, this male could be the death of me.

I tried to fight another blush. "Here, use this blanket again," I replied as I reached around him to drape it over his shoulders. I couldn't help but glance over the rest of his chiseled physique. His scrapes and bruises seemed to be healing well. I resisted the urge to touch him again as our eyes locked.

Pull yourself together, Ari!

He reached up and tucked a strand of hair that had fallen out of my braid behind my pointed ear. The motion was so intimate . . . Our faces were inches apart.

"It's perfect," he said, his eyes dropping to my lips.

I quickly pulled away. Here I was, on my matri-ritus to prepare for my upcoming marriage, and I was flirting with a strange male. It didn't matter that he was the most intriguing male I had ever laid eyes on.

"It looks like you had quite the fall yesterday. How did you end up here? Did your horse run away? Where did you come from?" I started rambling to distract myself. "If I didn't know better, I'd say you look like what I've heard an Adamas would look like, but that's not possible. The Adamas have been gone for millennia."

"Is that so?" he replied, his voice laced with a hint of irony.

"I mean, that's what I've been taught my whole life . . ."

"I see. Well then, I suppose you saved an extinct creature. Lucky you," he replied, voice dripping with mild sarcasm.

"Does that mean you *are* one of them?" I asked, eyes wide.

"Yes, my family hails from a long, unbroken line of Adamas, but we like to keep to ourselves. We don't answer to the Iris."

My mouth dropped open. A myriad of emotions flooded me as I tried to reconcile what I had grown up believing with what was right in front of my eyes.

"Wait, how is that even possible? Does anyone else know? Where do you live? Are there many of you? And you're actually free from the Iris' rule?"

The male shrugged slightly, as if he wasn't willing to answer.

Ignoring his lack of response, I continued rambling as my mind spiraled with the new information. "I can't even begin to imagine how nice it must be to make your own choices. Where to live, what to do, who to love . . ."

"Is it truly freedom to live in exile?" he asked, raising an eyebrow.

"Well, at least you're not slaves to the Iris' every whim."

"I'll give you that, but don't you realize it is all of *you* who give power to the Iris?"

"Easy for you to say when you're not ruled by them," I scoffed, feeling slightly angry and partly jealous.

"Arianwen."

I couldn't help but soften at the sound of my name on his lips. "Yes . . . ?"

He smiled gently. "I wish that all fae were free from the Iris' rule. Maybe someday someone will have the courage to stand up and fight them."

"Yes, for my children's sake, I hope so," I agreed solemnly.

"You have children?"

"Oh, no! Not yet. But I have an arranged marriage in my future, so they will come sooner rather than later."

"They will be lucky to have such a talented healer like you as their mother," he said warmly.

"Thanks," I uttered dryly.

"No, truly. I think you are a remarkable female to help a complete stranger. For all you know, I could be incredibly dangerous."

"Yes, so dangerous," I deadpanned. "You can barely sit up, and when I came upon you, you could hardly string words together and were deliriously calling me a 'star.'"

"Give me a few days, and you could find out just how dangerous I can be," he replied, slight daring in his voice.

I turned my head to hide my blush. This male already had a way of getting under my skin.

Trying to change the subject, I asked, "Can you really fly?"

I waited for his answer with bated breath. The Adamas were fabled to have control over the air, which had allowed many of them to fly.

He glanced up at the broken tree above us. "If you base it on yesterday's performance, yes, but not very well." His lips quirked into a smile. "I'm not exactly at my best right now," he continued, gesturing to his wounded shoulder.

"I think it would be terrifying to fly with just the wind at my back, I prefer the depths of the sea."

"We are worlds apart, you and I," he said, pursing his lips.

"Indeed we are," I replied, trying to picture him in the sky. Shaking my head to clear my thoughts, I rose from the ground. "Well, Mysterious Wounded Flying Fae, I am going to search for some plants to help speed your healing."

He chuckled and said with a faint smile, "You can call me Wynn."

"Wynn . . ." I repeated, liking the way his name felt on my tongue. "I'll be back soon."

Chapter 6
Prisma

Aella

I awoke groggy and homesick. Although we were afloat in a large vessel on the ocean, we weren't permitted to take a dive into the water. It left me with a horrible sense of unease, being so close yet so far away. Wondering if we'd have access to the ocean while in Prisma was another gnawing concern that kept circling around in my mind. I could not earn a straight answer out of Himmel. I wondered what the foreign city would be like—if it could ever feel like home.

We'd been sailing for over a month, give or take a few weeks. It was hard to keep track of time as all the days bled together. On the morning of our arrival, there was an increase of energy on the ship as the crew prepared to dock.

When we arrived in Prisma, we were ushered straight into carriages. The brief view I got of the port included only four massive, towering statues, taller than any building I'd ever seen. One bronze, one gold, and one silver to represent the three remaining elemental courts of earth, fire, and water. The fourth statue—which sported all three metals swirled together into intricate designs—represented the Iris, the ruling class sent to us from the stars. I wondered if there had ever been an Adamas statue for the Court of Air and what it might have looked like.

The city of Prisma felt both ancient and modern all at once. Towering buildings rose around us. The structures themselves were of a cool gray and white stone that showed little sign of the effects of weather. Intricate works of art marked the stone at the corners of the buildings. Faces of figures, past and present, forever etched into the walls. Ancient trees lined the streets in evenly spaced intervals. I'd never seen so much organization, so much symmetry. Where Iveria was a city of curves and fluid imperfections, Prisma was all straight lines and sharp angles. The carriage turned, taking us up a long, narrow bridge that appeared to separate the palatium from the rest of the city. When I peeked out the side window to catch a glimpse of what was below, I fell back, startled at the sight. The imposing height of the bridge we were crossing was overwhelming, so I closed the curtain and sucked in a breath, praying for an ending to the journey. Viera squeezed my hand, but her face displayed clear signs of discomfort too.

The Palatium Crystalis was monumental with sky-high ceilings and windows matching in height with long billowing curtains that fluttered as we marched by. Marble walls inlaid with gold lined the halls. Every inch of it was dripping in opulence.

Our footsteps echoed as we followed Himmel through the magnificent halls of the palatium. There was no art hung on the walls because the walls themselves were works of art, and the adjacent windows gave views of ornately designed botanical gardens.

Our first stop on our tour was the bathhouse.

Himmel spoke in an apathetic, unhurried tone. "It's going to take some time to wash the scent of Iveria off you lot, so you'll be spending a considerable amount of time in these bathing chambers every day, as well as drinking the teas provided and eating the prescribed diet. The goal is that even your perspiration will give off a perfumed odor as a result of your participation in these practices. We will make ladies of you, giving you the best possible chance at winning the favor of our prince."

As we entered, maids began peeling our clothing off with wrinkled noses. There were at least two of them for each one of us. Two maids working in tandem began to lather me up with scented oils and scrubs. I yelped, as the ladies were not in the least bit shy about scrubbing every inch of me, and a mitted hand shot between my thighs, a little too close for comfort.

"Stars above! I think I can scrub myself, thank you very much!" I said as I wrapped my hands around myself protectively.

I was eager to get into the bath and quickly made my way over. As I stepped into the bath, the shocking warmth sent me jumping back. I'd never swam in water warmer than a summer day in a lagoon. It did not feel right. Water should be cool. It would take me a minute to grow accustomed to the heat.

Feeling like a crab about to be boiled, I cautiously made my way in, and to my surprise, the heat was actually not half bad. My stiff muscles began to relax as I melted into the comfort of the water. All the tension in my neck and shoulders dissipated as I savored the sensation of being enveloped in the soothing caress of the bath.

Steam rose as flower petals floated around me, infusing their perfumed essences into the water and air. Shortly after I found a seat at the edge of the bath, one of the maids came over and began working scented oils into my hair. Startled by her touch, I spun away, nearly causing her to crash into the bath with me. She gave me a dirty look, and I glared right back at her while possessively holding my hair.

"You know, they're just trying to do their job," Viera said as she swam toward me.

I huffed, "I know. I . . . I'm not used to having people touch me like that. Besides, I'm perfectly capable of washing my own body and hair."

After I finished washing my hair, the maid begrudgingly handed me a comb, correctly anticipating I wouldn't allow her to do that either. I had wanted to stay in the pool for the rest of the day, but the heat started to make me feel lightheaded, and I was eager to cool off. As I exited, I was met with a set of plush towels and a robe.

"Thank you," I said, regretting the way I had first treated the females.

My maids nodded their heads and led me over to a cushioned seat.

"I'm sorry I started things off the way I did. I didn't mean to insult you," I added.

One of the maids handed me a cool glass of water with sliced fruit floating in it. The other brought over a set of grooming tools.

"I'm not used to people doing things for me . . . or touching me, for that matter. I'd like to apologize."

"It's not necessary. Now, may we please see your hands?"

I set down the glass, and they began filing my nails into delicate ovals. One of them got to work on my feet. I struggled not to jump as she filed at my heels.

"I'm Aella. What are your names?"

"My lady, please call us 'ma'am,'" one replied with her eyes pointed to the ground, the other nodding in agreement.

Once we were deemed clean enough, Himmel reappeared to take us to our bedchambers. The suite I was taken to had two spacious rooms connected by a shared living space full of plush seating areas, a dining table covered in trays of fruit, a fully stocked bar, and a wide balcony with lounge chairs overlooking the gardens of the palatium.

Upon entering the first bedchamber, I noticed five enormous canopied beds. There were five vanities, five wardrobes, and at the far end of the room, more doors.

"Due to the increased number of contestants, we've had to make a few slight alterations to our boarding arrangements. This should only be temporary until eliminations are made," Himmel announced, looking at her nails as if to avoid the unpleasantry of having to make conversation with one of us.

Even with five girls sharing the room, it was still one of the most spacious and luxurious places I'd ever seen. The beds were covered in plush silks and piled high with fluffy, lavender pillows and cream throw blankets.

Lambskin pelts padded the marble floors, and filmy canopies were draped loosely around our regal beds.

Heavy plum curtains hung from the high, vaulted ceilings around the floor-to-ceiling windows. In the center of the room hung an elongated chandelier made of lengthy, glass, teardrop-shaped bulbs suspended at different heights by wire so fine, they appeared to float in mid-air.

I went to explore what was behind the two doors at the far end of the room. One led to a small bathroom, and the other was locked.

"You are not to leave your suites unless summoned. If needed, pull the cord at your bedside to call your lady's maids, and they will provide anything you may require. Tonight, you will be expected to dress, then dine together in the dining hall where you will be meeting the contestants from the other courts."

As Himmel made her exit, I sighed a breath of relief. I always felt so uneasy when she was around. Something about the tone of her voice, like she'd been tasked with something so far beneath her. She never made eye contact and spoke down her pointed nose at us.

We had all mostly kept to ourselves on the journey. Viera and I were lucky to have each other, but some of the other girls seemed a bit more standoffish. I approached a petite Argenti female making herself at home by the vanity next to mine.

"It's Ulli, correct?"

She nodded her head warily.

"I'm Aella, and this is Viera." I smiled. "I figured we should get to know each other a little since we'll be living so close together."

"I wouldn't be wasting time making friends if I were you," said Ilaria, a taller female from across the room who had perfected a permanent glowering expression. "You realize we are all competing against each other, don't you?" she stated more than asked in a pessimistic tone.

"I'm Nickel," our fifth roommate chimed in. "And don't listen to Ilaria, she's probably just hungry. All they've given us is fruit since we arrived here. How are we supposed to survive on that?"

Ilaria narrowed her eyes at Nickel and then made her way out to the adjoining living quarters as though she were already tired of our company.

After meeting the rest of the Argenti in our living quarters, I went to check out the terrace. It had a magnificent view of the gardens, but we were a good three stories high. I could barely make out the sea in the distance, and it made my heart sink to be so far away from home.

There were a series of water-filled canals weaving through the gardens in a sort of maze. I wondered if the canals were deep enough for a swim and planned to find out.

An hour later, our maids and several seamstresses came to our rooms with an assortment of fabrics and gowns. The seamstresses carefully took our measurements, and our maids helped us into a variety of styles of gowns. Once the gowns were pinned in all the right places, they carefully removed them, and we returned to our silk robes.

My maids ushered me over to my vanity and began fussing with my hair.

"I'd really like to do it myself if that's all right," I said. They looked at me like I was crazy, then sighed and left me to it. I braided my hair into a fishtail braid which was simple enough, save for its remarkable volume and length.

My maid gave me a hopeless look, tsking. "It's almost as if you have no desire to win the favor of the prince. Would you at least allow me to make some minor adjustments?"

I sighed. "Minor adjustments?"

"Please trust me, my lady."

I hesitated. "All right, fine."

She opened a case filled with an assortment of glistening metals and jewels. Getting to work, she weaved pins with silver eight-pointed stars around the crown of my head. The centers of the stars were set with clear crystals. She fluffed the braid slightly, pulling out a few shorter pieces in the front to frame my face, and added more tiny stars into the length of the braid. Leaving my neck bare, she layered my fingers with multiple silver rings along different joints.

The corners of my mouth drooped as it brought back memories of my dawning.

"Is it not to your liking, my lady?"

"No, it's . . . perfect. I'm sorry." My voice wavered.

Fanning my face, I stared up at the ceiling. Once I composed myself, she smudged my eyelids with a rich, sapphire blue that had the effect of making my eyes double in size, and added a thick, shiny gloss to my lips.

My other maid returned with one of the gowns which had been swiftly tailored to my measurements. It was a simple, floor-length, silk gown with a deep v-neck. The straps crossed between my shoulder blades, then came around the front where they encircled my waist several times before tying into a knot in the front, long tassels hanging from the ends of the fabric. As I walked, the skirt of my dress parted, revealing the full length of my leg, while my sandals boasted braided silver straps that wound up to my thighs. The gown was flattering but did not leave much to the imagination as the thin blue fabric hugged every curve and slope of my body.

Seeing my expression in the mirror, my maid explained, "Don't you worry, we will have much more elaborate gowns for you in the future. This was one of the simplest styles to adjust on such short notice."

As I compared myself with the others, I was relieved to see that they had on similar-styled dresses. Viera's was like mine, except hers bunched over one shoulder, leaving the other bare. Mine seemed to fit tighter around the hips. I worried that, with a few wrong moves, my dress might split all the way up to my navel.

As an Argenti water fae, I was used to wearing thin and form-fitting clothes, but I'd never seen myself in something so sensual before. I hardly recognized myself.

◬

"Aereus," Ulli whispered urgently.

I tried not to gawk as we made our way out of our suite, getting our first glimpses of the other elemental fae. From the opposite side of the hall, Aereus contestants filed out. They were earth elementals from the southern tip of the continent.

None of us had ever seen other elementals before. Seeing them filled me with excitement but also apprehension about meeting them. Fae we'd been forbidden from mingling with our entire lives were standing right across the hall from us.

The Aereus ladies eyed us with the same wary expressions, whispering among themselves.

"Cease your ogling, and hurry along now," Himmel directed as she led the way, her footsteps clattering in the echoing halls.

Ilaria fearlessly led our group. The Aereus fae started walking beside us with their own leader, a well-built and poised female with dark bronze skin and lustrous burgundy hair. Her wine-colored eyes showed indifference, while the rest of us couldn't help but stare with wonder at the ladies who were so different from us. Their warm bronze skin with hair in coppery shades were such a contrast to our cool silver coloring.

It was said that the Aereus were the strongest of all elementals. With the power to split the earth, they could even move mountains. Us Argenti were considered quite weak in comparison with our water magic, but we too had our legends. The Aereus weren't just strong though, they had the power to make things grow and—over thousands of years—had turned the inhospitable desert of Ilithania into a tropical paradise, rivaling Prisma in its resplendence.

As we made our way through the halls, the Aurum fae joined our group. Fire elementals from the forest on the northeastern coast with cornsilk hair and golden skin with undertones ranging from green to rose. Not only could they make fire, they had the ability to control heat and light. The Aurum lived in the Easthen forest where they built homes high up in the trees. They were said to be excellent woodworkers, despite their reputation for being hot-headed and wildly destructive.

Himmel led the females from all three courts to a tremendous, two-floor ballroom with one long table arranged in the center. We were on the bottom floor, and I scanned the room to see the upper level balconies that overlooked the floor. Eager to eat since we'd been practically starved all day, we found our seats. The waitstaff entered the room, serving each of us small plates with grape-sized portions of food.

"I sure hope this isn't the whole meal," Nickel worried, and I nodded in agreement, my own stomach growling.

As our next course was served—a small bed of greens elegantly arranged with a paper-thin sliver of toasted bread—distant voices drew my attention. From above, Iris nobility began filling the balconies, looking down at us through narrowed eyes like spectators to a sport.

"Which one do you think is the prince?" I asked, my voice barely above a whisper.

The Iris, known for their vanity, did not disappoint as they were dressed in the finest silks in revealing styles, clearly attempting to show off as much of their radiant skin as possible.

"From what I understand, the more marbled and lucent they appear, the higher their rank. So that would mean the most radiant one of them is the prince," Nickel said before taking a small bite of greens.

The feeling of their eyes on me had me shifting uncomfortably in my seat. Viera placed a hand on my arm, signaling me. Leaning her head slightly toward mine, she whispered, "In the far corner, that must be him."

Trying not to be too obvious, I pivoted my head as if to converse with someone to my right. Smiling at Ulli as though not to appear too conspicuous, I slanted my eyes up to the corner balcony. My breath hitched in my throat as I made eye contact with the Iris male who was already staring directly at me.

Chapter 7
Contact Juggle

Aella

I couldn't breathe as I took in the details of the young Iris male with bronze, marbled skin in the corner of the balcony above. His silk shirt was unbuttoned, revealing tinted silvers and golds woven into an enchanting design upon his skin. He glowed with ethereal, yet intensely dark, masculine energy. His vivid green eyes were locked onto mine. I couldn't breathe as I stared back at him, the smile slowly melting from my face.

The male casually turned away, taking a sip from his crystal goblet as he conversed with the Iris female beside him. I let out a breath and stared at my food as if it were the most interesting thing I'd ever seen.

"I think you're right, V. I think that's him," I whispered breathlessly.

It was so awkward sitting and eating with all of the nobility looking down on us, but food was food, and I was starving. Eating always made me feel better. Besides, I wanted a distraction.

Our next course was served—a skewer of juicy-looking meat, vegetables, and edible flowers with a leafy-green dressing drizzled atop. I sucked bites of the meat right off the skewer, moaning in delight as they melted in my mouth, the savory flavors agreeing with my palate. Giggles echoed around me before I noticed how the few from wealthier families like Viera meticulously used their utensils to slice off and nibble small bites of their food.

Self-conscious now, I couldn't help looking back up at the far balcony, but I found it to be without the Iris male who had stolen the breath from my lungs. I didn't know if it was relief or disappointment I felt at that moment. Several more courses were served, and as our bellies filled with food and wine, we began to relax a little and make conversation.

"Is it true that you breathe water?" a slender Aurum female named Rae with greenish-tinted golden skin asked in our direction. Her jade eyes sparkled with curiosity.

"In a way, I guess," I began. "Though it's hard to explain. It would be like trying to describe instinct—"

"What I'd like to know is how you manage not to burn down the entire Easthen Forest with all of your fire," Ilaria cut in with an arched brow.

Another Aurum contestant, Kire, flared her nostrils in response.

Nickel rolled her eyes at Ilaria's audacity. "Maybe their ability to avoid burning themselves and their homes is similar to our own ability to survive underwater without drowning or being crushed by the immense pressure of the sea."

"I heard Ilithania was the most magnificent city on the continent, so much so that the Iris began modeling Prisma after it. How does it compare?" Viera directed her question to Elutha, the Aereus female with wine-colored eyes.

"There are differences. While Prisma is closer to sea level, our buildings are taller and raised up from the ground on cliff faces. Plant life thrives and grows abundantly in our city. Less manicured than what you would see here, more wild and beautiful. The Palatium Crystalis is actually quite similar in style to the architecture of our ancient palatiums." Elutha spoke in a thoughtful manner, skillfully choosing her words, as we all knew how dangerous it was to insult or outshine the Iris.

What everyone obviously wanted to talk about, judging by the occasional looks and expressions, was how odd it felt to be put on display. I could have endlessly speculated on what the Iris were scheming up above, but that type of talk would definitely not be wise.

We also didn't know who could be trusted among us since we were all in direct competition with one another. So we stuck to asking each other about our homelands, magic, and ways of life, hoping to gain answers to all of the burning questions we'd had since childhood.

Himmel returned to escort us back to our suites after the final course was served. We walked back, conversations flowing more freely between the ladies. The other elemental fae were not so different from ourselves, despite the fact that we lived such separate lives. In the end, we found many of us had similar curiosities, hopes, and desires.

As we returned to our rooms, our maids were there to help us undress and prepare for bed.

"Best to get a good night's rest tonight, my lady," my maid said to me. "We'll be back in the morning to dress you."

Our maids left through the far door after turning down our beds.

"There's no way they had us get all dressed up just to watch us eat," I said to Viera once we had some privacy.

Viera shivered. "It's almost as if they were expecting us to put on a show for them or something."

Our room was dimly lit with only a few candles on our bedside tables. Snuffing them out, I lay down in my enormous bed, staring up at the canopy. The bed was luxurious, with a pile of the softest pillows surrounding me. Velvety blankets and silk sheets enveloped me. I couldn't help thinking of my sister, Mila, how she would have loved it.

Out of habit, I reached for the seashell under my pillow that wasn't there, then squeezed my hand in a fist, taking a deep breath. I did not want to think of them, of the family I'd left behind. I could not allow myself to be crushed by loneliness in this oversized bed, surrounded by strangers in a place so far from home.

Memories of the little ones flooded my brain and the way they'd cried when my name was called. And my parents.

Grabbing one of the many plush pillows on my bed, I squeezed it to my chest as I let out a silent sob. I was supposed to be an adult now, but I still needed them. Regret filled me as I thought of all the time I'd wasted being angry with my mother for the distance that had grown between us. Perhaps it hadn't only been her fault but also mine.

I curled up onto my side as I thought of our last moment together. When she'd held me and whispered in my ear, *"Trust in your heart. Trust your instincts."* But what had she meant by *"star-blessed?"* Why had that been the last thing she'd said to me? Surely she hadn't meant . . . No. That couldn't have been it. Could she have been talking about the prince? Or the "star-blessed" children I might have bore for him? The Iris had proclaimed themselves to have been sent from the stars, their multiple gifts and severe beauty evidence of this fact. Maybe it had been her way of giving me her blessing. Only the stars knew.

Being around the Iris, no matter how much they resembled stars, still set me on edge. Prince Kaleidos, if that had been him, was certainly worthy of all the adoration he received for his appearance. Full lips, strong jaw, vibrantly colored eyes which had locked with mine in that endless moment. Even the memory gave me chills. I tried clearing my mind of him, but every time I closed my eyes, I envisioned him again, standing proud up on that corner balcony, eyes on me.

After sleeplessly tossing around in my bed, I slipped out and wandered over to check if Viera was still awake. She looked far too peaceful to disturb, so I headed for the terrace.

In the dark, my view wasn't as clear as it had been the last time I was there. I had hoped to get a better idea of the layout of the palatium's grounds, but not much was visible by the glow of the fireflies and the pale moonlight.

I summoned some water from a nearby canal which appeared to snake its way through the garden in an interesting pattern. The water brought a smile to my face as it formed into a crystal clear orb the size of a grapefruit in my hands and then rolled up the back of my arm and over my shoulders as if in playful greeting. My mind calmed in meditation as I interacted with it.

While learning to harness my powers as a child, that had been one of my favorite techniques. It was a sort of dance, a contact juggle. It required a lot of concentration, as I needed to simultaneously maintain the water's shape while balancing and manipulating it in precise movements. A practice that had taught me to master both my elemental energy and my physical form. In this moment, it functioned to clear my head of all my troubling thoughts and emotions.

The orb glided across my skin in a smooth, fluid motion as I gracefully directed it with my body. I rolled it up the length of my arm and down my spine. The orb then traveled over my hip and down the length of my raised leg, coming to balance at the tip of my foot. I methodically raised my leg higher into the air, almost into a split, while maintaining the orb's position.

My powers were draining faster than usual. It was likely due to the stress and lack of access to a natural source of water. I desperately needed a swim under the stars, and there had to be a way down from the terrace.

As my eyes adjusted to the dim light, I was better able to make out my surroundings and found a trellis against the side of the wall. Covered in climbing roses, I'd have to chance sticking myself with a few thorns, but I decided it was worth the risk. If I climbed carefully enough, I might be able to avoid getting stuck.

"Ouch!" I sucked my thumb which had caught on a sharp thorn just as I reached the bottom. My feet fared a little better than my hands, thanks to my soft suede slippers, but a few nasty thorns had managed to sink through them. It had not been my brightest idea, but at least I'd managed to find a way down.

I removed my robe before entering the serpentine waterway in my nightgown. Staring up at the stars as I floated, the tiny injuries on my hands and feet started to heal as the water worked to restore me. I let the water carry me on a gentle current, watching the surrounding trees slip past.

The evening breeze carried the sweet and musky scent of night-blooming jasmine. It was so quiet and peaceful out there, the only sounds were that of nature and the tinkling of the stream.

"Now, that's a sight I haven't seen before." A deep voice with a sophisticated accent broke through the silence. Alarmed at the intrusion, I ducked under the water, even though I doubted it was murky enough to hide myself in. As I peeked up, an Iris male—*the* Iris male—stepped up to the side of the waterway, a small, amused smile tugging at the corners of his lips.

Chapter 8
The Prince

AELLA

I had no choice but to confront the male who stood at the edge of the water staring down at me, so I emerged with as much grace as I could manage. The fact that my nightgown was white and nearly translucent with water did not help.

The prince, or rather the male who I assumed was the prince, stood with his well-fitted silks unbuttoned halfway to his navel. What showed of his darker complexion glimmered iridescently in the soft moonlight. His hair was a mess of dark onyx waves reflecting colors in a kaleidoscopic fashion.

"Were you spying on me?" I blurted out before I could think better of it.

His eyes narrowed slightly followed by a soft chuckle. "I like to stroll the gardens at night. This coincidentally happens to be one of the paths I frequent for the night-blooming jasmine . . . but now this new . . . *water feature* has me captivated." He winked. "Do you always perform for the fireflies?"

My cheeks burned when I realized he must have been watching me the entire time. I marked my distance from my robe, plotting an exit for myself.

Returning my attention to the prince, I slicked the wet hair out of my face and feigned what little confidence I could muster. "I should head back inside. If you wouldn't mind turning around while I fetch my robe . . ."

The male cocked a brow at me, likely unaccustomed to people making such requests of him, then sighed before pivoting his head away from me. I swiftly emerged from the water, pulling the thin fabric of my robe tightly around me.

When the male turned back to face me and took in my shivering form, heat began to swirl around me like that of a flame. It surrounded me, invisible tendrils licking at my skin like tiny rays of sunlight, evaporating virtually all of the remaining moisture. Despite the comforting presence of his warmth, a chill ran up my neck at this foreign yet intimate sensation. I shuddered lightly.

"I can't have you catching a chill now. It's only your first night here." The corner of his lips rose into a taunting grin before he turned to walk away.

Something about him set off a current in me. I couldn't tell if it was good or bad, but whatever it was, it rallied like a hurricane of emotions swirling around in my stomach and chest. My knuckles whitened as I gripped my robe tighter around me. The male began walking away, then paused mid-stride, tilting his head as if he sensed I had something to say.

"You're the prince, aren't you?" I asked.

A flicker of displeasure flared in his eyes as he faced me again, his expression quickly returning to a mocking facade.

"At your disposal," he said.

"I would have expected you . . . you of all people . . . to know it's poor manners to use your powers on a lady without her permission," I said with a huff, thrown off by how much his sneering gaze affected me.

His eyes widened and then narrowed at my accusation.

"You were shivering and wet. I was doing the chivalrous thing," he said, his tone carrying more than a hint of frustration at having to explain himself to me.

"I am Argenti, I like being wet!" I shouted back at him, my brows furrowed.

The prince threw back his head in a roar of laughter. His laughter piqued my irritation before being replaced by humiliation as the realization of what I'd said occurred to me. My hand came up to cover my slack jaw.

"I don't know how long it's been since I've had a good laugh like that. Thank you, my lady," he said.

I couldn't allow him to win. I had to walk out of this with some dignity. Dropping my hand back down, I stood as tall and as regally as possible. While forcing a smile on my face, I replied with little humor, "I am delighted that I could be of assistance, Your Highness."

He seemed to balk at the formality, looking away in disinterest as if I'd somehow offended him. My pulse quickened at the sense, although I was uncertain why.

The wind picked up, blowing loose flowers and leaves off the trees and into the air. My hair flew around me, and my robe threatened to expose me as it flapped in the wind. The prince looked around curiously at the sudden change in weather.

Then he looked back at me. "I shall head back to my wing now. But before I go, would you tell me your name?" he asked.

Still mortified, I was tempted to give him the wrong name, but it was not a ruse that would hold up for long. Begrudgingly, I offered my name to him. I really should have been more careful with my words in his presence. I might have gotten myself into waves of trouble if he'd had more of an ego.

I turned to leave, but my name on his lips stopped me.

"Aella."

I paused. I'd never heard my name uttered like that before. His deep voice, velvety smooth and beckoning.

"Goodnight, My Prince," I said without looking back.

I made my way back to the thorny trellis which cracked under my weight, threatening to come loose as I climbed.

A flash of lightning lit up the sky. Thunder followed less than a breath later, sounding too close for comfort. A torrent of rain battered down on me, making it harder to climb.

A few more cracks pulsed through the trellis as it started to pull away from the wall. Realizing I was going with it, I propelled myself, rolling into the fall for protection before the trellis came crashing down.

With the next strike of lightning, thunder cracked almost instantaneously, making me jump. The ferocity of the storm was utterly frightening. Tree branches waved relentlessly in the strong winds, evoking a wicked dance of shadows across the expanse of the garden.

While I could barely stand due to the fierce gusts of the howling storm, the prince stood under a ledge that provided a small shelter. His powers acted like a force field to protect him against the weather.

I immediately regretted being out there, unsure what I'd been thinking when I decided using the trellis was safe. The prince leaned against the wall, seemingly unaffected, legs crossed at the ankles as he watched me recover myself back onto my feet. *Useless male.*

Lightning struck again, and I crumpled down into a low crouch, hands over my neck and head. Another shock of lightning flashed through the sky, shining a blinding light on all the surfaces around me. I risked a peek, only to find the prince no longer under the ledge.

My heart hammered in my chest, vibrating with the roar of thunder. Powerful arms pulled me into an embrace—not loving or gentle but strong and protective.

As another sweeping gust of wind struck toward us, the prince created a dome of protection, insulating us from the storm. My head burrowed into his marbled chest as I sought safety in his arms. His scent reminded me of sea salt and oak, and his skin was warm in contrast to the violent storm around us. My breath was uneven, and my skin tingled at the sensation of our touch.

The prince stared off into the distance. But as I gazed up at him, he tilted his face down toward mine until our faces were mere inches from one another.

My heart quickened as I took in the colors of his eyes. The combination of rich forest green and bronze with gold and silver chaotically mixed in made them the most mesmerizing sight.

His strong, lean body pressed firmly against mine as he held me tight, making me feel small but safe in his arms.

The wind quieted, and the rain began to slow from a downpour to a drizzle. I pulled back sheepishly.

Everything about his actions and the way he made me feel was wrong. It was so at odds with my perception of the Iris. He was supposed to be self-centered and vain, not gallant.

"I didn't need your help," I said, balling my hands into fists.

"Clearly," he replied, whipping his wet hair from his face.

I opened my mouth to retort, but as I couldn't come up with a decent comeback, I closed my lips and let out a frustrated breath.

The prince turned, putting space between us. Thick vines began growing and twisting furiously as they made their way up the side of the wall, creating a ladder-like shape up to my balcony.

Hating that he had been right and that I obviously did need his help made it worse, frustrating me even more.

We stood in the light rain, water dripping down our faces while we stared at each other. His eyes appeared to shimmer and glow in complement to his iridescent complexion. His chest rose and fell in a controlled pattern as if he was trying to hold back his temper.

"What are you so bothered about?" I asked with a tone of condescension in my voice to rival his.

His voice darkened. "You think you can handle yourself? Clearly, you don't need my help." He gestured to the fallen trellis and the new vine ladder.

"Is that all you followed me here to do? To scold me?" I challenged him.

"A little thanks would be nice."

I laughed haughtily.

The prince stalked toward me, and I shrank back as he towered over me. Slowly, he spoke, his tone sharp and biting. "I had to make sure that my potential bride didn't get herself killed on her first night here."

I recoiled at his words. The prince turned away, making to leave. He looked me over once more, eyes scanning me from head to toe, and then scoffed, a cruel sound. I blinked as it hit me like a slap to the cheek.

Wrapping my arms around myself, I wanted to scream. I was insulted that he had the power to draw out so many different emotions in me and make me feel so insignificant. I sat down on the ground, pulling my knees into my chest, and let the rain envelop me like sympathetic tears.

The skin on my cheek still tingled, a reminder of where it had made contact with his chest just moments before. I stood up in determination. He did not deserve my tears, and I would prove that to him.

Chapter 9
Divergence

Arianwen

As I hiked through the woods, I kept an eye out for specific plants I needed for healing and anything edible. My stomach rumbled, reminding me that I had yet to pull out any of the food my mother had packed for me after all the excitement of the evening prior. I was relieved to have a moment to myself away from the stranger—from Wynn. He made me feel on edge, and I wasn't sure if that was because he was a strange male or because being around him brought my feelings of discontent to the surface. It was as if I was caught in a strong current and was about to be pulled in a different direction.

Come on, Ari, time to focus. Get this fae back on his feet and continue with the plan. Make it to the villages and meet with the healers and return home in time to get married.

My head knew what I was supposed to do, but my traitorous heart couldn't help but wonder what it would be like to let that current divert my path.

Perhaps the stars sent me to help him.

I continued walking, stopping every so often to pick up a plant or forage for some of the winter berries that were in season. My stomach rumbled again, and I figured it was a sign to head back.

※

"Wynn! I'm back!" I called out as I neared the copse of trees where I'd left him. When no response came, I hurried my steps toward him. "Wynn!" My heart stuttered as I came upon his unconscious form.

Stars, I was gone too long.

He appeared sicklier than before, his skin pale yet flushed with fever, moisture beading around his temple. I didn't have the proper supplies with me, so I chewed up some of the plants I'd found to create a paste to put on his wound. Part of me was grateful he wasn't awake to watch me do it. Gently putting the paste on his injury, I pushed more healing power into him, willing the infection to leave his body. Fae bodies usually healed faster than his was healing. I silently prayed to the stars that whatever had poisoned him would be neutralized by the paste. Not knowing what poison had been used limited my ability to help him beyond that.

I shook him lightly. "Wynn, you should drink some water. Please wake up."

His eyes fluttered open, and he tried to crack a smile. "Sorry I'm so much trouble, my star."

I summoned water to me and cupped it in my hands for him. "Please, try to drink a little."

He took a few sips from my hands and then closed his eyes again. Unable to stop myself, I brushed some strands of his white hair away from his brow. It shimmered a little in the light. I continued to brush his hair back, my hands cool from the water I had summoned, and he seemed to relax under my touch.

"Don't stop," he mumbled. "Your hands feel amazing."

His words made me smile, and I continued to soothe him with my touch over the next hour, letting as much healing power flow into him as I could spare. His color started to improve, and he started sweating more profusely as his fever broke. As he drifted off to sleep, I sensed his rest becoming more peaceful.

Pulling away from him and leaning back against a tree, I breathed out a sigh of relief. Healing took a lot out of me, and I was still feeling weak after unintentionally fasting since the day before. I pulled out some of the food my mother had packed for me and moaned quietly at the taste of the delicious crusty bread and cheese. After a little while, I grabbed the winter berries I had found and popped them into my mouth one by one. As my strength returned, I glanced over at Wynn and caught him watching me with faint amusement.

"Oh! You're awake! I think your fever broke. You'll be feeling better soon, I hope." I wiped at my mouth, hoping I didn't have food stuck somewhere.

"Yes, thanks to your ministrations, I'm feeling much better."

"Are you hungry? I have some food to spare."

"I could watch you eat all day," he teased. "Looking at you, I'd have thought you were eating the greatest of delicacies."

My silvery skin flushed at that. "I hadn't eaten in a while . . . I think any food tastes better when you've been deprived of it." I scooted a little closer to him and held out a handful of winter berries. "Would you like some?"

He nodded, opening his mouth for me to feed him, a dare in his eyes. Before I could talk myself out of it, I fed him a berry with my fingers. His lips closed around them and small flutters moved from my stomach to my toes at the sensual feel of it.

What am I doing? This is totally inappropriate . . .
Why do I like it?

Our eyes met, and I was drawn into his gaze. I had never felt that way before. Was it arousal? Was I going to be sick? My heart rate started picking up, and I panicked knowing he could probably hear it, which only made it worse. He opened his mouth for more, a knowing smile on his face, and I continued feeding him the berries. When they were gone, he sighed in pleasure. I would have thought feeding a male like that would feel demeaning, and perhaps it would have, had it been anyone else, but with Wynn . . . it somehow felt right.

Stars, I'm in trouble.

"What are you doing so far from the sea, Arianwen?" Wynn asked.

"My people have a ritual called the matri-ritus that every female partakes in before she is to be wed," I replied. "I'm supposed to be meditating and preparing for marriage as I make this journey."

"Ah, yes. The arranged marriage you mentioned," he said. "I gather that marriage is not something you are looking forward to?"

My brow furrowed slightly. "I wish I was free to make my own choices and not be rushed into something because the Iris demand it," I replied. "Though merely voicing my displeasure would be cause for treason."

Wynn's face lit up with understanding. "You may speak freely with me if you wish," he said reassuringly. "The Adamas are not on speaking terms with the Iris, and I would never subject anyone to their punishment if I could help it."

Looking at him, I believed that he spoke the truth. Perhaps it was naive, but I wanted to trust him. "You never told me what you were doing here . . . I know you don't know me, but I would never turn you in to the Iris either. I have the impression it would not go well for you if I did."

"You assume correctly. The bolt you removed from my shoulder was one of theirs."

I gasped, my eyes going wide. "The Iris did that to you? They're aware of your existence?" I jumped to my feet and started pacing. "Stars! So many lies, so much control. I don't know what to believe anymore. I loathe everything about them, everything they stand for. So help me—"

I was cut off by Wynn's groaning as he attempted to stand for the first time since I had found him. He appeared a little pale, but I wasn't sure if it was due to his natural coloring or weakness from his injury. He braced himself against a tree and took a few breaths.

Stopping my pacing, I hurried back to him. "Take it easy, Wynn. You're still regaining strength. You lost a lot of blood yesterday and have barely eaten more than a handful of berries since then."

"Arianwen . . . Ari, I am all right, thanks to you. While I'd love nothing more than to remain and discuss our mutual hatred of the Iris, we can't stay here forever. Being with me will only put you in danger. As much as I have enjoyed your company, I do think we should part ways so that you can continue your rite."

My heart dropped even though I knew he was right. Staying with him was foolish and was keeping me from my journey. If an Iris patrol had shot him out of the sky, stars knew what they would do to us if they discovered us together. If they found out I had stumbled upon one of their best-kept secrets, I would be imprisoned or worse.

I'm not ready to leave him . . .

What is wrong with me?

"I'm not leaving you until you've recovered more," I replied.

"Traveling together is a terrible idea. I'll be fine."

"You can barely stand! Damn the consequences. I'm a healer, and I'm not abandoning my patient when he needs me."

Wynn reached forward and tucked a wayward strand of hair behind my ear, and I shuddered at his touch. "There's no convincing you otherwise, is there?"

I raised my chin as I stared him down. "Absolutely not."

If I was being completely honest with myself, the fact that being with him was so forbidden also held a certain appeal.

"Well then, we have stayed here long enough. You must be star-blessed considering they have not discovered us thus far."

I looked around a little nervously. "Do you really think they are still hunting you?"

"I don't believe they would assume me dead without confirming the kill and hiding the evidence."

The reality of the actual danger we were in sank in, and I quickly packed up my belongings and tried to erase any trace that we had been there.

"There's nothing I can do about the broken tree branches, but hopefully they won't be too observant, or maybe they won't even come this way," I said. He was still leaning against the tree, so I put my arm around his waist and looked up at him. "You can lean on me, I'm stronger than I look."

He stood to his full height, which was easily a foot taller than me, and put his arm over my shoulders. "I humbly accept your assistance."

"Where should we go?" I asked, still looking up at him.

"We need to head north, further up into the alps," he replied.

He leaned on me as we started moving in that direction, our pace sluggish. I could tell that he was trying to prevent me from bearing all of his weight, and considering the bulk of his muscles, I was glad for that. Though I would never have said it.

"Perhaps I can venture into the next village for some provisions. I wish we could stay the night at the inn there, but you are way too conspicuous to do so. There is no way you could pass for Argenti or Iris."

"True. Keep an eye out for caves, it will be getting colder at night the further north we go. With the patrols, it's not safe to build a fire."

I shivered a little at the thought, then almost immediately blushed, remembering how close we had gotten the night before.

Our progress was painfully slow, and I sensed Wynn trying to hide his growing weakness from me. His breathing became a little more labored, and we barely spoke as we made our way through the woods. What would have taken me a few hours took us most of the remainder of the day. It didn't help that we were off the path. As we rounded a bend, I knew we were nearing the village where I had planned to make my first stop when the trees thinned out and the ground showed signs of tread. My stomach grumbled at the thought of a warm meal, and my body ached at the thought of another night on the hard ground, but I could manage. I refused to complain.

"It'll be dark soon," I said as we stopped near a stream. I knelt and filled up my empty flask with the icy water. I could summon the water to me at any time, but I wanted Wynn to have access to water without relying on me. I handed him the flask which he took with a thank you, and then I splashed some of the water onto my face. I wished I could submerge myself, but the splash would have to do. The water felt amazing on my flushed skin, especially after the arduous walk through the woods supporting Wynn's weight. "I'm fairly certain the village is not far from here."

"We can still part ways, you know," Wynn reminded me. "I would not hold it against you."

"I already told you that I'm not leaving you, so stop trying to get rid of me."

Wynn sighed, sounding exasperated. "There is nothing wrong with a little self-preservation."

Ignoring him, I said, "I wonder if I can find you some clothes, considering how much colder it's getting. The blankets I have won't be enough without a fire."

"Good thing there is such a thing as body heat," Wynn said with a wicked grin.

I looked away, fighting the blush that was coming over me. This male had my stomach erupting with butterflies with his suggestive words and glances. It was all so new.

"You are very easy to tease, Ari . . . but I hope I'm not making you too uncomfortable."

"Don't worry about it," I replied. "I'm not as naive as you might think."

But I was lying. I was way out of my depth.

Chapter 10

Lakehaven

Arianwen

After finding a small cave to shelter in, I left Wynn and hurried toward the village to look for supplies. I had always wondered why some Argenti fae were willing to live over a day's hike from the sea but understood as soon as I made my way into the heart of Lakehaven. A dozen or more homes and structures were built around a beautiful shimmering lake. Seeing the water brought a calming peace to my soul.

Despite the energetic commotion in the streets surrounding the lake, the water itself was still like a mirror, perfectly reflecting the silhouette of mountains around it. Small children played near the lakeshore, chasing all manner of freshwater critters as their parents called for them to return home for dinner. The sun's last rays hit the water as it crept below the horizon.

I made my way down the length of a dock that jutted out into the water, checked my pack to make sure it was properly fastened to protect the contents, and dove in. It felt like a home away from home as the water soothed my sore muscles and washed away some of the anxiety I'd been feeling. The lake was much calmer than the sea, and there were no underwater homes, but I still relished the feeling of weightlessness as I explored the lakebed. I spotted small creatures burrowing into the sandy bottom and some Argenti fae foraging for plants.

Despite wanting to linger, I made my way back to the surface. My power reserves had been filled, and I felt a little more like myself. I climbed the ladder back onto the dock and used my power to siphon the water out of my clothes and hair while glancing around to get my bearings.

Warm light and the sound of music poured out of one of the structures, which I assumed to be some kind of tavern. I made my way toward the welcoming atmosphere, the scent of freshly baked bread causing my mouth to water, tempting me more than I wanted to admit. Wynn was waiting for me in the cave, and I needed to get what I came for and not let myself get too distracted.

As I walked into the tavern, heads swiveled toward me, giving me a brief once-over before returning to their meals and conversations. I made my way over to the bar, knowing that was where I would most likely find the information I needed.

"Evening," I said, nodding my head in respect to the male behind the bar. "I'm here on my matri-ritus from Iveria and was hoping to replenish some supplies. Do you know where I might be able to find some extra clothing?"

"Take a seat," the older fae replied gruffly. He poured me a giant tumbler of ale, scrutinizing me, his brows furrowed. "Our village has one shop that might have what you need, but they closed at nightfall. You'll have to wait until tomorrow."

I clutched the tumbler, disappointment crashing through me. Wynn needed clothes, especially because we couldn't build a fire. I took a giant swig of the ale, enjoying how it warmed my insides. "The sun just went down, is there any chance they might be willing to sell me a few items now? I really need to be on my way." Looking at the bartender, my eyes pleading, I hoped I could sway him to help me.

The bartender frowned at me. "It's not safe to travel through these woods at night. Many beasts wouldn't mind taking a bite out of a female traveling alone." He leaned toward me and spoke quietly, looking around furtively to make sure he wasn't overheard. "There's talk of Iris patrols. I wouldn't want my daughter wandering on her own with those dangers. If you were smart, you'd stay here tonight."

I fought back a shudder. Wynn had been right, they were looking for him. I was anxious to return to him, despite—or maybe because of—the danger.

"I appreciate your concern, sir, but I really must be on my way tonight. I guess I can make do without." I took another swig of the ale, wishing I could stick around for a meal. "You wouldn't happen to have any food ready that I could take with me?"

He eyed me a little suspiciously but nodded his head. "I'll check what I have in the back and wrap something up for you. I still think you're making a mistake," he grumbled, walking away.

While finishing my drink, I was startled by a gentle tap on my shoulder. I spun around and took in the Argenti female. She appeared to be a little younger than me with deep amethyst eyes and a friendly smile.

"Hello! I'm Siris!" she chirped. "I couldn't help but overhear that you need some supplies?"

"Hi," I replied with a smile. "Yes, I was hoping to purchase a few things, but it appears I'm too late." I gave a slight shrug.

"My mother owns the village store, and I'm sure she wouldn't mind if I helped you out," she offered.

A big smile broke out on my face. "Really? That's so kind of you. You'd be doing me a huge favor."

"We don't get many outsiders here in Lakehaven. Word of a visitor travels fast, and I had to see for myself."

The bartender returned with a small bundle of food and placed it in front of me. "Siris, not getting into trouble, are you?"

"Oh, not at all, Grandpa Jesse. Just trying to help a stranger in need!" she replied excitedly.

I pulled out some coin and placed them on the counter. "Thank you so much for your hospitality, sir."

He nodded at me and then moved down the bar to help another patron. I placed the bundle into my pack and turned to Siris. "Lead the way!"

We left the tavern, and I followed her toward the village store. She chattered away about the weather and how she wished she could travel to Iveria, asking me lots of questions about my home and the city.

"Nothing exciting ever happens here," she lamented. "We are so far from the city, we aren't included in any of the marriage drafts."

"Consider yourself lucky," I replied. "I'd trade excitement for more freedom any day."

"You say that now, but you'd change your mind if you had to actually live here." She led me into the store and turned on a few lights. "Let me know if you need help finding anything! I'm going to let my mother know I'm here so she doesn't worry."

I took a quick inventory and found a couple of oversized shirts that might fit Wynn. Spotting a flask, I pulled it off the shelf then grabbed another warm blanket.

I hope she doesn't ask too many more questions. I don't know how I'll explain why I need such large clothes for myself. If the Iris show up and question people...

I bit my lip, starting to worry.

"Siris? I found what I need!" I called out. The clatter of feet pounded down the stairs, and she bounded back into the room.

"Wonderful!" she exclaimed. Siris inspected my selections, an eyebrow raised in question, and named a price higher than I'd anticipated.

Handing back one of the shirts, we renegotiated before I placed the coin in her hand.

I put the clothing and flask into my pack and wrapped the blanket around my shoulders. Giving her a smile filled with warmth, I hoped my gratitude showed through.

"Thanks for your kindness and for opening up the shop for me after hours."

"It was no trouble at all," she replied. "I'm sorry to see you go. It really is unusual that you are not staying the night. How very adventurous of you."

"The matri-ritus is all about meditation, and I don't do well behind closed doors," I lied, feeling somewhat guilty.

"Well, please stop by and say hello if you ever make your way here again."

"You can count on it," I said with a smile.

She let me out of the door, and I waved as I made my way back to Wynn.

With a spring in my step, pleased I had found what I needed, I approached the tiny cave we were settling in for the night. Stars willing, we would be left alone by the beasts and Iris patrols I had been warned about. I was excited to see Wynn, which surprised me, considering I barely knew him. My matri-ritus had taken such an interesting and unorthodox turn. I'd bet all my coral that my mother would faint if she knew I had spent the night with a strange male and was planning on doing so again.

It's not like anything is going to happen. He knows I'm getting married, and our flirting is totally innocent and just for fun. Nothing could ever come of us anyway. The stars would curse us, and the Iris would put us to death if they found us getting involved.

"Wynn, it's Arianwen!" I called out as I approached the cave, keeping my voice soft. I didn't want to scare him.

I crouched a little as I entered. The small space made me feel somewhat claustrophobic.

"I was beginning to think you might have taken my advice and stayed away," Wynn joked half-heartedly.

"Wild seahorses couldn't have kept me away," I teased in return. He was huddled up under blankets at the back, looking exhausted with dark smudges under his eyes. There was no light in the cave, but my eyes were able to see well enough in the dark, so it didn't bother me. "I brought you some clothes and picked up something warm to eat from the tavern."

"That sounds wonderful," he said.

I sat down next to him and opened my pack, handing him one of the shirts I hoped would fit him. He unwrapped himself from the blankets, and I couldn't help but admire his broad shoulders and sculpted chest once again. His wound looked like it was healing well, which pleased me. The shirt was a little snug, but it was better than nothing.

I pulled out the food the bartender had wrapped up for me and opened it eagerly. "It looks like I have some smoked trout and roasted potatoes here—more filling than a bunch of berries."

Wynn chuckled. "The berries were my favorite part of the day, but that does sound delicious."

There he goes, flirting again. At least I think he is?

I shook my head as I placed the wrapper with the food on the ground between us and picked up a portion of the fish. "Mhmmm, this is cooked to perfection." I moaned softly, the buttery, tender flesh melting in my mouth. Wynn gave me an indecipherable look as he picked up a piece and started eating. "What," I deadpanned.

"Just . . . you and food. I've never seen anyone enjoy it as much as you do."

"You've got to be kidding me."

"No, I'm serious. You have a certain light and joy to you that hasn't been quelled by your unfavorable circumstances. It's a wonderful quality."

"Thanks, I guess . . ." My brow furrowed. "Is your life so challenging that it's lacking in joy?"

"My life is dangerous and full of responsibility, but I do occasionally have time for simple pleasures . . . like watching you eat." He smirked at me.

"Glad I could be of service to you," I said dryly.

We continued eating, enjoying each other's company in companionable silence. I liked that about Wynn. He didn't seem to find it necessary to fill every moment with ceaseless chatter. There was a certain peace that came over me in his presence that I hadn't expected to feel, despite the frequent chest flutters and chills that coursed down my spine when I was around him.

Maybe something is seriously wrong with me and I should find a healer to check me out. This can't be normal.

"I heard talk of Iris patrols when I was in the village, so we do need to be cautious," I said, breaking the silence.

"I was afraid of that," he replied.

"Are they strong trackers?"

"The fact that they haven't caught up to me so far is a good sign, but we need to be on guard. I also can't risk leading them back to my people . . . or you."

His concern for my well-being flooded me with warmth. "Where is home for you, Wynn?"

"Home is north, but I can't give you more than that in case they do manage to capture us. I don't want you in possession of any information that would put my people in danger. I hope you understand."

I felt a pinprick of hurt, but I understood. I would do anything for my family as well, and I didn't know what forms of torture the Iris might use to gain information—better I had no information to lose.

"I do . . . I'd hate to be the reason anyone was put at risk."

After demolishing the food I'd bought, I pulled out my flask and handed Wynn the extra one. I gulped down the fresh, cold water and sighed in satisfaction. The water tasted better in the mountains somehow, maybe because it was closer to the source.

"We should try to get some rest so we can make more headway tomorrow," Wynn said. "I was holding us back today."

"Give yourself some credit, you lost a lot of blood and had a raging infection. Your fever had barely broken when you wanted to start walking!"

"I credit all of my healing to you, Ari," his low voice murmured, doing funny things to my insides.

My lips broke into a shy smile, his praise giving me a sense of satisfaction. "Yes, rest sounds good. Especially so you can have more energy tomorrow and continue healing."

Wynn spread out one of the blankets on the ground and lay with his back against the cave wall. He patted the blanket-covered ground in front of him. "Come, lie next to me so we can be warm. I promise I won't bite or do anything you don't ask me to." His eyes glinted in the dark with a hint of daring.

All of the blood rushed to my face, and I was grateful for the cover of darkness as I considered his offers, both spoken and implied.

"I suppose proximity makes sense, especially with the lack of a fire . . ."

I lay down next to him, making sure no part of our bodies were touching, not sure if I should face him or turn away from him. I tried to lie on my back, but the rocky ground was digging in uncomfortably as I fidgeted, so I decided to lay on my side, facing away from Wynn. I was satisfied with my decision, realizing that lying that way was the best way to avoid the awkwardness and intimacy that came with sleeping next to him.

"Arianwen, body heat only works if we're touching," Wynn said, amusement clear in his voice. He reached out to put his arm around my waist and pulled me closer so my back was nestled against his chest. He settled the remaining blankets over us and shifted so that our bodies were completely flush against each other. "Much better," his voice rumbled through me. Then he seemed to hesitate. "Is this okay?"

"It's fine," I squeaked.

This is totally not fine!

I had never been this close to anyone other than my siblings when we'd cuddled together in bed as children. It felt like my heart was going to race out of my chest. How in the stars was I supposed to fall asleep with him surrounding me like that? I tried to calm myself by taking a deep, cleansing breath, but all it did was make me more aware of Wynn as his crisp, woodsy scent filled my nose.

"Don't worry, you're safe with me," Wynn murmured against the back of my neck, the breath from his nose tickling the pointed tip of my ear. I didn't respond in hopes that he'd just fall asleep and we could end the awkward conversation.

He eventually loosened his grip around my waist, and I felt his breath grow slower and deeper as he drifted off to sleep. With that, I finally allowed my limbs to loosen and felt my heart rate begin to slow. My body relaxed into the warmth of him. True to his word, he hadn't tried to do anything, even as a small, traitorous part of me wished he had.

You're in so much trouble, Ari.

Chapter 11
The Wager

Arianwen

"Arianwen... Ari!" Wynn spoke urgently in a whisper while shaking me gently.

"What is it?" I yawned, not yet awake enough to comprehend his tone. The cave was dark, it had to still be the middle of the night.

"You need to be very quiet, and you need to trust me," he whispered.

I looked up at him, and my whole body jumped to alertness as I registered the alarm in his voice and the tension in his body.

"Wynn, you're scaring me. What's going on?" I leaped up as I questioned him, reaching for my pack.

"There is a patrol nearby. We need to go. Now."

My heart began racing at the fear of being caught with him. I started shoving everything into my pack as quickly as possible, not wanting to leave any trace of having been there.

"How do you know? How did they find us?"

"I'll explain later. They haven't found us yet, but they could at any moment if we don't get out of here."

Wynn crawled toward the cave's entrance and motioned at me to follow him. I crept as silently as I could, and he held a finger up to his lips to remind me not to speak. I rolled my eyes and followed him out of the cave.

He leaned down and whispered, so softly I could barely hear him, "This is where you need to trust me."

Before I could even think to respond, Wynn pulled me tightly to his chest, and I clung to him as the ground suddenly dropped away. Biting down on my tongue so hard I tasted blood, I fought every instinct telling me to scream as we rose swiftly into the air. Right before we broke through the top of the trees, Wynn stopped our ascent and set my feet onto a sturdy branch.

"A warning would have been nice," I whispered angrily.

Wynn chuckled softly. "I'm sorry, my star. We didn't exactly have time to debate the escape plan, but I will let you know well in advance next time we need to fly."

"There won't be a next time!"

"Feel free to climb down and join the Iris then."

I glared at him in the dark. His calm demeanor was somehow making me even more irate. This was not what I'd signed up for, but, to be fair, he *had* tried to give me an out multiple times.

Taking a deep breath, I asked, "How long do we have to stay up here?"

"Hold on, I'm trying to figure out how many we're dealing with."

"How did you know they were coming? I didn't see or hear anything!"

Wynn looked exasperated with all the questions. "I could hear them in the wind," he tried to explain. "If I set my mind to it, I can hear a whisper that is miles away. Knowing the Iris are hunting me, I've had to use most of my power to try to stay alert to noises that don't belong." He stiffened. "Shhh . . . they're here," he whispered into my ear.

I strained to hear what he could, afraid to look down from such a great height. A gentle breeze carried voices up toward us.

"I could have sworn I got that birdstain with one of my bolts," a male voice stated. "We should have found a body by now."

"Caelum will be furious with us if we don't bring him a head," another male voice replied.

"The locals said there are some caves around here. If he's still alive, we'll find him," the first male said.

"Faex, I am so sick of this patrol duty. All I want is to get back to my wine and some tasty females. Caelum is supposed to give me furlough to Prisma, and I am so ready for it. I need a break from all the fishy Argenti whores," the second male spoke.

I bristled at the derogatory comments.

Why, oh why did the stars send them?

Looking up at Wynn's face, I could see hatred stirring in his eyes. He held a finger up to his lips as a reminder to be quiet, and I blew out a breath, glaring at him. I was annoyed at his insinuation that I lacked common sense. He wrapped my arms around the trunk of the tree and then dropped silently toward the ground.

Risking a peek at the ground below, I instantly regretted it as a wave of nausea swept through me once I saw how high up I was. Clinging to the tree, I observed as Wynn landed behind the two Iris males. Within seconds, they were gasping and clutching at their throats before falling to the ground.

What in the stars . . .

Wynn dragged them one by one into the cave we'd vacated.

Did he kill them? Oh, stars. I'm going to be sick.

I started hyperventilating, and my knees went weak.

Get it together, Ari. You cannot fall out of this tree!

I tried slowing my breaths and closing my eyes—praying the nausea would pass.

"Arianwen, are you okay?" Wynn asked.

His voice took me by surprise, and I nearly jumped. Before I could respond, he swept me up into his arms. I clung to him in fear, my arms wrapped tightly around his neck.

"Did you kill them?" I whispered accusingly. Despite how much I hated the Iris, the healer in me struggled with the thought of their deaths.

"They won't be bothering us anymore," Wynn replied while we descended toward the ground.

"What? How?" I sputtered. "You don't have any weapons on you, and you didn't even touch them, but I saw them collapse . . ."

"I stole the air right out of their lungs," he said, avoiding my gaze.

"Stars, I'm going to be sick . . . Put me down!" I exclaimed as we landed.

He gently set me on my feet, and I dashed away from him to empty my stomach onto the ground. I summoned water from a nearby stream to cool my face and soothe my sore throat when the retching finally stopped. Wynn's footsteps alerted me to his presence, and I turned, glancing at him warily.

"Are you all right?" he asked, concern knitting his brow.

"I will be," I said, wringing my hands together. "I know they were disgusting and vile, but did you have to kill them?"

Wynn raised his eyebrows, his eyes pinning me where I stood. "They would have gladly killed both of us without a thought if they'd caught us unaware. There would have been no trial, you would just be dead. Your family would have never known what happened to you. My existence is a secret they would never allow to get out. I did what I had to do to keep you safe. I warned you I was dangerous." He practically sneered at the end of his rant.

Chills skittered down my spine, and I felt myself cowering away from him. Looking down, I took a few breaths before I said something I'd regret. I knew he was right about the situation, but I'd be lying if I said he didn't scare me at that moment.

Straightening my posture, I raised my chin and caught his eyes. "I understand, but I don't have to like it."

He prowled toward me, and without realizing it, I took a few steps back before hitting a wide tree. Wynn huffed a dark laugh as he boxed me in, raising one large muscular arm to lean on the tree over my head. He bent his head down to my face, his breath coasting over my lips. "Afraid? You should be. This wasn't the first time and most certainly will not be the last time I kill someone."

I shivered at his proximity and the warring feelings flooding me. Fear. Curiosity. Revulsion. Arousal.

There must be something seriously wrong with me.

"I know what you're doing, and you're not going to scare me away," I replied, not breaking his gaze, hoping I wouldn't give away all the conflicting feelings that were flowing through me. His mouth was so close to my own, our lips would have touched if one of us moved an inch. My breath hitched, and his gaze dropped to my lips, his own tipping into a sardonic grin.

"My star, do you really have no sense of self-preservation?" He gripped my chin with his right hand and locked eyes with me again. "I am not at my full strength, and those Iris could have caught us by surprise," he said, sounding almost angry. "I think, perhaps, you have no real desire to return home to your unhappily arranged marriage. Staying with me could get you killed, yet you're still here."

"You have no idea what I'm thinking or feeling!" I spat right back, ducking out from under his arm and putting some distance between us.

"Oh, really?" he mused. "I think you can't help thriving on this danger, and you don't know if you want to hit me or kiss me."

He smirked while I blushed furiously, hating that he wasn't far from the truth. But he had one thing wrong. Despite having left only two days before, I desperately missed my home. The sea called to me, but I couldn't deny that Wynn had somehow caught me in his thrall.

"You think way too highly of yourself. I will never kiss you."

"I wager you'll be begging me to kiss you before we part ways."

"Oh, really now? If I had anything to wager, I'd take that bet. There is no way you could win it."

"I'll just have to prove you wrong then."

"If you say so," I huffed angrily at him, rolling my eyes, then decided to change the subject. "We can't stay here—you filled our cave with dead males! So what's the plan now? I don't think I could sleep anymore tonight unless someone knocked me unconscious."

"Is that a request?"

"Can you be serious?"

The humor left Wynn's eyes. "There could be more patrols, so we need to continue north. I would fly us, but I don't have the strength to fly all night, especially with an unwilling passenger."

Placing my hands on my hips, I said, "I would prefer my feet remain on the ground for the remainder of this journey."

"I'm sure you would, but you surprised me and did fairly well earlier. You didn't scream. Consider me impressed."

Stunned at his praise and sudden change of attitude, I didn't know how to respond. I couldn't trust my feelings around him. One minute, he was making me feel all flustered and infatuated, and the next, he was making me angry. I had never spent so much one-on-one time with a male, and I couldn't help but wonder if Verus would make me feel that way too. Would he get my blood boiling and evoke such passion? I couldn't imagine it, especially because I had never met—much less *seen*—the male. My parents weren't passionate unless they were fighting each other. I wouldn't say they had the happiest of marriages, but they seemed satisfied with their lives.

Ignoring my silence, Wynn started moving noiselessly through the forest. It was almost as if he pushed the sound away from him as he walked, and I wondered if it had anything to do with how his powers worked. Taking a deep breath, I followed after him, thinking some quiet between us might actually be a good thing.

Chapter 12

Faber Ludi

Kaleidos

The sun shone down on thirty elemental fae as they marched around the expansive arena. The ensemble of females were dressed in tailored bodices made of supple leather that tastefully accentuated the curves and contours of their bodies. Bronze, gold, and silver filigree accented the edges along with strategically placed clasps and studs that added to the fierce but elegant look of their outfits. They appeared ready for battle. The shortened skirts, which reached just above the knees, were made of overlapping layered tiers of leather and parted as they walked, giving a sensuous glimpse of their thighs.

It was midday in the late spring, and after the previous night's storm, we would all suffer from the humidity. The crowds cheered as the contestants made their way to the center, facing us in the king's box.

Around me, the Iris nobility looked down on the contestants, appraising them with the assessing eyes one would use for choosing a fine horse or another prized animal.

Accompanied by my Uncle Ventius and cousin Estrella, I sat in the foremost position.

"You have to at least *feign* interest, Kaleidos. Give them something to fight for," Ventius explained with a dark chuckle. "It shouldn't be too difficult for you to convince these females you care about them considering your record number of affairs."

"Careful, Uncle," I warned as I scanned the contestants, purposefully avoiding eye contact with any of the Argenti.

"Kaleidos, you are the biggest flirt I know." Estrella winked. "There is rarely an occasion I've seen you without a new female on your arm." Running her extra-long nails across my chest, she teased, "You know it's true. I'd wager to say you've courted half the noble houses in Prisma."

But that phase in my life had come to an end, as I was ultimately expected to take an elemental wife to ensure a strong and powerful heir. Duty before pleasure. Although I presumed I would still be able to get away with the occasional amorous pursuit. It wasn't as though my elemental bride could divorce me.

"To be quite frank, I too had a difficult time picturing myself stooping down to their level for my Matri-Ludus. They come so wild. Little more than savages if you ask me," Estrella added with a sneer.

"I am sure you will find that they are quite enjoyable once you take them to bed, nephew. Show a little affection, and you'll have them eating out of the palm of your hand, begging for you to cast your glow onto them," my uncle said, his voice brimming with enthusiasm.

The whole thing sounded so contrived.

Mistaking the reason for my objection to the whole process, Estrella chimed in, "Don't worry, cousin, despite how plain and weak they are, it is quite satisfying, the feeling of dominance."

Like all Iris, I had been raised to see elemental fae as lesser beings. We were superior to them in every way—faster, stronger, and even their magic couldn't compare. And now I was expected to wed one of them. A task that would turn out to be infinitely more challenging, considering my encounter with the little water nymph last night. An encounter I refused to give any more thought to.

The events of the Matri-Ludus would weed out the weakest of them, ensuring only the strongest would continue the royal line. I had little choice in the matter, my power was limited to small favors I could hand out which may or may not help the one I'd choose. It wasn't simply strength we valued. Appearances mattered as well—as beauty was prized among my people as though it were power in and of itself.

"I think you should go for an Aereus female. A bronzed beauty to add more strength and richness in color to your family line," Estrella added matter-of-factly.

She had a mate of her own. One she hardly ever appeared with or spoke of. She had wanted an Aereus, but her favored had not been victorious in the final event of her Matri-Ludus two years ago despite her best efforts in helping him along. So she had ended up bitterly taking an Aurum male to wed in the end. We could only do so much, the rest was up to the stars.

The Iris were slow to produce offspring, so siblings were uncommon, and even having cousins close in age was a rare occurrence. Because we had only been born a couple of years apart, Estrella and I were often paired up for lessons or play. We had a close bond, even if we did not always see eye-to-eye.

Since Estrella's mating, she seemed to prefer spending most of her free time in my company, most likely to avoid the Aurum male whom she did very little to hide her displeasure with. She'd made it her unofficial project to help me choose a suitable mate to favor in my Matri-Ludus.

I hadn't slept much after the storm the previous night, so the high-pitched and breathy sound of my cousin's voice was as triggering as metal scraping against marble. Like a sister, she had always been around, but it was getting excessive. I stepped away from her, making my way over to the refreshments.

To my dismay, the headmaster of games, the Faber Ludi, approached, his heavy slate robes sweeping the floor as he neared. "Your Royal Highness." I wanted to turn the other way but could not keep shirking my duties. "Have you made your selection for the first event?" he asked.

I wasted time pouring myself a chalice of wine and drinking it slowly while contemplating my options. The Faber Ludi hovered so close, it made my skin crawl. He did not seem to understand what personal space was, buzzing around like a mosquito. Despite his marbled complexion, his skin appeared waxy and pale in the bright daylight.

I scanned the contestants again. The Aereus females stood out from the others, even the earth they stood upon appeared to thrive in their presence, sprouting up soft grass in place of sand.

I couldn't bring myself to look at the Argenti. I would not risk making eye contact with Aella. *Foolish, ignorant Aella.* I could not stop thinking of Aella. My grip tightened on the chalice, warping it in my hand. The elemental fae were meant to serve the Iris, to humble themselves before us, to submit to us—*she* had done none of that.

"Fifth one from the left," I said, letting out a breath before turning to leave.

"Excellent choice, Your Majesty," the Faber Ludi said, closely trailing me. He eyed one of his many lists. "Elutha, from the Aereus line. She comes from one of the higher houses in Ilithania. She will be given an advantage in the first competition in light of your favor. And what of your preference for the events?"

"I haven't given it much thought. What do you suggest?" I sighed.

"If it's not too bold of me, might I suggest starting the Matri-Ludus with a hunt?"

Chapter 13
Hunt of Shadows

Aella

They paraded us in front of crowds of thousands in Prisma's great arena. All around us, people stared—leering, hungry looks from the males, and jealous, hateful looks from the females.

Instead of evening gowns, we were garbed in more athletic outfits made of soft, lightweight leathers that enhanced our curves while still allowing for ease of movement paired with sandals that laced up our legs.

They'd gone lighter on our makeup and jewelry as well. My handmaid had fitted me with a pair of plain, silver cuffs whereas Viera donned a braided silver band across her forehead. They'd painted numbers on the fronts and backs of our leather bodices. I was number twenty-three.

As we approached the front of the king's box, everything inside me wanted to stare down at my feet. Sweat dripped down my brow, and I was unsure if it was due to the weather or my nerves. The idea of locking eyes with the prince terrified me. *Egotistical, condescending male.*

Even the *thought* of our encounter from the previous night made me bristle. But looking down would have made me appear weak, and the last thing I wanted was to give him the satisfaction of winning our small battle of wills. Taking a few deep, grounding breaths, I held my head high, maintaining my focus straight ahead.

When we came to a stop, I fought all of my urges to run, but there was nowhere to hide. I found the prince in the king's box. He lounged crookedly on his throne, surrounded by Iris sycophants.

I stared up at him in triumph, proud of myself for refusing to let him see how much he'd affected me the night before. But it was he who refused to look in my direction. He seemed deeply focused on the Aereus females to my right, even as he rested his chin lazily on a fist.

I persisted, however, shooting daggers at him with my eyes. He still didn't bother to look. The longer I stood there, the less triumphant I felt, like he was the one who was winning. But I kept glaring, just in case. *He will look eventually.*

"Why do you think they keep parading us in front of them like this?" I asked Viera under my breath.

"Entertainment perhaps? They're probably making wagers on us," replied Viera.

The thought of people placing bets on us made me cringe. And the idea of competing against my friend was worse. It didn't matter though, because I had no real desire to win the Matri-Ludus anyway.

A pretty-faced, ostentatiously dressed Iris male made his way out to the center of the arena with a megaphone in hand, stopping in front of us. The crowd roared with excitement, chanting, "Nephos! Nephos! Nephos!" at his arrival.

Nephos began, bellowing, "Citizens of Prisma, we are here today to commence the Matri-Ludus for our prince, Kaleidos Stellaris, son of King Solanos, heir to the Iris throne and to all nations of Esterra!"

The audience erupted like a wave surging through the stands, their admiration for the prince evident as they jumped to their feet.

Nephos continued his speech, enunciating each word with such vigor. "Due to the nature of this event, which may very well be the grandest affair of your lifetimes, we have brought in thirty of the most eligible bachelorettes of the continent here today. Only the finest ladies of Esterra were selected for our prince. To carry on the Stellaris line and to bring glory to the Iris Kingdom!"

Some of my fellow contestants looked like they were buying into it. Maybe some of them actually wanted to be in the competition. Or perhaps they were simply better at faking it than I was.

"As is tradition, the prince may select a contestant to support," Nephos announced. "Today, the prince's favor goes to number five, Elutha of Ilithania!"

The Aereus female with a bronzed umber complexion and burgundy hair curtsied and smiled demurely at the prince. She was poised and alluring in every sense. It was no surprise she had been chosen, even though a tiny part of me was disappointed my name hadn't been called.

The prince's favor would give her an upper hand—although what that meant precisely, they had yet to explain to us. While the crowd was cheering for Elutha, it was clear by the chorus of hushed voices around me that the other ladies felt threatened by what it implied.

"At nightfall, we shall commence the festivities with the Hunt of Shadows!" Nephos declared.

The spectators went wild, drinking and chanting in the stands, drums and music egging them on. Himmel signaled us to make our way back to the exit where we'd come in, and dancers swiftly replaced us in the arena to keep the entertainment going.

As we neared the exit, onlookers spewed crude remarks at us, referring to us by the numbers painted on our chests as if that was all we had been reduced to. A lump formed in my throat that I couldn't seem to clear, and I found it almost impossible to continue plastering on that fake smile my handmaids had encouraged me to use.

The other females appeared to be either oblivious or indifferent. Elutha was all smiles, though—wide, gleaming, jubilant smiles—as if starlight itself was radiating off of her flawless face.

After a grueling parade through the humid streets of Prisma, we were brought to a courtyard revel within the palatium. The Iris in attendance were dressed in the finest clothing, in more colors than I'd ever seen before, dripping with fine jewels and precious metals, making the sight almost too much to take in. It was a grand and opulent affair with music, food, and drink.

Violet smoke wafted through the air from large crystal pipes, casting a gauzy haze about the courtyard. The music was rhythmically hypnotic and far too loud, as though its purpose was to discourage conversation. Elemental fae waitstaff roamed with silver trays of sparkling drinks and tiny bites of food. Scantily clad performers swung from hoops above us, and dancers swayed their hips on elevated platforms. They were all painted in prismatic glitter in various hues, giving them a faux Iris appearance.

We were led to a guarded alcove adorned with plush furnishings where Himmel was waiting. She signaled for some waitstaff to come pour drinks and bring us food.

I tried to refuse the drink, but the painted female forced the wine with sparkling dust into my hand whilst shouting over the music, "Trust me, you're going to need it!"

All around us, the Iris were partaking in the festivities. Several Iris females outside our alcove laughed together as they looked down their noses at us. Others danced to the tune of the music, carelessly sloshing their drinks about. Some of the revelers snorted glittering substances up their noses, wild looks in their eyes. In other alcoves, Iris shamelessly pursued their carnal desires, clothing becoming more and more sparse by the minute.

A guard led some of the Iris nobility, whom I recognized from the king's box, into our alcove. One of them had been at the prince's side. With a look of smugness on his face, he walked among us, eyes devouring and sinister. I dumped my wine in a nearby bush as I did not want to risk losing control of myself like the revelers I saw around me, especially not with predators like him prowling about.

We were supposed to partake in some kind of hunt that evening, so I was confused why they'd bring us to a revel first. It did not make any sense.

There was little point trying to talk over the music, so I became engrossed in watching one of the aerial performers weave herself in and out of the hoop up above. She appeared to be of Aereus descent, and I wondered if she had been brought to Prisma for a previous Matri-Ludus or if she had volunteered to come for work.

Viera grabbed my hand, yanking it for attention. I spun around to see the prince enter our alcove and leisurely start making his way around to meet all of the ladies. My hands became sweaty, and I started to regret dumping that glass of wine.

All of the contestants were so excited to meet him—preening, simpering, and blushing. I rolled my eyes at the sight. At least Ilaria looked as irritated as I felt. She was one of the few who had made it painfully obvious how much she did not want to be there, despite the risks of speaking out against the Iris. Although perhaps that was her strategy for winning: to turn the other contestants against our rulers.

I braced myself as the prince neared us. He made his way down the line of females, taking each one by the hand and air kissing them on the cheeks, as was the custom. I frantically wiped my hands on my leathers in anticipation, not willing to let him see how much he affected me.

I couldn't decide if I should smile politely or glare at him, but I was running out of time. I could give him a piece of my mind when he came in for the greeting. He had lingered a moment with a few of the others, making them giggle and blush.

Finally, when it was my turn, the prince stepped in front of me, and I could hardly breathe. His expression grew cold as he beheld me for a moment that felt like an eternity. When he took my hand, a slight tingling sensation traveled up the length of my arm from his touch. His hand was strong and warm, not like my father's thick, calloused hands used to hard work—smooth from a life of luxury yet still strong in the way that made it evident he had trained with a sword.

He bent down, closing the distance for the customary air kisses, but my gaze had drifted downward to our intertwined hands. In a dizzying moment, my mind strayed, and in that split second, I tilted my head, anticipating the direction of the air kiss, but misjudged it completely. Not realizing I'd mirrored the prince, our lips collided. I gasped, eyes widening as my cheeks burned.

The prince released his grip on my hand, backing away from me as though I had jolted him with some unseen force. I winced as the prince made a speedy exit. The lingering gazes of the last few females the prince was supposed to meet pierced through me like icy shards in silent judgment.

"Stars, they are going to kill me!" I shouted over the music into Viera's ear.

Viera shook her head. "What was up with that look you were giving him? You were practically staring him down!"

"I'm really bad at this," I muttered.

Viera tilted her head and gave me a reassuring smile. "A, you've got this. Just . . . maybe stop giving murderous glances to the prince. I need you here with me." She handed me a crystal goblet full of shimmering wine, and without hesitation, I took it.

△

It had been several hours, and only the stars knew how many glasses of that sparkly wine I'd consumed. Pretty hues of orange and pink tinted the wispy clouds overhead, marking the day nearly over. I was not sure how we were all going to do in the hunt, considering half of us were sprawled out on the furnishings while others still danced on the tables in wild abandon.

I was lying on one of the sofas with Viera, her head in my lap. The walls seemed to spin around us in slow motion. Or maybe our sofa was being carried in a circle. I didn't really care. Whatever was in the capital wine was something else. Nothing like what I'd had at my dawning ceremony.

I replayed my earlier interaction with the prince, and, instead of cringing, I burst into laughter.

Mother of pearl, I couldn't be fumbling this competition worse if I tried.

Himmel came a short time later to lead us to a holding area outside of the arena. Our ride back was dizzying, and I fought a lingering light-headedness even after we arrived. Some of the contestants were hardly able to walk, while others were more tolerant to the effects of the wine.

The prince's favored, Elutha, who had been summoned hours earlier, arrived separately, looking refreshed and well-rested unlike the rest of our sorry lot. I worried what that implied.

"When the trumpet sounds, the doors will open, and you will enter the arena. Make haste . . . and good luck," Himmel said with a hint of hesitation. "Line up now. Elutha, dear, you may take the lead."

We hurriedly formed a line, desperate to claim positions closer to the front, closer to the favored. Several of the ladies were tearing at each other to avoid being last in line. The real competition hadn't even started yet, and already it was getting ugly.

From within the chamber, I could hear the crowd chanting and stomping in the grandstands. Nephos shouted through a megaphone, the crowd cheered in response, but his words sounded muffled from where we stood.

"There are no rules . . ." Himmel made her way to the exit, a cruel inkling of a smile on her face. "Only, whatever you do, don't get caught."

The guards sealed the only exit behind her and pressed us toward the arena's entrance. A trumpet sounded, and we raced out, the door slamming shut behind us. The arena had been completely transformed. It was only from the light of the stars that we were able to faintly make out what lay before us: a maze of glass with ten entry points.

Elutha led us all, sprinting straight for the maze. Viera and the others raced ahead of me, following her example and entering the maze at various points. None of us knew if Elutha had been given any special tips, as there hadn't been time to ask, but she definitely had the advantage of rest and sobriety.

I jogged, indecision slowing me down. My head was still spinning, and I wanted to throw up.

They'd called it the Hunt of Shadows, but we hadn't been told what we would be hunting.

The crowd went silent, and an ominous feeling crept up my spine, almost as though I could feel movement through the way the wind gusted behind me. I slowed down to look, and from grated openings in the walls, ten black creatures—shadow fangs—prowled out toward the maze, their manes like wreaths of black smoke.

The realization hit me: we were not going hunting, we were the ones being hunted. I ran faster, straight ahead this time. I reached the entrance right as several of the other ladies rushed out, and they crashed into me, all of us falling to the ground.

"It's a dead end!" Ulli gasped, and then she shrieked as she spotted the nightmarish predators heading in our direction. I scrambled to my feet as the shadow fangs stalked toward us, drool dripping from their unholy maws. Ulli froze in place, tears streaming down her face.

"Ulli, you need to get up. Now!" I shouted as I tried to help her up. She was dead weight in my hands, not budging.

"Ulli!" I screamed at her, but she would not move. I had to run. Himmel's words echoed in my ears. *Whatever you do, don't get caught.* The dark predators prowled forward slowly as if toying with us as they neared, readying to pounce. Ulli still would not give way. I sobbed, realizing I would be forced to abandon her there.

I tried to summon water. If I could at least create some sort of distraction, maybe Ulli would still have a chance. But I felt weak, unsure if from the wine or because there wasn't a water source near enough. All I managed to do was shoot a light mist of water in the direction of the shadow fangs which served only to briefly distort their view. It wasn't enough, but it was all I could do. Then I ran.

I said a prayer to the stars and chanced a hopeful look back once more, only to see Ulli curled up in a ball on the ground, knees to her chest, just before the creatures pounced. Our screams were drowned out by the cheering in the stands. I gasped for air as I ran, making a sharp turn into the next maze entrance.

I ran for my life, knowing the shadow fangs would not be held up for long on Ulli's tiny body. I wanted to break down and cry, but I had no time for tears. All I could think about was Viera suffering the same fate. I needed to find her and figure out a way to get us out of this. What was at the end of the maze? Were they all dead ends but one? My mind raced faster than my legs, as if it might gain me speed.

I rushed through the maze, darting left and then right, no time to stop and think about which way I should turn. Inside, the glass was so crystal clear, it was hard to tell what was a glass wall and what was a path. But something in the air guided my steps. A slight breeze called to me, so I followed it, digging my feet into the dirt as I almost crashed into another glass wall.

Through the glass, I saw some of the beasts making their way into the maze like dark shadows, their amber eyes and white teeth gleaming in the starlight, their paws leaving a trail of blood. I had to block out thoughts of the state they must have left Ulli in, if there was anything left of her.

"Viera!" I shouted, my voice cracking.

"Aella! I'm over here!" she called back. About twenty paces to the right of me. I was so relieved when I saw her, I wanted to cry. But my relief was short-lived as I realized we were separated by walls of glass.

"I'm lost, I don't know which way to go. I think I might be stuck in a loop," Viera said.

I jumped as I heard another scream from a different part of the maze, and it spurred me into action. I ran through the maze, desperate to find a path that would lead me closer to my friend. Nearly reaching her with only one panel of glass between us, I pounded on the tempered wall, fists slamming over and over. Despite my efforts, my bruising hits only produced hollow thumps, not even a splinter on its sleek surface.

"Did anyone else run down this path with you?" I asked, looking around.

"Elutha was ahead of me, but she must have taken another turn. I don't know. She disappeared. I'm too scared to backtrack."

Viera's gaze darted in the direction she'd come from. Another shriek pierced the air before the cheering and stomping in the stands drowned it out.

Viera stared at me hopelessly, our hands reaching for each other through the glass.

"Aella, you need to go. At least try to get yourself out of here."

My eyes went wide. "No! Not without you!"

I blinked as a fourth scream echoed through the maze, sounding closer now.

"Stars damn you, Aella!" cried Viera as she pounded on the glass, tears streaming down her face. "You need to go, now!"

We flinched as the sounds of snarling and growling became louder, proof they were way too close now. Viera and I locked eyes, waiting for the inevitable. Then, from my left came an Aurum female, Jara. She used her element to melt a hole through the glass, now sharing the section of maze with me.

"Tell me there's a way out of here!" she demanded.

"Melt the glass for my friend, please!" I begged.

"I can't. I'm running low on source as it is," she said. "I'm sorry, but I'm not going to waste it on her."

"Melt the glass for my friend, and I'll show you the way out," I said with as much command as I could muster. I was bluffing, but I'd say or do anything to get to Viera. I wrapped both hands behind my neck while waiting for her reply. The metallic scent of blood filled my nostrils, alerting me that the beasts were nearing us. "Hurry!"

Jara wavered for a moment, then cursed as she melted a thin wedge in the glass. It burned Viera as she slid through it, the glass still hot. When half of her body was on my side, a shadow fang prowled into the clearing on the opposite side of the glass. I grabbed Viera, pulling her through the opening just as the beast pounced and slammed into the translucent pane.

Its paw slid through the gap, slicing ribbons into the back of my arm. I winced and held my shredded limb which was thankfully numb to the pain. The shadow fang fought viciously to break through, and the glass splintered around the opening. We scrambled backward and up onto our feet. Viera squeezed me to her chest in a sob.

"The way?" the Aurum female barked.

Pausing to sense the breeze again, I led the way. "We have to backtrack a little first."

"Are you kidding me?" the female whined.

I continued on, side-by-side with Viera. Back and forth we zig-zagged through the maze. It started to feel like we were going in a circle, and I began to doubt myself. But I continued to follow the draft as I couldn't think of any alternatives. At last, we made it out the other end of the maze.

There were Aereus-made holes in the ground, vines that hung over the tops of the maze at different points, and areas where the glass had been melted by the Aurum. I feared for the rest of the Argenti females, as there had been no advantage for us in the Hunt.

We ran to an open door, entering a room that mirrored the one we'd started in. Inside, we were handed goblets of wine as they praised us for our performance. The Aurum female we finished with placed 11th, Viera 12th, and I 13th. As thirsty as I was, I couldn't drink the wine. A lump blocked my throat as my stomach's contents threatened to leave my body.

Viera and I huddled together in a corner, shivering, our teeth chattering uncontrollably. We waited in silence as the medics came in to attend to our wounds. The aftereffects of adrenaline made it hard to think, let alone process my emotions. But as I sat, trembling and numb, I had to remind myself that I'd made it.

We survived.

Chapter 14

Secret Garden

AELLA

After the Hunt, they brought those of us who had survived to the throne room in the Palatium Crystalis. It was a circular room, its outermost walls lined with a mosaic of mirrors, and pillars created a triangular center. It was clearly made to resemble the emblem of Prisma, a triangle enclosed within a circle. While other parts of the palatium were more decorated with fabrics and colors, the throne room was cold and hard, every surface made from marble or plated in precious metals. It was an epic display of power and wealth.

The room was so vast, it was hard to believe we were indoors. Its lofty glass tetrahedron ceiling came to a point above us, showing off the stars in the night sky. I imagined that, during the daytime, the crystal ceiling would act as a prism, casting rainbows of light throughout the throne room. At this hour, the space was dark, lit only by the flickering flames of sconces.

King Solanos sat on a throne forged of gold, silver, and bronze. Crown Prince Kaleidos, to the right of him, harbored a bored expression. A slender male in heavy robes orchestrated the procession, ordering us to our knees. As we knelt before the king, Nephos and Himmel placed wreaths of ivy on our heads like mock crowns, ignoring our tear-stained cheeks and solemn expressions.

"You may rise," the king spoke, his words booming over us. I imagined he could knock someone over with the power of his voice if he so desired.

The Iris were in high spirits, as if their hunger for violence and blood had been satiated. I was unsure if I was delirious from the day's events, but the flickering light from the flames cast shadows on their faces, making them appear menacing, which was in complete contrast to their usual alluring state.

The host from the arena, Nephos, gestured toward us. "Out of the thirty elementals who entered the Hunt of Shadows, we have nineteen victors! The Aereus are in the lead with eight, next the Aurum with seven, and finally the Argenti with only four remaining contestants."

Eleven of us are dead. Shred apart. Has this been their plan all along? To eliminate us, one by one, until only the strongest of us remained?

"This one even fought off a shadow fang. Didn't you, Number Eighteen? She shot fire at the poor leo," the sweet-faced Iris male teased.

Rae flinched at the attention, a distant and pained expression on her face as if silently reliving her darkest moments. My own mind took me away, tuning out the voices around me. Ulli's face haunted me. Her look of terror as she'd become paralyzed with fear. The sound of her screams as the shadow fang had taken her.

Guilt ravaged me to the point I could scarcely breathe. My chest tightened, overwhelming shame closing in on me. As if I might collapse into myself like a dying star. Deeper and deeper I went. The room darkened around me until I reached complete isolation. Alone in a depthless void of darkness. I hated myself for leaving her. I hated myself for surviving. I would never be able to forgive myself. At the farthest reaches of despair, I fell. Deeper and deeper I fell. It would never stop, and I would never get up again.

A hand reached for mine like a tether pulling me out of the darkness. I gripped it tightly, the hand of my best friend, my lifeline. The room came back into focus around me as the darkness dissipated. Viera stood by my side, her presence giving me strength. She looked at me in a way that said, *I'm here for you*, as she squeezed my hand.

The Iris around us laughed as Nephos gave an animated play-by-play of the evening's events. Everything about it was wrong. How could they laugh and cheer at our expense, toy with us like we weren't even people? Were our lives worth so little to them?

Anger filled me to the brim, and I swore to myself that I would never forgive them for what they had done to us. I glared at the prince, unafraid to show the tempest of hate in my expression. His bold green eyes locked onto mine, a flicker of regret showing before it was replaced by a mask of indifference. A muscle in his jaw clenched—the only proof of his torment.

△

As we walked back to our rooms, Himmel lectured us. "Now, don't look so glum, my darlings. You should be very proud of yourselves for your success this evening. I am quite sure your performances impressed the prince."

"Are you going to kill us all?" I bit out.

Himmel stopped in her tracks, turning to face me, and, in a soft way that did little to hide the menace in her eyes, replied, "Kill you? What do you think we are, savages? We are not going to kill any of you." She picked a speck of lint off her shoulder as she continued, "Sometimes there are . . . casualties in the competitions. Of course, it is never intentional, but we must test your limits to prevent any weakness from entering the royal bloodline." Spinning on her heels toward the bedchambers, she warned, "I don't want to hear any more questions or complaints about our methods, or I will have to report it. And there *will* be consequences."

We walked in silence after that. I wanted to scream, I wanted to fight, yet I was at a complete loss for words. I squeezed my hand into a fist, allowing my nails to dig deep into my palm. It was all I could do to keep myself from losing it. Himmel had made it clear they expected us to be grateful we were chosen and that they did not want to hear any objections from us. None of us wanted to find out what kind of consequences they would dole out, especially after the evening's events showed us how little value they placed on our lives.

Is this what they have been doing to all of our drafted for all these years? How many young males and females had been torn apart in the arena for show? My mind was spinning, and I became more and more enraged as I walked down the hall, unanswered questions plaguing me.

Questions I feared I already knew the answers to.

The awareness of how powerless I was, how useless my anger was, washed over me. I released my clenched fist and continued walking, shoulders slumped the rest of the way.

When we made it back to our bedchambers, only three of the original five of us returned to the room. The space felt empty without Ulli and Nickel. Their vacant beds served as a reminder of the violence committed against us. We hadn't known them for long, but their absence was tangible.

It would have been easier to imagine that they'd left to go back home, but my memories would not allow it. Although I hadn't witnessed them all, I pictured every one of the shadow fang attacks so vividly in my head. Any time I closed my eyes, terrorizing images played in my mind's eye, intrusive thoughts filling in the blanks.

A knock at the door made me flinch, returning my awareness to that present moment. The last remaining Argenti female from the other room peeked her head in.

"Would you mind if I stayed in here with you tonight?" she asked, her voice dry. "I can't bring myself to stay in that room all by myself after everything . . ." She trailed off, looking as haunted as I felt.

None of us objected, so she entered, looking around the room for a moment before deciding where to settle.

"I'm Lewenne, from Lakehaven," she said as she padded over to the bed between Ilaria's and mine.

"I thought they didn't draft from the small villages," Ilaria jibed.

"They don't," Lewenne replied. "I traveled to Iveria to put my name in for the draft. Things were . . . bad back home." She laughed bitterly to herself. "I thought coming here might be a chance for me to start over."

"What could possibly be so bad for you to make such a foolish decision?" Ilaria spat out.

Lewenne took a deep breath, stilling for a moment before stalking toward Ilaria. "Perhaps for you, living your pampered life in Iveria, it's hard to imagine what it's like for the rest of us." She made a slow circle around Ilaria as she continued, "Have you ever had Iris soldiers take over your home? Treat you like a slave? Take everything from you?"

Ilaria stood with her arms crossed, her lips in a thin line, even as Lewenne stopped right in front of her.

"They took *everything*," Lewenne said, her voice breaking.

Ilaria continued staring down at her, chest rising and falling as she appeared to be holding herself back.

"Do you know what it's like living in a small town after something like that happens?" Lewenne asked. "The way people look at you, with pity and disgust in their eyes? They called me an Iris whore!" She wiped angry tears from her cheeks. "So, yes, maybe I wanted to come here. Maybe I wanted a second chance. Maybe I wanted . . . revenge."

Ilaria showed her no sympathy. In fact, she was fuming—steam was practically coming out of her ears.

Viera stepped between them. "Lewenne, what you did—coming here, I mean—it was very brave of you." She led Lewenne away from the red-faced Ilaria who stood wordlessly, hands in fists at her sides. "We may be brimming with emotions right now, but let's not forget who the real enemy is. Don't let them turn us against each other."

"She's right. We all need to stick together if we're going to get through this." I glanced toward Ilaria who glared back at me. "All of the other elementals had advantages tonight. It was almost as if it was rigged against us. We're lucky we still have the four of us left."

"Whatever you're thinking, leave me out of it," Ilaria said, climbing into her bed.

"I'm not planning anything. I just think we should at least try to help each other. We're stronger together," I said.

Lewenne nodded her head in agreement. "I'm in."

△

Later that night, Viera crawled into my bed. She laid her head down on the pillow next to mine and whispered to me, "I can't sleep."

I rolled over to face her. "Neither can I."

Although my eyes were burning and my body ached for slumber, anxiety and fear had kept me awake. My mind had been replaying the events of the Hunt on an endless loop. And when I'd managed to stop thinking about it, my mind had gone to all the ways the Iris might try to have us killed in the upcoming competitions.

"I've been thinking about tonight. If you hadn't found me, I—How did you know the way out?" Viera asked.

"I just followed the breeze. I assumed it must've been coming from the exit since the dead ends felt stagnant."

"A breeze?" She eyed me as if I'd just told her I had fins.

"Yes. I mean, it was subtle but definitely there. You couldn't feel it?"

"All I remember was how humid and muggy it was. I'm pretty sure I would've noticed a breeze if there was one," she replied.

I rolled onto my back, staring up at the canopy. "Hmm, that's weird. I could have sworn I felt one. Anyway, do you think Ilaria will come around?" I asked, changing the subject. I tilted my head to look at Viera for a response when she didn't answer right away.

She eyed me with suspicion, then turned her attention to Ilaria's bed. "We can't make her, but we can still try to help her. Maybe she'll change her mind." She yawned. "I think it needs to be her idea though." She then snuggled up close to me and pulled the covers up.

I ran my fingers through her hair as she drifted off to sleep, the way I used to for my sister, Mila. We had to find a way to work together, to protect each other. I would not accept any more losses.

△

My dreams were a series of nightmares from which I awoke sobbing and screaming. Every time I woke up, my hands shot out in a panic, feeling for Viera to make sure she was still there, still breathing, her heart still beating. I eventually gave up on sleep altogether to avoid the terrorizing dreams.

My stomach growled, so I carefully crept out of the bed so as not to disturb Viera. In the shared living space, I found a big bowl of fruit on one of the tables alongside pitchers of infused water. The fruits were different, some of them unrecognizable to me in an assortment of strange colors and textures. Most of them required a knife to cut through their thick, prickled skins to reach the edible centers.

I chose a shiny, purple fruit which appeared most similar to what I'd had back in Iveria, cut into it, and took a bite—its white flesh sweet and subtly tart. It reminded me of home, conjuring memories of floating in the cool water under the night sky where I could surrender to the current and let it take all my worries away.

I brought my bounty out to the terrace and settled myself onto a lounge chair. I could feel the stars mocking me as I reclined, engorging myself in self-pity. But they were right, I couldn't just lie there. I needed to do something. The familiar fruit suddenly tasted bland—I had to get back down into the garden again with its winding waterways. It wasn't the ocean, but it was under the stars at least.

I went to the far side to check if the ladder-like vines Prince Kaleidos had created were still present from the night we'd met. It was a small wonder they hadn't been cut down yet by the Aereus gardeners who kept the grounds so manicured.

I hoisted myself over the ledge and tested the strength of the vines before making my way down and to the flowing stream. I should have offered to bring the others as well, but if too many of us came then we would surely have been found out and possibly even punished. So, truly, it was best to keep one secret to myself, even if it served a selfish part of me to do so.

I stripped out of my robe, hung it from the branch of a jasmine tree, and dove in. Nothing compared to the feeling of submerging myself in the cool, refreshing waters. A current swirled around me, showing the water's delight in my presence. My body hummed as my powers renewed themselves, and I found solace in my mind as I lay there floating under the shimmering midnight sky.

Chapter 15

The Oath

Arianwen

Wynn and I continued our journey north through the dark forest. Dawn was still a few hours off. It was almost unsettling how easily Wynn took charge after he'd been unable to do anything but rely on me in his weakened state the day before. As the eldest in my family, I liked being in control, and it chafed a little to let him take the lead.

You have no one to blame but yourself, Ari.

Ever since I'd discovered my healing ability as a child, I'd been drawn to help any injured creature I came upon. It would drive my mother to madness when I'd insist on trying to save even the tiniest of crustaceans. Helping Wynn hadn't even been a question. There was no way I would have been okay leaving him to die alone in the forest. So I had to deal with the consequences.

As we walked, my feet started to drag. I was exhausted, and the adrenaline from our encounter with the Iris was wearing off. Not wanting to admit my weakness and ask Wynn to take a break, I stopped for a moment to rest my weight against a tree and close my eyes briefly. Traveling such a distance by foot was hard. I would much rather have been in the sea. Once again, I wondered what my crazy ancestors had been thinking when they decided this ritual was a good idea for water fae.

Groaning, I straightened and opened my eyes, knowing I had to get moving before I stopped moving at all.

Where in the stars is Wynn?

I looked ahead in the direction he'd been walking and didn't see him. How long had I been resting? It couldn't have been more than a few minutes. Calling out seemed like a bad idea, knowing the Iris could be anywhere, so I started walking in the direction I had last seen him.

I stalked through the forest, branches and brush crackling under my heavy footsteps. Anger roiled within me. Perhaps I was being unreasonable, but I thought Wynn would have realized I wasn't with him and come looking for me.

Infuriating male.

Maybe he was trying to get rid of me and thought I would just give up and continue my journey without him. That would have been the smartest course of action for me, but I had committed myself to seeing him arrive home safe and whole. He had been moving so quickly through the woods on his own, he probably didn't need me anymore, so my excuse of keeping him safe was gone. I could no longer deny that I was hoping he would lead me to his people. I wanted to see where he came from and experience how they lived apart from the Iris. There was no way I would stay, but I was curious all the same.

Suddenly, the forest went silent around me. My body stiffened as fear rushed through me. A few feet to my left, a large branch cracked, and a snarling growl filled the air. Peering through the darkness, I spotted a pair of glowing eyes. I cursed under my breath. My anger at Wynn had clouded my mind, and I had led the beast right to me.

I took off in a sprint, knowing it was futile. There was no way I could outrun the enormous warg. The black lupine beast howled, and the sound of its close pursuit filled my ears as I crashed through the trees, running toward the stream that called to me. Having never used my magic to harm,

I was unsure how to wield it to defend myself. My only other weapon was a hunting knife, but it was buried deep in my pack. I had to try something—I wasn't ready to die.

The warg snarled at my heels, and I cried out as I tripped over some rocks and went sprawling to the ground near the stream. Glancing over my shoulder, I saw the warg leap toward me. Summoning with barely a thought, I sent a stream of icy water right into the beast's open maw. The water pushed the beast away from me and onto its back, choking and sputtering for breath. It rolled over seconds later, recovering faster than I had hoped.

I pushed myself to my feet, slowly backing away from the warg and its predatory gaze. Stepping into the stream, the water's strength flowed through me, and I summoned a giant orb into my hands. The warg growled as it crept toward me.

"Are you sure you want to mess with me?" I postured, trying to cover my fear with false confidence.

The muscles in its haunches bunched right before it leaped toward me. Tossing the orb, I ducked down into a ball as the warg flew over my head. A whine and the sound of crackling ice filled the air, and I peeked up in horror as the now-frozen warg fell to the ground and shattered into a million shards of ice.

What in the tides just happened?

Something touched my shoulder from behind, and I shrieked before a hand covered my mouth and an arm banded around me. Recognizing Wynn's voice as he attempted to calm me, I started shaking at my close call.

"Ari, it's just me. Don't scream." Wynn removed his hand, and I gulped down air, trying not to hyperventilate.

"Are you all right? Were you injured?" he asked.

Looking up at him wild-eyed, I sputtered, "I lost you and was trying to find you and then the warg started chasing me and I fell but I'm fine I think . . . but . . . What . . . ? How? It exploded!"

Wynn held me tightly to his chest. "Shhh . . . you're safe. No need to worry. I used my power to freeze the water you summoned. I didn't realize you had fallen so far behind, I was trying to give you some space. You seemed so angry with me after our encounter with the Iris, I thought I would scout ahead. I was always going to return for you. Everything will be okay."

I took a few more shuddering breaths then finally relaxed into his arms. I was safe for the moment. "I can truly say my life has never been quite this exciting . . . until you crashed into it, that is."

Wynn chuckled. "I believe it." He loosened his arms and stepped back, looking over me appraisingly. "You were lucky. I don't see any major injuries."

"Thank the stars," I breathed. "And thank you for coming back for me. I think the water was only angering it. I would not have been able to hold it off much longer."

"That was quick thinking. You almost didn't need my help."

My laugh sounded hollow to my ears. "I'm not used to using my magic to defend myself. My powers are better suited for nurturing and healing than destroying."

"That beast would have torn you to pieces if you had let it get close enough. Don't waste any tears or regret over it."

"I'll try," I murmured while kneeling to wash my hands in the stream. The water soothed the scratches and abrasions from my fall.

Wynn stretched out a hand toward me, and I took it, letting him pull me to my feet.

"Let's be on our way before some other beasts try to make a meal out of you. Wargs travel in packs, so I wouldn't be surprised if there are more nearby. I can hide our scent with the wind, but you need to stay close."

Giving him a grim smile, I nodded. It would take a while for my mind to process the entire ordeal.

※

Hours passed as we continued our hike through the forest, stopping only for brief moments of rest and munching on anything we could forage.

What I wouldn't have given for a hot meal and some warm tea. The glacier water was refreshing, but I was starting to feel the iciness of the higher elevation seep into my bones, as the alpine chill was different from the cold of the deep sea.

The further north we went, the harsher the landscape became and the quicker the temperatures dropped. Where the trees had been golden and warm nearer the sea, the ones that surrounded us on our hike were monstrously tall, uninviting, prickly, and coarse. The ground became rockier, and my feet ached, unused to such terrain. It was hard to believe that another day had passed and evening was upon us again. The sky was clearer, and the stars appeared closer—it almost felt like I could reach out and grab one if I climbed a little higher.

We stopped at a rock formation that almost resembled an aquila nest if I used my imagination. The giant birds did not fly near Iveria. I had only read about them in books. I pulled out my flask of water and some leftover bread that had become quite stale. My lips turned into a frown, but my grumbling stomach forced me to satisfy it with something.

Breaking off a chunk, I held it up in offering to Wynn. "Would you like some? I wouldn't say I'd recommend it, but it's all I have left."

Wynn shook his head. "Thanks, but no, I'm fine for now." His face turned grave as he leaned against the rock formation, arms crossed in front of him. "You have a decision to make, Arianwen."

Despite myself, I loved the way my name rolled off his tongue. His baritone voice made it sound like a caress.

"Oh? What's that?" I replied, raising an eyebrow at him.

"If you continue traveling with me, you will see things you can never speak of should you choose to return home."

I nibbled at my bread, pausing to collect my thoughts.

Choose to return home? Why wouldn't I return home? What is he talking about?

Clearing my throat, I replied, "I understand that. You have spoken of the danger already, but surely you know I must return home at some point . . . That said, I do want to continue traveling with you and see your home and your people if you think you can trust me."

"This isn't about trust. If you choose to come, I would have to take certain precautions so that you could not lead anyone else to where I bring you. I'm only considering taking you with me because we could make use of your healing skills." Wynn paused, looking slightly uncomfortable, almost as if he was afraid to continue. "You would need to make a star-sworn blood oath to never reveal what you learn or see."

My whole body stilled, and the bread I'd been chewing turned to dust in my mouth. A star-sworn blood oath was significant—it was more binding than marriage. Giving blood was also an incredibly intimate act. Did I truly want to see his home that badly? Forcing a swallow, I decided I had come so far and wasn't willing to quit.

"I will swear it . . . on one condition."

I couldn't be sure, but it looked like relief swept through Wynn before he raised an eyebrow. "What condition would that be?"

"You swear an oath to me as well. An oath to leave me unharmed and to allow me to return home to my family."

He blinked. "What makes you think you have any bargaining power? I could just leave you here to make your own way home."

"You're right, but you did say you could use my skills. It would be foolish of me to swear an oath to you with no guarantee of safety for myself. For all I know, you could bring me to your home and then murder me like you did those Iris guards."

Wynn's face tightened, a muscle in his cheek twitching as he considered my request. "I suppose that would be fine . . . but I must admit, I'm wounded that you don't trust me."

I scoffed, "You already said this wasn't about trust, Wynn."

His jaw clenched and he gave a brief nod before he motioned toward the pack that rested beside me. "You have a blade?"

My mouth went dry and my hands shook slightly as I nodded and pulled out my hunting knife. I'd learned about such oaths in my studies but had never witnessed one. Many elemental fae rituals had been banned once the Iris seized power, and more were slowly disappearing. For the oath, verbal promises would be made, but it wouldn't be complete until we shared our blood with each other.

What am I getting myself into?

I rose to my feet and handed the knife over to him. Wynn held my left hand in his, my palm raised to the sky, and made a small incision with the blade. I hissed, tensing as the blood welled up, and willed my magic to hold off from healing the cut right away. He quickly made a small incision on his hand as well.

Looking into my eyes, Wynn spoke, his voice resonating through me. "Do you swear upon the stars to never speak of nor disclose any of the people or places you see associated with the Adamas, as long as the blood flows through your veins and breath resides in your lungs, unless I release you from this oath?"

His grip tightened on my hand, and I cleared my throat nervously, every sense heightened. "I swear, as long as there is breath in my lungs and blood flowing through my veins, I will reveal nothing of the Adamas people or the places I see unless you release me. May the stars witness my oath."

Wynn nodded at me to continue with his portion of the oath.

"Do you swear upon the stars not to harm me or my family and to allow me to leave whenever I choose?"

I held my breath, waiting for Wynn's response. His eyes darkened as he lifted my hand to his lips, his eyes never leaving mine as he replied, "I swear, as long as there is breath in my lungs and blood running through my veins, I will not harm you or your family and will allow you to leave when you choose. May the stars witness my oath."

The stars twinkled behind him as if in approval of our vows.

His mouth dipped and covered the incision on my hand as he drew some of my blood, some of me, into his mouth. A shiver ran through me at the sensuous feeling of his tongue and his mouth on my skin, and I felt a slight burn in my hand as the oath bound us together. He raised his hand toward my mouth, and I quickly licked the blood off of it, trying to ignore the sudden warmth pooling inside me. As he lowered his hand, the look he gave me made my toes curl. Smirking as if he'd won a prize, he licked a drop of my blood off his lower lip.

My face burned with embarrassment at all the conflicting feelings that were rushing through me. I was drawn to him in a way I didn't understand. If he kept looking at me the way he was, I might actually close the space between us and throw myself into his arms. Needing distance, I pulled my hand away from his and let my healing magic close the incision. There was a small, star-shaped mark on my palm, an eternal reminder of what had transpired. I looked at Wynn and noticed him staring at the twin scar on his own hand.

Does he regret his promise?

"So, what now?" I tried to break the tension as I twisted the end of my braid around my fingers nervously and turned away from him.

"Now we head to my home."

He whistled a sharp, melodic tune, and an answering trill of high-pitched notes sounded. I gasped as a giant aquila swooped down from above and landed on the rock formation next to us.

"Oh my stars! What a beautiful creature," I exclaimed, taking in the majestic bird—its plumage a combination of pure white and silvery gray. There was a keen intelligence in the aquila's golden eyes, and it chirped at Wynn as if asking a question.

"That she is," Wynn said proudly, reaching over and ruffling some feathers. "Her name is Luminara, and she will make our trip infinitely quicker."

"You expect me to fly on an aquila?" I exclaimed. "You know I am not comfortable flying!"

"I've already been gone far too long and can't waste any more time traveling on foot. My family might send someone after me, and I don't want to put anyone else at risk," he replied, sounding impatient.

"Well, sorry for holding you back," I retorted.

"Arianwen . . ." He growled my name with increased irritation. "For Luminara's safety and my own, I had to make sure we were not being trailed by the Iris. You know I am not at full strength. I had to make this journey by foot until now." Wynn looked exasperated. Apparently, I got under his skin as much as he did mine.

Looking warily at the giant bird, I rolled my shoulders back and prayed to the stars for courage. "Do you promise it's safe?"

Wynn chuckled. "Nothing in this world is truly safe, my star, but Luminara will see us home."

"You should really stop calling me that." I frowned. It was too intimate.

"You don't mean that," Wynn said, smiling.

"Excuse me?" I replied, wide-eyed.

"Every time I call you, 'my star,' your nose crinkles in the most adorable way, as if you can't believe I am calling you that, but you like it all the same."

I stared at him, my mouth open.

Cocky fae male.

He never ceased to surprise me, and an unwelcome warmth flooded my chest at his observation. He chuckled at my lack of a response and turned to adjust the saddle I had just noticed on the back of the aquila. Wynn tucked my pack into one of the pouches, and before I could protest, he hoisted me up onto the giant bird. He jumped up behind me and buckled us into the saddle's harness. Despite the straps that secured my legs and waist to the aquila, I felt far from safe up on her back. Wynn pulled me into his chest, his arms wrapped tightly around me, bringing back memories of our night in the cave.

I couldn't stop the shiver that went through me as he spoke into my ear. "Hold on tight, Ari."

Chapter 16
Forbidden Fruit

Aella

In the days following the Hunt, we were fed lots of sweet fruits and bathed in floral baths. They pampered us and treated us to all of the comforts of luxury. Thanks to the prompt administration of the antidote, my shadow fang wounds had healed quickly, only leaving behind a few bands of shiny scars across the back of my right forearm. My lady's maids had attempted to apply a healing balm to fade the scarring, but I'd refused. It hadn't felt right to cover them up, pretending like the Hunt hadn't happened.

Himmel explained that even the best dresses and grooming were not enough—we would also need to talk and behave like ladies. So she had us take lessons on manners and etiquette: how to stand, how to walk, how to eat. It made me feel like an infant learning how to swim for the first time.

While our days were filled with grooming and lessons in the mornings, every evening we had another revel to attend. The Iris debauched themselves tirelessly. It was as if their entire existence consisted of carousing and dancing their nights away.

There were always the same half-nude performers, mind-numbing music, and feasts with more food than needed to feed a village. So much excess, depravity, and waste. They didn't just drink the wine, they sprayed it in the air, making showers that left us stinking of sour grapes.

We were expected to attend every single evening. Kept safe in our guarded corner for most of the party but on display for all. The worst part was walking in. It was always crowded, and the Iris were not discreet with their hands. Hands grazed my lower back as I walked by—a pinch here, a grope there—sending unwelcome shivers down my spine.

One night, Elutha had swatted an Iris away from her as the male had made himself a little too friendly. She had been awarded ten lashes to the hand she'd swatted him with for the offense. Apparently, our bodies were no longer our own as we were now considered property of the Palatium Crystalis.

We walked swiftly through the crowds, praying not to earn any more unwanted attention. I had tried keeping my head down and avoiding eye contact as a method, but they often became even more aggressive when we ignored them. Saying things like, "Smile for me, pretty," or "Don't you know how to take a compliment?"

Many of the Iris considered ignoring them to be an offense, and none of us wanted to find out what else they might do to us if we fought back.

I learned to force a smile and pretend I didn't mind all of the hands on me as I walked by, feigning appreciation for their affections, even as my skin crawled and acid crept up my throat.

The first couple of nights after the glass maze, I had refused the wine. I hadn't wanted a repeat of the first night, never knowing when we'd be led to slaughter again. It had been almost a week since our last competition, and I dreaded that it meant another one could happen at any time. But soon enough, I'd given in, and the wine helped quiet the storm inside my head.

Prince Kaleidos always made an appearance, it was apparent he drew the attention of every fae in the room. Even the Iris looked at him with lust in their eyes, male and female alike. The iridescent Iris remained a sight to see, and I found myself marveling at their beauty despite all of the cruelty they had inflicted upon us. But the prince . . . he stood out from the rest. Like a dark star, he sauntered through the courtyard, making waves in the crowd with his comings and goings. Out of respect, they gave him a wide berth as he passed, but their eyes reached for him.

Prince Kaleidos sometimes entered our alcove, making small talk with some of the elemental fae. He avoided me, or perhaps we avoided each other. The truth was, I was glad to avoid the confrontation, because I had many things I would have liked to say to him. Things that could have led to my arrest and execution. Better he stayed away from me.

△

Himmel had the rooms rearranged after the Hunt so that each room was fitted with only two beds. Viera and I were together in one while Lewenne and Ilaria reluctantly shared the other.

Every night, after I was sure the others were asleep, I snuck out and swam in the gardens. Always holding my breath in anticipation until I found the vines still in place.

On a few occasions, I had almost awoken Viera to have her join me, but I worried she might feel hurt if she found out I'd kept secrets from her. I desperately wanted to tell her everything, but I feared it was already too late.

I grabbed some fruit for a snack before I snuck out again that night. Although I craved salt, the Iris seemed to think fruit was all we needed. In Prisma the only salt I frequently tasted was from my tears.

Setting the fruit at the side of the waterway, I disrobed then slunk into the water in my silk nightgown. The cool temperature was a perfect contrast to the lingering, humid heat.

Lavender flowers that had fallen from their trees floated around me. I plucked them up, weaving them into my hair and stared at my reflection in the water. My face was different, my bone structure more defined. There was a maturity in my eyes that hadn't been there before. The more I looked, the less I recognized. I couldn't see my mother anymore. It was almost as if a stranger stared back at me. A week in Prisma had changed me, not only on the inside.

I lay back into the water, the flowers coming undone as my loose hair floated around me like a black crown. I counted the stars, pondering if one day, I would join them. I wondered if Ulli and Nickel were up there twinkling in the night sky, all their pain forgotten.

I made my way to the edge where I had placed my snacks and sat with my legs and feet dangling in the water. My hair graced the full length of my back like a shiny cape, some of the flowers still dangling from my loose waves. I began working to remove the spiky rind of the small, round, green and magenta fruit. After the Hunt of Shadows, I'd had my nails filed into long, sharp points like claws as a form of self-defense. It didn't hurt that they also made my job of peeling strange fruit easier.

The juicy inside was saccharine but tart and left a syrupy glaze on my fingertips. Greedily, I dug into four more. I thought I was sick of fruit, but I couldn't seem to get enough of the foreign but delicious treats. They were mouthwateringly good. I didn't know if it was because they practically starved us or what, but each bite had me sighing, almost moaning in delight. Wishing I had more of them, I licked the juice from my fingers.

When I heard footsteps approaching, I looked up to find the prince striding toward me. I had wondered when we would meet again, considering he'd originally found me in the gardens. I'd prepared myself for our next encounter during the previous nights, so I would not allow his presence to throw me off. The prince sat down beside me, removing his shoes and dunking his feet into the water.

"My mother designed these rivers," he said.

Of all of the scenarios I had run through in my mind, that was the last thing I expected him to say to me. I hadn't anticipated something so personal from him and found myself at a loss for words.

"Your mother is Argenti?" I asked.

"Was," he corrected, his expression going distant.

"Oh." I took a sharp inhale at the realization. "I'm so sorry . . . What happened?"

"It was a long time ago."

All right, so he doesn't want to talk about it.

"Tell me about yourself, sea nymph." He cocked a brow at me.

I snorted in response to the nickname and then took a moment to gather my thoughts. "Well . . . I have a large family back in Iveria. We live beneath. I am the eldest, and I have three sisters and three brothers. They are all much younger than me, so I sort of helped raise them." My lips curved into a sad smile. "Stars, I used to resent all the hard work, but what I wouldn't give to spend another moment with them. Sticky hands and all." My eyes moistened at the thought, but I blinked rapidly, taking a deep breath to try to keep myself from getting emotional in front of this male I hardly knew. "My family was basically my whole life back in Iveria. My family and, of course, my best friend, Viera . . . I mean, it doesn't really matter anymore, because I'm here now and this is my life." I gestured to the palace and sighed, one of the remaining flowers in my hair releasing with the movement.

Kaleidos studied me, his eyes drifting from my face only to follow the flower as it floated down to the pile of fruit skins behind me. He reached back to pick up one of the many peels, raising an eyebrow at me. A small, knowing smirk grew on his face as he examined me.

"How many of these did you have?" he asked, not hiding the amusement in his voice.

"I don't know. A couple," I said, trying but failing to keep my expression blank.

The prince glanced at the pile and then back at me as if to say, *liar*.

"Okay, maybe four or five," I admitted. I tried to repress my smile, but it wouldn't budge. "What does it matter anyway? They are delicious, and your people don't feed us enough around here!"

"Is that so?" he asked. "Do you know what these are? Or rather, what they can do in high doses?"

"Fruit? They were in the assortment left in our rooms. I've been trying different varieties every night. They are all so different here than in Iveria," I rambled on, proceeding to suck the juices off another finger, moaning audibly this time. "I've never had anything like this," I said with a slight flutter of my lashes.

He reached for my hand, looking me right in the eyes, and said in a somewhat patronizing tone, "I think you've had quite enough."

Against my better judgment, I gave in to the inexplicable urge to be closer to him and reached my other hand out to trace the curve of his muscled arm. He grasped hold of that hand as well, but instead of pulling me in toward him, he flung me into the water.

My arms windmilled as I ungracefully fell into its depths.

Foolhardy male.

Without coming up, I darted for his still-dangling feet and yanked him in before he had a chance to see me coming.

After we both surfaced, he laughed wholeheartedly. Kaleidos brushed his wet hair back, the biggest smile spread across his face as he contemplated me.

"Fructus amare are delicious and typically harmless when eaten in small doses . . . but more than two? Now that would elicit interesting consequences." He grinned slyly while swimming backward toward the riverbank.

I drifted toward him, cornering him against the edge, and asked, my voice deep and sultry, "What kind of consequences?"

I trailed my finger lazily down his forehead then down his nose and over the silhouette of his full lips and chin, watching the water droplets ever-so-slowly snake their way down his godlike skin as if they too had an appreciation for his dark, shimmering complexion.

He remained perfectly still in that moment, allowing me to explore him so intimately. I breathed him in, his sea salt and oak scent mixing with the floral bouquet of the garden. I leaned in to close the distance between us as if begging him to kiss me.

"Let's just say my friends like to consume these before engaging in . . . passionate affairs," he drawled, his lips nearly on mine as he spoke. His breath danced upon my skin, making me shiver from head to tingling toes. Lightheaded as I hungrily breathed in his air, I yearned for him to take me into his arms, to devour me.

"Aella," he said, his voice gruff. My eyes fluttered open at the way he said my name, and I backed up ever-so-slightly to get a better look at him. To take in the sinewy contours of his form, the delineation of his muscles visible through the damp fabric clinging to his body. An ethereal radiance emanated from his skin, reflecting off the water's surface. He drank me in, eyes shimmering under the pale moonlight. Attempting to place some distance between us, he explained, "I know you may feel like you want certain things at this moment, but I suspect you would not be acting so friendly with me right now had you not indulged yourself on this particular fruit this evening."

"You speak as if you know me so well," I taunted, my hands now exploring my own skin, as if they needed to touch someone, something.

The prince raised a brow at me and shook his head as he laughed under his breath. "Come on, we need to get you back up to your bedchamber. A good night's sleep will do the trick, and you'll be back to hating me in no time."

"Oh, you have me all wrong, Prince. I still hate you. Oh, I loathe you. In fact, you are the worst person I have ever met," I said, my voice darkening but still full of lust.

"Tell me more," he urged. "Tell me why." His voice was softer now, his eyes narrowed as he studied me, flicking briefly to the band of scars on my right arm before connecting with mine.

"You're a self-serving, egotistical, vain person."

"All of those words basically mean the same thing. Tell me how you really feel about me," he challenged.

"You arrogantly sit up in that box with all creature comforts and pleasures—drinking, laughing, reveling, and feasting—utterly oblivious to the countless lives sacrificed for *your entertainment*. You let people die for you!" I finally blurted out, shocking myself sober as the words crossed my lips. A small cry escaped me, and I turned away from him.

As if satisfied with my reply, he climbed out of the water and reached his hand toward me as he said, "Come, let me walk you back."

I didn't want to take his hand, afraid the feeling of him would send me over the edge again. I could not allow myself to forget who he truly was for a fleeting moment of pleasure—the fact that he was Iris and his role in the Matri-Ludus was unforgivable. I climbed out of the water on my own, ignoring his outstretched hand.

Kaleidos draped my robe over my shoulders, making a joke about how he'd let me stay wet this time since he knew how much I liked it. I didn't laugh.

Walking back to the terrace, I fought the constant urge to rip off my clothes and jump on him. Repeating the sobering mantra in my head, *He killed Ulli. He killed Nickel.*

He offered to help me up, but I forced myself to say, "No. Thank you."

I ascended the vines at a sluggish pace, struggling the entire way, my body yearning to drop to the floor and writhe in the cushion of the soft grass.

"Are you sure you don't need help?" he asked, watching my painfully slow ascent.

About halfway up, I decided I was never going to make it and I should just give up.

"At this pace, you might make it up by sunrise, but I'm not betting on it," he quipped.

I sneered down at him, but the thought of finishing the climb to the top was growing more impossible by the minute. My traitorous muscles wouldn't budge. Whimpering to myself, I begrudgingly called down to him, "Fine."

"Oh, you don't have to tell me, I know I am," he said as he leaned against the wall.

"You're infuriating!" I shouted down at him, and he smiled.

"What was that? You find me intriguing?"

"I need your help, Kal. Are you coming or not?"

He smiled at my use of his name. "I thought you would never ask." Kaleidos chuckled, a boyish grin on his face as he deftly made his way up to me. When he reached for me, I swatted his hand away as if he would burn me.

"Use your powers. Float me up there on one of your plants or something."

"It doesn't work like that, Aella. Climb on my back and I'll take you the rest of the way."

I huffed, tentatively wrapping my arms around his neck before climbing onto him. I felt ridiculous hanging on his back like a small child, and as soon as he got me to the top, I dropped away from him.

Kaleidos lingered as I headed toward the door. I turned back to look at him one last time. Another competition was due, and I had no guarantee I would survive the next one. I needed to ask what was on my heart.

"How can you let this happen to us?" My voice broke.

"It is the way it has always been," he replied, his voice hollow.

"So you just let it happen? Don't you have any authority? You're the prince, Kaleidos! You could stop this."

"It is the way it has always been," he repeated, sounding resigned.

"You are just as bad as the rest of them," I accused, not caring that he could have had me killed for half the things I'd said. I somehow knew that he agreed with me, and deep down, he hated himself as much as I hated him. Still, I prepared myself for his anger, for him to put me in my place, but it did not come. He simply turned and climbed back down over the terrace.

Chapter 17

Zephyria

Arianwen

Luminara swept through the mountain passes with stealth and speed. If it hadn't been for Wynn's arms holding me close, I might have passed out in fright. Everything appeared so small from up above, and I marveled at the snow-capped peaks around us. Glancing over my shoulder at Wynn, the serenity on his face spoke volumes. Up among the clouds was where he found his peace, just like I found mine underneath the sea.

I had expected it to be much colder up in the sky, but Wynn had formed a protective shield of air around us which helped tremendously.

"See, it's not so bad up here," Wynn spoke, leaning his head down toward me. He gave me a little squeeze. "You're a natural."

"Right!" I scoffed. "I can't wait to be back on land, which is strange for me to say, considering I usually can't wait to get off land and into water."

Wynn's laughter rumbled through me, causing warmth to flood my body.

We flew for hours, and I found myself almost drifting off to sleep. If I hadn't been so terrified of falling to my death, I might have closed my eyes to try. When I could barely keep my eyes open, Wynn landed Luminara high up in the craggy peaks, and we spent the short remainder of the night in a shallow cave. Wynn shielded us from the harsh wind using his power, and warmth radiated from the giant aquila's body as she allowed us to sleep tucked under her giant wings.

❖

While I wasn't about to admit it to Wynn, I was grateful we were able to fly for the remainder of our journey. Just imagining how long it would have taken to traverse the land speeding past us as we flew was daunting.

The steep mountains and rocky passes looked treacherous from above. I imagined it would have been nearly impossible to bring any kind of significant force through them, so it didn't surprise me that the Adamas had been able to remain hidden from the Iris for so long.

As the day turned to night once again, Wynn squeezed a hand around my waist, pulling me closer. "We are getting close, so I fear I must take another precaution for your safety," he said, his voice becoming more serious. "I'll need to blindfold you."

"The blood oath isn't enough?" Though he couldn't see me, I rolled my eyes. Even without the oath, I doubted I'd ever be able to find my way back. We had covered so much land, and the mountains were starting to look the same to me. How he knew where we were seemed more impressive the longer we flew. Also, the idea of flying *blind* sounded even more terrifying.

He sounded apologetic when he spoke. "It's how it has to be, especially if you plan to leave. My people would not let you if they thought you could lead the Iris back to them, oath or no oath."

The possibility of not being allowed to return home made my body go rigid with fear. *He* had sworn to let me leave when I chose, but what if the rulers of the Court of Air held me captive? I berated myself for not being more careful with the wording of his oath.

There is no way Wynn would let them keep me against my will . . . right?

The reality was, I didn't know him. We had been traveling together for less than a week, and there I was, heading to a mythical city and putting my life in his hands. All I could do was hope that my decision wouldn't end in tragedy.

"If you must, go ahead," I begrudgingly agreed.

Wynn let go of me as he twisted and reached down to pull something out of one of the pockets hanging off the saddle. I shrieked as I leaned forward, clutching Luminara, feeling unmoored without his arms holding me close.

"A little warning next time would be nice!"

"Don't worry, my star, I won't let you fall," he said, sounding like he was holding back a laugh. "Now close your eyes."

He reached around me, placed a rolled-up tunic over my eyes, and tied it securely around the back of my head. Taking deep breaths, I tried to calm my racing heart as all my other senses heightened at the loss of vision. His scent hit me first—notes of pine and sage—as he wrapped his arms back around my middle. His muscled chest felt hard against my back, and I hated how much I loved the way his arms felt around me. The wind whistled around us, followed by trilling sounds coming from Wynn that Luminara responded to. Straining my ears, I thought I recognized the sound of swords clashing below and some faint shouts. My body tensed in preparation for a landing I couldn't see, and I silently cursed Wynn for needing to blindfold me.

Wynn brushed his lips against my ear. "Relax. We are almost there."

"Easy for you to say. *You* can see where we're going."

The sounds got louder, and Luminara's abrupt landing jolted me. I blinked at the sudden brightness as Wynn removed my blindfold. We'd landed in a snowy clearing with torches lighting a path toward a city built into the side of a mountain. There were aquila aeries around us, and the sound of squawks coming from nestlings and fledglings filled the air. Wynn unstrapped me from the harness and helped me climb off Luminara. He shouted at some young Adamas males—who appeared to have been training with swords—to come take care of the aquila, and they rushed right over to do his bidding. One of them gave me a shy smile, mumbling a hello before getting to work. I noticed guards wearing leathers in muted gray colors blending into the side of the mountain and armed with bows. One of the guards nodded at Wynn in some unspoken communication and flew off into the city.

"You're so quiet. What do you think, Arianwen?" Wynn asked, anticipation coloring his voice.

"I'm just taking it all in. I would have never guessed that anyone lived up this high, and it's not nearly as cold as I would have expected, even with the snow on the ground."

"Welcome to Zephyria and the Court of Air." Wynn chuckled. "There are many benefits to controlling the air. It would be miserable if we couldn't protect those who live here from the biting winds." He held out an arm. "Let's get settled. You deserve a warm meal and a good night's rest after the last few days."

Taking his arm, I smiled up at him. "Sounds perfect."

Wynn nodded at the guards, and they saluted him as we passed. I couldn't help but wonder if he was their superior officer based on the deference they showed him, and my curiosity had been piqued when one of them rushed off as soon as we'd arrived.

"Why were those young ones training this late in the evening?" I asked curiously.

Wynn looked back at them. "Ah, Peetrus and Henri are guards in training and often help out in the aeries when needed. Our population is smaller than you might think, and we begin training young so all will be prepared in case the Iris ever find us. They must be on the night rotation."

I frowned. "Have you had many altercations with the Iris since you parted ways?"

"As I've said, we try to keep to ourselves. However, we have run into patrols occasionally on our rescue missions and do not always come out unscathed, as you well know," he finished, gesturing at his shoulder.

"Rescue missions?" I asked, eyes widening. Wynn seemed hesitant to respond, so I pointed at my palm while rolling my eyes. "Star-sworn blood oath, remember? You can trust me."

Wynn gave me a pained smile. "Force of habit, I assure you. It's hard to speak freely."

I nodded in understanding. "Sorry, I don't mean to give you a hard time. I just want to know whatever you can tell me. It still amazes me that you have lived up here undetected for so long."

"Yes, I am grateful that we have had a fairly peaceful existence."

"So . . . rescue missions?"

"We take in refugees from all over Esterra, believe it or not. I was leading a small group from Ilithania when I was shot out of the sky," he replied, looking pained. "I tried to lead the Iris away from the refugees, but I have no idea if they got away. For all I know, they are rotting in an Iris dungeon or have already been executed for trying to escape. I'll need to find out if they made it."

I gently squeezed his arm. "I'm so sorry. Don't blame yourself, regardless of what did or did not happen. The Iris are monsters."

Wynn patted my hand. "You have a kind heart, Arianwen. Thank you for trying to make me feel better, but they were my responsibility, and I failed them."

"I'm still trying to wrap my head around the fact that you have refugees here! How do they even know you exist or how to find you?" I asked incredulously.

"Ah, my star, there are always some who will stand against tyranny. Those who are desperate will find each other."

Wynn's response was so cryptic, I wasn't entirely sure what to make of it, but I didn't think it was worth pushing him for more answers until after we had rested.

Changing the subject, I asked, "Where will I be staying tonight?"

"You'll be staying in my home. It is not too much further, I promise," Wynn replied with a smile.

The city was surprisingly warm and inviting. The homes and buildings were built into the mountain and the streets were narrow. There were flights of stairs that led to different levels, and we had climbed quite a few of them. Hardly anyone was out, but I saw a few guards patrolling the streets as we walked. Raucous laughter and music came from some taverns we passed, and I glimpsed flashes of gold *and* bronze skin.

"You were serious, there truly are other elementals here," I said in awe. "I thought Prisma was the only place in Esterra where the different fae races can live among one another."

"Does that not seem wrong to you, Arianwen?" Wynn asked. "Our differences make us stronger, and just think about what we could achieve if we were allowed to work together."

"I guess I never thought much of it. We have been kept separate for millennia, anything else would feel unnatural. We were taught that the Adamas were annihilated because they went against the stars' commands."

Wynn gave me a knowing look. "There is a saying that history is written by the victors. You cannot believe everything you have been told. I understand this is a lot for you to take in, and I have to admit, you have been surprisingly open-minded."

"I think a part of me always knew there was more to what we'd been taught."

We made our way to the uppermost level of the city, and I stopped to catch my breath and admire the view of the twinkling lights that made Zephyria glow.

"It's breathtaking here," I said, then joked, "literally and figuratively. All those stairs have worn me out."

Wynn smiled and teased back, "I'm glad you like it. I would have flown us, but someone here is not a fan of my flying."

"Ugh, don't remind me."

Wynn chuckled then guided me toward the pillared entrance of a grand palatium. Most of it was built into the side of the mountain, but some terraces jutted out of giant, arched openings. My mouth gaped at the incredible architecture. It reminded me of something I might have read about in a fable.

We were greeted at the entrance by an older Adamas male who gave me an appraising glance before he bowed before Wynn. "Your Highness, so glad you've returned to us. The king and queen request your presence in the study immediately."

My mouth dropped open.

Your Highness?!

Wynn smiled and handed him my pack. "Thank you, Emil. Can you please have a room prepared for our guest?"

Emil nodded and hurried away.

"I feel like you could have mentioned your station, *Your Highness*," I said, my voice dripping with sarcasm and surprise.

"This was so much more fun though," Wynn replied with an amused glint in his eyes. "Now come, we mustn't keep my parents waiting."

"Is there any way I can freshen up first?" I pleaded.

"They will be anxious for an update, so I'm afraid not." He led me up a grand staircase and down a hallway covered in beautiful tapestries that gave warmth to the gray and white stone walls.

"I probably look like I was dragged out of the deep."

Wynn's shoulders shook in silent laughter. "It's not that bad, I assure you."

We approached what I assumed was the study, and Wynn strode in confidently. I followed a little behind, nervous about meeting the king and queen of the Adamas.

"Mother! Father!" Wynn said, embracing the queen and pressing a kiss to her cheek before turning to acknowledge his father, the king. They both wore thick robes over sleeping garments, looking as if they'd been roused from their bed.

"Wynn!" the queen exclaimed. "I was so worried when you didn't return as planned. Are you well? Were you injured?" She glanced in my direction. "And who, pray tell, did you bring to intrude on our meeting?"

Wynn ignored her tone and turned, motioning for me to join him. "Mother and Father, meet Arianwen. I was shot down by an Iris patrol, and she took it upon herself to stop and help a stranger—she healed me. She is a fantastic healer. Arianwen, these are my parents, King Volare and Queen Astrid Sorensen of the Court of Air."

"Your Majesties, it is an honor to meet you," I said, curtsying before them.

"You may rise," King Volare proclaimed, sounding tired and unamused. "Wynn, we must speak with you in private. Have Emil show your guest to a room."

Wynn's jaw tightened, and his body went rigid, but he went to call for Emil as requested.

I stood before the king and queen, twisting my hands together while glancing around the room. "You have a lovely home . . ." I started to say before the queen interrupted me.

"Yes, yes. I am sure you are exhausted from your travels. There is no need for small talk."

I flushed, gazing down at my feet, wishing the ground would open and swallow me whole.

Wynn returned with Emil and placed a hand on my shoulder. "Emil will take care of you. I'll check in on you later, all right?"

Looking up at him I nodded, mumbled a thank you, and did a quick curtsy in the king and queen's direction before following Emil back out into the hall.

"Right this way, miss." Emil spoke quietly. "Will you require anything to eat?"

My stomach rumbled in response at the thought of food. "I don't want to be a bother, it can wait until tomorrow."

Emil frowned slightly. "You're a guest of the prince, it's no bother. I'll have something sent up."

"Thank you, that's very kind," I said in relief.

We wound through various hallways and up a few flights of stairs.

Everything was so unfamiliar, and I felt lost. The severity of my decisions hit me suddenly, settling like a huge weight on my shoulders. It was too soon for me to be missed, but I had no idea when I would be able to leave and return home. A silent tear rolled unbidden down my cheek, and I could taste its saltiness as it touched my lips, bringing a fresh wave of homesickness upon me.

Emil stopped in front of a door and opened it for me, then waved me inside. "Hopefully this will do. I will have someone prepare a bath for you and bring you something warm to eat."

I turned to him with a smile. "Thanks again for your hospitality."

He nodded and left me to admire the space. I was happy to see that it had a large, arched doorway leading out onto one of the balconies I had seen upon arriving at the palatium. Part of me had feared they would put me in a chamber in the depths of the mountain with no windows. A giant four-poster bed was in the center of the space, draped in snowy white, rich fabrics. The room was decorated simply with touches of blue and silver. A deliciously warm fire crackled in the fireplace, and I dropped onto a comfy chair situated next to it. I pulled off my hiking boots and groaned in relief as I stretched my toes. Feeling the need to relieve myself, I got up and padded over to the connecting room, delighted to find a bathing chamber.

Stars, my entire living room and kitchen could fit in here.

After I finished taking care of my needs, I went to wash my hands in a basin and made the mistake of looking in the mirror.

Faex! This is how I met the king and queen?!

I glared at my reflection. The flying had turned my hair into an aquila's nest on the top of my head. Dirt smudged my silvery cheeks, and there were dark circles under my eyes. A bath couldn't happen soon enough.

A soft knock on the door to my bedroom stole my attention, and I heard a cheerful voice call out, "Hello! My name is Mari. I brought you something to eat and am here to prepare a bath for you."

Hurrying back into the bedroom, I smiled widely at the Aurum fae. "Mari! Pleased to meet you. Thank you so very much. Perfect timing."

Mari set a tray of steaming food on the low table in front of the fireplace. "Please let me know if there's anything else you need."

I smiled and nodded at her as she passed me and went to prepare a bath. Having never met an Aurum fae before, I wanted to ask her all manner of questions, but my grumbling stomach reminded me how hungry I was. I sat back down in front of the fire and groaned in delight at the smell. It was simple—a big piece of crusty bread and a bowl of hot stew—but it was exactly what I needed.

Mari re-entered the room as I was sipping on a steaming mug of tea. "Your bath is ready, miss. I've left some fresh linens and a robe for you, as I'm not sure what you brought with you. If there is something else you need, ring for me." She pointed at a cord that hung near the door. She spied the empty tray and smiled. "Would you like me to bring up any more food?"

"No, thank you, I'm good for the night," I said. She nodded and left.

Not wanting to stay in my filth a minute longer, I rushed to the bathing room while undoing my braid and stripping off my clothes. The enormous bathtub was filled with bubbles, and the scent of lavender and rosemary mingled with the steam rising from the water. I reached my hand in to test it and flinched a little at the intensity of the heat. I should have told Mari that a cold bath would have been fine. Regardless of my trepidation, a bath was necessary, so I decided to climb into the tub and sink into the hot water. The heat soothed my sore muscles, and I felt my body starting to relax. *This isn't terrible . . .*

I took my time, picking up all the little vials of soaps and oils and smelling them before choosing one to lather into my hair.

I must have stayed in the bath for over an hour. By the time I climbed out, the water was tepid. The fluffy white linens felt wonderful on my body, and I dried off before wrapping myself in a sapphire robe made of satin. I had never worn something so luxurious in my entire life. Padding over to the mirror, I found a brush and began the task of working all the tangles out of my long mane before plaiting it back into a braid.

My mouth stretched into a yawn as I made my way back into the bedroom, heading straight for the bed. As I pulled back the covers, the sound of someone clearing their throat took me by surprise. I practically jumped out of my skin, curses flying out of my mouth at the realization that I was not alone.

Chapter 18

A Bitter Treat

Arianwen

"What in the dark depths are you doing scaring me like that!" I exclaimed.

Wynn sat, looking completely relaxed in one of the chairs by the fireplace, a smirk on his face. "Apologies, my star. I knocked before I came in . . . an hour ago," he replied, his eyes darkening as they swept me from head to toe.

Feeling self-conscious all of a sudden, I pulled my robe a little tighter. *Why is he looking at me like that? This robe isn't sheer . . . is it?*

I glanced down at myself, realizing the robe left little to the imagination. My face flushed, but I met his eyes. "I'm sorry to have kept you waiting, I lost track of time."

"The wait was worth it," he replied, biting his lip.

Warmth surged through me, and I quickly crossed my arms over my chest to hide any signs of my sudden arousal. Perching on the side of the bed, I crossed my legs, trying to look relaxed despite the tension that flooded my body. "Is everything all right?"

Wynn dragged his hand over his face. "I hope you forgive my parents for being so short with you. They were worried about me and had been woken from sleep, so they weren't their usual charming selves."

I grimaced. "You don't need to apologize for them. I'm sure it was a shock to have an unexpected visitor when they just wanted to see you. Not to mention, I wasn't at my best."

"Don't worry, you'll have another chance to meet them."

I groaned. "I knew I made a bad impression. It would have been nice to know you were a prince before you dragged me here."

Wynn raised an eyebrow. "Dragged you here? If I'm not mistaken, you were quite eager to visit my home."

"Well . . . I didn't have all the facts," I said, flustered.

Wynn rose to his feet and stalked toward me, his icy blue eyes locked on mine. Stopping right in front of me, he reached over and tucked a stray tendril of hair behind my ear. I trembled, his proximity and the intimacy of the simple act surprising me. It wasn't the first or even the second time he had done so. The brush of his fingers sent chills skittering down my spine, and I wanted him to do it again. I craved more. Wynn gave me the impression he wanted to say something, but before he opened his mouth, he stopped himself. He spun on his heel and went to the door saying, "You should get some rest. We will have a busy day tomorrow."

As the door clicked shut, I exhaled a breath I hadn't realized I was holding. Getting to my feet, I went to extinguish the lights.

My interactions with Wynn were getting more and more confusing. I climbed into bed and closed my eyes, wishing he had stayed longer . . . but to what end? Being alone with him in my room had been completely inappropriate.

Despite the comfortable bed, it took me a while before I drifted off to sleep, visions of icy blue eyes haunting my dreams.

The light of dawn woke me from my heavy slumber, and I opened my eyes to sunlight dancing off the snow on the majestic alps outside my balcony. I yawned as I stretched my limbs and tried to wake my body. I had not gotten as much sleep as I'd hoped to thanks to all the confusing thoughts keeping me awake.

A neatly folded stack of clothing on the table snagged my attention as I glanced around the room. I climbed out of bed, curious about what I'd find, and selected a cream-colored sweater and a pair of fleece-lined pants from the pile. A pair of warm snow boots rested by the door. I smiled at the thoughtfulness of whoever provided the weather-appropriate clothing as I went to the bathing room to wash my face and get changed. I undid my braid and let the waves fall around my shoulders, tying up a small section of hair to keep it out of my eyes.

I wonder what's happening today. Wynn said we would be busy. Do I ring for Mari? Should I wander around and try to find Wynn?

Satisfied with my appearance, I returned to the bedroom to put on the boots. Before I could sit down, someone knocked on the door, and I heaved a sigh of relief.

Thank the stars I don't need to figure out what to do.

Mari entered the room with a smile. "Good morning, miss! I hope you slept well. I'm glad to see you found the clothes I left for you! It looks like they fit."

"Thank you so much! It was very kind of you to think of me."

"You can thank Prince Wynn. He asked me to bring something for you," Mari explained.

"Oh!" I said, surprised. "I definitely will. Do you happen to know where he is? He told me we had a busy day ahead of us, but I'm afraid I have no idea when or where I'm supposed to meet him."

"I actually came to wake you. You are to meet Prince Wynn for breakfast in the dining hall. Are you ready?"

"Yes, I'm starving. Please lead the way!" I said with a smile.

Mari chuckled. "I can see why he likes you. You are very enthusiastic."

My mouth dropped open as I raised my eyebrows at her words.

Mari grinned as she continued. "Not that he's said in so many words, but I can tell that you're not just any refugee. Prince Wynn never brings anyone here as a guest as there is designated lodging for the refugees until they can be sorted into homes."

Wynn kept surprising me, but I supposed I didn't count as a refugee, considering I intended to return home.

"Will the king and queen be at breakfast?" I asked as I followed Mari down the hall and up multiple flights of stairs.

"No, they already ate. You will most likely join them at dinner."

I breathed a quiet sigh of relief. After my mortifying first impression the previous night, I was happy to avoid them as long as possible.

We stopped in front of a large door, and Mari turned to me. "You can head in, miss. He's waiting for you."

"Please call me Arianwen," I replied with a smile. "You've been so kind, and I'm not one for formalities."

Mari's eyes glinted in amusement. "I'm well aware, miss—Arianwen."

She bustled off, and I took a deep breath before opening the door, my nerves getting the better of me at the thought of eating a formal meal with Wynn.

I pulled the heavy door open and smiled at the sight of him sitting at a large, elegant table, shuffling through papers with a furrowed brow. He looked like a prince, no longer wearing the ill-fitting tunic I had procured for him but a rich gray leather jacket over a sapphire shirt. Glancing around the room, I noticed that it was decorated sparsely but had a rustic charm to it. Massive wooden beams went across the ceiling that sloped up on both sides. Intricate wooden chandeliers hung over the table, casting a soft glow. A wall made completely of glass gave a stunning view of the surrounding alps.

"Good morning, Your Highness," I said, as I made my way over to the table, wondering if I needed to curtsy. An extra place setting had been set next to his seat at the head of the table.

Wynn looked up, his eyes distant. "Good morning, Arianwen," he replied, forcing a smile.

My brows furrowed as I sat down, wondering at his begrudged pleasantry. "Is something wrong?"

"Nothing you need to worry about," he replied. "Please eat." He went back to studying the papers in front of him while sipping on a steaming beverage.

Feeling slightly uncomfortable, I obliged and piled my plate high with scrambled eggs and bacon. I was not about to turn down a delicious-smelling breakfast. "You said we were going to be busy today. What will that entail?"

Wynn glanced up, and I noticed his eyes appeared to be a stormy shade of gray instead of his usual blue. "If you recall, I told you that we could use your healing skills. It would appear that you're needed sooner than I had anticipated. There aren't many Argenti here in Zephyria, and the healers we have are stretched thin. I was informed last night that we have some seriously injured refugees from one of our recent rescues whom our healers have not been able to help. I'm hoping you might be able to."

"I'm happy to try my best, but you do remember that I am only a healer in training, right?" I said, then added, "Your *Highness*."

"Ari, please," he replied, looking exasperated. "You don't need to get all formal with me now, and don't act like I can't hear the sarcasm in your tone."

My face flushed as I retorted, "Forgive me for not knowing how to talk to you. With everything that has happened in the last few days and now finding out who you are, I just feel all out of sorts. And to be honest, I'm still a bit angry that you weren't more upfront when we met."

"I am still the same fae you stopped to rescue," he countered, his voice firm. "Yes, I am a prince, but I don't need to explain myself to you, and if you'd rather I start treating you differently, tell me now." His eyes simmered with pent-up frustration as he stared me down.

A wave of anger rose in me, but perhaps Wynn had been wrong and I did have a tiny bit of self-preservation in me. The realization hit me that if I angered him enough, he still had the power to keep me from returning to my family. While *he* may have sworn to let me leave, the king and queen had not. Trying to cool my temper, I lowered my gaze and mumbled a soft apology.

Wynn spoke, his tone softening. "You don't give yourself enough credit. You have a real gift for healing, and we could truly use your help if you are willing to try."

"Of course, whatever you need," I replied, slightly mollified. Desperately wanting to change the subject and trying to reclaim the sense of familiarity we'd had with each other, I asked, "What are you drinking? It doesn't smell like tea."

Wynn finally gave me a hint of a real smile. "It's coffee. Some refugees from the Court of Earth brought these beans and showed us how to roast them. I find it helps to wake me up, especially after a night of little sleep. Would you like to try some?"

My curiosity getting the better of me, I nodded, and he poured some of the black liquid into a cup for me. I took a big gulp of the coffee and almost spit it out, surprised by the intense, bitter flavor.

"That is interesting," I said, trying to sound polite and not show my utter disgust for the beverage. "I don't know if coffee is for me."

Wynn chuckled. "Here, before you give up on it altogether, try it like this." He added some milk and a few teaspoons of sugar then stirred them in, turning the dark beverage a lighter caramel color.

Looking at it reluctantly, I took a smaller sip, bracing myself for the bitter flavor.

"Oh!" I exclaimed. "This actually isn't terrible."

Wynn laughed loudly at my response. "I so enjoy watching you eat or drink. You are quite entertaining, Arianwen."

"So you keep saying," I said, trying not to feel embarrassed. I tried a few more sips of the coffee, realizing it was quite delicious the more I got used to it. A slight buzz went through my body as I started feeling more alert, and I quickly finished my meal. Wynn became distant again as he refocused on the papers in front of him.

I pushed my plate away and rose from the table. "I'm ready to go if you are."

Wynn set his papers to the side and joined me. "Let's find you a warm cloak and be on our way then."

I followed him down the hall and down a sweeping flight of stairs before seeing the entrance we had come in the previous night. Emil strode toward us. Wynn asked him to provide a cloak for me, so we waited by the door for him to return. I hated that the quiet between us had become awkward when it had been so peaceful before.

Breaking the silence, I said, "I'm looking forward to seeing Zephyria in the daylight. I'm sure it's breathtaking."

"Yes, it is," he replied, giving me nothing more.

Maybe I had imagined all the flirtation and ease from before. It almost felt like Wynn was angry with me. Right before I tried to speak again, Emil returned with a cloak for me.

"Here you go, miss." He handed me a beautiful, wool garment in the most vibrant shade of blue.

Wrapping it around myself, I thanked Emil and looked at Wynn with expectation.

"Let's go then," he said as he opened the door into the cold, snowy day. Despite the awkwardness between us, the idea of seeing a city that I hadn't even known existed brought me quite a thrill.

Chapter 19

Poison

Arianwen

Zephyria in full daylight was beyond my expectations. We were surrounded by snow-capped mountains, and the sky was the clearest shade of blue I had ever seen. It felt like I could reach up and touch the fluffy clouds. I would have never guessed a city was hiding among the peaks of the alps.

"Is there always snow here? Where do you get all your fresh food?" I asked.

"Yes, we are up high enough that the snow doesn't melt. We have some greenhouses where we grow produce, and we have teams go out to hunt for meat on the aquilas," Wynn explained.

We continued walking in silence except for the sound of our feet crunching in the snow. Suddenly, Wynn swooped me up into his arms, and we were airborne, flying through the streets.

"Wynn!" I shrieked.

He only chuckled as he held me tightly to his chest. "Walking was going to take too long—this is faster."

I beat my hand on his chest half-heartedly. "Ugh, you just better hope I don't lose my breakfast all over you."

"You'll be used to this in no time," he teased.

I clung to him, grateful his mood seemed to have lightened a little since we'd left the palatium. It felt like everything had changed between us once I'd found out he was a prince. His picking me up and flying out of nowhere reminded me of the Wynn he had been on the trail.

He landed in front of a large building somewhere in the heart of Zephyria. The front was covered in windows from the ground to the roof, allowing tons of natural light to pour in.

"This is the hospitium," Wynn explained as he walked me up to the doors. "We have a few Argenti healers who run the place, along with anyone else who has a healing affinity. As you know, Argenti tend to have the strongest healing gift among the elementals, but we have learned quite a bit from some of our Aurum and Aereus refugees."

"That sounds amazing. I have always longed to learn healing techniques that are different from what I know. If only the Iris allowed us to live among each other . . . outside of Prisma."

Wynn's jaw tightened. "Our world would be so much more advanced if we worked together. Have you ever considered why they keep us separate? My theory is that the Iris do it to weaken us. Maybe they're afraid that if we all joined forces, we might actually stand a chance of overturning their rule."

Wynn's passion ignited something in me. For the first time in my life, a tiny flame of hope started to grow. Hope that someday, things could actually be different.

As we walked into the hospitium, I immediately noticed pools of steaming water on the left, and then, on the opposite end of the building, a stream of running water cut through. With my element all around me, I could sense my power recharging.

"Was this place designed by Argenti healers?"

"Yes, it was, with the help of some of our Aereus fae. The Aereus are such gifted builders." He pointed toward the pools of water. "The hospitium was built around existing hot springs to make use of their natural healing properties."

I glanced around the room, loving how open and airy it felt with the high ceilings and floor-to-ceiling windows. Intricate woodwork filled the spaces in between, and eternal flames lit up the areas that led into the inner rooms. I had only read about the Aurum's eternal flames in textbooks and couldn't help but run over to take a peek.

"This place is incredible! I have always wanted to see these up close," I said, admiring how the flame gave off bright light but no heat. "You're right, there is so much we could benefit from if we weren't all separated."

Hearing soft footsteps approaching, I turned around and saw an older Argenti female walking toward us.

"Prince Wynn, so kind of you to check in on the refugees," she said, acknowledging him with a slight curtsy.

"Pluvia! I heard about the injuries, and I brought you someone who may be able to help." He motioned toward me. "This is Arianwen. We met near Lakehaven after my last run went badly. She healed me from a poisoned bolt to the shoulder and is gifted in the healing arts."

I blushed at the praise. "Nice to meet you, Pluvia. I'm happy to help however I can."

Pluvia scanned me with an arched eyebrow. "You appear so young. Have you completed your training?"

Shaking my head, I replied, "No, I have not, but learning from someone with your experience would be extremely valuable, and I would be honored if you'd teach me."

Looking pleased with my answer, she motioned for us to follow her. "Your Highness, I assume you have been brought up to speed?"

"Yes, I'm aware of what happened, but Arianwen isn't," Wynn answered.

"The Aurum refugee group coming from the Easthen Forest was almost caught by the Iris," Pluvia fumed, her upper lip curling. "They sent trained shadow fangs after them! *Children* were mauled, and some didn't make it."

I gasped, horror filling me at the thought. "How could they do that? Chase people down with savage beasts?" I asked.

"Come now, we are not worth much more to them than slaves, and they would rather we were dead than out of their control," Pluvia answered me.

I shuddered, and Wynn placed a hand on my back in comfort. Surprised, I glanced up at him and offered him a soft smile.

"How many injured are here?" I asked Pluvia.

"We have five in critical condition and others with minor injuries we were able to heal," she replied. Pluvia stopped in front of a door, turned to me, and said, "Brace yourself, my dear. It is fairly gruesome, and I doubt you would have encountered something like this in Iveria."

Dread filled me, but as a healer, I had to get used to seeing distressing things. I rolled my shoulders back and followed her into the room. The first thing that hit me was the putrid odor combined with the intense pain I could sense radiating off the patients lying in the beds. Some of them were missing limbs, and visible claw marks marred one male's face. There was a sickly sheen to them, and I suspected the shadow fangs' claws had been covered in poison.

The healer in me felt compelled to help them immediately, so I looked to Pluvia. "Do you mind if I examine them?"

"Please, go ahead. Unfortunately, we haven't been able to determine what has poisoned them. Their wounds aren't healing because of it," she remarked with a grim look on her face.

"The prince was wounded by a poisoned bolt—I wonder if it is the same substance," I said as I moved to examine the first patient. "What's his name?"

"That's Styx. He's ten years old," Pluvia replied.

I looked down at the young Aurum male. His golden skin was leached of color, the angry-looking claw marks down his face oozed blood. His hair was so light, it was almost white, and it was matted to his head in sweat, his body raging with a fever. The sight of him made me want to cry and scream all at once. No child should ever have to go through something like that. Involuntarily imagining one of my siblings in his place, I closed my eyes tightly, trying not to let my emotions get the better of me.

Focus, Ari. You can do this.

I placed my hands on his chest and pushed some of my power into him. His eyes fluttered, and he groaned as I tried to battle the infection in his body.

"Keep fighting, Styx. I'm here to help," I said soothingly, then turned to Pluvia. "Do you have any quercus alba and aralia spinosa? Those helped fight the prince's infection."

Pluvia shook her head. "I'm sorry, we don't grow them in our greenhouses here, and they don't grow this far north. Do you think they would make a difference? Someone would need to search closer to Iveria, which would be risky."

"If everything else you've tried to fight this infection with has failed, I would take the risk."

Wynn spoke up. "I will send someone immediately. Pluvia, do you have an apprentice who would be able to recognize those plants?"

"Yes, I have someone who is working in another wing of the hospitium. I'll go and fetch them, Your Highness," Pluvia replied before hurrying off.

I glanced up from the young male as I kept trying to push healing energy into him. "I don't know how much time they have left if they've been fighting this for days." My face started beading with sweat at the effort.

"I'm going to accompany the healer. We will need to head back toward where you found me. I know you came across the plants there, and we don't have time to waste," Wynn said.

A surprising pang of homesickness washed through me at the thought that he would be heading so close to my home.

"Maybe you can bring an extra guard with you? What if the Iris are still out looking for you? What if they found the bodies of the other guards?

Maybe I should go because I know the area?" I asked, my anxiety causing me to ramble.

"Are you worried about my safety, Arianwen?" Wynn raised a brow, a self-assured smirk playing at the corner of his lips. "The Iris got lucky when they hit me with that bolt. They won't be so lucky again. We can make the best time if it's just the two of us, and hopefully you can help stave off the infection until we return. You really are a gifted healer, and I think you are their best chance at surviving."

My heart warmed at the praise, but I worried I would just disappoint everyone if I couldn't save the patients. I straightened my posture, setting my mind on the task ahead instead of dwelling on feelings I had no business entertaining. "That makes sense. How long will it take if you can fly the whole way?"

"I'm not sure, but Luminara is fast. I think we can make it back in less than a week if we push ourselves."

My brow furrowed in concern as I glanced around at all the patients in the room. "I wish I could promise you that they'll last that long, but I can't."

Pluvia returned with a gorgeous Argenti female in tow. Her face glowed when she looked at Wynn, and she smiled shyly at him.

"This is Dorel. She is available to accompany whoever is going, Your Highness."

"Nice to meet you, Dorel. I believe I have seen you around these halls in passing. Lovely to put a name to your face," Wynn said with a smile. "We should be off so we can return as quickly as possible. Arianwen?"

"Yes?"

He paused as if not sure what to say in front of the other healers. "I will see you soon. Let Pluvia know if you need anything."

"Thank you. May the stars be with you."

Wynn looked at me for a moment, and I held his gaze, hoping my worry wasn't too obvious. He turned and left, Dorel with him. I shook my head and took a deep breath. I needed to focus on helping the injured refugees and stop worrying about Wynn's safety . . . and the fact that I didn't like how Dorel had looked at him.

❈

Hours flew by as I helped Pluvia care for the patients. We tried our best to keep the fevers at bay, and I poured as much healing magic into them as I could spare. Since their wounds weren't healing, we had to continuously remove the soiled bandages and replace them with fresh ones to prevent additional infections.

An older female who had lost one of her legs in the attack succumbed to the poison despite our best efforts. Her husband's sobs reverberated throughout the room when Pluvia broke the news to him. The sound and sight of him weeping over his wife would haunt me forever. Unable to continue watching, I made up an excuse and ran from the room, needing a moment to let my own tears fall. Had there been anything else I could have done? Had I missed something? I fought back my guilt and despair, knowing the other patients still needed me, and continued working.

As night fell, I began feeling weak before realizing that I hadn't eaten anything since breakfast. Pluvia saw me swaying on my feet and admonished me, "Arianwen, you must take care of yourself or you will be no good to anyone! Have you taken a break at all since you've been here?"

"No, I haven't. I'm sorry, I just can't help it. It's hard to sit back and do nothing when they are in such pain," I lamented, my voice starting to crack. "I can't lose anyone else."

Pluvia released a knowing sigh and laid a gentle hand on my shoulder, her voice softening. "We did everything we could for her. Do not blame yourself."

I swallowed my emotions and nodded before rolling my neck, trying to work out the tightness.

Returning to her original question, Pluvia straightened back up. "Well, the prince will have my head if he returns and finds you have run yourself ragged. Please take a break. I know you are used to recharging your power in the ocean, but the hot springs here are incredibly rejuvenating for our kind as well. I recommend you go and soak while I have some food prepared for you," she ordered in a tone that allowed no room for argument.

Raising my hands in surrender, I agreed and headed toward the hot springs. When I got to the pools of water in the ground, I noticed an Aurum female soaking in one of them. I looked around a bit awkwardly. I wasn't sure if I was supposed to disrobe or of any other protocol.

The Aurum female saw me standing there and spoke up while pointing behind me. "If you go into that room, you'll find light robes you can change into."

I nodded my thanks and entered the room she had mentioned. Along the wall were shelves separated into small niches for clothing, and there was a section that stored clean, folded robes in neat piles. Stripping off the smock Pluvia had given me earlier along with the rest of my clothes, I changed into a short, lightweight cotton robe.

My feet dragged as I returned to the springs and chose an empty pool. The stone steps were smooth and warm, and I sighed in relief as I slowly submerged myself. The water surrounded me while its minerals immediately made me feel more alert as my skin soaked in the healing power of my element. I found a ledge to sit on and tried to relax as all the stress of being unable to heal the Aurum patients hit me.

Feelings of hopelessness crept in, guilt that I hadn't been able to do more, that my magic wasn't enough . . . that I wasn't enough. Wynn's belief in my abilities was wrong. I was going to disappoint him. Who was I to think I could help where more experienced healers had already failed?

My mind continued racing with thoughts and ideas of how we could try to stave off the poison a little longer. If Wynn didn't return soon, we'd keep losing patients, and I didn't know if I could bear it.

Feeling eyes on me, I turned and noticed the Aurum female staring in my direction. Her expression was bleak, and I debated whether or not I should say something.

"Are you all right?" I asked, wanting a distraction from my spiraling thoughts.

She shook her head, looking down. "We were meant to come here for a better life, but now here I am in a strange city with a son fighting to survive and a dead husband and daughter. The fact that I escaped with only a few scratches . . ."

"By the stars, I am so sorry," I replied. Her despair was palpable, and I struggled to find words. What could I have possibly offered her amid such tragedy?

Tears started falling down her face. "I had to watch my daughter get ripped to shreds by the shadow fangs those Iris sent after us. My husband tried to save her, and they got to him too." Her voice broke into sobs.

I climbed out of my pool and went over to hers. "Do you mind if I join you?"

She shook her head, and her sobs continued.

I slowly approached her, putting a hand on her shoulder, and she turned and fell into my arms. Letting her cry, I held her close, my own tears finally breaking free. I pushed some healing magic into her, knowing it could never match the magnitude of her loss but still hoping it might help in some small way.

Chapter 20
New Purpose

ARIANWEN

The palatium loomed ahead of me as I trudged back through the icy streets of Zephyria. Pluvia had insisted I return and try to get some rest. I conceded, but I still felt guilty abandoning our patients. Despite the rejuvenating waters of the hot springs, I was drained emotionally and physically after my day in the hospitium. A darker side of me questioned why I would want to be a healer if that was what it was going to be like—helping heal some but losing just as many.

Despite my grim thoughts, I also recognized that I had never felt more alive and filled with purpose than when I'd used my gifts to try to help those in pain. Would I be willing to give that up and become just a meek wife? Content to take care of the home and pop out babies? I didn't think so. The thought of staying in Zephyria and having a purpose beyond being a wife and mother was starting to sound more appealing. Not to mention, there was Wynn, the infuriatingly handsome male who consumed my thoughts and had me thinking and feeling things I never had before.

Is he cuddled up in some cave with Dorel right now?

He's not mine. Stop it.

I hurried into the palatium, shivering a little from the cold. Despite the unseasonable warmth the Adamas created by shielding the city with their air, Zephyria was still significantly colder than Iveria. Emil appeared out of nowhere and took my cloak from me.

"Will you be needing any food sent up to your room, miss?" he inquired in his gruff manner.

"No, thank you. I ate at the hospitium. I'm going to go straight to bed."

"I'll have breakfast sent to your room in the morning," he informed me before walking off to wherever he intended to disappear.

He's an odd one.

I wondered if Emil would ever warm up to me or if he would remain so stoic. I also wondered if there was any chance of Zephyria ever feeling like home.

It's not like I've decided to stay. It's only been a day.

Making my way back to my room, I was relieved I wouldn't be expected to dine with the king and queen for breakfast with Wynn gone.

Despite all my worries, sleep came as soon as my head hit the pillow. My dreams were filled with sneering Iris males chasing me through the woods and snarling shadow fangs biting at my heels.

The skies were stormy as I made my way back to the hospitium the next day. Lightning flashed in warning, and I started running, praying to the stars it wouldn't hit me. Some Adamas children who were playing in the street saw my distress and started pointing and laughing in my direction. I glanced down at myself, wondering if I had forgotten to put the proper clothing on or had something stuck to me but couldn't find anything amiss. Deciding to ignore them, I continued my hurried run to the hospitium. Wynn had been right, flying was so much faster.

I rushed into the front doors and immediately headed back to the room where all the Aurum patients were being kept. I hung my cloak on a hook near the door and grabbed a clean smock. Pluvia entered the room behind me and said, "Good morning, Arianwen. I hope you got some rest. The rest of our patients made it through the night—"

"Thank the stars," I breathed.

"—but hopefully the prince will return soon. I don't know how much longer they can fight this," she continued.

"We will buy them as much time as we can," I stated as I walked over to check on the patients, determined not to lose anyone else.

"We appreciate your help," Pluvia replied kindly.

"I hope this weather doesn't travel south and prevent the prince from getting back," I said, concern filling my voice. "The lightning was flashing so intensely outside, I thought it would hit me!"

Pluvia looked at me peculiarly. "Lightning is the least of our worries here in Zephyria. In fact, the children often mess around with it to show off."

"I'm sorry, what?" I asked, my eyebrows raised.

"My dear"—Pluvia chuckled—"didn't you know the Adamas can control lightning?"

I blushed, feeling embarrassed. "No, I did not, actually. I only knew they could control the wind and sometimes fly . . . Hardly anything is taught about the Adamas nowadays, as I'm sure you're aware."

"I'm sorry, Arianwen, I don't mean to laugh at you. I've been here for so long, I forget what it is like for a newcomer who doesn't know much about them," she said compassionately.

"Well that explains why the children were laughing at me when I was running from the lightning on my way in earlier," I replied.

Pluvia's eyes glistened with mirth, but she didn't say anything else, so I got to work on making poultices, cleaning wounds, and doing my best to help soothe the Aurums' fevers and pain. We worked in companionable silence for a while, but my curiosity got the better of me.

"Can I ask you something?"

Pluvia looked up at me and nodded as she continued to work on the patients.

"How do you manage being so far away from the ocean? You said you'd been here for years, and I just can't imagine being away from home for that long. Did you leave anyone behind?"

A thoughtful look crossed her face as she considered how to reply. "Most of us here who left our homes felt as if we had no other choice. Yes, some sacrifices were made, but staying in Iveria wasn't an option for me. Some of us Argenti will make trips to the ocean north of Iveria on special occasions, and there are beautiful lakes in the mountains we visit as well."

She didn't offer any further information, and I didn't feel like I could ask for more, so I replied, "It's hard to imagine never leaving this place and never seeing my family again."

"Don't worry, my dear. You'll get used to life here sooner than later," she said with a sad smile.

I wasn't sure how to respond since I hadn't decided if I was going to stay, but I also didn't know if that was something I should even mention. Looking down at my palm, I remembered my oath to Wynn. Seeing the star-shaped scar reminded me that if I did leave, I could never speak of Zephyria or all that I'd experienced.

Chapter 21
Tithe

Aella

I awoke from a deep slumber and found my body was one with the bed, tempting me to spend the whole day there.

I could get used to this.

On our way out for the morning's activities, Viera snatched a fruit from the display.

"I wouldn't eat that one if I were you," I said as I traded her chosen fruit out with another.

She raised a brow at me. "Why not? They look delicious." She picked it back up from the tray, inspecting it.

"I may or may not have had one too many of them as a late-night snack earlier this week, and . . ." I blushed, then proceeded to lower my voice to a whisper. "I think it's a very powerful aphrodisiac."

Viera laughed. "What did you do?"

"I'd rather not go into details, but it made me *want* to do unspeakable things!" I cringed at the thought.

"Well, you *have* seemed a bit less high-strung lately, so maybe it did you some good," she teased, placing it back onto the tray. "I'll save it for later." She winked.

I blushed then replied thoughtfully, "Despite its embarrassing side effects, that wicked fruit gave me some of the most restorative night's sleep I've had since coming here."

We spent the first half of the day in more etiquette and manners lessons. Lessons that were so painfully boring, I'd confessed to Viera I would rather swim in a bloom of jellyfish than spend one more morning sitting through one of Himmel's lectures.

At one point, during another speech about acceptable conversation topics in social settings, Himmel paused mid-sentence with a stern expression on her face. "Do you have something to share with the rest of the class?" she asked the Aurum contestant, Jara, who had been talking in the back. The same female who had helped us melt through the glass panels of the maze.

Jara rolled her eyes, not caring to simmer down her fiery attitude. "We're putting all of this preparation into looking and behaving like ladies. Yet, I have not seen one elemental lady in the Palatium Crystalis. Where are all of the elemental lords and ladies of Prisma? Isn't that what was promised to us? Every year, we send our people willingly to your drafts so that they might become lords and ladies of Prisma, wed to the Iris nobility, to be respected and honored by the star-blessed. They aren't here. Our maids won't tell us anything. I guess I was just wondering, where do you keep them?"

The room tensed, and I held my breath in anticipation, positive that Himmel would not take kindly to her tone.

Himmel's eyes narrowed, her vibrant coloring seeming to flicker with her anger as she stalked unhurriedly down the aisle, her heels tapping the ground in an ominous slow beat. Himmel came to a stop in front of Jara, cupping her cheek tenderly in her bony, ringed fingers. Himmel's look softened, a hint of a cruel smile on her face as Jara began choking on a stream of water being directed down her throat.

Jara reached for her neck, her face strained as she fought to breathe.

Himmel was drowning her right in front of us as if it were nothing, and she looked to be enjoying the act.

"Please," one of the other Aurum females, Kire, cried out. "I beg of you! She didn't mean to offend!"

"Did I not say there would be consequences?" Himmel asked.

Jara was still struggling. She didn't look like she would last much longer, her golden lips turning dusky.

"The guards will escort you back to your chambers. We are done here for the day," Himmel said, releasing her grip on Jara before making her exit.

Jara collapsed to the floor.

"Somebody do something! Please!" Kire screamed, looking to the guards who stood at the doors, unalarmed.

The Aurum fae clustered around Jara, making it difficult to get near. They stood there helplessly as their friend lay unconscious on the ground.

Why isn't anyone doing anything?

"I can help!" I found myself saying. "Let me through." My voice sounded foreign, and I moved with an assertiveness I hadn't realized I was capable of.

Most of them turned to look at me doubtfully—anger still shining in their eyes from Himmel's actions—but Kire, in full desperation, reached out and made room for me.

"Please . . . do something," she sobbed.

I knelt down beside Jara who lay motionless on the cool marble floor. So still. Too still.

"I am not a healer, but I can siphon the water out of her lungs," I explained. I didn't know if it would be enough to save her, but I had to try. I focused on removing the water from the correct place, intent not to draw too much and accidentally leave her desiccated. I worked cautiously as a slow trickle began to leak from her mouth.

Jara remained unconscious even as I was sure I'd gotten the last of it out.

"Why isn't she waking up?" one of the girls asked.

"She still isn't breathing . . . She put out her fire . . . She put out her fire!" screamed another.

Kire's brows knotted and lips wobbled as she stared at me, searching, pleading. "Please," she murmured. "Do something."

I swallowed.

What else can I do? What else can I do? She needs to breathe . . . She needs . . . I leaned over her, placing my mouth over hers, giving her a breath of air. Her chest began to rise with the breath, then fall, but she remained unconscious. I tried again.

Come on, Jara.

I combed through all the times I'd seen healers work. I'd never seen them treat drowning before. Maybe I was doing it wrong. Maybe I was too late. I gave her another breath, preparing myself for the same response. Preparing myself for the worst.

Finally, Jara began to stir, coughing, her eyelids fluttering open. I almost sobbed in relief, my eyes lined with tears. I couldn't believe I had done it.

Kire cried, curling over her friend. "Stars, Jara. I thought I'd lost you!"

When I started getting up to leave, Kire grabbed my hand. "Thank you!" she said, her eyes brimming with tears. Some of the other Aurum fae nodded their heads in appreciation. I headed out of the room, picking up speed as I left.

Viera ran after me. "That was incredible, Aella! You saved her life. I could have never done what you did!" she exclaimed.

I did not want to accept the praise. Saving Jara did not feel like a victory to me. Everything had happened so fast, and the events were already starting to blur together, but Himmel's expression and her nonchalant attitude as she punished Jara replayed in my mind. One thing was clear: Himmel was not afraid of the consequences of killing one of us.

Himmel had told us that the Iris themselves would not harm us and that the contestants we'd lost had been nothing more than unfortunate casualties in the process to ensure a strong heir. But she had almost killed Jara . . . and would have, had I not been able to help her.

If that was how our guardian treated us, the supposed honored guests of the king, how did they treat the rest of the fae in the capital? For all I knew, they would keep toying with us until none were left. Take what they wanted, then discard us like forgotten playthings.

Jara had made a valid point, and Himmel had wanted her silenced. She'd wanted to discourage us from asking questions. But it had only served to make me more curious. What was done with the elemental lords and ladies once their services had been completed and their spousal roles fulfilled?

△

Later that day, I stood motionless as my maids fitted me into a sheer, silhouette-hugging gown. Delicate beads cascaded down its entirety in intricate and alluring designs. They'd left my hair down—one side pinned back with a matching beaded silver hair comb to reveal my jaw and neckline. It was much more glamorous than our typical evening wear, so I assumed they were preparing us to put on another show for the Iris.

Viera was fitted into a sweeping gossamer gown embroidered with floral patterns styled in strategic locations. We looked like a pair of goddesses carved from stone, faces expressionless. If our circumstances had been different, I would have been beaming at the beauty of the looks they had us in. Never in my life had I imagined myself adorned in such finery. But after everything, it all felt like a cruel joke.

No one spoke as we made our way behind Himmel to the throne room, only eighteen of us now. Jara had been taken back to her room after the *event*, and none of us had seen her since. I wondered if Himmel knew or cared that Jara was alive.

I needed to find Kaleidos and tell him what had happened to Jara. I needed to plead with him. I'd seen a flicker of remorse in his eyes, I was sure of it. If I could manage to get through to him, maybe there was something he could do to put a stop to our mistreatment. I was willing to try anything to persuade him.

As we entered the throne room, Himmel introduced us to the crown as ladies of the court—an empty title, as she had so painstakingly demonstrated to us. All of the fine fabrics, jewels, and titles were a part of their scheme to trick us into playing their games.

The throne room was brighter than the last time we'd been summoned, taking on a warm glow with coral-hued clouds visible through the crystal spire. King Solanos' usual steely demeanor softened as we lined up, a devilish smile curving the corners of his lips.

Before him stood eighteen exquisitely decorated elemental fae groomed in the fashions of the Iris—a far cry from the sad bunch we had been a fortnight ago. The king practically drooled at the sight.

Prince Kaleidos was absent. A knot formed in my stomach as I scanned the room, anxiously trying to figure out where he was and what we were doing there. It seemed off that he was missing—his uncle Ventius in his place at the king's right.

Beyond the royal family, the throne room was full of the Iris of Prisma. Their eyes gleamed with bloodlust. Dread filled me as I anticipated what they'd have in store. Everything was so secretive. They either enjoyed withholding information from us, or they thought we weren't important enough to bother telling.

The king gestured toward us as he conversed with an Iris male on his left. Though all Iris had beautiful qualities, something about the heavily robed male was insect-like and unsettling, making my skin crawl as his eyes scanned over us. The king pointed a finger at an Aereus female and then to an Aurum female. He kept his voice low so that we could not make out what he was saying. The spindly male next to him nodded, a wry expression on his face. The king then gestured to Viera.

I couldn't help but track his gaze to her. But even as his stare darkened, she did not falter. Where the others had bowed their heads in avoidance of direct eye contact, my friend stood firm. Head held high, never to be intimidated, even under the stare of the most powerful Iris ruler of our lifetime. She would never crumble, never be made to feel small. It made me proud, despite what I feared the special attention might mean. But whatever it was, Viera could handle it. She had a gift for making people bend to her will.

A dangerous thought occurred to me . . . Perhaps Viera could be the one to bring an end to it all.

The male who had been at the king's side came to collect the three females, including Viera. I grasped for her hand in a panic, but she smiled at me, a look of resolution in her eyes before following in queue. I held the back of my neck instead.

I will see her again.

A band of musicians began to play moderately paced music. It was very different from what we'd had back in Iveria. In Prisma, they seemed to have many more types of instruments. Strings they plucked with their fingers, others they threaded with long bows. In high and low rhythms, they harmonized and created a gorgeous symphony of sounds that made me feel like floating about the room.

We stood in a line as fifteen Iris came to lead us in a dance. The male who paired with me placed one hand on my back, taking my hand in his other. I had to fight the urge to recoil at his touch, doing my best not to exhibit any emotion—good or bad—as he led me in a series of circles around the room.

The music changed and with it, my dance partner. The next male I danced with was closer to my height, making it harder to avoid eye contact.

"Aren't you a pretty little thing?" he crooned.

I gave him a tight-lipped smile, but my eyes told another story.

"What? Can't you take a compliment?" he asked.

"It's hardly a compliment," I replied, failing to hide the bite in my tone.

"She has teeth!" he exclaimed. "Does she bite?" he challenged with a flirtatious smile.

"I take offense at being called little or a thing, as I imagine most females would. Maybe you should rethink your opening line," I said.

The male started laughing before I was through speaking which irritated me even more.

"What is so funny?" I asked.

"Just that you speak as if you're one of us. Most fae would be grateful to be spoken to by an Iris, much less considered attractive. As you know, we have the highest of beauty standards in the capital, as we make up the fairest of all Esterra."

I couldn't help rolling my eyes at his arrogance.

"You're lucky I am not one to retaliate," he said before switching partners with the change in music.

The rhythm began to pick up pace and so did the circles we danced in. Our partners swapped out with Iris onlookers. They spun us around and around at dizzying speeds, and my feet began to hurt as I tried to keep up.

While spinning in circles, I swore I caught a glimpse of Kaleidos weaving his way through the crowd. My heart rate picked up at the idea of him watching me. I kept turning my head to try to see where he went, until my dance partner took notice.

"Though you *think* you are being subtle with your glances, they are quite obvious," she expressed.

"I am here to compete for a place beside him," I replied, unsure why I felt the need to defend myself.

The female smirked. "He may take temporary interest in you, but spare your heart, dear child, for he could never truly love an elemental fae," she said, her lavender eyes cold and empty.

"I hope that the female who becomes his bride would earn his respect and affection," I replied.

The female scoffed, "Kaleidos is too good for any of you. He is only doing this because it is his responsibility. Do not think for one moment he would choose a fae bride by choice." She almost spat out the last few words as if they'd left a bitter taste on her tongue.

I recognized the female from somewhere. She was beautiful—her skin a gorgeous prismatic display of colors, glistening in the fading sunlight. Her hair was a voluminous pastel rainbow of tight curls that cascaded down her back. A series of three diamond-encrusted bands graced the crown of her head like a bonnet. It was evident from the complex marbling of her skin that she ranked high among the Iris. She must have been one of the females who I'd seen interacting with Kaleidos. It would make sense, as she almost sounded jealous. Perhaps she was his lover.

"You have a close connection with the prince?" I stated more than asked.

"He is my cousin," she said, then handed me off to another.

I was ready for a break. Sweat beaded my brow, and the balls of my feet burned, blisters forming at the straps of my heels. As the next song began at an even faster pace than the last, the male grinned as he spun me around.

"Please . . . I would like . . . to sit down . . . have a glass of water," I begged breathlessly.

"That won't be possible," he said before twirling me in a series of more circles. I tried at one point to pull away, but he only held on tighter, twisting and turning me at a nauseating rate.

One of the Aurum ladies collapsed, almost tripping us as we made our way around the floor. The revelers cheered as another pair collided with them and another contestant began to vomit on the floor. There were only twelve pairs of us left. As the tempo quickened, so did we. The next time the music sped up, five more females tripped and fell or fainted from the speed at which they were being spun. Their Iris partners folding over in laughter at their expense.

I was like a top whirling around and around. My feet went numb. One misstep and it would all be over. I thought about making myself fall just to end the nightmare, but I did not know what they would do to me if I failed. I had made a promise to myself to do something, so I needed to succeed if I wanted to have any chance at all.

Around and around we went, and I swore I would never dance again in all my life if given the choice. The Iris cackled and squealed with excitement as each female fell. My next partner was nothing more than a blur as I spun so fast, it was impossible to focus. Faster, and faster, and faster I twirled until it felt like the room was revolving around me and I was the one who was staying still.

I concentrated on my breath, as it was the only thing left I could control. In and out as the world went around. In and out as the cheering got louder. In and out. In and out. Around and around. Until, at last, the music stopped.

And with the cessation of the music, I folded into the arms of my dance partner. My vision took a moment to calibrate as my brain thought we were still spinning. Everything gyrated back and forth for a moment. I watched as multiples of the Iris male in front of me gradually merged into one. Slowly but surely, my vision corrected itself, revealing my partner to be none other than Prince Kaleidos himself.

Chapter 22

Stars in Your Eyes

Aella

Nephos grabbed my free hand, raising it in the air. I stumbled back up onto my feet, though standing completely upright was impossible, and if not for Kaleidos supporting me, I would have fallen flat on my face.

"We have a winner!" Nephos exclaimed, to which the crowd cheered. "This lucky female shall receive the prince's favor in the next event on account of her performance tonight."

The revelers became raucous with excitement—all but the prince's cousin whose eyes found mine from across the room, narrowing on me as if in warning.

"Can you walk?" Kaleidos asked in a low growl.

Attempting a step, I winced as the sensation in my feet had rudely returned. I hated to admit weakness, so I took another step in spite of the pain.

Kaleidos made a disapproving sound and then scooped me up into his sculpted arms. The surrounding Iris jeered as he carried me away. Kaleidos smiled and winked at them as if to confirm their crude remarks.

It made me want to push him away, climb out of his arms and run, but the state I was in meant I would have had to crawl my way out of there. All I could do was tuck my head in and close my eyes as the room continued to spin around me at a nauseating rate.

With my head pressed against his chest, I could feel the beating rhythm of his heart against my temple. Strong and steady it thumped, and my own began to slow down to match it.

Kaleidos carried me from the room and took a few turns I did not remember from my walk, moving at a swift pace. When the temperature dropped and the light faded, I opened my eyes to find we were in some kind of secret passageway with simple, pale sandstone walls and none of the palatium's ornamented facade.

"Servants' passages," he said as if reading my mind.

I relaxed a little knowing we were out of sight from all the leering eyes. Still, I hated being so helpless and small in his arms. Stars knew I wouldn't have been in such a vulnerable state to begin with if it weren't for him. But despite everything, I felt safe with him, even if he was the most frustrating male I'd ever met.

Kaleidos carried me back to my room, entering through the small door our maids entered from. Viera was not there, and from the sheer silence, it was easy to infer the others had not yet returned to their rooms either.

"Which bed is yours?" he asked, his voice deepening to a depth I hadn't thought possible, making an involuntary shiver roll over me in a wave.

I tilted my chin to show him the direction, and he carried me over, setting me down on the edge of the bed. Kaleidos pulled the cord on the wall, ringing for my maids, and then knelt before me. He untied the straps on my heels, and I whimpered as they slid off. My feet were red, swollen, and bloody where the curves of the shoes had cut into them.

One of my maids came in and immediately bowed flat to the ground at the sight of the prince.

"Bring a wash basin, and send for the healer," he commanded with all the authority of a prince but with a graciousness in his voice I did not expect from his kind.

My maid ran out of the room, returning hastily with some towels and a large, silver bowl of warm water. The prince asked her to leave, then helped me lower my feet into the bowl. It burned for a minute, and I bit down on my lip, trying not to cry. Tears beaded my eyes. I hated crying for myself, but that thought only made it harder to hold back the tears.

Kaleidos wiped away a tear, his thumb resting on my cheek. His bold eyebrows bunched together as he looked me in the eyes. I blinked back the rest of my tears at his attention, breath catching in my throat. His gaze shifted down to my lips for a moment before he averted it and let out a breath. I swished my feet in the bowl of pink-tinged water, releasing a sigh. Our hands touched as we both reached for a towel at the same time.

"Thank you," I murmured.

"Don't," he replied, his tone clipped. Kaleidos handed me the towel before getting up to leave.

I had so many things I wanted to say. My heart sped up as I considered demanding he not walk away from me again. He paused on his way to the door, his body going rigid for a moment, then he turned back to me. His furrowed brows and clenched jaw betrayed his inner turmoil, reflecting the storm surging inside of him.

"I am so very sorry, Aella," he said, covering his face with his hand. "And don't tell me it's okay, because I know that it's not. The entire system is cursed." He looked back up at me. "I am well aware of your sentiments toward my kind. And you have every right to despise us. To hate me." My stomach tightened as he uttered the words. "And I know it's too much to ask that you ever forgive me. I can't ask, fully aware that no matter what I do, I could never undo the damage inflicted upon you or restore what has been taken from you."

The silence stretched between us as I considered all he had said. On the one hand, I desperately wanted to believe him. Believe he was sorry, believe he was better than the other Iris. I could not deny that—despite all rational thought—there was a spark of connection between us, drawing us together. But on the other hand, he represented everything that was wrong with our world. Blood had been spilled in his name as a form of entertainment, and I did not know if I could ever see past it.

I could not allow my feelings to get in the way. I had a plan and I needed to stick to it. Keep my feelings out of it and use the opportunity to inspire Kaleidos to fight for us, for all of the elemental fae.

"You could start by canceling the Matri-Ludus, Kal. You have the power. You could put an end to this."

He laughed bitterly. "I have little more power than you do, Aella. While my father sits on the throne, I am just as much a pawn as all the rest."

"That doesn't make any sense . . . Why would he limit you?"

"It's a long story."

As he talked, I patted the bed next to me for him to come sit down, nodding for him to elaborate. But instead of sitting on the bed, Kaleidos knelt before me again so we were at eye level. "He will never give me an ounce of control, not while there is still aether in his veins," he explained, then motioned for me to hand him the towel I'd forgotten to use.

"But why? You are the crowned prince of Prisma." Tingles ran up my legs as he, *the prince*, dried my feet for me, one at a time as he spoke.

"In title, yes, but that means little to him. My father holds power over my head, always just out of reach, demanding I earn it from him."

"How does he want you to earn it?"

"It does not matter because it will never happen . . . at least not for a very long time."

My brows converged.

"My father has resented me since the day I was born. I don't expect you to understand," he snarled.

"You're right, I don't understand what that's like. But listen to me, Kal, you are not your father. You have the potential to surpass him." I took his face in my hand and whispered, "Be better than him."

Kal shuddered under my touch, closing his eyes as he nuzzled his cheek into the palm of my hand, then refocused his gaze on me. My heart quickened as he looked into my eyes—as if he saw right through them, straight to my soul. As if he could read all of my secrets if he stared long enough.

"You have stars in your eyes," he said.

I couldn't help but blink nervously at his observation, his close attention overwhelming. The intimacy of the moment surprised me, his willingness to open up to me. His vulnerability, the way he responded to me as though starved for affection.

"I've never seen eyes like yours," I said. Unable to suffer the weight of our continued eye contact, my gaze dropped down to his full lips, noticing his slight smile.

Kal closed the distance between us, lips brushing against mine. He hovered there for a moment, our breaths mingling in the hair's breadth of space between us. His scent intoxicating, his proximity electrifying. If I could have spent the rest of my life suspended in time, I would have lived in that moment . . . but time belonged to the stars. I tilted my face ever-so-slightly, lips parting, waiting for him. And with that tiny invitation, his lips came crashing into mine, molding into them as if they were made never to be apart. I moaned, enraptured in his kiss, wanting him closer, wanting more of him.

Meeting his intensity, I grabbed a fistful of his shirt, pulling him into the bed with me. I drew in his lips, capturing his mouth with my own. I could feel the smile in his kiss as he delighted in the passion emanating from me. Kal pulled back slightly, leaving me gasping for air in his absence. He looked down, his eyes darkening in hunger as he studied me. I took a sharp inhale of breath as the line of his body pressed into mine.

My body responded to him with an intense, throbbing heat. It was more than passion, more than pleasure. I wanted every part of him, body and soul. My heart reached for him, ached for him, even as I struggled to reconcile my feelings on all the things I blamed him for. I pushed all thoughts aside, allowing myself to fully luxuriate in his affections.

His hands explored my waist lazily and patiently before somehow pulling me closer to him. Our bodies merged in a passionate embrace, fitting together perfectly but somehow still not close enough. Kal placed kisses along my jaw and then down my neck, pulling the strap of my dress from my shoulder and tearing the delicate fabric down the center, sending beads scattering across the floor, exposing more of me. He trailed kisses along my collarbone, my skin pebbling to his touch. I gasped as he lowered his mouth to my chest, my back arching for him in need. Feral with desire, I dug my hands into his unruly hair as my whole self threatened to come undone.

When a knock came at the door, I shoved Kal to get him off of me. Embarrassment burned through me at the thought of being caught in such an intimate position. My push did nothing to move the hulking mass of him. His devilish smirk showing me he had little intention of stopping.

"Get off of me!" I whispered furiously while still panting for air underneath him.

Kal ever-so-slowly removed himself but not before placing one more heart-stopping kiss on my lips before rising to stand at the side of the bed.

Pulling together what remained of my tattered gown before the healer could enter, I tried to calm my breathing. It was hopeless to hide what we'd been doing. Anyone with eyes could have taken one look at our swollen lips, mussed hair, and fast-paced breathing and known.

Kal didn't even bother trying to wipe that stupid grin off his face, even through the wince that escaped when he readjusted himself in his trousers. I couldn't help the blush that spread across my cheeks when he caught me staring. Kal winked at me with a wry smile. A look that said, *just wait*, with a promise in his eyes.

Stars, he is the most beautiful male I've ever seen.

The healer, to her credit, did not draw attention to it. After making a quick assessment of my feet, she told me they should be able to heal themselves without issue, but I needed to remain off of them for at least a day or two to prevent any delays in the process.

"That won't be possible," Kal said with regret. I questioned him with my eyes. "The second official event is tomorrow. She won't be allowed to miss it."

My skin prickled, a chill washing over me. I'd known it was coming, but still, I felt betrayed. It wasn't his fault, and yet it still was.

He looked at me, acknowledging the hurt in my eyes, and urged the healer, "You must heal them for her. Expedite the process."

The healer gave me a look of pity. As if she felt bad fixing me just so I could go die the next day. Perhaps she'd hoped the injury might let me sit out of the next competition.

"I can seal the wounds and reduce some of the bruising, but it won't be a full recovery. She still needs rest, and, if possible, being near her element will help speed up the healing."

Kal nodded eagerly in agreement, then reached for my hand as the healer got to work. My hand recoiled from his touch, and I braced myself for the burning sensation that often came with healing. Within minutes, the blisters and bruises began to fade. The healer again urged me to stay off my feet as much as possible until the event.

After she left the room, Kal climbed back into the bed as if to resume our previous activities. I couldn't help flinching when he touched my face.

"Aella," he said, pleading.

I turned my head away from him, closing my eyes. *How could I be so foolish? To let him have such power over me?* My heart was torn between wanting him and hating him. I needed to be strong though. I needed to stick to my plan. I needed him on my side.

I looked back into his guilt-filled eyes, and it angered me. I wanted to scream at him that his inaction was just as bad as willing participation in the slaughter. Surely he had more power than his father made him believe. But it didn't matter, I needed to play it right. I could not let my emotions get in the way. I would need to keep the prince at arm's length. No closer, no further.

I spoke with as much poise as I could muster. "I am tired and would like to sleep now."

"Of course," he said with a furrowed brow before backing away. "Goodnight, Aella."

Chapter 23
A Different World

Arianwen

Four days passed with no sign of Wynn or Dorel. The patients were barely holding on. All of the healers, myself included, had been sleeping at the hospitium and taking shifts to try to keep the patients alive for just a little while longer.

It was late afternoon when I heard a disturbance outside in the hall. Relief crashed through me as Wynn came rushing through the door, Dorel in tow.

"You're back! How did everything go? Did you find the herbs?" A million more questions raced through my head, but I was so relieved to see him, I had to fight back tears.

Dorel had a big smile on her face and nodded excitedly. "Yes, we were able to find a decent amount of them, and I brought some bare root plants to grow in our greenhouses. Now we just need you to show us how you administered them on Wynn."

The second Wynn's name dripped from her mouth, a jealous monster started writhing under my skin.

She's on a first-name basis with him?

Fighting to keep my face pleasant, I replied, "We can go create a poultice with it, which we should do as quickly as possible. I don't know how much longer these patients can hold on. It's been a rough few days."

"Let's go prepare it in our apothecary. I'll show you where to go," Dorel replied.

Catching Wynn's gaze when we passed, I offered him a wan smile and whispered, "Glad you made it back safely."

Wynn caught my hand and squeezed it, causing a slight flutter in my stomach.

Focus, Ari. You have work to do.

Letting go of his hand, I rushed after Dorel so we could—stars willing—save the remaining Aurum patients before it was too late.

※

"Would you like to get something to eat?" Wynn asked me as we left the hospitium together.

"That sounds wonderful," I replied, stifling a yawn. "I am exhausted but starving. I have barely eaten this week."

"There's a local tavern here that makes incredible food I'm sure you would approve of," Wynn teased.

"I can't wait," I said, ignoring his tone and thinking about the last few hours.

We had been able to administer the medicine to the Aurum patients, and—thank the stars—their fevers had finally started to break. Pluvia had insisted I leave with Wynn for the night, as the long days had taken their toll.

Wynn and I walked in comfortable silence toward the tavern, and I couldn't help but breathe deeply, taking in the crisp, cold air. Since he had returned and the patients were on the mend, it was as if a huge weight had been lifted off my shoulders. I was also incredibly relieved they hadn't run into any trouble on their trip.

"So you didn't see any Iris?" I asked, breaking the silence.

"No, we were able to remain undetected, and the trip was uneventful. Dorel is a lot of fun. I'm glad I had a chance to get to know her."

"Oh, really?" I squeaked, then cleared my throat. "That's nice."

"Do I detect a hint of jealousy?" Wynn asked, his voice implying he found the idea humorous.

"No! Of course not," I scoffed. "You're the prince, I'm sure all the girls are throwing themselves at you, but that doesn't mean I am too."

"My apologies, I must have misread the dirty looks you've been shooting Dorel's way ever since we returned," he replied with a smirk.

"You're imagining things. Why would I even care? I'm betrothed, remember?"

"Ah, yes, the arranged marriage. Just how well do you know the male you are supposed to marry?"

Am I completely crazy or is he *acting jealous now?*

"I don't know him, actually. We come from two separate parts of Iveria, and I'm fairly certain our paths have never crossed."

"Yes," he replied drolly. "That sounds exactly like what you want in a mate, someone you've never laid eyes on."

"I already told you, I don't have the luxury of choosing someone for myself. My time to *fall in love* ran out. Better I marry Verus than be drafted into marriage with one of the Iris."

Wynn shuddered in disgust. "Arianwen, consider yourself star-blessed that you were never selected in the draft. It's not what you think it is. The Iris are far more vicious than you realize, and they love to play games with their elemental servants. Many elementals who live here left their homes and families because they did not want to take part in the farce they call the Matri-Ludus. They never would have seen their families again regardless. Better to take their chances and try to escape than meet whatever horrific fate awaited them in Prisma."

"It's always made out to be such an honor to be chosen," I said.

"Yes, the Iris lie so prettily," Wynn replied, voice dripping with sarcasm.

"Well, thank the stars that's not my fate. I just have to marry a male I don't love, lucky me."

Wynn stopped and turned to me, gently gripping my chin, his eyes capturing mine. "You can stay. Make your own fate."

I stared up into his eyes, my pulse racing at our proximity. "I don't know if I can, Wynn . . . but there is a part of me that is considering it."

Wynn smiled and lowered his head to speak into my ear. "I was hoping you'd say that. I still have my wager to win."

Before I could answer, he spun around and kept walking down the street, leaving me staring after him, flustered.

Wynn led me to a quaint tavern in the heart of Zephyria. Joyous laughter greeted my ears, and the aromas that assaulted my nose had me salivating for whatever it was they were serving. Tinkling sounds of a piano filled the air, and I spied a young male staring at the musician with rapt attention. Most wondrous of all was seeing the various elemental fae all laughing and spending time together, not separated by the color of their skin or the power in their blood.

This is how all of Esterra should be.

We sat down at a table and were almost immediately served two tankards of sweet-smelling ale and a basket of bread.

"Thank you, Kristel," Wynn said with a smile.

"It's fortunate you're here to eat tonight. The meal I had the cook prepare is one of your favorites! I'll be back in a bit with the main course, My Prince," Kristel replied, flashing her gorgeous amethyst eyes at him.

Ugh, every female here wants him. I guess I should get used to it if I'm going to be spending time with him.

I pasted on a smile, despite the fact that Kristel had completely ignored me.

At least she brought me my own ale.

I took a large swig of the drink, and it warmed me from the inside out. "This is delicious! What kind of ale is this? I've never tasted anything like it."

"It's a spiced wine actually. We call it glogg."

I downed the rest of my glogg, and my mind started to feel a little fuzzy as my body relaxed. "Stars, that's amazing. Another please!"

Wynn chuckled. "You may want to slow down, Ari. There *is* alcohol in it."

I blushed, but I wasn't sure if it was the glogg flushing my skin or the way Wynn was staring at me. Toying with the tankard, I glanced up at Wynn curiously. "Does every female in Zephyria want to be your princess?"

"Ha, one would think that, but no. I don't have much time for females. I'm off on rescue missions most of the time or helping my father with whatever he needs to run the Court of Air. I don't have a lot of spare time, but when I do, Kristel's is the best tavern around for food and entertainment."

"Yes, she is quite lovely," I said, watching her float around and serve the patrons with smiles and flirtatious glances.

Feeling a tug on my tunic, I turned in my seat, surprised to see a child grinning up at me.

"Why, hello there!" I crooned. "Who might you be? And where are your parents?"

The girl smiled shyly, but before she could speak, Kristel swooped over, admonishing her. "Aya! What are you doing out of bed? I told you not to disturb the guests." She ushered Aya out the rear door of the tavern after giving us an apologetic look.

"That little girl was adorable," I said to Wynn. "Is Kristel married?"

Wynn shook his head. "Not that I'm aware of, but I guess anything is possible. I don't think the girl's father is still seeing her."

Perhaps my mind was just fuzzy from the drink, but something was different about the little girl, and I was trying to put my finger on it. Her alabaster skin had a golden shimmer to it, and her hair appeared more blonde than white. "Wait, was that little girl Iris?"

Wynn shook his head again. "No. She has no Iris blood in her whatsoever. She is part Adamas and part Aurum."

"What? How is that possible? Now that I think of it, how is *any* of this possible? I thought the stars cursed us to remain separate? What about the destruction of Concordia?"

Wynn raised an eyebrow at me. "Just chalk it up to another lie the Iris have ingrained into your minds for centuries."

"I feel like a fool," I lamented. "The Iris have us all brainwashed to keep them in power, but I don't see how that could ever change. No one would believe me unless they saw it with their own eyes, and it's not like I can tell anyone anyway," I said, glancing at the mark on my hand.

"Someday, we will be strong enough to take them down. That's what I pray to the stars for."

"Are there many like her here?"

"Some, but the lies are deeply rooted, and not many have ventured outside their elemental race."

"I think it would be beautiful to live in a world where our element or the color of our hair and skin didn't define us."

Wynn reached across the table to play with a strand of hair that had fallen out of my braid, pushing it gently behind my ear. "What a world that would be, Ari," he said.

I found myself leaning closer to him, the energy between us pulsing with possibilities.

"Here you go!" Kristel interrupted as she placed our plates in front of us, breaking up the moment we were having. Almost as if he were embarrassed, Wynn pulled away from me, and I felt hurt trickle in.

"Thanks, Kristel. If you could please bring more glogg and some water, that would be appreciated."

"Of course, My Prince," Kristel replied as she sauntered away, a smirk on her face.

Biting back my irritation at Kristel, I looked appreciatively at the food in front of me—root vegetables smothered in herbal butter and a generous piece of tender-looking meat.

"This smells amazing," I groaned in delight, digging into the food with reckless abandon.

Wynn chuckled. "Enjoy, Arianwen. You've earned it." He started eating his meal with more dignity than I was. "What do you think of the hospitium?"

"I love the rugged simplicity of it," I replied in between bites. "The facility at home feels so much more sterile and clinical while the hospitium here feels like a place of healing. The mineral pools are incredible."

"Well, I'm pleased that you like it. You are by no means obligated, but there is a permanent position available for you at the hospitium if you so desire. I've already cleared it with Pluvia. I want you to feel at home here, should you decide to stay," he said.

Warmth filled my heart, and I smiled at him across the table, at a loss for words. "I don't know what to say . . . but thanks."

"Were the other healers nice? I think you'd get along with Dorel."

Trying not to roll my eyes, I considered who else I had worked with over the previous two days. "I met this Aereus fae named Liisa, she was very kind. It was interesting working with her because she doesn't have the innate healing ability some Argenti have, but she has so much knowledge of healing plants and herbs I'd never heard of! Her earth element gives her this sense of groundedness that I think is very soothing to the patients. I hope I get to work with her again."

Wynn seemed pleased with my response. He crooked his head at me curiously. "Other than your family, are there friends back home you miss?"

I looked down, twisting my napkin in my hands. "Honestly, I've always found myself on my own. I love to study and read, which doesn't leave much time for socializing. No one would miss me if I never returned, other than my family."

"I find that hard to believe," Wynn scoffed.

"It's hard for me to open up to people," I admitted before hesitantly adding, "Perhaps that's why I've acted jealous of your attention. I've never spent one-on-one time with someone like I have with you, and I don't like to share."

Faex! Did I just say that out loud? How much glogg have I had . . . ?

Wynn reached across the table and gently tipped my chin up so I would look him in the eyes, grinning at me. "Oh, is that it, huh? A little possessive of me?"

Blushing, I knocked his hand away. "I meant as a friend. Obviously. Don't let it go to your head. "

"Too late for that," he teased. "Considering you are so discriminating about who you spend your time with, I feel honored."

His eyes twinkled with mirth, and I found myself returning his smile, feeling lost in his beautiful eyes. We stared at each other across the table, communicating without words. While I had not made up my mind yet about whether to stay or go, at that moment, I knew I was definitely not ready to leave.

Chapter 24

Never Walk Alone

AELLA

Waiting for Viera's return, I sat at the edge of my bed, eyes trained on the door. I had to tell her about what had happened while she'd been gone. Not only that, I had to tell her everything. I wouldn't keep any more secrets from her.

As the hours went by, my stomach churned with growing apprehension. I would not be able to rest until I knew she was okay. Another hour passed and still no Viera.

I paced the room on achy feet despite the healer's suggestion to stay off them. The longer Viera was gone, the more uneasy I felt.

We weren't allowed to leave our rooms unchaperoned, but I didn't care. I had to find her. Peeking out into the large empty hall, I was happy to find no one stationed outside our suite. I crept out, staying near the walls as I scurried along. When I approached the main hall, I noted heavy curtains that might provide a decent hiding place if needed. Revelers still roamed the palatium late at night, and I did not want to be caught alone by one of them.

As an Iris male rounded the corner, I ducked into an alcove. Not fast enough. Holding my breath, I stood still, plastering myself against the wall as if I could disappear into it if I tried hard enough.

The male chuckled at my failed attempt as he began to corner me, his cunning voice giving him away. The same male I'd danced with earlier that evening. Though he was not quite as tall as Kaleidos, he made up for it in muscle.

"Well, what do we have here?" He smirked. "A contestant? Hiding in the corner? What could she be doing out here all by herself?" He took me in, head to toe, fingering the fabric of my robe at my collarbone.

I trembled under his touch, which seemed to amuse him. That, combined with the way he spoke about me as though I were a small animal, infuriated me.

"I'm looking for my friend," I said to the male through clenched teeth. "She was summoned by the king before the dance this evening and has not yet returned."

"Of course, the tithe. In that case, I'm sure she's in very good hands." He winked at me.

I tried my hardest not to show my repulsion, but my eyes betrayed me, and I started to panic as the male closed in on me.

"The tithe?" I asked.

"The king selects a tenth of the contestants from the draft to use for whatever purpose he chooses. He can excuse them or keep them in the Matri-Ludus as he pleases."

"I need to find her," I choked out, a sense of urgency tightening my throat.

He took me in, scanning me again, a calculating tell in his eyes. "All right, fine. I'll take you to her," he said.

"Really?" I gasped in relief.

"Follow me." He sauntered off.

I hesitated for a moment, chewing my lip, debating whether or not I could trust him. Following the male was risky, and I probably should have run straight back to my room. But after everything Viera and I had been through, I was desperate to find her. She would have done the same for me.

"Forgive me, darling, but if you are planning on seeing your friend again, it will require the moving of your feet," he said without even looking back to check if I was following.

Faex.

I walked quickly to catch up to him, making sure to maintain a safe distance.

I had become somewhat familiar with the structure of the palatium, although I'd only actually seen a small portion of it. The Palatium Crystalis was like an enormous, circular city. There was one main hall so vast, it hardly appeared curved as it encircled the central throne room, gardens, and courtyards. The hall went around for miles with dozens of wings branching off like sunbeams on the outer walls.

While a few Iris still meandered about, it was late, and more palanquins—or, as my sister had called them, crystal boxes—filled the endless halls, most likely carrying those too inebriated to walk back to their quarters.

On our way to find Viera, Gaelor properly introduced himself to me, including his full title and station. He was twelfth in line to the throne—a fact he was rather proud of, despite the number of people who would need to either die or forfeit their positions for it to actually mean something.

"Tell me more about the tithe. Does it happen every draft?"

"For the most part. You know, your dear Prince Kaleidos himself is the son of the king's tithe." He chuckled.

I stopped in my tracks. "His mother was a contestant?"

"Like I said, the king takes his pick. She gave him an heir, so that granted her some extra time."

I didn't know why it felt so shocking to think of his mother as a contestant. It was obviously how things worked in Prisma, but still, it was hard to imagine. All Iris who had ever stood in those stands watching the slaughter had elemental fae mothers or fathers, yet they'd never batted an eye at the cruelty. Kaleidos was different somehow. He had felt remorse.

"Was the prince close to his mother?" I asked.

"Too close, if you ask me." He linked his arm with mine, and we began walking again. "She was a shell of a female, good for little more than pleasure. It's no wonder King Solanos got rid of her so promptly."

My heart filled with sorrow for Kal. That he had been forcefully separated from his mother, an experience I only too recently shared. An unexpected empathy surged within me for him and his mother, and I found myself relating to the female I had never known. A female who had fought for her life just like Viera and me. Was that why his father resented him? Not the son of a winning contestant but the son of a tithe. A pardoned contestant who had never proven herself. What had happened to all the rest of the tithed females over the years? I started sweating. What it all implied for Viera filled me with dread, making me even more anxious to find her before one more thing went terribly wrong.

We entered a wing of the Palatium Crystalis I'd never seen before: the entrance to the king's quarters. A majestic set of iron doors inlaid with precious metals and jewels were framed by entire walls of fountains that cascaded down like waterfalls. The amount of water magic needed to keep that constant flow . . . They must have had an entire team of Argenti behind those walls.

Gaelor had me wait at a distance as he approached a pair of guards stationed outside the doors. Knots twisted in my stomach, and I reached my hand around to squeeze the skin on the back of my neck. I prayed to the stars that I hadn't put my hope in the wrong hands. The guards spoke in hushed tones so I couldn't hear what they were saying, only how they sniggered.

Gaelor shook his head as he walked back my way, his arms outstretched in a helpless gesture.

"She remains in the company of the king. She'll probably be there until morning, if you know what I mean," he said with a lecherous wink before sizing me up with his eyes. "You appear as though you could use a distraction. Come back to my room. I'll give you a night you won't forget."

I blushed at his boldness. "Have you been partaking of the fruit?" I asked, foolishly thinking he'd need an excuse for his behavior.

He chuckled. "No, darling, but I can fetch *you* some if you'd like." He winked again.

"Why are you flirting with me? I am intended for the prince."

He laughed a dark, mirthless laugh. "You know he's never going to choose an Argenti, don't you? His mother was Argenti, and let's just say, after that disaster, his father would never allow it."

"But what about the Matri-Ludus? I was brought here to compete for the prince."

"Oh, love, you think the events aren't rigged by the Faber Ludi? Look, little siren, you're beautiful but clearly not the brightest star." He stroked a hand down the side of my face, and I trembled with fury. "You'll never win the Matri-Ludus. It's just not in the stars. You might as well enjoy the time you have left in the Palatium Crystalis. Come, you won't regret it."

"No, thank you. I'd like to return to my rooms now."

Gaelor's smile faded from his face. "Listen sweetheart, I've been awfully patient with all your demands tonight, but I'm starting to get tired of this game you're playing." He leaned in, his hot, liquored breath sending shivers down my spine.

"I said no!" I hissed.

Gaelor covered my mouth with one hand while pressing himself closer, his body forcing me against the wall as he began kissing and nipping at my neck.

I couldn't shrink away, so I fought to push back, but he was too strong and held me in place. I summoned water from the fountains, hoping the shock would give me a chance to get away.

The water slammed into him, knocking him off his feet and stunning him for a moment, giving me just enough time for a head start. I darted down the hall, adrenaline pumping through my veins, numbing me so that

I could not feel the aches in my feet. I tripped over myself as I looked back and saw him gaining on me.

He stalked toward me. "Oh, you filthy little Argenti whore."

I surged back up, running as fast as I could until I was almost certain I'd gotten a safe distance away. My heart stopped when, out of nowhere, Gaelor had me pressed up against another wall. I yelped as he grabbed at my body, his hands rough and demanding as he ripped at my clothes.

"I was going to bring you back to my room, but maybe I'll just take you here in plain sight," he sneered.

I pushed and kicked back at him, screaming.

"Stop fighting, you're no match for an Iris. You might as well give in. It'll be easier on you. And I'm sure you'll enjoy it, too. Let me taste those sweet lips of yours." He closed in on me, nearly placing his mouth over mine.

"Oh, Gaelor. Would you leave the poor girl alone?"

I cried in relief as I saw the prince's cousin, Estrella, emerging from a crystal palanquin.

Gaelor loosened his grip. A predatory look still in his eyes, he turned his head to face her.

"I'm just having a little bit of fun, dearest cousin," he panted.

"That's enough now," she said, waving him away with her hand. "I'm sure Kaleidos would not be happy to hear you had your paws all over one of his toys."

Gaelor snorted, retreating with a scowl.

I shivered, rubbing the tears from my eyes.

"Run along," she commanded, and he left us.

I heaved a sigh of relief. "Thank you . . ." I quavered.

"You're lucky it was me who found you, girl. Do you have any idea what they would have done to you had they caught you tainting yourself with another male?"

I could still smell the scent of him on me, and it made me want to crawl out of my skin. Worst of all, I couldn't shake the feeling that it was somehow my fault.

"Come now, no need to cry. You are safe with me."

Estrella invited me to her rooms, bringing me straight to her private bath. Though somewhat smaller, it was even more luxurious than the one they'd been letting us use. The pool of water was tastefully decorated with a mosaic of turquoise, blue, and gold tiles, reminding me of the ocean. The bath extended onto a balcony overlooking the city and the sea far below. The stars twinkled above, reflecting off the water.

Estrella had her servants bring us some cool, herbal waters with tiny flowers floating in them, which they set at the border of the bath on a shiny golden tray alongside an assortment of exotic fruit.

"You can stay here tonight," she offered as she swam over to me at the corner of the pool. The female gingerly stroked my hair, careful not to tangle her excessively long nails in it.

"Aedrus," she called out, her voice ringing. After waiting less than a second, she shrieked, "Aedrus!" which set my already heightened nerves on edge. A moment later, an Aurum male entered the bathing chamber, his wavy, golden hair a tousled mess, appearing to have just woken up.

I tried to cover myself, shocked and embarrassed to be completely nude under the water in his presence. Estrella rolled her eyes. She already appeared to be irritated at his proximity as if sharing the space with him was suffocating her.

Refusing to look at him while she spoke, a sharpness poisoned her tongue. "Come to my bed tonight, the girl will use your room."

He stared at her with a blank, unyielding expression.

"Do I need to repeat myself?" she threatened.

He grunted in agreement, then cast a cool glance in my direction before leaving the room. I wanted to say no and that I'd prefer to return to my own room, but it was clear she was not the kind of female to disagree with.

"Tell me, child, what happened after the dance?" Her voice dripped with honey, a sharp contrast to the way she'd spoken to her servants and her spouse. "You disappeared so quickly, I did not have an opportunity to congratulate you."

I wasn't sure what to say. She'd seen Kaleidos carry me out, and she was obviously prying for information.

"He took you back to his rooms, didn't he?" she asked in a patronizing tone. "Don't worry, your secret is safe with me. It's not like those kinds of things don't happen. I myself had an intimate relationship with one of the drafted males in my Matri-Ludus." She looked thoughtful for a moment. "Kaleidos, well, he's different. I'm sure you've seen the way others look at him. He could have a different female in his room every night if he so chooses." She picked up a piece of fruit inspecting it before discarding it for another. "And let's say, if by chance, you were to make it all the way to the end to win the Matri-Ludus, it wouldn't be long before he tired of you and went back to his ways."

Noting the sullen expression on my face, she feigned surprise. "Oh, you didn't know? Kal has quite the reputation. You didn't think you were his first love, did you? Oh, sweet and naive Aella, you have much to learn. Never mind that now. Let's dry you off so you can go and get some rest. The sun will be up soon, and you have a big day ahead of you!"

We dried off, and she gave me a tiny, black, silk robe with lace at the edges. It was so short, it left most of my legs exposed, the curves of my body making the robe split open more than I'd like.

"I'm sorry, that's the largest one I own," she said with a giggle.

She left me in the sitting room situated between both bedchambers. I sat stiff-backed, not wanting to go into Estrella's husband's room—it just felt wrong. But I couldn't chance going out into the halls again either and risk running into another Iris like Gaelor. So I lay down on a sofa in her sitting room and closed my eyes.

If only I'd stayed put and waited in my room, none of this would have happened. I could still feel the ghosts of his hands upon my skin, making me flinch. Not only had he assaulted me physically, he'd infiltrated my mind, filling it with feelings of shame and fear.

Before long, I started hearing the disturbing sounds of Estrella moaning and shrieking through the walls. It was hard to imagine after seeing how she'd behaved as though she couldn't stand his presence. I wondered how much fruit he'd needed to consume to be able to perform for her.

I finally gave in and went to Aedrus' room, closing the door and shoving a blanket at the bottom to block out as much noise as possible. I did not trust Estrella, but she had saved me from Gaelor. If she hadn't stumbled upon us . . . I didn't want to think about it. I climbed into Aedrus' bed, and through sheer exhaustion, sleep found me quickly.

Chapter 25
The Library

Arianwen

Clutching my cup of coffee and enjoying how it warmed my hands, I observed Wynn from across the table while trying to stifle back yawns. We had stayed out far too late the night before, walking the streets of Zephyria after our delicious meal at Kristel's. The endless hours at the hospitium had worn on me, and the effects still weighed heavily.

Wynn glanced up from his morning paperwork while I was mid-yawn and chuckled. "Did I keep you up too late last night, my star?"

"I think I'm just exhausted from the last few days, and it's catching up with me. I probably need to take a day off from exploring or working, if you don't mind."

"That's fine with me. I know there has been quite a bit of excitement since you got here." He leaned forward, resting his chin in one hand and looking pensive. "Actually, I think I have the perfect activity for you today."

"Oh, really? What's that?"

"You mentioned your love of reading last night, and we have an incredible library here in the palatium. We have books here that you would never be able to get your hands on in Iveria due to the Iris' censorship."

My eyes lit up. "Library! Yes! Take me there immediately!" I stood up, almost knocking over my chair in excitement.

Wynn, looking extremely pleased with himself, set down his coffee and proceeded to lead me to the library. I tried to pay close attention to the turns and hallways so I could make my way back on my own. We passed beautiful tapestries of the surrounding mountains as well as portraits of the royal family.

One family portrait we passed portrayed a younger-looking King Volare and Queen Astrid with two young children. There was a boy with silvery-white hair and vivid blue eyes next to an older girl with the same-colored hair but amethyst eyes. I paused for a moment, curious who the girl could be, seeing as Wynn had never mentioned having siblings.

"Is this you?" I asked.

Wynn had gone ahead of me, so he stopped and made his way back. He gave me a sad smile. "Yes, that was my family many years ago."

"I didn't know you had a sister."

"The Iris killed her."

He didn't offer any more information, and I hated to bring up something painful, so I rested my hand on his arm and gave it a gentle squeeze. "I'm sorry."

"She is my reason for helping people escape. I do it in honor of her."

"That's beautiful, Wynn. I think she would be proud of the work you have done and continue to do."

"I hope so." He cleared his throat and motioned down the hall. "Shall we continue to the library?"

"Yes, of course."

When Wynn opened the giant double doors into the library, I gasped. We were inside the heart of the mountain, and I took in stacks of shelves dozens of levels above me. When I peeked over the edge of the railing, I saw levels going down into the mountain as well. There were more books than I could ever have imagined reading in multiple lifetimes. Despite having no windows, the library had a warm glow throughout it, so it didn't make me feel claustrophobic. Wynn led me to the center of the room where an Adamas librarian sat behind an ornate desk, cataloging books.

"Good morning, Aarifa," Wynn said. "This is Arianwen, and she is my guest. She is welcome to look at any of the books we have here."

"Morning, is it?" Aarifa replied gruffly. "I must have been here all night."

"You must be very dedicated to your work to lose track of so much time," I indicated.

"This is all I live for," she replied, her eyes warming as she looked around fondly. "I know every single book and its contents in this entire library."

My eyes widened. "That's incredible."

Wynn chuckled at my awe. "Well, I will leave you to it. I have some work I need to get caught up on. I'll check on you later if that's okay with you?"

"Yes, thank you for bringing me!" I beamed.

"What kind of books are you interested in, my dear?" Aarifa asked once Wynn had left.

"Honestly, I would read anything. I love learning and have pretty much read everything available back in Iveria. If you have any texts on healing, I would love to read those as well as anything you have on Esterran history. Our history books are very biased, as I'm sure you know."

"Well, I can help you, but there are far too many books on those topics for me to bring you all of them at once."

"Can you recommend some for me then? I trust you know these books the best."

She preened at the compliment then took a moment to think. "Yes, I know the ones. Wait here, and I will be back in a moment."

To remember every book so well, she must have had an incredible memory. Aarifa walked over to the railing, then seemingly floated on the wind up to a higher level of the library where she proceeded to pull a few books from the stacks. She sent them flying toward me, and they landed gently on her desk.

Stars, what I wouldn't give to be able to do that.

I'd had no idea the Adamas could manipulate the air that way. She flew down to a lower level, and within minutes, a few more books flew up over the side and landed next to the others. She reappeared over the railing and returned to the desk, tucking in a few stray hairs as she walked.

"I can honestly say I have never seen a library like this or met such an impressive librarian before!" I said excitedly.

Aarifa piled the books into a large stack and handed them over to me. "There is a reading area to your left. Please do not take the books out of the library without my express permission. If you are done with a book, put it in the cart. If you would like to come back and continue reading any of these books, please bring them back to the desk so I can set them aside for you."

"Understood."

She went back to her task, and it was clear our conversation was over, so I walked in the direction she had pointed me.

There were a few desks and sitting areas to choose from, but I picked the most comfortable-looking sofa, as I was in the mood to relax rather than study. Maybe I should have asked her to find me a few novels as well. Perhaps the next time I visited, I would ask her for some. I wondered if any other librarians worked in the library or if Aarifa was the only one.

After lighting the gas lamps surrounding the sofa, I placed the stack of books on the table in front of me, looking through them to decide which one to pick up. I set the healing textbooks to the side, as I was particularly interested in reading some Esterran history. *The Abridged History of Esterra* appeared promising and a little less daunting than some of the other texts, so I decided to start there.

The beginning of the book was familiar to me, as it detailed our earliest history. Every fae was taught that Esterra had been formed by the stars. The stars had created every fae race and blessed them with elemental powers, then gave each race a corner of Esterra to care for. As I read the next section about the Iris, I paused and had to read it again.

Surely that can't be right.

In front of me, in black and white, I saw information that—once again—shattered my worldview.

> *An Adamas hunting party witnessed strangers entering Esterra from a portal in the mountains of the Court of Air. They appeared taller than the average fae and emitted a glow from the inside. King Odeo Sorensen met with their leaders and learned that they'd come from another world, looking for a way to save their species from extinction.*

"Stars above," I muttered to myself, anger rising within me. "What a bunch of lying monsters."

I continued reading about how the Iris had learned everything they could about Esterran culture from the Adamas before leaving to settle in what became Prisma. They'd visited all the other courts and awed them with their powers of light and illusion, telling people they had been sent by the stars themselves. The courts had been asked for offerings in the form of their sons and daughters so they could attempt to procreate with them. Those offerings had evolved into the marriage draft over time as the Iris' population stagnated. Despite successful procreation with the elemental fae, their birth rates remained low. As the elemental communities had grown, the offerings overwhelmed the Iris, so they developed the draft for their entertainment and the ability to be more selective in their choices.

What in the tides . . .

The more I read, the angrier I became. The Iris had swooped in and set themselves up as gods, and the Adamas had known the entire time? People needed to know the truth! At the mere thought of telling people, the star on my hand burned.

Faex.

The idea of going back to my ignorance was unimaginable, but part of me wished I had never taken that star-sworn oath.

How could I keep this information to myself?

Angry at Wynn and the Adamas and infuriated by the Iris, I slammed the book shut, pushing it away from me. Each paragraph revealed more knowledge that had been kept from me, and my anger was preventing me from fully understanding it.

Grabbing the next book off the pile Aarifa had given me, I opened it, hoping it would be a distraction.

Fates and Prophecies, let's see what nonsense you have to say.

I skimmed through the first few pages filled with prophecies that seemed nonsensical to me. The Iris forbade us from accessing prophecies. They believed *they* were the only ones anointed by the stars and therefore the only ones worthy of interpreting them. If I was being honest, I didn't put much weight on prophecy, as I was beginning to doubt the stars really had any interest in our lives. If they cared about our plight, wouldn't they have done something about the Iris who had lied about where they'd come from?

As I flipped through the pages, I came upon one that had notes in the margins. Curious, I stopped to read it.

Born of great defiance
Marked by the stars
Truth no longer silenced
The choice will be hers

Born of courts united
Illusions will crumble
One will rise to power
A mighty kingdom tumbled

Born with powers
Past wrongs to be righted
Stars grant their blessing
Once separate, now united

Born under cloak of night
A glimmer of hope shines
End of a kingdom's might
When the stars align

Reading through it over and over, I tried to make sense of it as it sparked something in me. Hope. It sparked hope. If I was reading it correctly, it spoke of a kingdom's downfall, and I could only hope it was referring to the Iris.

I tried to keep reading, but my focus was split. Not only was I angry with Wynn for keeping the information from me, but I was also confused. If he didn't want me to know, why would he have given me access to the library? I just needed to find him and ask him instead of stewing in my rage.

Stacking the books together, I carried them back over to Aarifa.

"Done so soon?" she asked, sounding surprised.

I had no idea how long I had been reading, as time seemed to slip by in the library and there were no windows to indicate the time of day. Shrugging, I put the books down on the desk. "Can you hold these for me, please? I need to find the prince."

She nodded and waved me away, focused on the task in front of her.

Making my way down the halls back toward my room, I kept hoping I would bump into Emil or someone who could direct me toward the prince, but the stars were not on my side. I decided to grab something warmer to wear and then head outside for a walk, hoping the fresh air would help me gather my thoughts.

Right as I turned the last corner to my room, I bumped into him.

"Wynn! I was hoping I'd find you."

He tilted his head to the side, looking at me curiously. "I'm surprised to see you already, I thought you'd be in the library all day."

Taking a deep breath, I tried to focus my thoughts so they wouldn't come out in too much of a jumble. Unsure of where to start, I finally just asked, "Did you know?"

"You're going to have to be more specific, Arianwen."

"Did you know that the Adamas were complicit in tricking all of the other courts into believing the Iris were gods sent by the stars?" I asked, fidgeting with my hands, unable to stay still.

Wynn closed his eyes, his hand pinching his brow, and heaved a loud sigh. "I can see how this looks to you," he started, nervously running a hand through his hair. "I knew there was a chance you might find the information before I was able to talk to you, but that's no excuse. I should have told you sooner."

"You made it sound like the Adamas were victims like the rest of us, but you knew all along? How could you turn on us like that?"

"First of all, this was not my doing. This happened millennia ago! Please do not hold me responsible for the actions of my forefathers."

"You're right, I'm sorry, but I'm just having a hard time wrapping my brain around all this new information. What really happened in Concordia? Last night, you said it was another lie. What did you mean by that?"

Wynn grimaced. "That is a horrific tale that I do not feel like getting into, but, essentially, the Iris decimated the settlement because they feared the elementals would become too powerful, as the children had started showing signs of dual elements. There was also something about them fearing a prophecy and trying to thwart it."

My eyes widened in horror. "It wasn't the stars?"

Wynn shook his head, his eyes filled with sadness.

"You're telling me the Iris wiped an entire settlement off the face of Esterra, and the Adamas knew and did nothing?" My voice had gone up an octave.

He grabbed my arm and pulled me into a room, shutting the door firmly behind us. "Arianwen, I can see you're upset."

Yanking my arm away from him to put some distance between us, I glared at him. "Upset? Of course I'm upset. I'm starting to think the Iris aren't the only evil race in Esterra."

Wynn's eyes darkened. "You think I don't hate what my ancestors did? It was despicable. I know this is new information for you, but you're not the only one who was angry after learning of it. I carry the guilt of my ancestors every single day. They were selfish and after power. All I can do now is try to right some of those wrongs in any way I can."

"I am so angry with you right now!"

"Angry with me?" Wynn sputtered. "I had nothing to do with the choices that were made before my birth."

"I'm angry because I feel like you tricked me into the oath so I could never enlighten anyone else, and here I am now, carrying the weight of all these secrets, unable to do anything about them."

"The oath was for your safety!" he exclaimed. "My father would never even consider letting you leave without it. I had no choice."

"There is always a choice!"

"Not if I wanted *you* to still have choices. I didn't want you to be forced to stay here! The oath I swore in return would not have protected you from my father." Wynn stared at me, his eyes filled with pain and something I couldn't quite decipher.

Looking at him with pleading eyes, I said, "You could always release me."

He looked away, unable to hold my gaze, and disappointment crashed through me. "You know I can't do that."

"How can you keep this information to yourself when so many elemental fae are suffering as slaves to the Iris?"

"What do you think I have been doing by risking my life on these rescue missions? Once I was old enough, my father educated me about the true history of the Iris, and I have been fighting with him to do more ever since. Do you think it's easy for the king and queen to let their only living heir go on dangerous missions to help rescue others? They have been begging me to stop and settle down so I can do my duty to our people and be ready to lead when the time comes."

My mind flashed back to seeing him on the ground, soaked in blood, the poisoned bolt in his shoulder, and I shuddered. Despite my anger, I recognized that he was stuck between duty and what he believed was right. I could respect that.

"I just wish you had told me. Since I met you, my worldview has been wrecked multiple times. I feel like I need to do something to right these wrongs, but who am I? I'm just a healer in training who has run away from her own duty in favor of an adventure."

Wynn stepped closer to me, his hand gently cupping my chin. "Ari, look at me. You are not just a healer in training. You are an incredible fae who was willing to take risks and leave everything you have ever known to help save lives. Those refugees you saved wouldn't be alive if you hadn't stopped to help a stranger—to help me. I will forever be grateful for that, even if you do leave."

Tears pricked my eyes, and I tried to blink them away, giving Wynn a faint smile.

He smiled back at me and gently drew his fingers along my jaw. "You can have a purpose here if you desire it."

I looked down, unable to hold his gaze. "So you've said . . . I need time to think and figure out how I feel about everything. This has been a lot to process."

Wynn tilted my chin back up and brushed away a stray tear with his thumb. "You can have all the time you need, my star. There is no rush."

Needing some time alone, I excused myself and headed back to my room. My desire for a walk had dissipated, as the intense emotions and revelations had left me feeling empty, drained. I picked up a cozy blanket as I made my way to the large balcony attached to my room. The outdoor settee looked inviting, so I bundled myself up, turning my face toward the sun and seeking its warmth. Despite the cool air, I found myself falling asleep, dreaming of portals and strangers from a far-off land.

Chapter 26
Star-Blessed

Aella

I woke up to the sound of crying, shrill and disturbing. Disoriented, it took me a moment to remember where I was. I sat up in bed, my eyes burning. It felt like I'd only just fallen asleep yet the sun shone brightly through the windows.

I looked down over the side of the bed and found Estrella balled up on the floor, weeping like a wounded animal. Kaleidos stood by her, glaring at me, something like outrage in his eyes.

"Kal?" I said as I sat up straighter. "What's going on? Is she all right?"

"I should ask you that," he replied, his voice gruff.

What did she tell him?

In the bed to my left, something glinted in the sun as it stirred. Someone. There was a male next to me—Aedrus, Estrella's husband, golden skin on full display. I shrank away from him on instinct, and my eyes widened in disbelief.

"Kal, please. This isn't what it looks like. I can explain," I insisted, climbing out of the bed. My disheveled appearance and too-small robe did not help my case.

Kal backed away, refusing to look at me.

"Please, Estrella, tell him."

Estrella only cried, "I invited you here as a friend, and this is how you repay me?" She sobbed some more.

"Aedrus!" I pleaded. "Tell him what really happened!"

He only shook his head, a resigned expression on his face. Like it had been a long time coming.

"They were together last night," I argued. "Kal, please. Estrella told me I could stay here."

"I don't want to hear any more," he said before turning to go.

"Wait!" Estrella hissed. "You must do something about this! They must be punished!"

Without turning around, Kaleidos paused at the threshold.

"Aedrus will be sentenced to death for his adultery."

"But he didn't do anything!" I insisted. I swore I saw a look of satisfaction in Estrella's eyes in between her feigned sobs.

"And what of the girl?" she asked, pointing at me.

"Aella's fate will be up to the stars in today's event," Kal said and then left without another word.

"Kal!" I begged, but he did not return.

Estrella wiped away her crocodile tears within moments of him leaving. She was completely unsuspecting as Aedrus came up behind her, wrapped his hands around her neck, and started to choke her. Estrella reached her hand out to me as if to plead for help. But I did not move, I just watched.

I watched as she struggled. Watched her body twitch as she fought for air. I was glad to see her suffer. I wanted her to. I wanted her to die in that moment for what she had done. I hated her. Hated all of them, even Kal for not believing me.

Estrella clawed at Aedrus' hands in a moment of feral desperation, to which he responded with even more force. Had she not been Iris, he surely would have crushed her spine.

But as her eyes reddened through the spasms and she slowly stopped fighting back, memories of Jara's struggle flashed in my mind. Standing there watching as Estrella fought for her life made me no better than Himmel, no better than any of them. They had taken enough from me already.

"Stop!" I shouted. "Aedrus, stop!"

He glared at me with so much anger in his eyes, anger that I knew was not intended for me. He had probably wanted revenge against her for so long, her latest ploy the last straw that tipped him over the edge. He didn't want to stop, and who was I to take this from him? But if I stood by and did nothing . . .

"It's not worth it, Aedrus," I tried. "You're better than this."

"They are going to kill me anyway," he snarled, his face red with exertion.

"Don't let them turn you into a monster, Aedrus, because you're not one."

Aedrus' eyes locked on mine for a moment and then he let out a visceral cry, his body shaking as his grasp went slack, Estrella collapsing to the floor. He stood there breathing heavily before storming out of the room. With a forceful slam, the door cracked and threatened to come off its hinges.

Estrella lay on her side, clutching her throat, wheezing.

I squatted down to her level, allowing her to catch her breath before saying, "You have not won today, Estrella."

And with resolute steps, I exited her room.

△

Viera still wasn't back, so only three of us followed Himmel to the bathing suite.

"Where's Viera?" whispered Lewenne.

"She never returned," I replied. "I tried to find her last night, but it was no use. They said she was with the king."

I'd never wanted a bath more in my life. After the night I'd had, I felt like I needed to scrub at least three layers of skin off to feel normal again. But I doubted even that would take the terrible feeling away. I scrubbed and scrubbed at my skin until it was raw.

"Calm down. If you rub any harder, there won't be any skin left."

I spun around at the familiar voice, my jaw dropping as Viera entered the bath. She was smiling and appeared unharmed.

"Where have you been? Are you all right?" I asked, looking for any signs of abuse.

"I'm fine. I'll have to tell you all about it later," she said. "You shouldn't worry about me. You know I know how to handle myself." She winked.

"Where are the others?"

"They were removed from the Matri-Ludus," she replied with a frown.

I covered my mouth. "Why?"

"It's a long story."

"Viera, I have so much I need to tell you."

"So do I."

△

In the privacy of our room, I opened up to Viera. I told her everything. About the first night I'd met the prince, my secret night excursions to the garden, the cursed dance, my conversation with Kaleidos after, the assault in the hallway, and then how I'd been set up by Estrella. She sat listening without interrupting. Tears welled up in her eyes, but she still did not say a thing.

"I understand if you never want to talk to me again after this. I should have told you everything from the beginning." I couldn't look at her anymore, I was so ashamed. Knowing I had betrayed her trust, I worried that I had effectively ruined our relationship, the last good thing I still had in my life. I feared she might never forgive me.

Viera lifted my chin with her hand. "Look at me, Aella, I won't pretend that all of the secrets you kept from me don't hurt. But I haven't been completely honest with you either." She hugged me fiercely. "I'm so sorry, Aella! I can't believe all you've been through." She drew back slightly to look me in the eyes when she said, "Last night was not your fault. Don't ever let anyone make you feel that way. It was *not* your fault. Remember that."

I nodded, rivers of tears flowing down my face. Viera hugged me again, and giving in to it, I wept in her embrace. It would take time to believe those words and heal, but her acknowledgement of what had happened marked the beginning.

As we withdrew from our hug, it was a different Viera staring back at me, and I was sure I was not the same in her eyes either.

Viera became very serious, and her voice dropped to barely above a whisper. "I couldn't tell you my secret before because I didn't want to put you in any more danger than we are already in. But since you've been meeting with the prince, I have no choice but to fill you in."

"More danger?" I frowned.

"What I am about to tell you . . ." She paused, thinking of the right words. "I knew you were sneaking out at night because I often waited for your return so I could do the same. I saw you in the rivers, lending to my belief that your excursions were innocent. But *my* affairs were not."

Goosebumps prickled up my arms.

"There is an underground movement of rebels who want to overthrow the Iris. My brother is a part of it, and so is my father. It's why he wanted my brother enlisted. Shortly after we arrived, I started receiving messages from my brother. I've been secretly corresponding with him to tell him everything I've seen and heard, and he's been relaying my messages back to the movement." Viera's eyes dipped to our clasped hands. She swallowed, and her gaze locked with mine again. "Our plan was for me to become close with the prince . . . so that I could assassinate him."

All of my muscles went rigid, her truth hitting me like a tidal wave. I didn't know how to process all that it meant, and on top of everything, my chest tightened at the thought of her killing Kal. He was one of them, and even though all my logic told me I should hate him, he still didn't deserve to be killed. And Viera wasn't a killer. An assassin? No.

"I know they want you to do this, but this . . . it's not going to change anything. You're not really going to do it, are you?" I felt myself unraveling. I thought I'd known the way the world worked, and then suddenly the parameters changed. The earth became unsteady. I didn't know who we were anymore. So many secrets. So many secrets.

Viera squeezed my hand tightly. "Everything you've told me about the prince leads me to believe we need to restrategize. We may be able to use your connection to Prince Kaleidos if you can reconcile things with him."

I huffed. "I doubt he'll ever talk to me again, let alone become an ally."

"But he hasn't taken any action to have you arrested. There's still hope that you might win him back over to our side."

That last look Kal had given me made it hard to imagine I could ever earn his trust again. I closed my eyes and shook my head. I could sulk in that feeling later.

"What happened to you last night? I was so worried that they would hurt you . . ." I searched Viera's face for answers. "Then Gaelor told me about the tithe . . . and he made it sound like the tithed contestants don't stay around for very long. I feared I might never see you again."

"The king had us brought back to his wing for a private audience. He wanted us to dance for him . . . He wanted *other* things from us." She laughed a dark laugh. "I knew better."

I let out a breath.

"When I was chosen by the king, I was scared at first, until I realized it was an opportunity. And if I played it right, it could be even more effective than my original plan."

My eyes widened.

"I knew not to give in to the king, because if I'd given him what he wanted, he would have just thrown me out once he'd gotten bored of me like he had with the others." Her gaze temporarily glazed over as she spoke, her eyes fixed as though on a point beyond the room. She blinked rapidly as if refocusing herself and straightened her posture. Viera returned her focus to me, but with an unmistakable glint in her eyes. "I played him like a harp, Aella. He said he wants to see me again, and the next time I'm with him, I will be prepared. This might be my chance to kill him, to end his reign once and for all."

My best friend was terrifyingly cunning, and it was clear how much she meant those words. She was right. To end it all, we needed to destroy King Solanos. And I would do whatever she asked me to do. Suddenly, everything seemed to make sense. I massaged the back of my neck.

A small, knowing smile spread across Viera's lips.

I pulled my hand away from my neck at the thought that maybe she was aware of even more than she'd let on.

"I know about that, too." She pointed to the back of her own neck.

"But . . . how?" The feeling of being found out was both terrifying and exhilarating. I wanted to simultaneously duck under the covers and scream my secret from the rooftop. But it could never be discovered, my life depended on it.

"The night of the Hunt when you told me about the breeze you sensed. There was none, or at least not a detectable one. The way you won't let anyone touch your hair. Or how you would struggle to dress yourself when help was readily available. You always touch the back of your neck when you're nervous. You're not as good at hiding it as you think." She laughed to herself. "One night when you were asleep, I looked."

I took a sharp intake of air.

"I had to know for sure," she continued. "And then I understood why you had always been a little bit different. Why you always tried so hard to blend in."

Chills went down my spine, and the small hairs stood up on the back of my neck where my white, star-shaped birthmark lay hidden as I waited for her to utter the words. A secret I'd kept for as long as I could remember. The suspicion that had never been confirmed.

"You are star-blessed, Aella. It's the reason you are here. And that means even the stars are on our side."

Chapter 27

Favored

Aella

I was buzzing with energy from my conversation with Viera. For the first time in my life, I'd been able to speak freely about my secret. It had been so liberating and exciting but also terrifying. We had to be so careful. If the Iris were to find out, it would mean a death sentence, and I did not want to think of what they might do to our families.

Shortly after dressing for the evening's event, I was summoned to the prince's chambers. My feet were numb as I floated through the halls, my heartbeat rapid at the thought of meeting with Kaleidos. After everything that had transpired that morning, I'd fully expected him to dismiss our meeting.

I couldn't fathom what he would say to me, or if he would say anything at all. *Maybe he's changed his mind and wants to have me punished.* A maelstrom of fearful thoughts ran through my mind, and as we passed through familiar corridors, I started hyperventilating, my fingers tingling. I'd become so lightheaded, I thought I might pass out.

Outside the windows, fronds of trees whipped in the wind. The sky darkened, looking like a storm was upon us.

I asked Himmel to stop for a moment to let me catch my breath.

"What is the matter with you?" she snapped. "You will never hold the favor of the prince if you behave this way. Get yourself together before I send someone else in your place!"

I took a deep breath. Thinking of my mother, how she used to place my hand over her heart and breathe with me. *In through the nose, and out through the mouth*, she'd say while syncing her breaths with mine. *In for four seconds, hold, then out for six seconds.* I placed my hand over my heart as I counted. With my eyes closed, I could almost sense my mother's presence. After a few moments, my heart rate slowed, my anxiety faded, and with it, the wind outside seemed to calm down.

Himmel glared at me before walking again.

Brought to a great room in the prince's quarters, I was left alone and told to wait. As soon as Himmel left, I felt like I could breathe again and start to appreciate what was around me. The interior wall was lined with bookshelves that reached up to the lofty ceiling. I'd never seen so many books in my life. Literature was far too valuable for a common Argenti to own.

I slid my fingers across the books, reading the titles imprinted on their spines: *Forgotten Magic of Esterra's Artifacts*, *Fabled Histories of Our Past*, *Legends and Enchantments of the Ancient World*. Many of the books showed signs of wear, not only from their age, but from heavy use—as though the pages had been poured over many times.

I wondered if the prince had read all the books in his library and how much time he actually had to relax and read. I pulled out a well-worn book titled, *A Journey Through the History and Traditions of Esterra's Oceanside Lands*, and flipped through the pages. Passages were underlined, and in the margins were an abundance of handwritten notes and insightful thoughts about the text. Putting it back, I reached for another book. As I went to pull it from the shelf, a large hand covered mine. A thrill raced up my arm.

"Kal . . ." I spun around to face the prince who was standing so close, my breath bounced off his bare chest. His hair was wet like he had just come in from a swim. His expression cold and unreadable except for the tightness in his jaw.

"Have a seat." He motioned to the cushioned chairs in the center of the room.

"Would you please give me a chance to explain what happened this morning?"

"I'd rather not," he expressed while still holding his arm out in the direction he wanted me to go.

My hand curled into a tight fist. He may not have wanted to hear it, but he was going to anyway.

"Your cousin set me up—"

"Do you think I'm so dense that I would not be able to see through her schemes?"

My lips parted slightly. Perhaps that explained why he hadn't had me immediately arrested. I had come to him fully prepared to defend myself and plead my case but found myself speechless again.

"What I'm trying desperately to understand, Aella, is how you ended up *there* after I left you in your bed last night." His eyes bored into me. "You told me you were going to sleep. I do not need to be lied to."

"I was worried about my friend, Viera. She didn't come back last night. I waited, and I waited . . . She is my best friend. I had to find her."

The prince remained silent.

Why am I still defending myself?

"What about Aedrus?" I implored. "You would have him sentenced to death, knowing he was guilty of nothing?"

"Estrella has been trying to find a way to get rid of him since the night of their marriage bond. So it came as no surprise to find him in bed with another female. But to see *you* . . . lying in bed with another male . . ." His voice darkened to a growl.

I stood firm.

"You could have come to me for help. The palatium is dangerous for your kind. What were you thinking?" he chided.

"If you are so angry with me, then why bother bringing me here?" I countered.

Kal gave up waiting for me and ambled across the room, making himself comfortable on the velvet divan. I swallowed at the sight of him shirtless, his sculpted physique affecting me in more ways than I'd like to admit. I would not allow myself to think of the way his sinewy muscles had felt pressed against me.

This arrogant male just had *to show up half-naked.*

I considered if his choice of clothing—or lack thereof—was his way of getting back at me for kicking him out after the cursed dance. As though he were trying to show me what I had missed out on. I hated that it was working. Averting my gaze to regain some semblance of control, I continued my tour of his room.

Whether he'd picked up on my reaction, Kal did not give away. He still eyed me with a look of ambivalence as he spoke. "You need not worry about Aedrus, his life will be spared."

I sighed a breath of relief.

Sheepishly, I walked over and sat on one of the cushioned seats opposite the prince, doing my best to keep my eyes on his face and not the gorgeous, proud display of muscles that appeared to have been meticulously carved by the hands of an artist. The play of light on his skin unveiled the intricate network of marbling that proved his lineage.

"Are there any other matters you feel compelled to discuss?" Kaleidos asked, though it came across as more of a taunt.

I blinked rapidly, clearing my head. "I know you have little reason to trust me after what you saw this morning, but, as you should know by now, my intentions were pure." I closed my eyes while trying to figure out how to put the words together. "After I snuck into the hall . . . a male . . . an Iris male found me. He told me he'd help me find Viera. We walked all around the palatium." I paused, taking several deep breaths before continuing. "And then he . . . and then he . . ." I started hyperventilating. Just talking about it, I could feel his hands on me again. It was all still too fresh.

"Estrella . . . your cousin, she protected me from him, she—" My voice broke, and I could no longer hold back tears.

Kal stormed across the room and, in a heartbeat, knelt before me, reaching for my hand.

I placed mine in his as I struggled to get my breathing under control, and he cradled it so gently before drawing it to his heart. The strong and steady thrum and the rise and fall of his chest soothed like gentle waves serving to calm me down as I synced my breathing to his.

When he finally spoke, his voice was soft but sinister—another side of him I had not seen yet. "Who did this?"

I opened my mouth to respond, but the name tasted bitter on my lips. Torn between the feelings of wanting Gaelor punished for what he'd done but also feeling so ashamed, like I could have somehow prevented it.

I shouldn't have gone out alone.

No. No. No. It is not my fault. It is NOT my fault.

If I say nothing, how many more females might he harm in the future?

Finally, I coughed out his name like it had been choking me. And with it, a sense of relief flooded over me. Like I could breathe again. And I could feel his power over me fading.

Kaleidos, on the other hand, was furious. The room rumbled. Books fell from the shelves. I feared the windows might burst. I took his face in my hands.

"Kal, it's all right. I'm safe now."

He closed his eyes at my touch, and the shaking stopped.

"Was that an earthquake?" I asked.

"Just a little one." He sighed. "Come now, we don't have much time left. You are here because, as my favored, you are allowed one advantage." Kaleidos rose to stand, holding his hand out for me. "What would you like it to be, Aella? A hint or a tonic?"

"What would be most beneficial?"

"It depends on your strategy."

"Which would you choose?"

"I would have no use for the tonic, so I'd go for the hint."

"So I should choose the hint, then?"

"I did not say that."

I narrowed my eyes at him. "Fine, I'll take the tonic."

The prince got up and withdrew a small vile from a desk across the room. It hung from a thin, leather string. He motioned for me to join him.

"May I?" he asked.

I nodded, and he looped the string over my head. The tips of his fingers brushed against my hair, sending a ripple of tingling sensations all the way down to my toes. Pulling my hair out from under the leather necklace, I examined the tiny, teardrop-shaped ampule before tucking it into the bodice of my gown.

"What does it do?"

A knock came at the door. Himmel had arrived to take me away.

Not knowing if I'd see Kal again, I wrapped my arms around him, burying my face into his marbled chest. Kal stood stiff and awkward as if stunned, his hands to his sides for a moment before wrapping his powerful arms around me.

Another hurried knock sounded at the door, making me withdraw from our embrace. I didn't want to. I wanted to stay there forever. Linger in his warmth, high on the scent of him. I wanted him to hold me tight and tell me it would all be okay and that he would protect me, but I knew he would not make me a promise he could not keep.

His pupils dilated as he took me in one last time, and it was like I could see all of the walls he'd put up come tumbling down. He reached for my face, tilting it up toward him. He leaned in close enough to feel a whisper. I wanted to bridge that gap, to taste him, languish in his presence, let him carry me away into a dream where I would not have to compete for his love. But the events of the previous night were still too fresh in my mind. And he would not protect me in the Matri-Ludus. So I pulled away.

Kaleidos dropped his hand, and in an instant, his expression hardened, walls going back up.

"You may enter," he called out.

Himmel made her entrance into the room, her expression foul as usual with pursed lips and narrowed eyes. "Your Highness." She curtsied, handing the prince a scroll. "From the Faber Ludi." She snapped her fingers at me. "It's time to go, girl. Don't be greedy! Come along now." Her voice was sweet in a manipulative way but had an edge to it, her irritation coming through.

As we left the room, I glanced back at the prince one last time. His back was to me, but he did not bother to turn around. His hand was balled into a fist, knuckles whitening as he crumpled the paper in his hand.

△

In the arena again, I stood side by side with Viera and Lewenne. Our plan was to work together in this event. United, we felt stronger. The small ampule hidden between my breasts gave me hope, even though I did not know what its contents did nor when to use them. It seemed I would have to trust my instincts.

The arena was packed. Somehow, it seemed like there were even more spectators than the last time, their iridescent skin making them glitter and sparkle like a rainbow of stars in the night sky. They stomped in the stands, chanting in an eerie ancient language. My heart quickened at the sound of the drumming, ominous as a war song.

Only seventeen of us remained as two had been removed from the competition the previous night by the king's tithe. Instead of a maze, before us was an expanse of sand, empty except for a curtain-covered display at the center. My mouth went dry, not knowing what might be hidden underneath. Not knowing what foul beasts they may send after us.

Up above, Kaleidos sat in his usual seat next to the king with his cousin, Estrella, at his side. She was in good spirits, and when her gaze found mine, a wicked grin spread across her face, her lip curling to show her canines which she'd adorned with pointed silver fangs. I met her glare with defiance, showing she had not defeated me.

It was unclear what Kal was thinking, his expression bored, and he appeared more interested in toying with the goblet in his hand than what was going on around him.

Nephos entered the arena riding a horse whose coat was painted in the same glittering designs they used on all the servants in the Palatium Crystalis. How vain the Iris were that they felt the need to make everyone and everything resemble themselves.

Nephos wore a dazzling cape of dyed feathers that fluttered behind him like a purple flame as he trotted in. The crowd went wild for him, even after the music had stopped. He feigned bashfulness and fanned himself as he waited for them to quiet down.

"For our second official event of the Matri-Ludus, we have prepared a special challenge for the elemental fae standing before you tonight. A challenge that will put their endurance and willpower to the test. Tonight, we shall test their strength of mind, body, and soul."

Chapter 28
Cousin

Kaleidos

Cousin Estrella leaned in close, her voice grating on my nerves. She was delighted with herself, knowing she had finally found an excuse to be rid of Aedrus. Little did she know, her lover would not be executed as she had so desired. He would be placed in a lesser station outside the palatium, but at least his life would be spared.

It didn't surprise me how much joy Estrella took in Aedrus' downfall, but her actions incensed me, making it difficult to suffer her company. I attempted to ignore her sneering remarks, but the more she spoke, the more my blood began to boil. My tolerance was wearing dangerously thin.

Knowing Estrella's conniving nature and what she had put Aella through, I had to keep a blank expression, feign boredom. Not let it show who I was most concerned for. Aella, the singular person in my life who had seen me for more than my title. Unlike the others who saw me as the male my father wanted me to be, she saw a different side of me, a side that I hadn't even known existed. In her eyes, I found inspiration. She made me think I could be better, made me *want* to be better. No, I could not let it show that the one person in all of Esterra whom I cared for was in danger *again*, and I was powerless to protect her.

I downed my wine, signaling for a refill.

She's a fighter. She will get through this. She must.

Estrella placed her hand on my thigh, leaning in closer as she giggled more salacious remarks about the contestants. When I didn't respond, she chided, "Why are you so dull this evening? Don't tell me that little Argenti whore sunk her claws into you."

I snapped, gripping her wrist so her fingers curled in on themselves, her long nails digging in like talons, drawing tiny drops of blood from the palm of her hand. I was tired of her, tired of being surrounded by our gluttonous culture of violence and depravity.

"You're hurting me, Kal," Estrella whined.

Speaking so low that only she could hear me, I said, "Hold your tongue, lest I rip it from your venomous mouth."

Estrella shrank back, still whimpering after I let go of her.

I was so angry with her but tried to remember that she was my closest cousin. We had been raised together like brother and sister. So as much as I wanted to be able to make good on my threat, I knew I never could. Gaelor, on the other hand, had not been so lucky. He'd never lay his *hands* on anyone ever again.

"But Cousin—" Estrella sulked.

"Not another word."

Once she'd calmed down and stopped tending to her hand like a wounded kitten, it was clear from the devious look in her eyes that my outburst had been a mistake. I could practically hear the wheels turning in her head as she plotted her revenge against my Aella.

Chapter 29

The Pit

Aella

Before us in the arena stood a weapons rack complete with a selection of swords, daggers, spears, and bows and arrows. Nephos had drawn the sheet to reveal the display before making a quick exit on his horse. The females did not hesitate to run toward it, hoping to obtain the weapon that suited them best.

I ran on aching feet, trying my hardest to ignore the searing pain from the dance the night before. As I reached the weapons rack, I claimed one of the spears at the end. I had never been trained to fight but considered myself to be a decent spearfisher. The few times my father had taken me along with him, he'd told me I was a natural. A memory that, at any other time, would have brought a smile to my face.

He'd taught my siblings and me how to defend ourselves from predatory sea creatures in case it ever became necessary, although it was always taught as a last resort. We were not a violent race and had learned to respect the large creatures we shared our waters with.

If I were to use the spear, I would stick to the principles of defense my father had taught me. To protect—never to provoke.

The spear was a smooth but solid weight in my hands. Holding it was both terrifying and exhilarating. I spun it around, giving it a few quick practice thrusts. It felt different using it on land—heavier but also quicker without the effects of water inhibiting its movement.

Shouting drew my attention away from the spear, and I was surprised to see some of the other females fighting over weapons—two of them left defenseless, as they had arrived last.

"You do not need two swords, Jara. Give one to me!" one of the females shouted. But Jara would not yield.

I scanned the arena for any sign of what we would be up against. The arena doors remained closed to us and the crowd went quiet in anticipation. The silence became deafening, and I braced myself for what was to come.

All at once, my heartbeat slowed but strengthened at the same time, so much so that it was palpable. *Thump thump, thump thump, thump thump.* My mouth went dry, and the space around me stretched as if my vision had expanded, making things appear both closer and farther away at the same time.

Spectators had started laughing and cheering in the stands, but I couldn't hear them. The only sound, my pulse thrumming in my ears—strong, steady, loud—in tune with the pounding in my chest, *thump thump, thump thump*, like a drum.

Was it my heart, or were they playing the drums again? I couldn't tell the difference anymore.

Spinning around to find Viera, I discovered I was alone. Where the weapons rack had been moments before was a depthless pit of darkness, and Viera was on the other side.

The pit began growing in size, luring me to it. I wanted to see what was inside, curious about what was waiting for us at the bottom. A few others were compelled to do the same, one of them getting close enough to see over the edge. Her face paled when she peered over, and she let out a blood-curdling scream. She turned to run, but the pit opened three feet wider, the ground falling beneath her feet and sucking her in. Her scream echoed as she fell, before going silent, snuffed out like a flame.

The rest of us backed away, terrified by what we'd just witnessed. I started running to reach the other side. I needed to be close to Viera so we could work together.

As I ran around the perimeter, the pit continued to grow at a slow but steady pace. Yet even with its growing size, the bottom remained out of sight.

I narrowly dodged a few Aereus contestants while trying to maintain my distance from the pit. "Watch yourself!" one of the females warned.

The sound of combat and screams tempted me to look back, but I kept my focus on Viera. I had to reach her and Lewenne before anything else happened. I would not allow myself to get distracted again.

"Viera!" I shouted as I was in the final stretch. How had she gotten so far from me in the first place? She stood in a stupor, swaying slightly, looking as if one small breeze could knock her over.

"Viera." I grabbed her by the shoulders, giving her a small shake. Her eyes were locked on the king and the two females attending to him up in the box.

"Are those . . . ? They can't be," I said. "Weren't they sent away after last night?"

Viera's hands were shaking. She held a bow with a set of arrows slung over her shoulder. She had started reaching for one but couldn't complete the motion. "I could do it right now, aim for his heart. But what if I miss and strike one of them instead? I won't get a second chance. But what if this is my *only* chance?" she said, her voice small and frail.

I'd never heard her sound so unsure of herself. Viera was the confident one, the one who never took no for an answer, who always had a solution for everything.

"If you're not one hundred percent certain, then don't do it. Chances are the guards will strike you down the moment you aim in his direction. Better to think it through. We have a plan, remember?" I said and looked around for Lewenne.

"But what if I don't make it out of here today?" she replied.

"Viera, you're going to make it out of here because you're with me. We're together in this." I squeezed her hand.

Then I suddenly remembered the tiny, tear-shaped ampule! But why couldn't Kaleidos have told me what it was for? *Whatever it is, he said he would not have needed it, which means it must allow me to control something that he already has power over.*

I'd seen him command earth and fire. And it was common knowledge that the Iris had more magic than just the elements we ruled over. *Could he also bear Adamas blood and powers?* He did not know that I was star-blessed with more than one power. Perhaps I did not need the tonic since I already had the power of air. I was willing to take the risk.

I snapped off the tip, handing it to Viera. "You should take it," I said.

She gave me an incredulous look.

"I'm serious. You need it more than me, and if anyone should make it out of here, it's you," I said while pushing it toward her mouth.

Viera slapped my hand away, almost dislodging the ampule, some of the liquid spilling over my fingertips. Anger crossed her face. "I don't need your help, Aella. You don't always need to come and save me. I can handle myself just fine! You think you're so special because you're the prince's favored? Well, I'm sure by the next event, he'll have chosen a new one."

Her words stung, making me want to cry. She was supposed to be my closest friend. How could she say those things to me? I was tired of letting the Iris make me feel small and powerless, but hearing that from her was the worst of all. My face flushed, and my shoulders tensed.

"I can't believe you are jealous of me," I goaded. "Or maybe you just hate that I finally have something of my own and that I'm no longer dependent on you. You just wanted to keep me in your shadow, but now I've come out, and that scares you. I—"

A scream caught our attention and the ground rumbled beneath our feet. In one corner of the arena, two Aereus females fought each other. The earth shook and cracked with their combat.

In another corner, Jara was on the offensive, fighting off her fellow

Aurum contestants, her twin swords ablaze with fire as she backed one of them toward the pit. Her friend begged and cried, but she would not stop.

Something was off. I shot back the remaining drops from the ampule, and when I noticed Viera again, she was aiming her arrow at my heart, her eyes red and glazed over. It took me a moment to recognize it, but once the tonic began working, it was evident that she was under some kind of spell. How quickly the Iris turned us against one another.

"Viera, put the arrow down."

"Why? So you can kill me?"

"You don't want to do this. They are in your head."

Viera continued aiming the arrow at me while backing me toward the pit. I held my arms out to the sides, dropping my spear in surrender.

"I am not your enemy."

Her eyes darkened and she let the arrow loose. As it shot toward me, I managed to blow it off course, just barely, so that it skimmed the side of my neck. As she went for another arrow, I ducked down for my spear, spinning it around low to the ground, knocking her off her feet. She fell with a grunt, and as I came to her side, she tried attacking me again.

"Stop, Viera!" I wanted to shake it out of her, but it was no use, so I yanked the bow and arrows from her and threw them into the pit. She screamed at me and started throwing punches and kicks. "Remember who the real enemy is," I shouted.

The gaping pit had become larger than the strip of remaining land that circled it. All around it, contestants had begun attacking one another or pushing each other into the pit. We would all end up killing each other if I could not stop the poison from infecting their minds.

Viera blinked her eyes at me as if waking up from a dream, and then I realized—it was attached to the weapons. The weapons carried a spell. They had known we wouldn't fight each other willingly, so they spelled our weapons. At that moment, I was the only one who wouldn't be affected due to the tonic. *Kaleidos must have known.* He'd known I wouldn't have been able to live with myself if I hurt one of my friends, so he had made sure I chose the tonic that would help me see through it.

"Aella?"

"Listen, we need to disarm the others. *You* can't touch the weapons without being affected, so you distract them, and I'll take them away."

Viera nodded to me in understanding, and we ran toward our friends first. We needed to stop Lewenne and Ilaria from trying to kill each other. Lewenne was smaller than Ilaria but faster, able to easily outmaneuver the swings and thrusts of Ilaria's broadsword.

Lewenne clutched a small dagger and sliced the back of Ilaria's leg as she dove under. That angered Ilaria more than hurt her, but the next time Lewenne took a swing, Ilaria had caught on to her method. As Lewenne dove down again, aiming for her other leg with the dagger, Ilaria caught her—stomping down on her arm with one foot, making the dagger clatter to the ground, and kicking her in the face with the other. Lewenne panted, spitting blood onto the sandy gravel as she attempted to catch her breath.

Ilaria, ready to make the kill, had raised her sword up to strike when Viera came crashing into her from behind. Ilaria fell to the ground but managed to keep her hold on the sword. She rolled back onto her feet and charged at Viera in a rage, not even the injury to her leg slowing her down.

Lewenne lay there, stunned and grunting from Ilaria's attack, fingers reaching for her dagger. She roared as I kicked the dagger into the pit. She would thank me later, I hoped.

Ilaria swung her sword at Viera, which she scarcely managed to dodge. Viera tried to run, but somehow Ilaria was faster, and guilt twisted my stomach at the thought that I had left Viera defenseless.

"Ilaria!" I shouted to distract her. She only faltered for a moment, but it gave Viera a chance to dive out of the way. "She is weak and defenseless, Ilaria. Fight me instead. We are better matched."

Ilaria scowled and then turned to confront me.

"Why don't we fight without weapons?" I suggested, hoping she would take the bait. I held my spear out as if to drop it.

Ilaria scoffed at the idea.

"Are you too afraid to fight me one-on-one? Without hiding behind the strength of your weapon?" I continued to taunt her even as she charged toward me. "Oh, that's right, your hands are probably too soft. Wouldn't want to break a nail."

Ilaria roared with fury, then threw down her sword just before colliding with me. I swore my thanks to the stars even as Ilaria tackled me to the ground and the wind knocked out of me. I counted my heartbeats, waiting; *thump thump, thump thump.* She would snap out of it at any moment.

Ilaria wrapped her hands around my neck and squeezed. My heartbeat quickened and then slowed, my fingertips began to tingle, and a dizziness swept over me. *She should let go soon, she should remember. The spell should be wearing off.*

Viera tried to pry her off me, but Ilaria's grip was so tight, too tight. My vision started to go black around the edges like I was looking through a long tunnel and everything was swimming and becoming farther away.

"You're killing her!" Viera howled. She kept fighting Ilaria—kicking and punching, pulling at her hair, nails digging into her flesh—and finally managed to wrestle her off me. I took a big, choking breath, gasping. I willed the air to fill my lungs and replenish my body. I felt weak, but there was no time to rest. It was not over. Ilaria's brows furrowed and her face paled as she looked down at her hands.

"It's . . . not . . . your . . . fault," I choked out between heavy breaths.

"The weapons are spelled to make us fight each other," Viera explained to both Ilaria and Lewenne.

Only about half of the contestants remained. Their victims lay dead on the ground, others swallowed up by the pit.

"We need to get their weapons away from them?" Lewenne asked. "That is the only way to stop them?"

"As far as we know," I admitted.

"We go for the Aurum first," Ilaria said while helping me to my feet.

"There are less of them, and once we get them on our side, they can help us stop the Aereus."

"Good call," Viera agreed. "Let's go!"

The four of us ran to where the Aurum were battling each other.

"Figure out how to disarm them. Don't touch any weapons!" I shouted.

It appeared that Jara had defeated every Aurum contestant besides Rae. Like a goddess of war, her two swords shined red, and the blood of her friends dripped down her face and arms.

I was the only one among us with a weapon, and I had no time to question how my spear might compete against her twin blades. When they noticed us coming, they stopped fighting each other and turned to meet us, waiting. A sick smile crossed Jara's face as she set her swords ablaze.

I looked up to the heavens and gave a quick thanks to the stars as thick storm clouds began to gather above us.

"Make it rain!" I commanded as we charged into them.

With the four of us working together, the rain came hard, and it came fast. Like buckets of water, it drenched the arena—Jara and Rae's flames extinguished by the sudden onslaught of rain. The sand turned into mud, making it difficult for them to run. But we had momentum, and we knew how to maneuver through the wet and slippery.

As they tried to charge at us, they lost their footing, giving us the perfect opportunity to knock the weapons from their hands. Ilaria and Lewenne held Jara down as I wrenched the swords from her, tossing them into the gaping pit.

Rae had managed to get back onto her feet and stood in a low stance with her sword aimed toward me.

"Drop it," I warned as I stalked closer to her, spear in my hand.

"I'd sooner drown," she replied and then thrust her sword at me.

As I spun out of reach, Viera came from the side, kicking right into Rae's hand where she held onto the pommel. A crack sounded at the impact, and Rae screamed, holding her hand in pain, still grasping her weapon. I used the moment to knock her down with the blunt end of my spear. She finally lost her grip on the sword and I was able to rid her of it.

I picked up a bow and arrow from the side of a motionless Aurum female—I couldn't make out her identity through all the blood and bruising. On the other side of the pit, Elutha was fighting off two other Aereus females. The earth around them jutted up and apart, creating an elaborate topographical terrain.

I aimed for their hands, hoping to use the wind to guide my arrows. Ready to shoot, I hesitated. I'd never intentionally used my air powers before. It had always been luck or something else. What if it didn't work and I accidentally killed them? I let out a choked sob, lowering the bow. I couldn't bring myself to let those arrows fly.

Jara began coming out of the trance and let out an anguish-filled scream. "Kire!" she sobbed as she scrambled over. She bowed over her friend and wailed, "No, no, no, no, no, no!" The sound was gut-wrenching. Jara frantically swept her hands over Kire, as if she could wipe up all the blood. As if she could put her back together. Breathless, she looked down at her hands, at the thick coating of blood, and let out a raw and primal sound. "Kire! What have I done? What have I done?"

Rae wrapped her arms around Jara and held her as they both wept, curling over their friend, bloody tears streaming down their faces. I found myself frozen in place as I watched them. Their anguish tore through me, paralyzing me, making me forget what I needed to do. Thoughts of my earlier conflict with Viera hit me. *That could have been us.* Bile rose in my throat and I lurched over, spilling the contents of my stomach onto the ground.

All of the commotion drew the attention of the Aereus females, and they stopped attacking each other and started toward us. Viera came to my side.

"Come on," she said, shaking me out of it. "This isn't over yet."

Elutha led her group toward us, the earth splitting behind them in warning. As the three Aereus females approached, the four of us stood together in front of Jara and Rae. The earth began to shake harder the closer they got and the wind picked up around us. The arena darkened and the temperature dropped.

Something inside of me hummed. Something powerful and explosive was building up inside my chest. Though my body was exhausted, I felt a well of power waiting to be set loose.

The Aereus were close and began charging at us at full speed. Elutha threw her spear, which sank deep into Viera's shoulder. Viera cried out as she dropped down. But when I came to her side, she only pointed forward and shouted, "Go!"

Emotions flooded me. Fear and anger. Without thought, I let go of that power building up inside me, and I growled. With that, a bolt of lightning shot down from the sky, striking Elutha. She spasmed and then collapsed motionless to the ground. Her face burned beyond recognition.

Using that much power had felt good, dulling my senses to the reality of what I had done. The two other Aereus females, Ramalia and Ona, charged forward, unphased by the loss of Elutha. The earth rumbled as they drew nearer. I screamed a rallying cry as I stormed straight toward them. I spun my spear, fending off their blows as Ilaria and Lewenne circled around. Ilaria made use of the slick ground, sliding under the swipe of Ona's sword. She yanked on Ona's leg, pulling her off balance and giving Lewenne a chance to disarm her.

Ramalia fought on, pressing me toward the edge of the pit. The earth tilted at her command, sliding me closer to the gaping hole. A glance over my shoulder almost caused me to lose my balance and fall right into her trap. She was stronger than me, and I was losing more ground every second. I was only feet away from the edge. With her last blow, I grasped on to her spear, my body flinging back with the jab. I held on to the spear for dear life as I hovered briefly, my body dangling over the pit, only the tips of my feet still on the ledge. Simultaneously, Ramalia and I realized that she would fall with me unless she released her spear, but the spell kept her holding on. Ramalia struggled back as the ground began to splinter and crack, and I was losing my footing. Lewenne caught Ramalia by the waist and pulled her back with all her weight. Ilaria reached for me, and with the combined effort, we were all back on firm ground. The three of us managed to finally disarm Ramalia, and I hastily made my way back over to Viera.

Viera was lying there in pain but alive—her eyes wide with fear as I approached. I pulled out the spear in one swift motion, pressing the palms of my hands into her shoulder to staunch the bleeding. Everything suddenly became so still, so quiet, all except for Jara and Rae's sobs which had been joined by Ramalia and Ona's as they began to understand what they had done.

I waited for my tears to come. Maybe the tonic had worn off, making me blood-hungry. Maybe it had stopped working when I spilled my stomach contents upon the ground. But I was no longer holding any weapons. The spell should have had no effect on me. Viera could see the question on my face. But neither of us said a word.

Chapter 30
Honeyed Tonics

Aella

The event was over the moment we all stopped fighting each other. The Aereus females dropped to their knees in tears when they came to their senses, keening and striking at the earth in sorrow. The music picked back up again in attempts to drown out the sounds of mourning. Nephos rode out to announce us all winners, but the crowd responded with subdued applause followed by a chorus of boos. The sobbing contestants put a damper on the event, but Nephos tried his hardest to make light of it. Pushing the narrative about how it was all for Esterra, to ensure the strength of the royal Iris line, blessed by the stars, for the good of all fae.

Those were just the excuses they told us while they used us for entertainment. Maybe they had told those lies so many times, they'd even started to believe them.

Nephos did little to hide his surprise at how well the Argenti had done. I'm sure it came as a shock that not one of us had been lost, making us the majority. As if they had expected, or even hoped, to have eliminated more of us.

Only eight contestants remained—four Argenti, two Aereus, and two

Aurum. It had started to look like they might kill us all in the cursed competition, despite all they'd led us to believe.

No one said anything about the lightning strike. They must not have suspected it had come from any of us, as the Adamas had been extinct for millennia. They must have assumed it was an act of nature. I did not want to find out what they would have done if they'd known it was me.

As we exited the arena through the winner's hall, Viera was bandaged up and carried out by a team of healers. Himmel threatened to mute the remaining contestants if they did not stop crying. She then offered sparkling wine and honeyed tonics, her mood and affect appearing to change in an instant.

Her voice softened as she crooned, "You have not done anything wrong, my dears. Look at how blessed you all are to stand here in the winner's hall. One of you will be so fortunate as to claim a position beside the prince."

Himmel tilted a glass to Jara's lips, forcing it down her throat. Half of it dribbled down her chin, but she opened her mouth to it. Silent tears ran down Jara's cheeks as she attempted to gulp down the shimmering liquid. The rest of us took our own glasses, sipping the liquid down, careful not to be made examples by Himmel. Still, I was glad for the effects—the mind-numbing sensation, not having to care about what had happened to us . . . and what they had made us do.

The hours that followed bled together as we paraded through the streets, crowds cheering at our dirtied and bloodied appearances, the signs of our savageness. We smiled and waved back at them as if pleased with ourselves, proud of our triumphs, slap-happy from the tonics given to us. They threw flowers at our feet and sang praises as we passed through, worshiping us like heroes.

It felt like a dream, as though my legs were not my own, like I'd floated all the way up to the Palatium Crystalis. Everything after was a blur.

△

Back in our rooms, Himmel explained to us that there would be one final event at the end of the month. Since only eight of us remained, we would have the privilege of arranged meetings with the prince. Each would be given one private meeting with Prince Kaleidos where he would be allowed to dismiss any of the females whom he did not find most suitable.

Those females he dismissed would be granted life in servitude to Iris nobility in Prisma. I couldn't help thinking that it sounded better than remaining in the Matri-Ludus.

Jara had earned the right to meet with the prince first because she had killed the most in the last competition, making her the apparent victor. But Jara wasn't the same. Gone was the fiery, strong-willed female. She was a collection of broken pieces that Rae was struggling to hold together.

Jara did not make an appearance at our dinner that evening, and when Rae was asked about it, she told us Jara had been summoned before the prince. I doubted Jara would be dismissed, considering she was the most recent winner. Her strength and fierce fighting skills would have made her a popular choice, a strong elemental wife to bear children for the Iris throne. The thought of Jara spending time with Kaleidos sent a pang of jealousy through me, a feeling that I abhorred.

"Do you know what became of the others selected by the king on the night of the dance?" Rae asked Viera.

"What happened that night anyway? How come *you* were the only one to return to us?" Ilaria cut in.

"I don't presume to understand the decisions of the king," Viera replied. "But Aella and I spotted them up in the viewing box with him last night."

The two Aereus females, Ramalia and Ona, gasped and then whispered to each other in hushed tones.

"You mustn't have pleased him very much then," Ilaria muttered.

I shot up out of my seat, sending the chair flying back. Viera grabbed my hand and gave me a look that said, *let it go*. I huffed, trying to rein in my temper. If Viera didn't want me to fight for her, I wouldn't, but I was fed up with Ilaria's attitude. It took almost everything in me to keep myself from climbing over the table and taking my fury out on her. Begrudgingly,

I picked up my chair and returned to my seat, all while avoiding eye contact with Ilaria.

"Thank the stars they were spared from the pit," Ona spoke up, breaking the tension. "Zaita was too weak and wouldn't have stood a chance."

Ramalia blinked back tears, afraid to show weakness. We were all still competing against each other, and some did a better job of setting aside emotions than others. I wondered if anyone still wanted to win the Matri-Ludus or if it was just self-preservation setting in. But winning would mean a lot more than just surviving. One of us would end up marrying the prince.

As I lay awake in bed that night, I pictured myself standing next to Kaleidos, our hands entwined, his devilish grin, his scent, his lips. I sucked my bottom lip. Thoughts of all that a marriage to him would entail filled me with a dizzying warmth. Stars. I hated him, but I couldn't deny how much I craved him. How I longed to be wrapped up in his arms again. Tangled up with him. To feel the energy between us like a glitter of stardust humming between our skin, pulling us together. Like we were meant for each other. The insatiable feeling of having him yet still not having enough. I could wrap myself up in him. Up in this feeling. Let it swallow me whole like a silky bed of clouds. I could drown in him, and I would be smiling, pure bliss all the way to the deepest depths of the sea. I buried my face in my plush, silk pillow. Oh, but I hated him. I hated him for being Iris. I hated him for doing nothing. If only he could live up to his title and end it all. Why did I have to feel so much for a male who did so little? It made me want to throttle him. I had to do something. I had to find a way to ally him to us, to convince him . . . No matter the cost.

◬

When Jara joined us in the baths the next day, everyone swarmed her, asking her questions about her time with the prince. She gave vague answers and refused to go into detail. Jara shooed everyone away, keeping to herself, even avoiding Rae. She was the first to reach for honeyed tonics and was quick to drink herself into oblivion.

I did not blame her for using the tonics, as they were probably the only things getting her through. After her time with the prince, the jealous part of me forced me to see her in a new light. Her shiny, pin-straight, cornsilk hair, how it caught the morning sunlight in a way that resembled a crown atop her head. She was tall and strong, slender-built with elegantly defined muscles in her arms and legs and delicate feminine curves. Regal and glowing, she would fit well beside the prince. I tore my eyes away when she turned in my direction, embarrassed to be caught staring.

"Who do you think he will summon next?" I wondered out loud.

The remaining females turned their heads away as they began to follow Jara's example, keeping to themselves. It was clear that things had changed after the last event, and they were all only looking out for themselves. At least Viera and I still had each other, even if every day in the Matri-Ludus threatened to be our last.

Ramalia was selected to meet the prince that afternoon, and Viera, not even fully recovered from her injury, was summoned to see the king. She made me promise not to come looking for her again after what had happened the last time and assured me that she would be all right.

That evening, I snuck out to the balcony again, needing something to keep my mind off things, and—as the healer had said—a swim under the stars would help my beat-up feet heal faster.

I'd made a mess of them with all the running in the arena, and I'd hardly had a chance to stay off them as she'd recommended.

My heart sank when I found the vines cut down, but I'd known it had been too good to last. The gardeners would have been bound to find the out-of-place, ungroomed vines and prune them to restore the Palatium Crystalis to its pristine and manicured state.

I decided to stay out on the balcony regardless, looking out toward the sea. It wasn't visible like it had been from Estrella's rooms, but I could sense its presence just beyond.

Standing there wistfully didn't help my mood. It was too painful to think of home, and I did not want to let my mind wander to all of the terrible things that had happened in the arena, or think about whether I'd see my friend Viera again. I had to make a plan. I needed to practice my gifts.

What happened in the arena had felt out of my control, and I could not allow it to occur again if I valued my life. A power like that was unstoppable. If I could learn to harness it and direct it at will, *I* would be unstoppable.

Chapter 31

How to Please...

Arianwen

Days had turned into weeks, and I'd found myself falling into a comfortable rhythm. I'd spent most mornings in the hospitium learning from Pluvia and Liisa and helping whatever patients came in.

We'd all cheered when the Aurum patients recovered and were able to move to the refugee housing. The Aurum female, Rasa, who I'd met in the springs, had clung to me, weeping with joy as Styx was released. I was grateful they had each other to lean on as they walked through the grief of losing their loved ones.

The other healers had been so kind and welcoming to me. Though Wynn had been sure I'd get along with Dorel, I just couldn't bring myself to be more than cordial with her after seeing how her eyes would light up any time he was mentioned or whenever he'd show up at the hospitium. Jealousy was a newer emotion for me, as no males back home had ever really caught my interest.

While Wynn and I would flirt and tease each other, he'd continued to keep me at a distance, which was disappointing. A significant part of me yearned to experience what it would be like to choose someone for myself, but the terrifying risk of being rejected held me back.

When Wynn was available, my afternoons had been spent exploring Zephyria and the surrounding alps. I was grateful that I no longer had to wear a blindfold when traveling in and out of the city, though flying was still something I was getting used to.

He'd shown me a ruined city that had once been a part of the Court of Air but had long since been abandoned. Standing there surrounded by rubble and bits, I couldn't help but feel somber. A dingy white curtain fluttered in one window while destroyed belongings spilled out of the wreckage of another. Ghosts of the past seemed to flutter around as people's memories were left to rot and decay.

Seeing the lost city had reminded me of the legends I'd been told about the Adamas' extinction. Wynn had explained how it had once been their capital city, but the Iris had destroyed it in an attack long ago. They'd tried to wipe out the Adamas because they were the only ones who knew their secret.

I couldn't help but wonder how many of the other stories I'd been taught were completely false. It saddened me that an entire people lived in forced exile—yet perhaps they were the lucky ones. Zephyria was well-guarded and unknown to the Iris, which was why Wynn had to be so secretive about its location.

Zephyria had started to feel a little more like home, especially once my chambers began to overflow with books and new belongings. I could tell, however, that the king and queen merely tolerated my presence, not pleased I was staying in the palatium. I had managed to avoid them for the most part, often taking my meals in my room if Wynn was gone.

Whenever he was on a rescue mission, I found myself filled with dread, worried the Iris might capture or kill him. I wasn't sure when he had started to mean so much to me, but I knew the more time I spent with him, the more I wanted to be around him.

"You should buy this!" Liisa squealed, holding a beautiful, violet scarf to my face. "It goes perfectly with your coloring and makes your eyes sparkle."

Liisa and I were perusing the shops in the market area of Zephyria after our shift at the hospitium. I had been given a small salary for the work I was doing, and it was so freeing to have my own coin to spend how I wanted.

"I don't see how a scarf could make my eyes sparkle, but I do love the color," I said, then picked up a beautiful, emerald green one. "Here! You can buy this one. It makes your copper hair look like a living flame."

We burst into childish giggles. After bartering down the prices, we left arm in arm, our brand new scarves wrapped around our necks.

"Would you like to check out the bookstore next?" Liisa asked, her amber eyes gleaming.

"Absolutely. What's your favorite kind of book to read?"

"I love a chilling mystery," she admitted then lowered her voice, "but I also can't resist a steamy romance novel."

"That's nothing to be ashamed of!" I exclaimed with a grin. "Considering my lack of *actual* romance back home, I may have picked up a novel or two. I enjoy the genre . . . when I'm not too busy studying medical texts, that is."

"Ari, you're allowed to take a break from studying now and then. I insist you buy a book that has nothing to do with medicine."

"Then I insist you proudly purchase a romance novel," I declared right back.

Her bronze cheeks flushed, and she pursed her lips before holding her hand out to me. "All right, it's a deal."

"Good."

"Why do you feel the need to study all the time anyway?" she asked as we continued walking to the bookstore.

"Honestly, with my arranged marriage looming ahead of me, I've always felt like I was running out of time. There's a high chance my betrothed could make me stop my work to stay home and take care of his needs and raise his children."

Liisa rolled her eyes and scoffed, "That is such antiquated thinking. I'm so glad my family escaped Illithania."

"Me too." I smiled. "Otherwise, I never would have met you."

"I'm so very glad to have met you, too."

We continued walking in companionable silence before Liisa spoke up. "You've never met your betrothed, right?"

"Yes, Verus grew up in a different part of Iveria. In most arranged marriages back home, you don't meet your betrothed until the wedding day."

"Maybe he would have surprised you. You're such a gifted healer, and there are males out there who aren't completely primitive."

I rolled my eyes. "I guess I'll find out if I return."

"I really hope you stay, Ari. Now that we've met, I can't imagine not seeing you every day. Your family would survive without you, you know that right? If you had been drafted to Prisma, you would have never seen them again either."

"That's true, but at least I would have had the chance to say goodbye. If I never return, they will have no idea what happened to me, and I'm not sure if I can live with that."

Liisa squeezed my arm as we walked into the bookstore. "You're right. It's just . . . you were about to get married and start your life, a life you didn't choose. If you stay, you can decide what life you want and who you want to spend it with. What parent wouldn't want what's best for their child?"

I nodded at that thought. While I wanted to believe my parents would want me to be happy, I was filled with shame thinking of their disappointment in me if I broke my betrothal by choosing not to return. The longer I stayed away, the greater the chance they would assume something horrible had happened to me. If I did return to say goodbye, what would I even tell them? The oath would prevent me from sharing what I had seen and experienced, so how would I even begin to explain?

Perhaps the betrothal would be dissolved either way. My heart was torn between my duty to my family and my desire to live my own life.

Am I being selfish?

Liisa's excited squeal at a display of new books broke me from my spiraling thoughts. "Ari! It looks like someone smuggled some books from my favorite Aereus author! You have to come look."

"That's amazing! I have been wondering how they get new books here."

"Well, there are some local authors here in Zephyria who will occasionally write new books, but we also have raiding parties that smuggle supplies from all over Esterra."

"That sounds dangerous."

"It is, but some people enjoy a little danger." A deep rumbling voice surprised me from behind.

I spun around and smiled in delight at Wynn, who had somehow managed to sneak up on me. Playfully smacking his arm, I teased, "Don't you know it's not polite to eavesdrop?"

Wynn shrugged. "We're in a public place, and it's not like you were whispering. You're both quite exuberant in your love for books."

"When did you get back? And how did you find us?"

"I got back a few hours ago, and before you ask, everything went smoothly. I stopped by the hospitium, and Pluvia mentioned you two were planning on shopping this afternoon, so I decided to come find you."

"You know us well to have found us so quickly," I said.

"I caught your scent on the wind," he said, his eyes full of unspoken words. "I could find you anywhere, Arianwen."

A delicious chill went down my spine. The way he said my name felt like a caress, and I found myself wondering what it would be like to give in to our wager and beg him to kiss me.

"So . . . Prince Wynn, have you come to whisk Ari away?" Liisa asked, breaking the tension that had been building between us.

Wynn chuckled. "No, feel free to continue with your shopping. I just wanted to say hello and invite Ari to join me for dinner later. You are welcome to join us if you'd like, Liisa."

"My Prince, that is such a generous offer, but I must decline," Liisa replied. "I already have plans of my own."

"What plans?" I exclaimed. "You didn't tell me about any plans!"

Liisa shrugged. "I'm sorry I forgot to tell you, but you know the Aurum male I told you about?"

"The golden god you've been raving about with eyes like pools of water?" I replied with a smirk.

Liisa blushed and looked around to see who else might have been listening, pointedly ignoring Wynn. "Ari! I told you that in confidence," she said, feigning anger.

I laughed and saw Wynn trying to hold back a grin at Liisa's embarrassment. He winked at me before walking to another part of the bookstore to give us some privacy.

"Please forgive me, but do go on. What about him?"

"Well . . . he's been trying to get me to spend time with him, and I finally agreed to meet him for dinner tonight," she explained, voice brimming with excitement.

"Liisa! I can't believe you have been keeping that from me all day. I would have been bursting to tell if I were in your shoes."

"I'm sorry, but, truthfully, I keep almost talking myself out of it. I'm not sure I have the guts to go tonight."

"But you've been so enamored. Why wouldn't you want to have dinner with him?"

"I guess I'm afraid he'll end up disappointing me. You know, the idea of him might outweigh the actuality."

"It sounds like you're just nervous. Everything you've told me about him makes me think you should at least give him a chance. Especially with those eyes you could drown in," I said, dramatically fluttering my eyes.

Liisa laughed nervously, then squeezed me into a hug. "You're right.

I'm going to give him a chance, but that means I need to go home and start getting ready. See you tomorrow?"

"You've got it," I replied, hugging her back.

She smiled and waved goodbye before dashing out the door.

I turned around to go look for Wynn, admiring the beautiful displays of books as I walked around the bookstore. Rounding a corner, I found him leaning against a bookcase, his arms crossed, looking at me with a playful grin. "Well, it appears your afternoon is suddenly free."

Without looking, I picked a random book off the shelf in front of me and pretended to peruse it. "I don't know. I quite enjoy being alone in a bookstore full of wonderful things to read."

"Oh, really?" Wynn plucked the book out of my hands and chuckled. "Should I be jealous?"

"What?"

"*How To Please Your Male*," he said, reading the title of the book I had chosen.

I swiped it out of his hands and put it back on the shelf, blushing. "Well, I suppose it would have been an interesting read."

Wynn smiled, his eyes lit up at my playful response. He rested his arm on the shelf above me and leaned in. "You know, if you were curious about how to please a male, all you had to do was ask."

Backing up a step, I blushed even more, my pulse starting to race at his proximity. "I prefer to learn from books."

"But it's so much more fun to learn by doing," Wynn teased, his eyes full of mirth and something more.

My body was hot all over, and I caught myself staring at his lips, wondering again what they might feel like pressed against mine. "Well . . . I guess I'll keep that in mind," I replied, stumbling over my words.

Wynn looked like a shark circling its prey as he caught me staring. His lips turned up into a grin as he leaned closer and whispered into my ear, "I can leave you to read your educational books and meet you for dinner later if you'd like. Maybe after, you can get some hands-on experience."

Flabbergasted, I pulled back and stared up at him, my face burning with embarrassment but also curiosity. He kept flirting and teasing me, but would he ever follow through?

Needing to cut the tension before saying something I wouldn't be able to take back, I tried changing the subject. "Actually, I think I'm done here. There's a little cafe that sells coffee and pastries down the street. Would you like to get some with me?"

"I would be delighted."

Wynn ushered me back out into the crisp air which helped cool my flushed cheeks.

"So, Ari, tell me something about you that I don't already know."

I smiled at his question. It had become something of a game between us during our times together, a way to get to know each other better.

"Well . . . when I was fifteen, I had the brilliant idea to run away from home to one of the islands off the coast. I even stole my father's seahorse," I replied.

"You rebel!" Wynn chuckled. "So this isn't the first time you left home?"

"I *tried* . . . I didn't actually succeed," I confessed, looking down at my feet.

"Tell me more . . . if you want to, that is," he said, gently nudging me with his arm.

"My younger brother saw me sneaking away in the middle of the night, and my father caught up with me right as I was leaving the underwater stables." I palmed my face in embarrassment. "One of the drawbacks to growing up in a large family is that there is always someone watching or getting in your way," I griped with mild annoyance. "I was so furious at him for giving me up."

Wynn sighed, and I looked up at him. His eyes appeared sorrowful. "You know little brothers only want to keep their sisters safe, right?"

Stars, I'm so insensitive. Wynn lost his older sister, and here I am complaining about having a large family.

Stopping in my tracks, I turned to him, gently squeezing his arm, even though I really wanted to wrap my arms around him and give him a giant hug. "I know, Wynn . . . and I'm really sorry for your loss. I'm sure she loved you very much."

Wynn gave me a sad smile. "Thanks, Ari. I only wish I could have saved her." He cleared his throat, shaking his head slightly. "What in the stars made you want to run away from home?"

Recognizing his need to not talk about his sister any further, I continued my story as we started walking again. "I was fifteen, what *wouldn't* make me want to run away from home?" I joked, trying to lighten the mood. "But in all seriousness, I didn't think anyone would care if I was gone. I already told you that I don't have a lot of friends, but that was never more evident than when I was in school. I was always pushing boundaries, asking too many questions, and catching the eyes of our Iris Guardians." I glanced down at the faint scars on my hands. "After the public humiliation and punishment, no one wanted anything to do with me. They were too afraid of being noticed as well."

Wynn grabbed one of my hands and squeezed, gently rubbing his thumb along the back of it.

"I'm so sorry that happened to you," he said, his voice low and soothing. "They were fools not to be friends with you." We stopped in front of the cafe, and he turned to face me. "I count myself blessed to have you as a friend. Your strength of character and love for life is such a pleasure to be around." He lifted my hand and pressed a soft kiss to it, causing butterflies to flare up in my stomach. His eyebrows flicked upward, and he smiled. "Shall we go inside?"

I wanted to melt into a puddle on the ground right where we stood, but I simply nodded and smiled back, trying to memorize the feel of his lips on my hand.

※

We'd spent the rest of the afternoon and evening together and had a delightful time. It was so easy to talk to him about anything and everything.

He'd continued asking deeper questions about my life growing up as well as lighter topics like what my favorite book or color was.

Everything about spending time with him felt easy and right except for the lingering tension between us. It connected us like a thread, drawing us closer with every heated glance he sent my way. The idea of us being anything more than friends seemed ludicrous—he was a prince, for stars' sake—but my body and heart disagreed.

I remembered the sensation of tracing the pathways of scars on his skin when he'd been injured in the woods and wondered if I would ever have the chance to touch him so intimately again. Perhaps I was forever destined to want things not meant for me. Maybe I had been made for a different world.

Chapter 32
Homesick

Arianwen

"So, how did it go?" I asked Liisa as we restocked supplies in the hospitium. "Did your golden god sweep you off your feet?"

Liisa's bronze skin blushed while she busied herself with a stack of clean linens that needed to be sorted. "He has a name, you know, and if I hear you call him 'golden god' one more time in front of someone, I will wring your neck!"

"I'm just teasing you." I laughed. "You make it so easy."

"Char was perfect. He was so polite and kind, easy to talk to."

"But was there a spark?"

"You mean did he light something on fire?"

I gaped at her. "Please tell me you're joking. I didn't mean actual flames, but did you have chemistry?"

"Look who's easy to tease now!" Liisa crowed.

"You're ridiculous," I said, rolling my eyes.

"That's what friends are for." She smiled widely.

I couldn't stop the answering grin. It was freeing to have someone I could be myself with. My friendship with Liisa made me realize what I had been missing back home. After all of the rejection, I had completely closed myself off from friendships, even after enough time had passed and people had likely forgotten.

"Will you tell me what I want to know now?"

"Because you asked so nicely," she said, giving me a stern look before it dissolved into something more dreamy. "After dinner, we were sitting under the stars, and he put his arm around me and asked for a kiss."

"And . . . ?"

"I said no, of course."

"What!" I almost shouted.

"Oh, come now. It was only our first time alone together. I'm going to make him work for it," she replied with a devilish grin.

I laughed, prodding her shoulder. "You are going to drive the poor male insane with longing."

"That is precisely the plan, Ari. But to answer your original question, yes, there is most definitely a spark. I had to use all my willpower to stop myself from jumping into his lap and putting my mouth all over him."

"Liisa!" I gasped, my face blushing.

"Don't be ridiculous. I see the way you stare at Prince Wynn. I bet you would love to be all over that fine specimen of a male, with his rippling muscles and stormy eyes."

My blush intensified, and I glanced around to confirm we were still alone. "Shhh! You can't say things like that about the prince when someone could hear you. Can you imagine what people would say if they thought something was going on between us?"

"You mean anyone with eyes? It's so obvious you and the prince are obsessed with each other. He treats you differently than anyone else he has ever brought back from one of the rescue missions. You live in the palatium, for stars' sake." Her face spoke volumes, the loudest expression being that she was unimpressed by my naivety.

Mortified didn't even come close to describing the embarrassment that flooded through me. Was it that obvious I was attracted to Wynn? Was there even a chance he felt the same way? A ridiculous part of me thought if I admitted to myself how much I wanted something serious with him, I was deciding to stay. I'd rather be in denial than make that choice.

I looked down, avoiding her direct stare. "Sure, we flirt and tease each other all the time, but he's the prince. I don't honestly think there could ever be anything real between us. As much as I would like to give in to our attraction, I believe I deserve more than that. I want to be with someone who loves me, not just someone who lusts after me."

Liisa smiled sadly, nodding in understanding. "I think one of the reasons I want to take it slow with Char is because I *can* take it slow. I'm not being forced to be with him in any kind of time frame, so taking my time is a luxury I'm trying to enjoy."

"That's really great, Liisa. I'm happy for you . . . but I give it a week before you aren't able to hold yourself back from 'putting your mouth all over him,'" I teased, trying to lighten the mood again.

It was her turn to blush, and she rolled her eyes at me as we laughed together and continued stocking the supplies.

⁂

The sunset that evening was spectacular as I walked back toward the palatium—a beautiful display of orange and red fading into a darker shade of violet and blue. Clouds lit up from within, appearing on fire as the sun dipped beneath them. Wanting an unhindered view, I left the street and made my way to an outcropping.

Liisa and I had worked late that day due to an outbreak of illness among the refugees. In between caring for patients, we'd spent most of the day constituting medicine in large quantities, which had been exhausting but also rewarding because it made me feel useful.

As I stood at the edge, in awe of the view, pangs of homesickness crept in. As beautiful as Zephyria was, I longed to dip my feet into the ocean. A few tears rolled unbidden down my cheek.

"It's an incredibly beautiful sunset tonight, isn't it?"

Startling at the voice behind me, I quickly wiped my face and turned.

"Wynn! You've got to stop surprising me like that. What if I had fallen off the edge of this mountain?"

"I would have caught you, of course," he replied. "Would you like me to demonstrate?" He took a step toward me, a mischievous glint in his eyes.

I held up my hands in front of me. "Don't you dare even think about it!"

Wynn stalked closer to me and swept me up into his arms before jumping up and flying to a higher ledge of the mountain.

"Wynn! What in the stars do you think you are doing?" I yelped, my heart pounding with adrenaline.

He set me down facing out, sweeping his hand in front of me. "The view is so much better from up here, isn't it?"

Our bodies were only a hair's breadth apart—the ledge so narrow, I didn't dare take a step away from him. "You know how I feel about flying without being asked, Wynn."

Liar. You enjoy being in his arms.

He put an arm around me, holding me close. "Teasing you is so much fun, though. Don't you trust me? I would never let any harm befall you."

I turned to stare up at him. "I do trust you. You just caught me by surprise."

"I apologize, Arianwen. If it bothers you that much, I won't do it again," he said, eyes full of sincerity.

"A little warning would be nice, but thank you." I turned my gaze back to the view, watching as the sky continued to darken and a few stars started to appear.

"Is everything all right, my star?" Wynn questioned.

"Yes, why do you ask?"

"You looked a little sad when I came upon you . . . I also tease you because I like to cheer you up."

Warmth flooded me at the realization that he cared about how I was feeling, and I smiled at the knowledge that he was starting to read my moods. "I was feeling a little homesick for the ocean . . . I can't help but notice there aren't many Argenti refugees here. It's probably too difficult for them to leave the water behind."

"You're probably right. We do have a lot more Aurum and Aereus refugees here. I'm sorry you're feeling homesick. Is there anything I can do? Maybe we can take a trip to one of our lakes when I return."

"You're leaving again so soon?" I asked, hating my disappointment.

"Yes, I leave at first light tomorrow for Ilithania. I should be back within a fortnight."

"Take me with you!" I blurted as I turned back around to face him.

"I don't know. It's not the safest journey . . ."

"Please, Wynn?" I begged. "It would be amazing to see the Court of Earth, and I know I would be safe with you there, and perhaps we could stop near the coast so I could visit the ocean?" I held my breath, hoping he would let me come against his better judgment.

"I should probably be saying no to you right now," Wynn started, pushing one hand up through his hair, the internal war he was waging evident on his face. He blew out a breath. "You know what? Fine. You can come. I'll need to clear it with my cabala, but we can make it work."

"Really?" My eyes lit up with excitement as I threw my arms around him and squeezed. "Thank you, thank you, thank you!"

"If I had known this was how you'd respond, I would have taken you on a trip sooner," Wynn teased, his arms tightening around me. "I'll take you home so you can get some rest and pack a few things for the trip. May I?" he asked tentatively to which I nodded.

He picked me up again, and I wrapped my arms around his neck as we swiftly flew back to the palatium. His defined jaw was clenched, and I wondered what was on his mind. He peered down and caught me staring, his eyes flicking to my lips. A flood of heat rushed through me, and I tilted my face up toward him, daring him to close the gap. He looked away from me, his eyes on the path ahead, and I fought the sudden disappointment. How could he not want to give in to the attraction between us?

Leaving me at my door, Wynn said goodnight and told me to be ready to leave at sunrise. I grabbed my pack and filled it with a few clothing items and some medical supplies. I wanted to be prepared for anything.

Still exhausted from my day and knowing I needed to rest, I tried to hurry my bath, but my thoughts kept drifting back to how I'd thought Wynn was going to kiss me.

Come on, Ari. Stop thinking about how much you wanted that kiss. You're going to be traveling with him for weeks. If he was going to kiss you, he'd have done so by now. Try to let it go and not make things uncomfortable for the foreseeable future.

As I climbed into my large, comfortable bed, I forced myself to relax. I imagined rest would not come easy while traveling, and I should enjoy every moment of sleep while I could. We wouldn't be able to stop at any inns on our journey.

It had been impulsive of me to ask to go on the trip, but I couldn't quench my curiosity, and the hope of seeing the ocean had been too tempting to ignore. Despite my hesitations and my disappointment at Wynn's lack of action, I was excited about my next adventure.

Chapter 33
The Cabala

Arianwen

Wynn knocked on my door bright and early the next morning. The excitement about our upcoming journey had made it hard for me to sleep, and I had awoken as soon as dawn started to break and the sky began to lighten outside my window.

"Is what I'm wearing appropriate?" I asked Wynn. I had no idea how much we would be traveling by aquila, or if we would be traveling on foot.

Wynn perused me from head to toe, my cheeks flushing as I noticed the approval in his stare. I had chosen form-fitting pants—made of a thick material that was comfortable but also strong enough not to tear easily—and a warm sweater layered over a cotton tunic. My violet scarf was wrapped around my neck, and my hair was braided tightly down my back so that it wouldn't go flying in my face.

"Um, yes . . . that should do just fine," Wynn replied, clearing his throat, his gaze lingering on my legs before he tore his eyes away. "We'll be flying as much as we can, so the layers are a good idea. It'll be warmer down south, so make sure you have something lighter to wear as well."

"Perfect, that's what I thought." I bounced lightly on my heels, full of energy. "I'm so excited that I get to see the Court of Earth! Thanks again for bringing me."

Wynn nodded as he held the door open for me, his eyes crinkling in amusement, and we wasted no time making our way to the aquila aeries. The stillness of the city's empty streets had a certain beauty to it, enriched by the glow of the rising sun reflected off the snowy mountain peaks. With my permission, Wynn picked me up and flew me through the city. I realized that flying in his arms didn't scare me quite like it used to. As we neared the aeries, I glimpsed two soldiers waiting for us with saddled aquilas nearby.

"No other females will be joining us?" I asked Wynn in a soft voice, hoping the other males wouldn't overhear.

"No, my star, you're it. I hope you're not intimidated," he teased.

I punched him lightly in the shoulder. "No, of course not . . . Well, maybe a little."

Wynn chuckled then caught my gaze, his eyes sincere. "They are two of my *most* trusted soldiers and friends. You will be safe with us."

"I trust you," I smiled.

Once we landed in front of the males, he made introductions. "Arianwen, meet Valerik and Helio."

Feeling somewhat shy in the presence of the hulking males, I nodded demurely and waved a quick hello. Valerik, an Adamas male who was taller than Wynn, held his hand out to me in greeting. Emboldened by his friendliness, I shook his hand and smiled at him. "Nice to meet you, Valerik." His white hair was cropped to his head, and his eyes were a steely gray.

Not to be outdone by his fellow soldier, Helio grinned and shoved Valerik aside, grasping my hand in his and squeezing tightly. "How wonderful to have a pretty face to look at on this trip instead of being stuck staring at these ugly males," he said, his voice full of teasing. Helio was a handsome Aereus male, his bronze skin and bright, shoulder-length auburn hair made him stand out among all the grays and whites of the mountains.

"Nice to meet you too, Helio," I replied with a grin. "I personally find the view to be quite satisfactory."

Wynn put his hand on my shoulder, somewhat possessively, and said, "I expect you both to be on your best behavior. Keep all the sordid tales of past rescues to yourselves."

That piqued my interest. "Sordid tales, you say? Oh, please! Don't you dare hold back. I want all the dirt you have on Wynn."

Valerik and Helio chuckled.

"I've known Wynn since we were babes," Valerik said. "I'm sure there are some embarrassing stories to be told. If you fly with me, I would be more than happy to share them."

"Arianwen will fly with me," Wynn replied, a hint of a growl in his tone.

Valerik held his hands up in surrender, a knowing glint in his eyes. "Of course, My Prince. We'll save the stories for camp," he drawled out irreverently.

Helio looked amused at the whole exchange, and I could have sworn I heard him mutter, "*Idiot,*" to Valerik as they went to mount their aquilas.

I was simultaneously annoyed and intrigued by Wynn staking his claim on me to his friends. There had been so many times when he could have said or done something about the attraction that had been building between us, but something had always been holding him back. While the males were both very handsome in their own right, I only had eyes for Wynn. But I would've at least liked to have had a say before he went all feral male on them.

Wynn tucked our packs into the saddle bags and then helped me climb onto Luminara. After he climbed up behind me, I spoke for his ears only. "You could have asked me who I wanted to fly with, you know, instead of instigating a pissing match." He stiffened, but I couldn't stop myself. "Maybe I would have liked a chance to get to know your handsome friends better."

Wynn leaned forward and purred in my ear, "Just say the word and you can join either one of them. I won't stop you. I didn't want you to be uncomfortable, so I assumed you'd want to stay with me."

"Liar," I breathed as he wrapped his arm around me and pulled me closer to him.

Would it be so hard for him to just admit that he wants me too?

Wynn ignored my comment, gave trilling commands to Luminara, and we were off. Luminara led the way, wings outstretched as she dove off the side of the cliff. I couldn't help but hold my breath as the sensation of falling overtook me before we leveled out and coasted on the wind.

Seeing Esterra from above always took my breath away. Being up among the clouds and witnessing the vastness of the landscape below made me feel so small. I almost wanted to pinch myself to make sure I wasn't dreaming. If anyone had asked me weeks before how I viewed our world, it would have been so much smaller. To think that visiting a few villages on my matri-ritus would have been my grandest adventure if I hadn't come upon Wynn . . . The idea was unfathomable.

The Iris wanted our world to remain small and for us to keep to ourselves, all in the name of control. At that moment, my quiet rebellion toward them felt good. Even though they had no idea, I was proud that I was helping in some small way by healing the refugees who were fleeing them, and perhaps I would be of some use during the rescue mission we were on.

⚜

We flew for hours and hours and I grew tired, unused to flying for such a long time. While I knew Wynn wouldn't let me fall, I still didn't feel safe dozing off. Rolling my neck, I tried my best to stretch my limbs while in the cramped position.

"Are you all right, my star?" Wynn's voice rumbled through me.

Twisting, I peered up at him and gave him a quick nod. "Just feeling a little tired. I would kill to be able to stretch my legs properly."

"So vicious," he said with a chuckle. "We can take a break soon. I know of a place."

Wynn signaled to Helio and Valerik, and before too long, the air grew warmer as we descended below the clouds and drew closer to the ground. We landed on some cliffs right on the western coast. We were still north of Iveria, but seeing the ocean below brought me joy. Wynn helped me dismount before heading over to chat with Valerik. As I stood near the edge of the cliff, I found my legs wobbling as I stood for the first time in hours.

"Whoa there, careful now! We'd hate for you to fall off the side of the cliff," Helio teased while steadying me with an arm. "It takes a while to get used to flying for such long stretches on the aquilas."

"How long have you been in Zephyria?" I asked, unable to hold back my curiosity.

"Quite a while now, actually. My family was part of Wynn's first rescue mission. Once he learned the truth about the Iris, he traveled south looking for anyone who might be dissatisfied with their rule, and the rebel network was born."

"That sounds incredibly brave but equally dangerous," I replied.

Wynn huffed a laugh as he walked back over and said, "You should have seen my father's face when I told him my plans. He was furious but also terrified that something would happen to me."

"How in the stars did you make it around Ilithania undetected, Wynn? I'm surprised the Iris didn't capture you on sight," I said.

Helio laughed, slapping Wynn on the shoulder. "He didn't make it undetected, but he's lucky that it was my father who noticed him and not anyone else. My father caught him creeping around in the dark wearing a deep hood and gloves, which already made him stand out considering how warm it is down south. You can imagine his utter shock at finding an Adamas fae in our city."

Wynn grinned widely at his friend and his teasing, and I couldn't help but smile at the lightness and ease that exuded from him. Back in Zephyria, he'd often seemed to carry the weight of the world on his shoulders.

"You lot thought the Adamas were extinct. It's not like I could have walked around with all my ivory skin showing," he replied.

"So, what happened next?" I asked. "Was it hard to find people who were willing to rebel against the Iris? I've never even heard a whisper of rebels at home in Iveria."

"Helio's father hid me in his home, and I eventually told him about my plans to take in refugees who wanted to leave Ilithania. As I'd suspected, there were plenty of Aereus fae who were unhappy with the Iris' rule, and some were willing to leave everything behind for the chance at a better life," Wynn explained. "The rebel network has to be cautious, Arianwen. You'll find more rebels among the poorer sections of the cities, the ones who are most overlooked and ignored by the Iris."

"I wish I had known," I said quietly.

Wynn reached over and gently squeezed my shoulder. "I wish we could save everyone, but there is only so much we can do without drawing too much attention."

I nodded in understanding, filled with admiration for everything they were doing. Despite that, a small part of me was bitter that, if I did return home, I would be unable to inform anyone because of the star-sworn oath I had taken.

"Does everyone in Zephyria know the truth about the Iris? How do the other Adamas feel about all the refugees coming in?" I asked.

Valerik had been quiet during our exchange but finally spoke up. "Only some heads of families and Wynn's trusted cabala know the whole truth of the Iris' origins. Most of the fae in Zephyria are just happy to be out from under Iris rule and are fairly welcoming to the refugees we bring in. They see the Iris as tyrants worth escaping, regardless of where refugees come from."

"But what about Concordia, the settlement the Iris destroyed out of their fear of the prophecy? Do the fae in Zephyria know about that? Or do they still believe the lie that it was the stars? I met Kristel's child. Wouldn't everyone be afraid of the stars' wrath if they didn't know the truth?"

Valerik appeared thoughtful as he pondered my question. "While the truth of Concordia is not known to all, I do think that most fae in Zephyria believe they can't trust everything the Iris tried to ingrain into everyone. The rare fae who have been gifted with mixed-elemental children see them as a blessing from the stars, not a curse. Some may suspect the truth but find it's easier to live in denial."

"This is all still so much for me to take in. My whole worldview has been shattered many times over in the short span I have been here. I am glad though. I can't even fathom going back to my previous ignorance."

Taking a deep breath, I rolled my shoulders back, trying to shake off the heaviness that had come upon me during our conversation. I wanted to move forward and stop dwelling on the things I couldn't change.

"So, how are we getting into the city?" I asked, trying to keep my tone light as I changed the subject. "I'm assuming gloves and deep hooded cloaks are out."

All three males chuckled, and Helio threw an arm around Wynn, a teasing glint in his eyes. "Definitely not one of Wynn's brightest ideas," he ribbed. Wynn shook him off, rolling his eyes.

"We actually have an Iris ally in Ilithania who has been a valuable asset in our rescue missions," Helio continued. "I don't know if you know this, but some of the Iris have glamouring capabilities. Our ally is willing to help glamour Wynn and anyone else, like Rik here, who need help blending in while in the city."

My eyes almost bugged out of my face. "You have *Iris* involved in these rescue missions? How do you know you can trust them?"

"The Iris are more long-lived than us, and while many of the older generation grow increasingly cruel and heartless as the years go by, some of the younger Iris don't agree with their treatment of us," Wynn explained. "We have a few Iris allies in Ilithania and Iveria. We had one in Easthen Forest, but I suspect they were discovered after our last mission became so compromised."

I shuddered at the memory of the horrific wounds I had helped heal after that catastrophe. I still couldn't get over how evil it had been for the Iris to send shadow fangs after children.

"Here's hoping that doesn't happen on this mission," I said.

Helio slapped a hand over his eyes and groaned. "Now you've done it, Ari. You better hope the stars weren't listening."

I scoffed, "Surely you don't believe that a few words would change the outcome of our trip. After everything I've been learning, I don't know if the stars even care about us at all."

Helio appeared somber, not a hint of a smile in sight. "Words have power. Thus far, I believe the stars have been on our side, but they are fickle beings. I wouldn't want to test them."

Helio's words stuck with me, and I couldn't help but wonder how much the stars were involved in our lives. It was easier to trust in the things I could see and control than to believe that higher powers were directing our steps.

We spent the rest of our short break stretching our legs and snacking on food from our packs. After Valerik and Helio began sharing funny stories about some mishaps Wynn had experienced on previous missions, the atmosphere became lighter once again. Sooner than I would have liked, we continued our journey south.

✤

The days of travel passed slowly, but I found my rhythm with Wynn and the two members of his cabala. They told me there were a couple of other fae in their close circle of trust, but Wynn liked to keep the rescue missions smaller to attract less attention. The other members of his cabala also helped lead raids and other missions, and they were currently in the middle of a scouting trip to Easthen Forest. We flew above the clouds during the day, and at night, we made camp wherever we could hide.

The biggest benefit of traveling with various elemental fae was their usefulness. Valerik had lamented on one of the colder nights that he wished Glint was with us to provide warmth with her fire element, but we made do. Helio could build a shelter for us with his earth element while Wynn and Valerik used their element to create a shield of air to block our noise from the rest of the world. I contributed by summoning any water we needed so that we didn't have to scout for it. Being a part of their team and feeling useful filled me with a sense of contentment.

As we sat huddled together on a particularly cold evening, I nudged Wynn's shoulder. "Wynn?"

"Yes, my star?"

"Thank you for bringing me even though I know you didn't want to."

He nudged me back, and I could hear the smile in his voice. "It's been my pleasure. Your company has been quite enjoyable. You've been an invaluable asset with your water-summoning, and it's nice to know that we have a healer on hand in case something goes wrong. Not to mention, you're certainly more appealing than Rik or Helio."

"Hey, I heard that," Rik muttered loud enough for us to hear.

I bit back a giggle, my body shaking with mirth. "I've enjoyed getting to see a different side of you, and I admit, I am somewhat envious of your close friendships."

Wynn's brow furrowed as he caught my gaze and said, "You're a part of us now. There's no need to be envious. You're stuck with us."

"Being with your cabala and meeting Liisa has made me realize that something significant was missing from my life back home. I was so closed off from everyone to protect myself, but I think it caused more harm than good."

Wynn reached down and grabbed one of my hands, giving it a light squeeze. "Opening yourself up to another takes courage . . . and you are braver than you think you are. It's a great honor to be your friend."

My heart surged with warmth and a sense of belonging as Wynn continued holding my hand, his thumb making small circles on it. I laid my head on his shoulder, relaxing into the comforting touch, enjoying the companionship of a friend.

❦

After a week of riding Luminara, I was ready to swear off flying for life. I desperately missed the ocean and traveling underwater. We were only hours away from Ilithania, but Wynn had wanted to arrive after dark to draw less attention to ourselves. He signaled to the others to land.

We stopped high up on the southwestern cliffs. As the others tended to the aquilas, I walked closer to the edge, gazing at the water below with longing. Wynn had kept us on a punishing pace, so we hadn't had a chance to go down to the ocean.

Someone approached from behind, and I immediately knew it was Wynn. His scent and a distinct awareness of him surrounded me.

"Would you like to go for a swim now?" he asked, his breath tickling my ear as he leaned closer to me.

I turned and flung my arms around him. "Stars above, you have no idea how incredible that sounds!"

Wynn grinned down at me, and suddenly I was embarrassed at my brazen display of affection. My face flushed even more as I noticed Helio and Valerik approaching. I dropped my arms, stepping away from him while Wynn cocked his head, confusion at my abrupt movement evident on his face.

After they reached us, Valerik leaned toward me and whispered loudly for everyone to hear, "I wouldn't want to hug him either with the stench of travel all over him."

Helio laughed heartily while Wynn made his irritation clear, his lips pressed firmly together. I cracked a smile, appreciating Valerik's attempt to make things less awkward.

"I think we could all do with a dip in the ocean so the Iris don't smell us from a mile away," I joked.

Everyone agreed. Wynn held onto me and we swiftly descended to the beach below. Valerik flew solo, and I was curious how Helio was going to make his way down. I gasped as Helio summoned a pillar of earth, stepped onto it, and lowered himself down the side of the cliff as the pillar shrunk back toward the ground.

Wynn chuckled in my ear and said, "I'm pretty sure my face wore that same look when I first saw an Aereus fae manipulate the earth. It's incredible."

We landed in the sand, and I started stripping off the top layers of my clothing, eager to jump into the ocean as quickly as possible. When I was down to my undergarments, I ran and dove right in, the water welcoming me home for the first time in weeks.

When I surfaced and glanced back toward the beach, I noticed Valerik and Helio looking anywhere but at me, a slight flush in their cheeks. Wynn's body was rigid, his hands clenched into fists, but I laughed, calling out, "What? Have you never seen a female in her undergarments before?"

Valerik was biting his cheek, trying to hold back a smile. "Arianwen, do us a favor and give us some warning next time you decide to start taking off your clothes please? I think Wynn is about to gouge our eyes out, and I like them where they are."

Helio started laughing but quickly stopped when Wynn glared at him. I dove back under the water, laughing at the whole situation. Argenti fae often wore very light clothing because we were in and out of the water so much. Our sense of modesty was obviously very different from other elementals'.

I swam deeper into the ocean, delighted to see various plants and sea life that differed from those back home. A pod of dolphins were swimming together, and I watched as they played and jumped in and out of the water. I called out to one of them and she soon joined me, allowing me to grasp onto her fins and race through the water at high speeds. A smile split my face as the dolphin and I leaped out of the water and I breathed in the salty air, the soaring cliffs blurring past. My body thrummed as the power of my element surrounded and filled me.

Looking back toward the shore, I watched as Wynn and his friends messed around in the shallow water, dunking each other and splashing like children. I smiled at the sight and found myself admiring their strong warrior bodies and the way the water glistened on their defined arms and chests.

The dolphin I had been swimming with brought me closer to the group of males, and I thanked her before wading into the shallower water.

"Anyone want a ride?" I called out.

Wynn whipped his head toward me in surprise before realizing I was referencing the dolphin.

Valerik shook his head. "I much prefer the skies, Arianwen."

"You have no idea what you're missing!" I teased.

Helio laughed and said, "Maybe I'll take you up on that offer another time, but we should probably head back to shore so we can make it to Ilithania at nightfall. Flying is too conspicuous, so we are going to journey the rest of the way by foot."

As I waded closer to the group, Wynn's eyes darkened as he took me in, looking me up and down appreciatively. I blushed at his attention. I loved the power that came with feeling beautiful and attractive, and I added an extra sway to my hips as I walked past him back onto the beach.

Before I could will the water to leave, I shivered as a current of air swirled around me, drying my undergarments and hair so that I could get dressed again. I peeked over my shoulder and caught Wynn looking at me with hunger in his eyes and a hint of a smile on his lips. Another shiver of awareness swept through me as he walked past me toward his belongings.

I wanted to say something, to ask him about all the subtle and not-so-subtle looks he'd been giving me and the way he had pulled me closer to him every time we rode on Luminara. It was as if our bodies were screaming our attraction at a deafening level, but our stubbornness kept us apart. The real question was, who would break first?

Chapter 34

Ilithania

Arianwen

The sky was lit up in crimson and violet hues as we made our final descent down the mountains and into Ilithania. The vast city on the southern tip of Esterra was made of towering buildings that ran from the coast deep into the surrounding jungle. The earth-wielding Aereus were known for their incredible architectural skills, and I stood in awe of their artistry, which was evident even from a distance.

Helio left us waiting in a small copse of trees as he went to meet the Iris who would glamour us for our trip into the city. I found myself nervously pacing, twisting my hands together in front of me. For the most part, I'd tried to avoid any interaction with the Iris in Iveria, as they made me so uncomfortable.

Wynn pulled me aside. "Having second thoughts about being here?"

"No, not really," I replied, biting on my lip. "I'm just nervous about putting my trust in an Iris, ally or not."

"We've been working with Kalev for a while now. I am confident he won't betray us," Wynn said, trying to reassure me.

I nodded in response, my arms wrapped around myself.

Wynn came closer and tilted my chin up so that I would meet his gaze. "Arianwen, I will make sure you are safe. You have my word."

My jaw clenched, and I tried to smile. "I know. I trust you."

Wynn smiled at me and looked like he was going to say something more when the sound of Helio's whistle signaling his return stopped him.

Standing in front of me protectively, Wynn turned to wait for Helio and Kalev to arrive. I could see some of the tension melt from his shoulders when he saw that no surprises had appeared with their arrival.

I peeked around Wynn to scrutinize the Iris male. He was wearing a guard's uniform and was a few inches taller than Helio, which made him tower over me. His skin was a beautiful rose color with artistic swirls of gold marking his face, neck, and arms. His golden eyes gleamed despite the dim light. He was beautiful to look at, but his beauty exuded danger and I was still wary of him, perhaps even more so because of it.

"I can't stay long, so let's get this over with," Kalev said, walking over to Valerik.

My eyes widened as Valerik's glamour took effect and his skin changed from a cool, opalescent ivory to a warm, bronze tone. His cropped hair changed from white to copper, but his eyes remained the same.

Kalev walked over to Wynn and me and worked his magic on the both of us. Looking down at my arms and seeing the bronze color was startling.

"How long will the glamour hold?" I asked.

"It will last for about an hour, which should be plenty of time for you to get to the safe house. I wouldn't make any extended stops, though. I won't be traveling with you, so I can't maintain the glamour," Kalev explained. "I really do need to go. May the stars be with you."

He disappeared down the path and I breathed a sigh of relief.

Knowing we couldn't waste time, Helio led us into the city using mostly unpatrolled paths. I tried to keep my head down to not attract too much attention, but it was hard not to gape at the tall buildings decorated with vibrant flowers and the colorful fabrics draped in windows and over entrances.

Despite the glamour, I found myself fidgeting with nervous energy. My fear of being discovered dampened the excitement of experiencing a brand new city.

"Are you doing all right, my star?" Wynn asked, leaning in toward me. "Your hands are shaking."

I chuckled, twisting my hands together in front of me. "I'm sorry, I'm just so anxious that we might get caught."

Wynn stopped, grabbing my hands in his. "Try to take a deep breath and act natural. We don't want to attract the wrong attention, and right now, you're sending out signals that we don't belong."

Inhaling a deep breath, I closed my eyes, allowing myself to focus on the calming strength of Wynn's hands around mine. "Thank you . . . I'll be fine. Just give me a minute."

As we continued to walk through the city, we passed an Iris patrol. My whole body stiffened, but they didn't even give us a brief glance and I found myself finally starting to unwind. The glamours were holding. My fears were for nothing.

We passed a market square where all the vendors were busy putting away their goods. A few Aereus fae flitted around the market making last-minute purchases, but the majority of shoppers had left for the day. My stomach rumbled as the aroma of spiced meat filled my nose. The food we had eaten while traveling had left much to be desired, but considering Ilithania was where coffee came from, I was betting the food was incredible. Since my nerves had calmed down, I realized just how hungry I was after our long day of travel.

"Your stomach is rumbling loud enough to wake a bear," Wynn teased.

"I am a bit hungry . . ." I said sheepishly. "We probably don't have time to stop though."

"Helio, do you think you could find us something to eat? I bet Arianwen would love to try an Aereus specialty," Wynn said, a smile in his voice.

Grateful for his thoughtfulness, I looked up and smiled back.

"I'm sure I can scrounge up something around here," Helio replied before he headed off deeper into the market.

Wynn motioned for Valerik and me to follow him, and we turned down a dark alley to wait for Helio to return. Although our disguises were holding up, we still didn't want to draw too much attention to our group.

"Won't this look more suspicious? A group of Aereus hiding in an alley?" I questioned. "I still can't get over how different you . . . I mean we . . . look."

Wynn reached over and tugged on one of the copper curls framing my face. "Yes, this definitely takes some getting used to . . . but to answer your question, we're fine back here. I just don't want to take any unnecessary risks."

Valerik shifted around, unable to stay still. "Helio better get his arse back here soon. I hate not knowing the exact amount of time this glamour will hold. It's making me nervous."

Relating to his discomfort, I gritted my teeth. I silently cursed my grumbling stomach for drawing attention to itself, as I wouldn't feel completely at ease until we made it to the safe house undetected.

I nudged Valerik with my elbow. "You didn't strike me as a worrier, Rik," I teased, using the nickname I had heard Wynn and Helio calling him. "Where's your sense of adventure?"

A huge grin broke out on Valerik's face. "Wynn, I think she's finally warming up to us!"

"Don't get ahead of yourself," I said, feigning annoyance. "I still haven't decided whether I like you."

"If you can put up with Wynn, you can put up with the rest of the cabala," Valerik joked. "Wynn is the most annoying of the bunch."

Wynn rolled his eyes, crossing his arms while leaning against the building. "Don't listen to Rik, Arianwen. He's just jealous that he hasn't spent a week flying with a beautiful female."

"Well, we could always make that happen," I said, trying to get a rise out of Wynn.

His eyes glared daggers at me, but he shrugged and replied, "If you wish to switch things up, it's your call."

Infuriating male.

Before I could respond, Helio joined us with some delicious-smelling food in hand.

"We don't have time to sit and eat, but this food is perfect for on the go," he explained, handing out pocket-shaped flatbreads stuffed full of savory meat and vegetables.

"Stars above, this is incredible," I moaned, as I began devouring mine.

Wynn laughed as we started following Helio down the alleyway toward our destination and said, "Your reaction does not surprise me in the least."

I elbowed him as I walked past him. "Hush, Wynn. Don't ruin this for me."

"I wouldn't dream of it, my star."

We arrived at the safe house which was located in an impoverished section of Ilithania. The buildings were still in decent condition, but everything seemed old and worn down. Helio knocked on the door and a young Aereus female let us in, leading us down to a basement meeting room.

"Thank you, Ene," Helio said to the young girl, and she blushed before rushing out of the room.

An elderly Aereus couple entered, and greetings and introductions were made all around. Enixus and Indre spent time filling Wynn in on the state of things in the city, and we found out we were going to be transporting a family of four back to Zephyria.

Wynn had explained to me that the groups needed to remain small so that the Iris would be less likely to notice the missing people, as well as the fact that a larger group traveling north would be much easier to spot. We had arrived a day earlier than they'd expected, so we would need to lie low and leave the following evening.

I had to admit, I was grateful we could take a whole day off from traveling, and I was looking forward to sleeping under an actual roof and, stars willing, in a bed. The exhaustion from our travels started sinking in, and I found myself nodding off in my chair.

Startling awake at a soft touch on my shoulder, I blinked my eyes open to see an unglamoured Wynn giving me a concerned look. I glanced down at my arms and breathed a sigh of relief that they were back to normal. After an hour had passed and the glamour had held up, a tiny part of me had worried about it never wearing off, which seemed ridiculous once I considered it now.

"Indre, are rooms available for us?" Wynn asked. "I think we are ready for some rest."

Indre bit her lip. "My apologies, Prince Wynn, we only have two rooms available tonight. Will that be a problem?"

Wynn shook his head and replied, "Please don't worry, it's no problem. We will figure it out."

Indre looked apologetic but said goodnight, and I followed Wynn and the others down the hall.

"Are all the rooms here below ground?" I asked, anxiety creeping in.

"Why? Does it make you uncomfortable?" Helio asked. "Don't many Argenti live underwater?"

"Being underwater and underground isn't even close to the same thing," I retorted, trying not to roll my eyes at him.

Helio shrugged. "I guess it doesn't bother me as it makes me feel closer to my element."

No kidding.

I glanced over at Wynn and Valerik and said, "I'm surprised you two aren't struggling, considering you love the open air."

"Rik and I are used to it now, but I can't say we didn't hate it the first few times we had to stay here," Wynn replied. "We usually like to pick up the refugees and leave immediately so that we lessen our time here."

I shivered, trying not to let the claustrophobic sensation overwhelm me as we walked down the hallway. Wynn stopped in front of one door and gestured for Rik and Helio to take it before he opened the door across the way and ushered me in.

The room was small but quaint. There were no windows because we were below ground, but I tried to ignore that fact. As I perused the room, I realized there was only one bed, and Wynn had followed me in, closing the door behind us.

Looking at me apologetically, he said, "The rooms are quite small, and I didn't think you'd want to bunk with Helio or Rik. I can go sleep on their floor if you are uncomfortable, but, to be honest, I don't feel completely safe leaving you on your own."

"Oh?" I asked, trying to swallow back the sudden nerves that had overtaken me. "What could happen?"

"The Iris know there are rebels in Ilithania and conduct surprise raids on people's homes, looking for something to incriminate them. We should be all right, but if anything were to happen, I wouldn't be able to forgive myself."

I hugged my arms around myself, the reality of the danger we were in hitting me. I had almost forgotten the fear I'd experienced when we'd nearly been caught by the Iris scouts weeks before. Being around Wynn and his cabala had made me feel safe enough that I'd brushed off the risk.

"I think I would feel more comfortable if you stayed," I said quietly.

"Don't worry, Rik and Helio won't spread any rumors about us, if that concerns you."

"Believe it or not, I trust them," I said.

Wynn smiled at me, brushing a stray hair back behind my ear. "I'm glad to hear it." He cleared his throat and continued, "There's a washroom two doors down if you'd like to freshen up before bed."

Hurrying to the small washroom, I was eager to use the basin of clean water to wash off some of the dirt and sweat after our walk in the intense humidity of the Court of Earth. I longed for a full bath, but that would have to wait. After seeing to my needs, I returned to the room and found Wynn sitting shirtless on the edge of the bed, wearing low-slung, gray pants that showed off his taut stomach and tapered waist. His opalescent skin glistened in the dim light, highlighting each groove between the muscles on his abdomen. Looking away to hide my blush, I hurried over to my pack to grab something to sleep in. It struck me as funny that I'd had no qualms about walking around in my undergarments at the beach, but the thought of sharing a room with him completely clothed felt intimate. I had seen plenty of shirtless males, but something about Wynn's bare chest and chiseled abdomen stoked a fire underneath my skin.

Wynn cleared his throat behind me and spoke. "I'm going to clean up. I'll be right back."

I acknowledged him with a nod and watched as he left, my throat suddenly dry. Taking advantage of his absence, I stripped off my traveling clothes and put on the lightweight sleeping gown I'd brought with me. It was made of soft cotton and was a beautiful aqua color. I slipped under the covers and waited for Wynn to return, anxious but also a tiny bit excited that we were going to be alone after being surrounded by his friends for a week.

Wynn came back from the washroom and grabbed a pillow from the bed.

"What are you doing?" I sat up, my eyebrows raised.

"I'm just getting a pillow so I can sleep on the floor. You don't need it, do you?"

"Don't be ridiculous," I scoffed. "There is plenty of room in the bed, and I would feel horrible making a prince sleep on the floor. It's not like we haven't slept next to each other before . . ." I trailed off, thinking of that night in the cave when he'd pulled me up against him.

Wynn rolled his eyes. "Being a prince means nothing when it comes to you and me. You should know that by now."

"I know," I said, my voice going soft as I fought back the niggling hope that it could actually be true.

Isn't his being a prince the most reasonable explanation for why nothing has happened between us?

"Are you sure it's all right?" Wynn asked, his brows furrowed as he approached the bed, pillow in hand. "I just don't want you to feel uncomfortable."

"I'm sure," I said emphatically. "You didn't seem too worried about comfort and proximity when we were in that cave . . ."

Wynn's lips curled into a teasing smile. "Well, I didn't know you then. You were just some beautiful, intriguing female. I had no idea you would stick around."

"You thought I was beautiful?" I batted my eyelashes, my voice saccharine.

Wynn replaced the pillow and climbed into bed next to me. His sapphire eyes gleamed as they perused my face. "Beautiful?" he purred. "I'd say stunning is a more accurate description. Not even the stars shine as brightly as you."

Every word was a caress. I could sense him everywhere even though our bodies were not near enough to touch.

Why am I so nervous? This is what I wanted . . . right?

"We should get some rest," I stammered.

Wynn nodded in agreement and reached over to extinguish the light before he lay back on his pillow. "Good night, my star."

"Good night," I whispered as I slid back under the covers, turning away from him.

In the pitch-black darkness of the room, my entire body grew tense. How in the stars was I supposed to fall asleep? The walls were closing in around me, and my breathing became rapid and uneven. We were below ground and I had no idea what the fastest way to escape would be. I squeezed my eyes shut, trying to slow my breaths and calm my body down, but my brain wouldn't shut up.

"Arianwen, are you all right?" His voice was a lifeline in the dark.

"I'm feeling claustrophobic, Wynn. The thought of being buried underground is getting to me. I don't know if I can sleep."

"Would it be all right if I touched you?" he asked, his voice soft.

I nodded before realizing it was dark and he probably hadn't seen it with my back toward him. "That's fine."

The sheets rustled, followed by a gentle touch on my shoulder. Wynn trailed his fingers up and down my bare arm, and I tried to relax into it. The fear and anxiety slowly melted away under his soothing touch, and a gentle wind caressed my skin alongside the smooth strokes of his fingers. The air smelled of sage and pine, reminding me of being up in the sky surrounded by his scent.

"Thank you," I whispered. "That really helps."

The bed shifted as Wynn moved closer to me, his breath on the back of my neck sending different chills down my spine. "Just try to relax, my star. I won't let anything happen to you."

The caress of Wynn's element reminded me of a breeze coming off the ocean, and the soft touch of his fingers lulled me to sleep.

※

Strong arms surrounded me, and I felt the soft rumblings of a groan as Wynn nuzzled his face into my neck and hair, his breath tickling my sensitive ear.

"Why do you smell so stars-damned good, Ari?" he murmured as he nipped slightly at my ear, sending shivers down my spine. His fingers started to trace patterns on my stomach through my flimsy nightgown, and all I could think was that I wished there was nothing between us. Heat rushed through me as his hand trailed lower, making me feel like I was on fire. I arched back into him, the feeling of his arousal unmistakable as he groaned again. Reaching up with my hand, I dug my fingers into his hair and pulled him closer while he pressed kisses onto my neck. "What am I going to do with you? I'm beginning to think *I* might have to beg *you* for that kiss."

"Wynn . . ." I sighed as I slowly turned onto my back so I could face him. His eyes glinted in the dark, and I could see the hint of a smirk on his face.

"Would you like me to stop?" he purred as his hand continued the torturously slow exploration of my body. My nightgown had shifted during sleep and had ridden up high enough that most of my thighs were showing. His hand reached my bare skin, and I held my breath as the sensation sent more heat flooding through me.

"No, don't stop," I whimpered as he dragged his hand back up toward my waist, his fingers teasing me as they dipped underneath my bunched nightgown and met the soft skin of my stomach. I bit my lip and arched up into his touch, unable to hold back a quiet moan, fisting my hands in the sheets as he gently cupped and squeezed one of my breasts. The soft touches were driving me wild, and I wanted more, so much more. I needed to touch him too. If he kept teasing me, I'd be begging him to kiss me in no time.

A sudden boldness overtook me, and with a surge of strength, I sat up and pushed him onto his back, then climbed on top of him.

"My turn to explore," I said, a wicked smile on my face as I ran my hands over the swells and dips of his muscular chest.

Wynn chuckled, his eyes dark with lust. "I like where this is headed . . . Do your worst, my star."

I dipped down and licked a trail up and over the ripped plane of his abdomen, up his chest, all the way to his neck. I closed my mouth, gently sucking, feeling pleased with myself as Wynn's body tensed and he groaned, his hands gripping my thighs as I straddled his waist. I kissed my way up his neck before pulling the lobe of his ear into my mouth and gently biting down while my hands gripped his biceps.

"Ari," he growled.

Pushing up, I met his gaze. "Yes, Wynn . . . ?" My tongue flicked out, wetting my lips, and his eyes immediately darted toward them. I wanted him to claim my mouth and finally kiss me, but I wasn't going to make the first move. When he didn't say anything, I resumed my careful exploration of his chest and started kissing my way back down his body.

Wynn suddenly snapped, flipping me onto my back, his hard body pressing into mine as his lips met my neck and he kissed his way up my throat, stopping when he reached the corner of my mouth. He rolled his hips into me and I whimpered.

"Just say it and I'm yours," he panted.

"Wynn . . ." I groaned, my body trembling beneath him. "I want you to—"

I opened my eyes and sat up suddenly, my heart thundering in my chest. I turned and looked at the indentation his head had made on the pillow next to mine. He was gone. Grabbing my pillow, I shoved my face into it and cursed loudly.

It had all been a dream. A wondrous, torturous dream that had felt so incredibly real and only made me want him more.

A small part of me mourned the fact that I hadn't woken with my body entwined with his like that first night we had met.

What would it be like to spend every night next to him?

Are his lips as soft as I imagine?

Groaning and irritated by my train of thought and my too-realistic dream, I got out of bed. I needed a distraction, and finding breakfast sounded like the perfect one.

※

I was dying for some fresh air, but Wynn informed us over breakfast that increased Iris activity had been reported around the city. There were more patrols than usual and he didn't want to risk any of us being caught.

Every time I looked at Wynn, flashes of memory from my dream brought a slight flush to my cheeks. It had felt so real, I had to keep reminding myself that it hadn't actually happened. I hadn't tasted his skin. His fingers hadn't mapped the dips and curves of my body . . .

"Ari, are you all right?" Wynn asked, his brow furrowed.

Unable to meet his gaze and hoping no one could scent my sudden arousal, I nodded while shoveling more food into my mouth. Helio started discussing the best routes out of the city, and I was grateful the attention had been drawn away from me for the moment.

After breakfast, Indre brought me some books to read as a distraction, and I thanked her profusely for her thoughtfulness. I wasn't sure I could have acted naturally around Wynn with how my thoughts kept drifting back to him wearing those low-slung, gray pants and nothing else.

The day had dragged by, but dusk was finally upon us. Kalev had just come by the safe house to reapply our glamours. The Aereus family who would be traveling with us had arrived earlier, and we'd already discussed our exit plan. There was a meeting point outside the city where another rebel would be waiting with horses to take us part of the way.

The tricky part was leaving the city, as a group of people could draw too much attention. We decided to split up into four groups, and Wynn paired me up with Helio as Helio knew the city best and would know where to go if something went awry.

Nervous anticipation filled me as Helio and I left the safe house. We tried to keep our gait casual, but the anxiety coursing through me made me rush my steps. A prickle of unease trickled down my spine as we wove through the streets, as if in warning that something terrible was about to happen.

Trying to distract myself, I asked Helio questions, keeping my voice low enough not to be overheard.

"Is there anyone here who would recognize you from before you left?"

"That was quite a few years ago, so I doubt it. My immediate family left with me, and any old friends have likely moved on with their lives."

"Isn't it hard to be away from your home? Ilithania is so different from Zephyria, so much warmer and more colorful. How did you manage to adjust?"

"I can't say it was easy, but being out from under Iris rule makes it worth it. My family had very little here and were struggling to provide for all of our needs. I would have ended up in Prisma if Wynn hadn't come along. I'd have much rather left my home than to be married off to or have to work for one of their noble arses."

"I'm grateful my name wasn't chosen, but an arranged marriage isn't that great either."

"I can imagine."

We continued walking in silence, my mind drifting to the risks Wynn was constantly taking for others and how much I admired him for it.

"Arianwen, this might be too forward, but what are your intentions?"

"What do you mean?"

"Are you planning on staying in Zephyria? Wynn seems to have grown quite attached to you."

I blushed while staring at the ground. "He's grown on me too . . . but I don't know yet. My duty is telling me I need to return home, but my heart . . ." I took a deep breath—trying to think about what I was actually willing to reveal to one of Wynn's closest friends—when we turned a corner and ran into an Iris patrol.

"Whoa! Halt there!" an Iris soldier commanded. "What do you elemental imbeciles think you're doing wandering around this time of evening? You're breaking curfew!"

Chapter 35
Nameless

Aella

Late at night, I paced on the balcony outside my rooms. I needed to find a way to fully harness my magical capabilities. I figured I should start small with my air gift as I had when I'd first begun learning my water gift. It wouldn't be easy without anyone to train me, though.

How do I command it?

Water had become easy to summon and manipulate after many years of practice. It was as natural as moving my fingers. Like an extension of my body, my water power was there.

My hidden power felt different, more intrinsic in a way, not as physical of a sensation. I'd also spent most of my life suppressing that part of me, so the idea of working with it came with a feeling of wrongness.

First, I tried to summon a breeze. I took a deep breath, centering myself, imagining it. I called to it, focusing on drawing it to me with my source, but nothing happened. Perhaps I was foolish to think the wind would respond so willingly after so many years shunning it. I didn't blame it for holding a grudge.

Mighty wind, I honor you, respecting all you freely give.

I waved my hands rhythmically through the air as though to entice it to join into a dance with me, but still nothing happened. I sighed. It probably saw right through my pathetic attempt at flattery.

Okay, maybe a breeze is too ambitious.

I tried to make a single leaf flutter, but still nothing happened. Frustrated, I decided to try warming up with my water element, hoping it would allow me to relax a little. I summoned a globe of water and practiced rolling it along my body in smooth, precise movements, allowing it to glide silkily across my skin. It helped to steady my mind, allowing me to come up with some other strategies.

After some time, I decided I was ready to give it another go. In the past when I'd managed to control the wind, it seemed to just show up on its own in response to some greater need, and I wasn't even sure if I had been the one controlling it. Other times, it had seemed to appear when I experienced strong emotions—as though controlled not by my mind but by a deeper, subconscious part of me. I figured it would be easier to try the emotion route since I wasn't sure jumping off the balcony would quite count as a life or death scenario.

Fickle wind.

The first emotion that came to mind was anger. I had plenty of it, so it wouldn't be hard to trigger. I started thinking about Himmel and how she'd punished the girls when she'd perceived them stepping out of line. I thought of Gaelor, how he'd put his hands all over me. I thought of all those wicked Iris in the stands cheering and applauding as the shadow fangs took down Ulli.

Soon, I was breathing heavily, the anger simmering in my chest like a cauldron bubbling over. My whole body energized with a need to act, a need for revenge. A tornado of emotions flooded my head and made it difficult to remember why I had been so determined to control my power in the first place.

I was ready to destroy Prisma, crumble it to the ground. My emotions were so fierce, I thought I might even have the strength to do it.

"Aella," came an alarmed voice from behind me.

I turned to find Viera standing at the cracked door, her eyes wide. Clouds rolled in, blotting out the stars, and a tempestuous wind began to howl against the walls of the Palatium Crystalis. My hair and gown whipped around me, but I was unphased by it, electrified, even.

My smile was as wicked as the thoughts of vengeance and destruction swirling through my head.

"Are you doing this?" she asked with a wave of her hand.

"Yes, isn't it wonderful?" I asked. "My whole life, I've been afraid of it. But look at me. I am a force to be reckoned with."

"This is reckless, Aella! This isn't you. You're letting your magic control you."

"So what? I'm tired of hiding. Tired of doing nothing. If this is what it takes, so be it."

"It was you in the arena, wasn't it?"

I looked away.

"With the lightning . . . You shot down—"

"Don't say it," I cut her off.

Viera shook her head.

I didn't want to talk about it. I didn't want to think about what I had done. I'd tried to justify it.

"We were competing," I said with gritted teeth. "She struck you down!"

Viera remained silent.

"I was defending you," I argued. "I was . . ."

It was *out of my control.*

"This is all *their* fault!" I pointed at the palatium. "*They* put us in that situation. *They* killed her! Not me! Not my powers."

But deep down, I knew it was still my fault.

I had let my power slip.

I was responsible for her death.

I dropped down onto my knees. The wind slowed down, and the clouds became so heavy that they poured down on me, drenching me in what felt like tears.

"You're right. I did it. I killed Elutha. It's my fault," I said, my voice cracking. "I'm sorry. I'm so, so very sorry. I killed her. She's dead because of me." I stared at my hands as though they were to blame.

Viera came to my side and hugged me. "You are going to learn control, Aella. You have to."

△

Viera and I dried off and climbed into her bed together, bundling ourselves up in her blanket as if it had the power to make us feel whole again. We lay in silence for some time as we both processed what I had almost done.

"Enneli and Zaita were with the king." Viera broke the silence. "I didn't recognize them at first because they'd been painted with glittering, marbled designs like the dancers we've seen. They were personal servants to the king—feeding him and watering him with wine, rubbing his feet and such. When I tried to speak with them, they acted as if they didn't know me. When I said their names, they looked confused."

"I don't understand."

"I think he took their names," Viera said in a hushed tone, eyeing the servants' door.

I gasped in horror. I'd only ever heard about it in fables. The kinds of stories of monsters and legends told to children at bedtime.

"Do you remember the fable of the nameless key?" Viera asked.

I recalled the story I'd heard so many times before.

Long ago, in a faraway kingdom, there was a powerful fae warrior who fell in love with the daughter of a noble and longed to marry her. He came without pedigree, the son of a farmer, all his wealth earned through his service to the kingdom.

After being rejected for his lack of good breeding, he used all of his source power to craft the Nameless Key, an enchanted artifact with the power to erase his own identity. He believed that if he erased his name, he would be given another chance to prove himself to the family of his lover and would be permitted to take her hand in marriage.

At last, the warrior used the key to steal his own name and start over as a new man, but it came at a great cost. It turned out that whoever held the key would lose not only their name but also their identity, memories, and all connection to others.

The warrior became nameless, not even remembering the female he once loved. Alone and forgotten, his magic drained from the creation of the key, he spent the rest of his days forever wandering the lands, searching for what he had lost.

That was just a parable used to teach children the importance of preserving one's name and individuality. Could it have possibly held any truth?

If the mythical object were real and someone had discovered how to wield it, it would be very useful for keeping people in servitude. It would explain why word had never traveled back to our cities about the events and debauchery that went on in the capital. It would explain why the people who lived and worked in Prisma never fought back. If they couldn't remember who they'd been before, why would they have had any reason to?

It all suddenly made perfect sense: why our servants would never tell us their names, why it upset them when we asked questions about their lives before Prisma.

"Do you think that is the fate of those the prince releases from the Matri-Ludus? To become nameless servants?" I asked.

"I don't know, but it's a possibility."

"If it happened to Enneli and Zaita, how can we keep it from happening to you?"

"So far, I've been managing to keep the king intrigued, and I think he's interested enough in my charms to not want to turn me into a blank canvas. At least not yet."

"Have you seen such an item in the king's quarters?"

"No, but I'm sure if they possessed it, it would probably be locked away somewhere secure."

"Of course."

It was disheartening to think about all of the fae working in the palatium who could not remember who they were. To think of their families back home missing them. But in reality, they didn't even remember they had a family.

Was that what Gaelor had meant when he called Kaleidos' mother a shell? My mind went to the book in Kaleidos' library about the seaside lands with all the notes in the margins. Had she been nameless too? Had she been trying to remember?

Viera had been walking a thin line every time she'd gone to see the king. One misstep, and she could end up like the others. The thought made me curl up around her, holding her tight, as if that might be enough to keep her safe.

Chapter 36
Escape

Arianwen

Curfew? Faex. How did the rebels miss that crucial information? Did Kalev betray us? Did Enixus and Indre betray us?

I lowered my head, trying to hide the nerves that were firing through every cell of my body.

"You have our sincerest apologies, sirs," Helio said, bowing his head. "We just arrived yesterday from one of the outer villages and had not heard. We will head inside at once."

Keeping my eyes trained on the ground, I sent silent prayers to the stars, willing the Iris to let us go and not ask any further questions.

"What did you say your names were?" the Iris guard asked, pulling out a logbook to write them down.

"It truly was an honest mistake, sir," Helio countered. "We'll be on our way. No need to file paperwork. I'm sure that would just be extra work for you. I promise we won't be out late again."

The other Iris guard tilted his head, examining me with an odd expression. Glancing down at my hands, I noticed they were changing back to their usual silver. The glamour was failing.

Helio was still trying to sweet-talk his way out of being written up when the guard interrupted. "Stop talking. Down on the ground! Now!"

I raised fearful eyes toward Helio as he quieted and we lowered ourselves. He shook his head slightly, a signal not to say anything. My hair fell over my shoulder as I leaned forward, the onyx strands sealing my fate. In the dim city lights, my skin might not have been as noticeable, but the black hair was a dead giveaway.

The guards were quietly muttering, and I saw gestures in my direction, the words "Argenti" and "rebels" clearly on their lips. There was no talking ourselves out of it. We had to run.

Helio whispered, "Get ready." Before I could respond, he summoned his element and a wall of earth burst through the ground, separating us from the guards. He grabbed my arm, hauling me to my feet. "Run!"

We sprinted through the streets, the shouts of the guards following us as they broke through the barrier Helio had erected. Adrenaline pumped through my veins and fear unlike anything I'd ever felt threatened to lock my legs in place, but we didn't stop—we couldn't stop.

Flaming firebolts shot past me and the ground became uneven as the Iris guards used their elemental powers to slow us down. Helio cried out in pain and stumbled to the ground. I turned back, my eyes wide in horror as he ripped a scalding firebolt out of his calf, hissing as he burned his hand. The Iris guards continued toward us, their eyes gleaming with malice. Wincing as Helio's unimaginable pain swept through me, I knelt beside him and used my scarf to tie off his wound, trying to numb it with my power.

"Ari, look out!"

I spun around a moment too late as one of the Iris guards clamped a giant hand around my bicep and pulled me up, his other arm pulling me into his chest in a firm hold as I struggled to get away. Helio's eyes widened, and I felt the pointed tip of a dagger at my throat. My body stiffened in fear as I froze.

Helio rose slowly to his feet, favoring his uninjured leg. His eyes darted around, assessing and hopefully planning an escape.

"Stay where you are, unless you want your pretty little Argenti whore bleeding out on the street," the guard holding me sneered while the other guard approached.

Raising his hands in surrender, Helio said, "Now, now, let's not be too hasty. You've got us. We're not going anywhere."

What in the deep is he planning? We can't just go with them!

Panic flooded my body and my heart started racing faster and faster. Helio's eyes darted to the ground in front of me so quickly, I almost missed it. He raised his hand into the signal that meant "hold position" which I recognized from our week of flying.

"Hands behind your back, rebel," the Iris guard closest to Helio commanded as he continued his approach, holding iron shackles in one hand.

Faex. If Helio's powers are dampened, we won't stand a chance. There's got to be something I can do. I mentally berated myself. *I should have asked Wynn for lessons on wielding my element offensively.*

"What's a pretty thing like you doing so far from home?" the Iris guard behind me whispered into my ear. "It's been a while since my last rotation in Iveria, maybe we can make a little stop on the way back to the guard station."

"I'd rather be buried alive than let you anywhere near me," I spat, trying to mask my fear with anger.

The Iris guard chuckled cruelly. "I never said you had a choice."

He started dragging me backward and I stared at Helio in desperation, hoping for a way out. I didn't scream because I knew no one who might have heard me would put their life at risk. I didn't scream because I didn't want to give the Iris guard the satisfaction of my fear.

I watched as the other guard wrenched one of Helio's arms behind his back, but before he could lock the first half of the shackle in place, Helio roared, "Drop!"

The ground beneath me started to soften and ripple as Helio sent shockwaves in our direction. Making my body into a deadweight, I lifted my arms and dropped toward the ground, trying to slide out of the Iris guard's grasp. The guard's dagger sliced through my arm and I cried out, but the uneven ground had destabilized him enough that he lost his grip on me. I kicked out behind me, catching him in the knee, and heard a sickening pop. The guard groaned as he lost his balance, his useless leg collapsing underneath him.

The dagger hit the ground and I grabbed it, spinning around to face the Iris guard who had planned to assault me.

He leered up at me, unafraid despite the visible pain he was in. "Oh, look, she bites. This should be good."

Without stopping to think, I lunged forward, stabbing the dagger into his femoral artery, right near his groin. The Iris guard howled and reached for the dagger.

"I wouldn't pull that out if I were you. You'll bleed out in seconds."

The Iris guard swore angrily as I pushed to my feet. I ran toward Helio who was locked in combat with the other Iris guard. Despite his injuries, Helio's body moved fluidly and he was holding his own. A loud crack sounded as Helio's elbow connected with the guard's nose, finally knocking him to the ground.

"We need to get out of here before more reinforcements come," Helio said as he grabbed my arm and tried to run down the street. I wrapped my arm around his waist, trying to support his weight as his steps slowed and his limp became more pronounced. We'd made it only a few paces before we heard shouts coming from behind us.

I looked over my shoulder and cursed. "Reinforcements have arrived."

"Ari, is there anything you can do to slow them down?" Helio asked through gritted teeth as he leaned heavily on my shoulder.

Looking around frantically, I spied a fountain ahead of us and summoned the water to do my bidding. Within seconds, it was rushing toward the Iris in a torrent that knocked them off their feet.

Helio whooped a laugh even as he grimaced through the pain, and we ducked down a side street.

"Stars, are you all right? I won't be able to treat you until we make it out of here," I said.

Helio grunted in affirmation and continued directing me through the city streets, his injured leg slowing us down. Taking turns at random, we tried to throw off our pursuers. I was grateful he knew where we were going because I was completely lost.

Helio's breathing became more labored, his face gleaming with sweat. Suddenly, we heard shouts coming from a street over, and I pulled Helio down an alley. The scent of rotting food and garbage filled my nose and I tried not to gag. Lacking options, we tucked ourselves between the heaps of trash.

Pulling my pack off my back and thanking the stars that the guards hadn't taken it, I grabbed a poultice and clean bandages. Helio sat, his back leaning against the wall, his eyes shuttered in pain.

Unwrapping my scarf from his leg, I winced at the sight of his destroyed calf. It wasn't bleeding heavily because the firebolt had effectively cauterized it, but the burns were horrific.

"Helio, this is going to hurt, but you need to be quiet," I said. "Do you need something to bite down on?"

He shook his head.

"It's fine to admit weakness, you know," I said, trying to distract him as I pulled out a flask of water and poured it over his wound. Helio hissed through his teeth as I tended to it. Using my magic, I tried to numb the pain while rooting out any contamination. After I had packed and bandaged his first injury, I took care of the hand he had burned pulling out the flaming bolt. I sat back to catch my breath as everything that had just happened started replaying in my head.

"Arianwen, you're bleeding!" Helio exclaimed quietly, pointing at the cut on my arm.

"Oh, yes . . . I kind of forgot about that while we were running for our lives."

Helio looked at me with concern. "What happened, Ari? I couldn't hear what that prick was saying to you."

"You don't want to know." I grimaced as I cleaned out the cut on my arm and bound it with a clean bandage. "But I stabbed him. I didn't even think. I just stabbed him in a place that could kill him if he doesn't get help soon." Tears started to stream down my face. "I'm supposed to be a healer, but I might have just become a killer!"

My shoulders shook with silent sobs as Helio put his arm around me, and I let myself cry for a moment. As much as I wanted to continue crying and processing everything, we weren't safe yet. Sucking in a breath, I tried to center myself, knowing that it was not the time for me to break.

"I'm fine. Everything is fine. I'm all right. Now, how are we going to get out of this predicament?" I asked as I wiped the tears from my face.

Helio huffed a strained laugh. "Thank the stars they haven't checked this trash heap of an alley yet." His face turned serious as he looked me in the eyes. "Arianwen, I know you're not telling me everything, but, whatever you do, do not blame yourself for his fate. You had every right to protect yourself. Try not to judge yourself too harshly, please."

I looked down, knowing it wouldn't be that easy, but I would at least try. "Do you think they've blocked all the exits to the city?"

"That would be the smart move, but, lucky for us, I know some hidden ways to get out."

"Will you be able to walk? Your leg is a mess, and while I did the best I could, it's going to take some time for you to get full use of it again."

"I get to keep the leg?"

Patting his arm, I stood, needing to move away from the noxious scents of the alley as soon as possible. "You will keep the leg, but you'll have a beautiful scar if I'm guessing correctly."

"I can't wait to show it off," he joked.

Offering my hand, I helped him back to his feet, and he groaned at the pain.

"I can give you a sedative as soon as we find a safe place to rest," I said. "Unfortunately, for now, I need you to be alert so we can get out of this place."

Chapter 37

Safe

Arianwen

True to his word, Helio was able to lead us out of the city without running into any more Iris patrols. While we hadn't come out unscathed, I was grateful we'd made it out at all.

As we got to the rendezvous point, the sound of horses snorting and nickering greeted my ears.

"That was a close one," Helio said, clapping a hand on my shoulder. "Wynn would've had my head if I'd let you get captured."

"More like the *Iris* would have had your head if *you'd* gotten captured," I tried to joke. My hands started shaking as the adrenaline wore off.

"If Helio had managed to get you both killed, I would have brought him back from the dead just to kill him again myself," Wynn growled from behind us.

I turned and gave him a wan smile, relief flooding me at the sight of him. "Oh, good. I'm so glad you're safe."

Wynn looked me over, checking for injuries, concern etched in his brow as he took in the blood on my clothes and my bandaged arm. "What in the stars happened? Are you injured? Stars, what is that stench?"

"We ran into a patrol, and, unbeknownst to us, there was a curfew in place," Helio explained.

Wynn's eyes dropped to Helio's bandaged hand and leg, his anger bleeding into concern.

"Ari's glamour failed while we were stopped. Why didn't Enixus or Indre warn us about the curfew? Or Kalev?" Helio asked.

"They better not have known," Wynn seethed.

"The guards shot firebolts at us, and one of them grabbed Ari. She was able to fight him off and even stabbed him with his own dagger!"

Wynn's eyes darkened as Helio described the rest of the attack and our escape.

"Then reinforcements came, and Arianwen was able to take them out with a flood of water. She was brilliant," Helio finished.

"You were supposed to protect her," Wynn growled at Helio. His anger radiating off him in waves.

"Wynn, it wasn't Helio's fault. We made it. That's what matters. Please don't blame him," I pleaded.

"I promised you I would keep you safe, and I failed. We should have never split up." Wynn paced in front of us.

"I *am* safe. We made it out, but now we need to get out of here. Where are the others?"

"Rik and Fabra should be here any minute. Luckily, none of the rest of us ran into patrols."

Hearing faint voices, I turned and sighed a breath of relief as Fabra and Valerik rounded the bend. We had all made it to the first checkpoint—I hoped the stars would remain on our side.

There were six horses and eight fae, so two of us were going to have to double up. Wynn lifted me onto a horse and got me situated before he mounted behind me. The limited space in the saddle squished us together even closer than when we'd flown on Luminara.

As his scent and warmth washed over me, I was reminded of the night before when he had held me in his arms during my panic attack. Being with him filled me with a sense of safety, and after my close call earlier, safety was what I craved.

"Let's move out," Wynn said. "Arianwen and Helio ran into some trouble, and I don't know how long we have until they start searching these woods. We can't waste any time."

Clinging to the saddle in front of me, my legs ached as I used every muscle to stay put. We raced through the dark, and I muttered prayers to the stars that we wouldn't crash into anything or fall off any cliffs. Wynn had explained that we would be heading toward the western cliffs on horseback, then the aquilas would take us. I never thought I'd be looking forward to flying again, but traveling the rest of the way by horse sounded horribly uncomfortable.

"How far are we traveling tonight?" I leaned back and asked Wynn when we slowed from a raging gallop to a canter.

"We'll need to travel as far as we can in case the Iris are on our tails. We'll probably fly until dawn." He paused and cleared his throat, the sound rumbling through me. "Arianwen, I'm sorry for getting so angry before. I feel responsible for your safety, and hearing how close you came to being dragged off for questioning was just too much. Are you really all right?"

"I'm not going to lie and say I wasn't scared. The Iris guard . . . I don't think I can talk about it, but it's over now. Let's just focus on getting back to Zephyria."

"If you need to talk about it, I'm here."

His arm tightened around me, and we continued the rest of the way in silence. The closer we got to the cliffs, the more we had to slow down. The trails were steep and treacherous, but eventually, we made it to the top.

"What will happen to the horses?" I asked, stifling a groan as Wynn helped me dismount. My inner thighs ached and my rear was sore after our grueling ride.

Wynn looked at me with concern. "You all right there, my star?"

I glared at him. "I'll be fine. I dare say it will be a relief to get back on Luminara after that experience."

Wynn smiled and replied, "I'm sure she'll be happy to hear that. As for the horses, they know their way back home. This isn't the first time we have gone this route."

Helio cursed as he awkwardly dismounted from his horse. I couldn't believe he had held on with only one working leg and a burnt hand.

"How's your pain, Helio? Would you like anything before we go airborne?"

"Thanks, Ari. I'll survive. Believe it or not, I've had worse injuries."

I squeezed his arm. "Please try to take it easy if you can." I checked his bandages to make sure they didn't need to be reinforced before we left.

Uncertain of how long of a break we would have and how long until we'd get another, I started stretching my legs and rolling my neck, trying to work the kinks out. Wynn and Valerik disappeared into the clouds to summon the aquilas. The Adamas could send messages on the wind that would travel quite a distance, which is what I assumed they were doing. Luminara and the other aquilas wouldn't have gone too far though, as they'd known we would be returning.

The refugee family huddled together with their meager belongings. Fabra had her arms wrapped around her teenage daughter, Lule, comforting her as she cried silent tears. I couldn't imagine leaving everything behind, bringing only what would fit into the small packs they wore. Leaving Ilithania was no minor sacrifice for them. I hoped Zephyria would treat them well and that the freedom they sought would be worth it all.

The rustling of wings sounded, and I looked up to see four beautiful aquilas diving our way. Luminara chirped a joyful sound as Wynn met her in the sky and jumped onto her back. The aquilas landed and we swiftly mounted the giant birds. Wynn hopped down and helped the refugees secure their packs into the giant saddle bags, and then we were on our way.

My exhaustion started to catch up with me and I found myself nodding off as we flew.

Wynn pulled me closer to him and whispered into my ear over the wind, "It's all right, my star, sleep if you need to."

I smiled to myself once again at the safety he exuded. For perhaps the first and only time, I felt safe enough to relax and sleep while riding a giant aquila on the wind.

※

Our trip back to Zephyria seemed to be going faster than our trip down to Ilithania had. I couldn't wait to return and have some time to myself. The introvert in me was growing tired of the constant noise and chatter of our group. I longed to curl up in my big, comfortable bed with a good book that I could get lost in for hours. I was also looking forward to having actual alone time with Wynn.

Traveling with him in such close quarters had only made the tension between us stronger, and I couldn't stop thinking about that dream. Every glance he sent my way spoke volumes. Sometimes I thought I might have felt the softest of caresses on the back of my neck from Wynn's lips, but it had always been so brief, I wasn't sure if I'd imagined it or if it had been his breath causing shivers to go up and down my spine. Wynn had started to gently tug on my braid to get my attention and would often tuck my hair behind my ears for me. It seemed like he'd use any excuse to get closer to me, and every small touch had begun adding up. I was burning up with desire for him.

Across the small fire we had built to roast the game we'd caught, Wynn's smoldering gaze finally pushed me too far. Unable to handle the tension any longer, I got up and excused myself. I had to get away from him for just a minute so I could breathe again. All the torturous closeness without ever being alone with him was putting me on edge. It had been far too long since I'd been with a male.

I snuck off into the woods, not straying too far from the camp, just hoping to find a moment of peace and solitude. The trickling sounds of a nearby stream brought comfort. I made my way over to it and knelt down near the edge. The water was icy cold but refreshing as I washed my heated skin. It already felt like an eternity since our brief romp in the ocean a week earlier.

"Why am I not surprised to find you here with your element?" Wynn's deep voice rumbled from behind me.

Turning so he could see me roll my eyes at him, I tried to bite back my annoyance as I sat back on my feet. "Why am I not surprised to find you following me?"

Wynn prowled closer before leaning against a tree, his gaze watchful. "These woods are not safe at night, my star. I had to make sure you were all right."

"I didn't go very far," I scoffed. "I'm perfectly safe."

"Are you though?" Wynn asked. His piercing gaze was intense as if he could see straight through me. "There are terrifying predators in these woods. Your lovely scent could draw them right to you . . . You'd make a delicious snack."

I shuddered but not from fear. He crouched down to my level but still seemed to tower over me.

"I'm not afraid of you, Wynn," I said, not shying from his gaze.

"You should be. I'm not good for you. I will only cause you pain in the end." He leaned closer, his face inches from mine, and his gaze dropped to my lips.

"Maybe I'm a glutton for punishment," I breathed, tilting my head up toward his, hoping he would cross the divide between us.

A branch cracked, and Wynn spun around, jumping to his feet, looking for danger.

"Oh! Hi, Wynn. Arianwen," Rik called out. "Sorry, I didn't mean to interrupt." He raised an eyebrow and then sent a wink my way. My body flushed from head to toe, and I was grateful for the dark.

Trying to hide my disappointment at the interruption, I rose from where I knelt by the stream. "You have nothing to apologize for, I was just freshening up in the water." I summoned an orb. "Here, have some," I teased as I sent it flying toward Rik.

Rik sputtered as the icy water hit him square in the face. "By the stars,

Ari, that water is way too cold to play in." He sent a gust of wind my way that had my hair whipping around my face.

Pushing it out of my eyes, I groaned. "I'm never going to be able to untangle my hair now!"

"Don't dish it out if you can't take it," he said.

Laughing, I playfully shoved Rik aside before I ran back to camp, afraid to meet Wynn's eyes and see what he was thinking. Was he mad at the interruption or relieved? Despite all the glances and touches, he still hadn't made a move. What was really holding him back?

Either way, it had probably been for the best. We had a long flight the next day, and we all needed our rest.

❖

"We made it!" I exclaimed, tired but happy as we finally landed back in the aeries in Zephyria. It was late in the afternoon, but my body was so exhausted, I was sure I could collapse into bed and sleep until morning. "I need a long bath, food, and sleep as soon as possible."

Wynn chuckled as he turned to help me dismount from Luminara. "I'm glad you're happy to be back." He paused, our bodies momentarily flush as he lowered me to the ground much slower and closer than necessary. Heat rushed through me from my head to my toes as our bodies met—my skin tingling at the contact despite all the layers of clothes. His hands squeezed around my hips before he let go and stepped away, leaving me flustered.

We gathered our belongings and started the walk back into the city. I was pleased with how Helio's leg was healing—his limp was no longer as pronounced. The Aereus family's eyes were wide in wonder at the sight of the city built into the surrounding mountains. Helio and Valerik played tour guides and explained how the city was built and where things were. I smiled at how Lule stared at Rik in rapt attention as if he were the sun.

"I think Rik has found himself an admirer," I whispered to Wynn. We had fallen back a little, but I knew our voices could easily travel on the wind.

Wynn grinned broadly and replied, "She's been making eyes at him since we left Ilithania."

I smiled as we continued to walk in companionable silence, despite all the unspoken words I had rushing through my head. As we made it to the heart of the city, Wynn stopped me.

"You can head straight back to the palatium, Ari," he said. "I'm going to make sure the family gets settled into refugee housing. Just let Emil know to send up some food for you and I'll check in on you later."

"That sounds perfect. Once I bathe and eat, I think I could sleep the rest of the day."

He chuckled. "This was a long, eventful trip. I think we all could use some good rest."

"Thanks again for bringing me. I won't ever forget it."

"You handled yourself well on this mission, and I think you fit in nicely with the cabala. I hope you can meet the others soon. I want you to have people you can trust here, and I trust them with my life."

His praise brought a warm glow to my cheeks. "Rik and Helio are amazing. I'm so glad to have gotten to know all of you and everyone at the hospitium too. I'm starting to envision what life would be like if I stayed . . . and it's not bad." I looked down at my hands, unable to meet his gaze. I wanted to ask him about all the confusing things I felt around him, but I didn't know how to start, nor did I want to do it with all the others in earshot.

Wynn tucked a stray strand of hair behind my ear and I smiled as I realized the gesture had become second nature to him. He leaned closer and whispered, "I'll see you soon, my star."

※

After taking the longest, laziest bath in the history of Esterra, I threw on a satin robe and meandered into my room. It had taken forever to scrub myself clean after weeks without a proper bath. I was grateful for all the luxurious oils and soaps the palatium was stocked with. My hair smelled amazing and fell in soft, silky waves around my shoulders.

Emil had sent up a generous spread of food, and I'd gorged myself before my bath, so I was more than ready to climb into the large bed and take a much-needed nap. I yawned as I pulled back the blankets, but before I could climb in, I heard a knock at the door. Glancing down to make sure my robe was tied properly, I padded over to see who was there. Mari usually let herself in, so my pulse quickened at the thought that Wynn might be outside.

Cracking the door open, I peered out and saw him pacing. He was wearing clean clothes, and his fresh, woodsy scent filled my nose.

"Wynn, is everything all right?" I asked, opening the door wider for him.

"Oh, good, you're awake. I was worried you'd be asleep . . ." He stopped pacing and braced an arm on the doorframe. His eyes widened, suddenly registering the fact that I was standing there wearing nothing more than a robe. I found myself blushing as his gaze became hungry with need.

Unable to help myself, my eyes blazed in challenge as I stepped closer to him, placing a hand on his chest. "Is there something you need, Wynn?"

"You . . ." he growled quietly. "I need you."

Chapter 38

Butterfly

Aella

Two weeks had passed, and I still hadn't had my meeting with the prince. The way things had ended between us in his room before the competition had left more to be desired. I still didn't know if I could ever forgive him for being Iris, and he hadn't done anything significant enough to prove himself to me.

But I needed him. We needed him on our side. The next event was approaching, and we were running out of time.

Viera had been summoned almost daily to the king's chambers. Every evening before she left, I had squeezed her to my chest, begging her not to forget. Her memory hinged on her ability to keep the king intrigued, and I knew it was only a matter of time before he took her name from her too.

Our desire to bring down the king was not enough, we'd needed a plan. We had spent countless hours brainstorming ways for Viera to kill him during her visits but had never come up with a solid ploy that wouldn't involve Viera getting caught in the process. There had been too many ways for us to fail and not enough ways to succeed.

I'd not been willing to agree to any idea that left her in harm's way, so we'd decided that I would be the one to do it. That meant our mission depended upon me harnessing my powers to end King Solanos' evil rule.

No one else knew I was able to harness the air element, so no one would have any reason to suspect me. All I would need was another lightning strike . . . but directed at the king. He would never see it coming.

I'd spent countless nights lying awake in bed with nowhere to go since my access to the garden had been cut down. I'd been hesitant to summon my powers again after they'd proved to be out of my conscious control the last time. But Viera had continued to bring me out onto the terrace every night without fail. She was relentless and determined, unwilling to give up on me, even when it felt hopeless. My wariness had made it a challenge, but we'd kept at it. Viera would not let me give up. She had a strength and persuasiveness about her that was impossible to say no to.

After many fruitless nights of trying, I finally managed to control a minuscule amount of my other power. Such a tiny wisp of air, barely enough to blow a strand of hair out of place. Viera was so excited, she had to stifle her screams. It was small, but it was progress.

△

The next day, my maids brought me an embroidered tulle gown which was adorned with silk butterflies that looked ready to take flight. The diaphanous gown had sheer, off-the-shoulder puff sleeves gathered at the forearm and a thick, full skirt of many layers. The material was gauzy, showing off the fine, silk, lavender bodice cinching my waist underneath. I raised my brows at my appearance—the dress was over-the-top. We decided to leave my hair down, sleek and straight, with tiny, silver butterfly earrings dangling to my collarbone.

"We went with a butterfly theme because the prince loves the gardens so much," one of my maids said.

"It's beautiful, thank you!" I hugged them both, a tear threatening to run down my subtly shimmered cheek. I couldn't help thinking about what they'd lost, wondering what their lives had been like before coming to Prisma.

Himmel came to escort me to the prince's quarters where we would finally be dining alone together. I was left to wait on a grand, picturesque terrace overlooking the gardens, the great city of Prisma, and the ocean beyond.

The terrace was adorned with blooming, ornamental trees and plants, the scent of flowers mingling in the balmy air. Flowers hung down on vines overhead, wild and natural, so at odds with the manicured gardens of the rest of the Palatium Crystalis.

In the center was a table made of raw edge wood with hundreds of tiered candles on top, ready to be lit. I felt like I was in a dream. The evening skies were a smear of pink and yellow, and the moon and stars were starting to make their appearance in the far east.

I missed my nights floating in the sea, watching the sun disappear into the horizon. I didn't know if I would ever see the sun set over the water again.

I felt Kaleidos' presence as he entered the terrace, almost as if there was an aura radiating off him. I hesitated before turning to face him, unsure of what to say.

He broke the silence instead, walking over to stand next to me at the edge of the terrace. "Do you like it?"

"I should probably be polite and say it's the most beautiful sight I've ever seen . . . but I'd be lying."

"How so?"

"Nothing compares to the sight of home."

"What is it like in Iveria?" he asked with a wistfulness in his voice.

"Well, it's a big city, much larger than Prisma. Located right on the coast, the homes are built on the cliffs above and below the water. It feels older, more lived in than Prisma. It's messy, overcrowded, and dirty, but we have precious coves and lagoons left untouched by the fae, spiritual places where magic roams freely. And the horizon's fading light as the sun sets over the water . . . there's nothing like it," I said. "But beyond that, it's community, family. I never fully appreciated it before. Now—really, every single day since arriving in Prisma—I think of how much I've lost. It's hard to believe I ever took it for granted."

"You light up when you talk about it," he said with a sad smile.

I blushed at his focus on me, wringing my hands to control my nerves. I had wanted to ask him questions about the Matri-Ludus and find out if he would help us end his father's reign, but I didn't know how to bring it up, and I didn't really want to change the subject either.

"What's the matter?" he asked. "Your face dropped as if I said something wrong."

"You didn't," I said. "It's just . . . I have a lot of things on my mind."

The prince leaned casually against the balustrade and cocked a brow at me. "You've never had qualms about speaking freely with me before."

"I don't want to ruin the mood," I said with a small, appeasing smile.

"Is it because I didn't see you sooner? I had duties to attend to . . ."

I huffed. "Why do you assume it's about you?"

"Is it not?"

"Well, sure, I may have *some* questions for you, but I do happen to have more on my mind than just you," I said with a little too much pride.

"I would imagine you do." He shook his head. "Come, let's sit and eat. Then you can tell me everything that plagues you . . . if, of course, that's what you would like to do."

I forced myself not to return his flirtatious smile but was grateful for the offer to eat, as I was practically starving on the bird-food diet they'd had us on.

Kaleidos lit the candles on the table with a snap of his finger, and I startled. It would forever amaze me to see him wield so many powers.

The table was spread with an assortment of fine meats, cheeses, and fruit. Kaleidos noticed me eyeing the fructus amare with a wary expression, and with a chuckle, he picked them up, tossing them over into the garden. I gaped at him.

"Better?" he asked with a teasing smile.

I wanted to cover my face, the embarrassment coming back and making my cheeks burn. Somehow I'd hoped it had all been just a dream and that he wouldn't remember or bring it up again, but it was clear he would never forget that night. Nowhere to hide, I had to fight off my shame and face him with as much dignity as I could.

"Thank you." I nodded, then began filling my plate with food, avoiding eye contact for as long as possible. Servants came out promptly, filling our glasses with wine and bringing out more dishes with colorful salads and other small bites of food. I smiled at the sight.

"What is it?" he asked, noticing my facial expression.

"It's just every meal here is a sort of presentation. It's entertaining and beautiful. The foods are so carefully curated into looking like more than food. The variety of colors and shapes you eat. And the way they all come out at different times. It's just strange."

Kaleidos gave me a curious expression. "How else could it be?"

I laughed because he actually had no idea and likely couldn't imagine it any other way.

"You really need to get out more, Kaleidos. If you only ever see the world from your perspective, how can you expect to rule one day? You need to know how the rest of the world lives . . . and eats," I said with a wink.

"I shall have you take me on a tour then," he replied.

"I don't know much about Prisma," I snorted, "so, I'd be a pretty poor tour guide."

"What about a tour of Iveria?"

My breath caught in my throat. Disbelief at what he'd said and of the implications. *He can't possibly mean it.* I studied his face, looking for a sign of humor or teasing but found none.

"How?"

"Well, as you know, I am heir to the throne. It does come with *some* perks. We could travel all of Esterra if you'd like. Perhaps explore distant lands far beyond the sea."

"I'd like that very much," I said. But his promise felt empty as I would still have to win the competition for that to happen.

The sky continued to darken, and as if on cue, the hanging flowers began to bloom, filling the air with a sweet and sensual perfume.

"What is it like?" I asked. "Your ability to control so many elements?"

"Well, I don't give it much thought," he replied, his eyes narrowing a bit as if in deep thought. "I suppose it is mostly instinctual now . . . but when I first learned to master the elements, I had to focus on different feelings to trigger them. Controlling them is another matter entirely. There's a fine line between using the elements and letting them use you."

"This might be a dumb question, but I have to ask . . . Is it true that you have mastery over all four elements?"

"It's forbidden for any Iris to wield air powers, even if they carry Adamas blood. Although, as you might imagine, if anyone still carried Adamas blood, it would be quite diluted."

"It would be forbidden even for you?"

"You seem to think rules don't apply to me, but I assure you, I live with as many, if not more, restrictions than most citizens of Esterra."

I snorted. "That's doubtful."

Kaleidos' eyes blazed with a fire that seemed to consume him from within. But when he replied, he spoke in a controlled and measured tone. "You think you know so much." His voice darkened as it slowly began to reveal his pent-up rage. "Tell me then, Aella, why I have so little choice in the female I am to wed. Tell me why I am forced to watch as you tear yourselves apart for my 'pleasure.'" He finished his statement with a growl through gritted teeth.

He placed both of his hands on the table, pressing his palms into it, his breathing ragged as he attempted to reel himself back in. "While most Iris are shielded from the Matri-Ludus as children and develop their taste for violence as adults, I have been forced to endure these tournaments ever since I was a child. My father thought it necessary to shape me into a cruel monster like himself. When I tried to close my eyes or turn away during an event, my father had them hold me in place, *made* me watch."

The prince went unnaturally still for a moment, gaze distant and voice softer as he continued. "He made me watch as he threw my mother back into the arena as punishment for my tears, for showing signs of weakness." His expression hardened. "There is no room for a soft-hearted prince on the Iris throne."

Kaleidos cleared his voice and focused his piercing eyes on me again. "So while you sit and judge me, believe me when I say I have little more power than you do. This will not change until I have the strength to overthrow my father and take his place on the Iris throne, as he did to his father before him, as it has always been."

His voice softened then, anger replaced with defeat. "If I had the power to end this, I would. I would end it all."

My throat ached, and a sense of heaviness weighed on me. I reached toward him, taking his hand in mine. I felt terrible for making assumptions about the kind of person he was. Instead of jumping to more conclusions about his character, I had to ask him. I needed to hear from him how he envisioned the world. If he were to replace the king, how different might it be?

"What would you do then, if you had a choice? If you had the power to end it right now?" I asked.

"I would do everything in my power to restore the draft to its original intention. No more fighting, no more bloodshed."

"But there would still be a draft?" I asked, incredulous he thought that was still necessary. "Why not give us a choice in the matter?"

"What you don't realize is that we need you more than you need us, Aella."

"If you need us . . . couldn't you ask for volunteers?" I racked my brain for a better argument. "To continue taking all authority away from us . . . it's . . . it's not right, Kaleidos, and I believe you know this."

"Perhaps you have a point. Perhaps there should be more balance in power between the elemental fae and the Iris. A shared democracy or an alliance of some sort."

"Exactly. Now you are talking like a king." I smiled.

"It would not be easy to change the minds of all the Iris. There would be a lot of pushback."

"Change is never easy."

"No, I suppose it is not. But you have given me a lot to think about. Now, why don't we go for a walk."

"I'd like that." I beamed up at him. For the first time in a long time, I felt hope. If the Prince of Prisma was willing to consider alternatives, other Iris might as well.

△

As we strolled along the riverbank, I feigned interest in the flowering topiaries that so elegantly lined our path. The gardens sparkled with the soft glow of fireflies reflecting off the waterway like twinkling stars in a full spectrum of colors. With such a romantic atmosphere and memories of our last encounter in the gardens, I felt a blend of nervous desire. When the tips of his fingers brushed against mine, it sent tingles running up the length of my arm. I clasped my hands together and gave him a quick nervous smile, betraying the part of me that wanted to lean in closer to him. A knot coiled in my stomach as the touch made me long for his hands on me once more. Would I give in if he asked to kiss me again?

Afraid to find out, I needed a quick distraction, so I attempted to steer the conversation in a way that would serve my purpose. "Your library was quite impressive. I was hoping I'd get another chance to visit your collection."

"I'd hardly call it a library."

"What would you call it then? I've never seen so many books in my life. They are quite rare and valuable in Iveria. We have a small public library, but you can't take any books home with you, and, well, the selection leaves much to be desired."

"Anything in particular you're interested in reading about? I might be able to lend you something."

I considered for a moment whether it was worth the risk of asking, then, before I could second guess myself, attempted to speak in a casual tone. "You wouldn't happen to have anything on the Adamas would you?"

"The Adamas?" he replied, his tone conveying astonishment at the inquiry.

"It's just . . . I've only ever heard about them in cautionary tales, and I can't help but find the history fascinating."

"I don't have any that focus specifically on the Adamas, but I may have some older texts that mention them."

"I wouldn't mind looking through the older texts you have in your . . . *not-library*."

He chuckled and then sighed. "All right, is that truly how you'd prefer to spend the rest of our time together?"

I nodded my head with an overly enthusiastic smile to which he laughed some more before steering us back in the direction of his wing of the Palatium Crystalis.

⟁

Kaleidos' library felt more intimate after sundown. The room was dimly lit, the pale moonlight silhouetting us through the floor-to-ceiling windows. I kept my gait close to his, resisting the temptation to reach for his hand as we walked into the shadowy space.

Kaleidos snapped his fingers, lighting sconces around the room which cast warm shadows along the rows and rows of books and the rich velvet drapes lining the windows.

"How do you even find a book in this collection? There are so many of them!" I exclaimed.

"You know how everyone has at least one useless talent? Well, organization is mine. It will never help me to prove myself worthy of my title or to overturn my father's rule, but, hey, at least my books are organized."

"Well, I don't see it as useless at all," I said while admiring the collection of books we passed.

"What's yours?" he asked.

Caught off guard, I immediately thought of my air magic. Although it wasn't useless, it felt that way to me as I hadn't learned to harness it yet. I worried he might have been able to read the secret on my face, so I quickly spun away, and tried to make myself appear interested in the books in front of me.

"I don't think I have one," I said dismissively.

"Oh, everybody has one." He smiled. "Maybe you're too embarrassed to share it with me."

"I am not!" I blurted. "Fine, if you must know . . . I'm pretty good at swimming."

The prince laughed. "All Argenti are, I think you can do a little better."

I chewed on my lip, trying to think of something other than my impotent air magic but couldn't think under all the pressure. He closed in on me, and I felt as though all my secrets would spill out if he only laid a hand on me.

"Uhhh . . . How about this one?" I pointed to a random book to change the subject. "This looks promising!"

Kal raised a brow at the title, then pulled it out, reading the cover out loud. "*Tales of Starlight and Shadow: A compilation of romantic poetry*. Not a book about the Adamas, but you may borrow it. It might teach you a thing or two." He winked at me while handing it over, and I melted under his flirtatious smile. I had to stop letting him affect me that way.

"You said you know where all the books are, so do you have what I asked for or do you not?" I said, glancing between the book and my surroundings.

"Why do you really want to study the Adamas?" he asked, cornering me. He had one hand pressed against the bookshelves above me, his face tilted down so that he could gaze directly into my eyes.

My heart sped up as I opened myself up to him. I was captivated by the metallic sheen of interwoven gold, silver, and bronze which appeared to swirl around his green irises as his pupils dilated. His gaze darkened, and my lips parted slightly in anticipation. But rather than kiss me, he trailed his finger lazily down the silhouette of my face, stopping at my lower lip. I could no longer keep my breathing still. It was impossible to hide the signs of nerves firing all over my body, making me want to give in to him and run away all at the same time. He tilted my chin up even higher with his thumb and forefinger, just a hint of a smile creasing the corner of his lips.

This cocky male is trying to tease an answer out of me.

Doing my best to cover any signs of distress, I had to work my way around his question again. I swallowed and collected myself as much as I could before I started my nervous rambling. "Before coming here, I never thought I'd get a chance to meet Aurum or Aereus fae. And now that I have learned more about *them*, I can't help but wonder about the lost fae. Don't you? How do you feel when you think of Iveria, or of the many other places you have never been?" I was afraid I had spoken a little too much and a little too fast, the way I'd always done when I was trying to hide something. It wasn't like I'd lied to him though, I just hadn't shared the entire truth.

Kal stared at my lips once more before nodding, stepping away, and walking to the other side of the room. Conflicting feelings of disappointment and relief flooded me. Had he not restrained himself, surely I would have given in to him with everything I was, despite all rational thought. But it was better this way. It was good that he'd simply nodded and had not pushed any further. *Wasn't it?*

"I have a book on the bestiaries of Esterra—it doesn't have much about the Adamas, but they are mentioned in their connection with aerial creatures." He climbed a ladder and pulled a tome from a high shelf, bringing it over to his bureau.

Flipping through it, he came to a page with illustrated compendiums of the aquilas, an avian species so large, they could carry fae riders on their backs. It detailed how the Adamas had been the only ones to ride them, as no other fae could fly up to the heights of their nests in the alps.

"The Adamas could fly?" I asked, wonderstruck. I wasn't sure why I'd never considered that before. Dizzy at the idea I might have that ability as well. "May I borrow this?" I asked, trying not to sound too eager.

Kal curiously tilted his head before handing it to me.

"I'll have to take a look later to see if I have more, but most of their history has been lost with their people."

"Thank you," I said, clutching the two books to my chest as if they were the most precious items I'd ever held.

Kaleidos had thought it comical at first that I was so eager to return to my rooms, showing more interest in the literature than in him, but when he saw how much the books excited me, he added a couple more. It seemed to make him happy to spoil me with—what were, in his eyes—such simple pleasures.

I wanted to ask him to take me back via the gardens where I'd plead with him to regrow the vines up to my bedroom terrace, but when I looked down at the stack I was carrying, I decided I'd better not.

Kal escorted me through the hidden passages again, saying it was a shortcut. I wondered if he'd taken any of the other girls down the dark tunnels. Somehow, I felt they were just for me and that I had a special connection with him that the others did not.

When we arrived, the memory of the last time he'd brought me back to my rooms played fresh in my mind, and my breathing quickened. As I placed my hand on the doorknob, I paused. *This encounter could be our last.*

I dropped my hand down, and in a heartbeat, the prince dropped the books, took my hand, and spun me around so that I was pinned between him and the door. His hand pressing mine above me, leaving me feeling vulnerable to him. With his face so close to mine, he stared deeply into my eyes while expertly sliding his hand through the slit in my dress and lifting my thigh, pulling our bodies together seamlessly. I whimpered at the sensation, so thrilling but terrifying at the same time. While I wanted so badly to give in to the desire—wanted him to touch me, kiss me, drown me in pleasure—I couldn't seem to let go of this other part of me that kept holding back, afraid to give in, afraid to let him in.

I met his gaze as he pressed himself harder against me and couldn't help myself when my hips rolled in response. He hummed a low vibration of approval, then released my hand, scooping my other thigh up so that I had both legs wrapped around him.

"Are you going to kiss me now?" I asked breathlessly.

Kaleidos quirked a half smile. "Is that what you want, little nymph?" He thrust his hips against mine in a wave that had me aching to rip apart the thin barriers of fabric between us. His nose brushed against mine in a teasing caress, then his lips slid across my lips, so close I could feel their warmth.

"Don't close your eyes," he whispered against my lips.

And in that moment—our hearts pressed up against each other, our eyes locked together, that almost kiss—I surrendered myself to him, letting go of everything that had been holding me back. I wasn't sure how, and I wasn't sure why, but I trusted him. And with that notion, my body relaxed into his hold.

Kaleidos pressed his lips against mine, over and over again, tenderly exploring the contours of my lips.

"I could kiss you forever," he said, then licked my upper lip in a playful manner. "I never cared much for kissing until I tasted you . . . and now I can't seem to get enough."

"Liar." I nipped at his lower lip.

He chuckled. "It's true. Can you think of anything better?"

"As terribly romantic as it is stealing away with you in a dark passageway, there are a few things I can imagine that might involve a bed."

"Oh, but it's so much fun like this, isn't it?" he drawled, working his way down my neck.

"You're going to make me beg, aren't you?"

Kaleidos abruptly set me down. "On your knees," he ordered.

My jaw dropped open, and I looked at him in impudent disbelief.

"I'm only kidding. You should have seen your face."

I threw a fist at his rock hard chest, which he took with a grin.

"So terribly defiant you are." He then scooped me up into his arms and carried me into my room. As he set me on the bed, I tried to pull him into it with me. He started to lean in over me, but halfway, he paused. His eyes raked over me—but no longer in the ravenous way he'd been looking at me in the hallway—as an indecipherable look crossed his face and he backed himself off the bed.

"I can't believe I'm actually doing this." He shook his head while emitting a dark laugh. "Aella, I want this . . . but . . . not this way."

I wanted to ask him why, but my pride wouldn't let me.

"I'm . . . ehhh . . . I'm going to let you get your beauty sleep." He turned on his heel and headed for the door where he began collecting the books he'd dropped in the passageway, setting them neatly on a side table.

Faex. If this is how it's going to end . . .

This might be my only chance.

I shimmied my way off the bed, chasing him to the door. "One last thing before you go," I begged, my heart racing.

"Yes?" he replied, stepping closer to me.

"I need you to promise me something."

"Aella . . . you know I can't." He tilted his head back as though looking to the stars for answers.

"Promise me you will favor Viera for the final event."

His brows cinched together. "My favor is the only thing I can offer to help protect you. Without it, there is no guarantee—"

"There's no guarantee either way. Promise me, Kal."

He sighed then dropped his forehead down to mine, cradling my head in his hands. I held my breath, waiting for an answer. He pulled back, searched my eyes for a moment, then nodded. "I will favor Viera, for you."

I gasped in relief and wrapped my arms around him in a tight squeeze. "That means more than you could ever imagine. Thank you!"

Kaleidos squeezed me to his chest in a big bear hug that left my feet dangling as he carried me back to the bed.

"Is this what it will be like if I win the Matri-Ludus?" I teased. "I have legs, you know."

"I know you do," he said with a devilish grin as he set me at the edge of the bed.

He kissed me once more, in a slow but reverent manner, eyes closed. It was a goodnight kiss, but it might as well have been a goodbye kiss, as I never knew how many days I had left. Our kiss became deeper and more desperate as those thoughts manifested.

Don't go, I wanted to say.

Kaleidos withdrew then dropped to his knees, burying his face in my lap. "Heavens, you're making this so hard!" he groaned into my skirts. I ran my fingers through his tousled hair, and he hummed another deep, vibrating sound. The prince straightened himself back up again, then pointed a finger at me. "Stay there," he said. "Or I'll throw you over my shoulder next time."

I slapped his finger away and huffed a laugh. Kaleidos gave me a smug grin then swiftly crossed the room, wishing me a good night before departing. But even after he'd left, I couldn't help the smile that remained plastered across my face.

The following morning, more books had been delivered to my room.

Chapter 39

Defy the Stars

Arianwen

With Wynn's declaration of want still ringing in my ears, my heart started racing as he pushed further into the room, gripping the back of my neck. His eyes burned into mine as he sent the door slamming shut with the force of his power.

"You," he growled, "are under my skin. My every thought is of how I want nothing more than to claim you, body and soul. Your scent tortures me day and night, and the thought of tasting you consumes me."

He wrenched himself away, pacing before me. "Ari, when I'm with you, I feel alive. I can't have you, but I want you more than I have ever wanted anyone in my entire life. Tell me you don't want this, convince me I don't see the same desire in your eyes. I will walk away and let you choose your path," he finished, his eyes pleading.

"Wynn, I . . ." My voice broke. I stared at him, speechless, my heart thundering in my chest. I wanted nothing more than to fall into his arms and give in to the attraction between us, but my heart was still torn between duty and want.

This is what I have been waiting for all these weeks. I wanted him. My entire body thrummed in his presence, but crossing that line would change everything.

Why did he think he couldn't have me? Was it because of my betrothal? Verus was nothing to me. Meant nothing.

Seeing the indecision warring on my face, Wynn's eyes shuttered as the walls he had torn down were rebuilt.

His vulnerability broke something in me. I crossed the divide between us, reached up, and placed my hand on his face.

"I can't . . ." I whispered.

Growing still beneath my touch, Wynn whispered, "Can't what?"

"I can't tell you that I don't want you."

Something like hope filled his gaze. "What are you saying, Arianwen?" His voice lowered to a purr, wreaking havoc on my insides.

Slowly trailing my fingers down his cheek, I brushed my thumb along his full lower lip. "You win. Kiss me."

A multitude of emotions shone through his eyes. Relief. Joy. Hunger.

He pulled me into his arms and crashed his lips against mine as he began to slowly devour me. His lips firm yet soft as they captured my own. I groaned and his tongue delved into my mouth, finally claiming me. My body felt tight and loose all at once as I sunk into his kiss.

I grasped the corded muscles of his forearm, my other hand at his waist as he sunk his fingers into my hair. Our tongues twisted around each other as if in some kind of dance as he cradled the back of my head with one hand and gently wrapped his other hand around my throat, leading me through the steps.

My pulse thrummed erratically under his thumb, and I gasped as his tongue flicked the roof of my mouth. I had never been kissed like that before, so all-consuming. It was everything I had dreamed it would be yet better than anything I could have ever imagined.

I arched into him, needing our bodies to be closer, needing some kind of friction to sate the want pulsing through me. Wynn started kissing his way down my neck, one hand moving to the small of my back to pull me closer, the hard proof of his desire pressing into me. His other hand moved to my chest, squeezing, his thumb teasing me over the thin material of my robe. Needing to touch him, I ripped his shirt open, eagerly running my hands over the firm muscles of his chest. *Finally.*

"Ari," he groaned as he continued kissing my neck.

"Yes, Wynn?" I gasped, each kiss heightening the sensitivity of my skin. His soft lips and tongue contrasted by the sharp rasp of his stubble.

"If you keep touching me and making those noises, I'm afraid this will be over far sooner than I had hoped."

I let out a breathy laugh, then whimpered as he gently bit down on the shell of my ear. He rolled his hips into me, the heat surging through me almost unbearable. Turning my head to meet his lips, I started kissing him again, pouring every ounce of myself into it. All my fears and doubts fled as I immersed myself fully in the moment, each stroke of his tongue igniting the fire that burned inside me. I reached up, digging my fingers into his hair, and Wynn growled his approval as he kissed me like his life depended on it.

Backing me up, my legs hit the table and he lifted me, setting me on the edge. I instinctively wrapped my legs around his waist as he deepened the kiss, our bodies molding perfectly like they were meant for each other as he rocked against me. I was being consumed, and I couldn't get enough. Breaking away from my lips, he kissed and nipped his way down my neck and across my collarbone as I leaned back on my elbows, and he bent further down with me, keeping our bodies flush. I moaned, writhing against him, completely undone.

"Are you sure this is what you want?" Wynn asked after coming up for air. He cradled my cheek in one of his hands while the other pressed flat against the table.

"The stars couldn't stop me if they tried," I breathed.

Lifting me off the table, he walked me over to the bed and gently laid me down, his eyes darkening with approval as my robe slid open just enough to reveal my lack of clothing underneath. I stared up at him, my eyes hooded with desire as he groaned and bit his lip, watching me untie it slowly.

"You're exquisite, Arianwen. Still sure you're not a fallen star?" He smirked as his eyes traced my body while he trailed a finger down my chest, down the planes of my stomach, to where I desperately needed him. "I've dreamed of this moment for a while now, and I want to take my time."

Completely bare before him, I had never felt more exposed. At the same time, I had never felt more beautiful and desired than in his reverent gaze.

His grin was almost feral as I reached up and pulled his body back onto mine, needing to close the distance between us. Tugging his shirt off, I raked my hands over his shoulders and down his back, pulling him even closer. The feel of him pressed against me, all his hardness against the softness of my curves, created the delicious friction I'd craved. He trailed kisses down my body, causing heat to pool in my core.

"Wynn . . ." I groaned. "I need you . . . all of you."

His blue eyes met mine with a wicked gleam as he pulled back, unlacing his pants and letting them fall to the floor.

"Then you shall have me, my star," he purred.

Every breath, every touch lit me on fire, and I burned. I said his name like a prayer as he brought me to the edge, and I shattered into a million shimmering pieces.

We were insatiable. Every free moment in the following weeks was spent exploring each other's bodies and getting to know each other better. I woke up every morning wrapped in his arms with a happiness I'd never thought could be mine. Lingering doubts would be kissed away, and I could tell Wynn was trying to make me fall in love with his way of life as surely as I was falling in love with him. Whenever the subject of returning to Iveria would come up, we'd somehow always get distracted, and I'd find myself lost in a haze of bliss. It felt like we were living on borrowed time, and I didn't want to waste a moment.

Propping myself up on my elbows on the bed, I glanced over at Wynn, who appeared completely relaxed with his hands cradling the back of his head. A fine layer of sweat gleamed over the muscles of his chest and abdomen. He had skipped his afternoon training session in favor of exercise of a different sort. My lips twisted into a satisfied grin, and I briefly considered staying in for the rest of the evening instead of us meeting up with the cabala as planned.

"My star, your thoughts are written all over your face." Wynn smirked as he sat up and stretched. "If we stay in this bed another minute, we'll never make it in time."

I smiled suggestively for a moment before groaning, "I know . . . I guess I'm just a little nervous about meeting the others."

Wynn leaned down and pressed a kiss to my forehead before he got out of bed and strutted toward the bathing chamber. "They're going to love you. Stop worrying . . . and stop staring at my arse or I'm going to pick you up and throw you into the bath."

"Is that a promise or a threat?" I called back.

Looking over his shoulder, Wynn winked at me. I groaned into the sheets then pushed myself up, knowing he was right and we needed to get ready.

Sooner than I would have liked, we were dressed and ready to head over to Rik's for dinner and drinks. I hadn't seen Rik or Helio since our trip to Ilithania and had to admit that I missed their company.

"Ari!" Helio exclaimed as he picked me up and twirled me in a hug. "What have you been up to? Has Wynn been keeping you all to himself?"

I grinned as he set me down. "I missed you too, Helio. I've been quite busy in the hospitium most days, but Wynn and I have definitely kept ourselves occupied as well."

Helio's brows rose as he glanced between us before a knowing smile crossed his face. "I had a feeling . . ."

Before I could respond, Rik came over and gave me a quick hug, and

I was distracted by the arrival of—who I assumed was—the rest of the cabala.

"Ari, I'd like to introduce you to Glint, Kairi, and Eden," Wynn said with a broad smile as he gestured to the Aurum, Adamas, and Aereus females.

"Hello." I smiled shyly, giving a quick wave.

"Looks like the males are finally outnumbered," Glint teased. "And it's about time we had the Argenti represented. It's lovely to meet you, Ari."

The trio of ladies surrounded me and pulled me into the sitting room, peppering me with questions about my life and interests. My nerves dissipated as they quickly made me feel like part of their group. Eden handed me a drink, and as I thanked her, I caught Wynn watching me from the other side of the room. He raised an eyebrow in silent question, as if to make sure I was all right. Giving him a slight nod and a smile, I returned to the conversation, feeling fulfilled in more ways than one.

※

One bright and sunny afternoon after finally meeting the entire cabala, Wynn came up behind me while I was putting away supplies at the hospitium and wrapped his arms around my waist.

"My star, let's go on an adventure today," he said into my ear. Shivers went through me as they always did when his lips were on me.

"An adventure, huh? What do you have in mind?" I asked, turning in his arms and reaching up for a kiss.

He captured my lips and nipped at them teasingly. "Let's go so you can find out!"

I couldn't help the childish giggle that escaped. "All right then, My Prince, take me away!"

Wynn and I walked out of the building before he picked me up and went flying toward the aeries. Luminara was ready for us, and I greeted her warmly. She chirped at me, and Wynn grinned. "You have won her over, my star. I bet she would let you take her out on your own if you wished to."

"That is not happening," I said vehemently. "I need you with me to catch me if I fall."

"Never say never. Remember when you considered accepting the wager that you'd never kiss me?"

I rolled my eyes. "Don't act like you're not benefiting from me losing that almost-wager."

Wynn reached down and flicked my nose, a smirk on his face. "My star, you are the light in my darkness. My every breath is yours, but I love seeing you out of sorts."

"You're insufferable, but I still like you."

Wynn chuckled as he lifted me onto Luminara. The best part about flying was having Wynn wrapped around me, and I sunk into him as we took off through the alpine pass. With him, I felt safe and cherished. I could almost imagine a future with him, despite the odds stacked against us.

Wynn leaned down and spoke into my ear before pressing a soft kiss to my neck. "Close your eyes, Ari, I want this to be a surprise."

Closing my eyes, I shivered then smiled, his words bringing me back to our first flight together. "They're closed, My Prince."

I felt Luminara descend and held tightly to Wynn as we landed. Excitement built in me as I wondered what surprise he had in store. Keeping my eyes closed, I felt Wynn jump off the aquila, unbuckle me from the harness, and swoop me into his arms.

"You can open your eyes," he whispered into my ear.

Blinking, I opened my eyes and gasped. We were at the most beautiful, shimmering lake I had ever seen, surrounded by pine trees and nestled into a small valley. There was not a soul in sight, we were completely alone. My heart swelled with the knowledge that Wynn had sensed my need to be in my element.

"My stars, Wynn, this is incredible." My eyes lit up with pure joy. "What a wonderful surprise . . . Thank you."

"I would do anything for you, my star. I know how much you miss the ocean, but I hope you can find some peace here," he said with sincerity.

"It is so beautiful."

Wynn leaned in and captured my lips with his own. I could never get enough of his kisses. He pulled back far too soon, gently nipping at my lips. "How about we go for a swim?" He gave me a mischievous grin and started walking toward the lake, stripping his clothes off until he was bare.

My face flushed even though I had already explored every inch of his beautiful body, and I admired the view as he slowly walked into the lake. I was not nearly as graceful as I stripped off my clothes, but his gaze darkened as he beheld me from the waist-deep water. I ran in, my senses awakening, and I dove into its depths. I couldn't hold back my smile and the utter joy flowing through me from being in the lake with him.

Turning my head toward Wynn, I saw him watching me under the water. He had formed a pocket of air around his face so he could breathe and was grinning as he watched me enjoying myself. I swam over to him and wrapped my body around his, breaking into his bubble to kiss him deeply, hoping he could sense my gratitude.

We swam for hours, exploring the lakebed and learning just how long Wynn could hold his breath without his pocket of air. As the sun began to set, Wynn gave me a look that I knew meant we had to return. Despite my disappointment about leaving, it felt like nothing could take away how blissfully happy our afternoon had been.

"Thank you, Wynn. I needed this more than you know," I said.

"We can return any time, my star, all you need to do is ask," he replied while tenderly brushing tendrils of hair off my face. His face took on a pained expression. "Have you been unhappy in Zephyria with me?"

Pausing to think how to best explain, I squeezed his hand before capturing his gaze. "I have been homesick for my family and the ocean, but my time with you has been full of love and light. Don't mistake my utter joy at being here to mean that I have not enjoyed my time with you."

Wynn pulled me in for a deep kiss that took my breath away. It felt different somehow, as if all the words we weren't saying were being poured into it. I realized I would need to make a decision soon before my heart became any more involved.

Chapter 40
Forbidden Literature

Aella

"So you're telling me there's a chance you might be able to learn how to fly?" Viera asked.

"Well, let's not get ahead of ourselves. But if the Adamas could do it, and I have their gifts, wouldn't that mean I should be able to do it too?"

"This is a lot to take in," Viera said, picking up the book of poetry Kal had given me. She casually flipped through the pages before stopping on a random passage, her jaw dropping open.

"What is it?" I asked, swiping the book from her hands.

Viera began laughing hysterically, unable to speak. Every time she tried, laughter cut off her words.

As I read the "romantic" poem, my face burned with embarrassment and I wanted to scream.

Viera's giggles only intensified once she saw my reaction, and when I opened my mouth to defend myself, all that came out was laughter. The fact that the book had been in the prince's personal library made it even funnier.

"I've never heard . . . *anatomy* described in such a way before." Viera giggled. "Wait, it gets better on the next page." She pointed and I paled at the subject matter, unable to utter the words out loud.

"Do you think that's something he'll expect his wife to do?" I asked. My stomach knotted at the memory of Kal telling me I might learn a thing or two from the book. I wasn't *that* inexperienced, but the acts described in the book were on a whole other level. I couldn't help imagining myself in one of the roles which had been so painstakingly depicted in the poetry. The idea that Kaleidos was privy to that sort of literature was a bit nerve-racking, and what was worse was the fact that he'd given it to me knowing I was going to read it. I slammed the book shut. "Okay, that's enough of that."

"But it just started to get interesting," Viera teased. "Besides, I might need to know what to do when I have *my* turn with the prince."

I knew she'd meant it in jest, but the pang of jealousy that shot through me made my eyes burn.

Viera picked up on my change, her brows cinching together as she spoke. "Stars, you really do like him, Aella . . . I hope you know I was only joking. I would never—"

"No, I don't like him like that! I mean, faex, I don't want to! He is *Iris*, Viera. The very people who watch us slaughter one another for entertainment. The idea of loving him would mean I have to forgive all of that, and I could never . . . would never . . ." I found myself lost for words.

Kal is not like all Iris.

I rubbed the back of my neck as my mind drifted to the way he'd looked the previous night, and I sighed. "Besides, he's way too pretty for his own good, and he knows it."

Viera folded her arms, unconvinced.

I rolled my eyes. "Ugh . . . Fine, I do feel something for him, but it's mostly physical. I swear!"

"You're a terrible liar!" she teased. "You kissed him again, didn't you?"

"A little," I admitted sheepishly. Viera squealed.

"Words can't describe how perfect it was." I sighed. "When I was with him, I just had this overwhelming sense that I could trust him. But now, the more I think about it, I really don't know what to believe. I know he's had outings with almost all the other contestants already, and with his charm, I'm sure he's managed to make them all feel this way."

"To be fair, he does need to play his part in the game. He could end up with any one of us," Viera said.

"True. I guess I just don't want to admit to myself that he's holding a piece of my heart when I know he can't give me his. The whole thing is all so confusing. Things were much simpler when I hated him." I buried my head in a pillow and let out a scream.

"Judging by the stack of books he had sent over, I think there's a good chance he feels something for you. I mean, look, he must have been up all night tabbing them for you."

I sighed. The books he'd sent that morning had been bookmarked on all the pages with mentions of the Adamas. It was kind of sweet.

"Come, let's use all of this pent-up energy to practice your magic," she said.

△

With less than a week left until our third and final competition, only two contestants had been let go by the prince. One of the Aurum females, Rae, and one of the Argenti females, Ilaria. Disbelief had coursed through me upon learning of Ilaria's dismissal. Although she hadn't always been the most pleasant to be around, she was one of us, and her absence felt unsettling. Rumors circulated that Ilaria and Rae had requested dismissal, but I was skeptical considering Ilaria's character. Ilaria would never have chosen to concede the Matri-Ludus, so it had to have been Kal's choice to dismiss her.

Both of them had vanished without a trace, and it left so many questions in my mind. I wondered where they went, if they had been made servants in another noble household, if they'd had their names taken from them, if Kaleidos knew what had become of them. Most of all, I wondered if they were safe.

Strangely, the knowledge that I had less competition brought no comfort—it instead added to the ominous atmosphere.

It'd also been a while since Viera had received word from her contacts, and she was starting to fear they had abandoned her . . . or worse. It felt like we were running out of time and options.

Whatever alliance we had formed with Lewenne before, she made clear was no longer valid. Everyone was out for themselves, and I was just grateful I still had Viera on my side.

As far as my air magic, I had not improved much, but it was becoming slightly easier to summon and control the tiny wisp of air. I was still afraid of unleashing my full power. Better to control something small than let my magic consume me again.

Chapter 41
A Night to Remember

ARIANWEN

Wynn and I walked hand in hand, making our way back to the palatium at a leisurely pace after our relaxing afternoon at the lake. As we reached the entrance, the door opened before us as if someone had been waiting for our arrival. We were greeted by a flustered Emil.

"Your Highness, you are late for dinner and the king and queen are most vexed. You must hurry and change! Come, quickly now!"

Wynn's jaw tightened as he paused in the entryway. "Emil, I lost track of time and forgot they asked me to join them tonight. Please let them know I will be there shortly."

Feeling some guilt at having kept him distracted all afternoon, I asked, "Should I have Mari bring me something to eat in my room? I know your parents aren't exactly fond of my presence." Part of me wanted him to agree and let me hide in my room while another part of me hoped he would ask me to join him. If there was any chance of me staying, his parents needed to accept my presence. Our interactions had been awkward at best but generally more on the unpleasant side.

"Arianwen, don't be ridiculous. Of course you should join me," Wynn said.

"Your Highness, maybe you should let Miss Arianwen eat in her room, your—" Emil faltered.

"Nonsense," Wynn cut in before striding off. "I'll meet you outside your room in five minutes, Ari."

"Faex," I cursed under my breath as I rushed toward my room. That wasn't nearly enough time for me to get ready for dinner, but I would have to make do. Something about Emil's hesitation for me to join Wynn at dinner struck me the wrong way. My gut was telling me not to go, but I didn't want to let Wynn down.

Flinging the door open, I was relieved to see Mari bustling around the room.

"Arianwen! You're back!" Mari exclaimed, seeming surprised to see me.

"Mari, thank the stars you're here. Apparently, Wynn was supposed to dine with the king and queen and he forgot because he had planned this surprise outing for me today," I rambled. "I need to be ready in five minutes and my hair is a disaster after swimming and flying and—"

Mari's eyebrows rose up to her hairline. "Take a deep breath, I am here to help. Go ahead and undress, and I'll find something for you to wear."

"You're heaven-sent. Thank you," I said while removing my clothes.

Mari returned from the closet with an evening gown over her arm, a hesitant look on her face. "Here, try this."

Surprised at the lack of her usual enthusiasm, I wanted to ask her what was wrong but decided to wait. My time was running out.

I stepped into the luxurious dress and she pulled it up over my curves. While she fastened the back, I glanced up into the mirror and gasped at my reflection. The gown was made of fine satin, the color a deep amethyst. It hugged my figure in all the right places, emphasizing my slender waist and full hips. It had long sleeves and a modest neckline, but the back had a gratuitous cutout that went dangerously low, showing off my glimmering, silvery skin. Tiny crystals adorned the seams and hem of the gown, sparkling in the light. I felt like a princess.

"Mari, this gown is incredible. Are you sure this is appropriate for dinner?"

Ignoring my question, she tamed my hair into a simple updo, pinning it up with more rhinestones that glittered in my dark tresses. I let her add a little rose tint to my cheeks and some lilac color to my eyes that made the silver pop. A knock sounded at the door as I slid into silver heels.

"You're a miracle worker. I never would have thought I could look like this in so little time. Thank you so, so much," I said, pulling her into a quick hug.

"You're welcome, Ari. You look incredible," she replied, squeezing me back. "I just think—"

Another loud knock at the door interrupted her, and I spun to leave. "Thanks again!" I called out as I exited the room.

I will make sure to sit down and chat with her later to find out what's bothering her.

"Ari—" Wynn stopped as he took me in. "You look like the night sky at dusk," he said in reverence, offering me his arm.

I smiled broadly, feeling exquisite, not just because of the gown. The way he worshiped me with his gaze made me feel like the most beautiful fae alive.

"You don't look so bad yourself," I teased. And he did look amazing in his sapphire waistcoat and silver-gray dress shirt.

I hurried toward the formal dining room on Wynn's arm, hoping we wouldn't invoke any more of the king and queen's ire at our tardiness. Wynn, being an only child, was their pride and joy and, for the most part, could do no wrong.

Pausing in front of the double doors, Wynn turned to me and tilted my chin, capturing my gaze. "Don't let them make you feel like anything less than the amazing, beautiful fae you are. I want you here, and nothing they say or do will change that," he promised. "Oh, and dare I say it, I cannot wait to take you out of that dress later. I'm debating right now if I even want to go to dinner or just take you to my chambers and—"

"Wynn!" I gasped with a laugh, grateful to him for the distraction that eased my nerves. I took a deep breath as he opened the door and we entered the room.

"It's about time you joined us," King Volare said in a loud voice. I dropped into a quick curtsy, lowering my head. "Did you forget that Lady Katye was returning and would be here tonight?"

Who?

My head snapped up, and I caught sight of Wynn's face as he blanched. His fair complexion lightened a shade or two, which I would have thought to be impossible if I hadn't seen it with my own eyes.

Who in the stars is Lady Katye, and why does Wynn look like he wants the floor to swallow him whole?

I glanced around the room, noting the king and queen seated at the table, but rising from her seat to greet Wynn was a striking Adamas female. Her hair fell like a river down the length of her back, and her violet eyes simmered with desire as she raked her gaze over Wynn, ignoring me as if I did not exist. She wore an emerald green dress that showed off her shimmering, white skin and perfect curves.

"Wynn!" she cried out as she floated across the floor, covering the distance between them and brushing quick kisses to both of his cheeks. "It's been too long! I am so glad to be back so we can start planning."

Recovering, Wynn returned the greeting. "Katye, always a pleasure to see you." He turned to me and said, "I'd like to introduce you to Arianwen. She has been staying at the palatium and assisting the healers."

I feigned a smile as I nodded at her, unsure if I needed to curtsy before her as well. A sickening sensation filled me as I tried to piece together the nature of their relationship. Why hadn't he introduced me as more? My jaw clenched as I forced myself to hold it together and not spiral because he had not attempted to claim me as his—what would he even call me? His lover? No formal declarations had been made, but I wanted to believe that with all we had shared, with what he had *just* told me before walking into the room, I was more than just someone who had been "assisting the healers."

Ugh, pull it together before you embarrass yourself in front of the king and queen again.

"It's lovely to meet you, Lady Katye."

Lady Katye eyed me up and down, and I caught a slight sneer before she covered it up. "Likewise, I'm sure." She turned away, heading back to her seat. Addressing the queen, she said, "I thought this was a family dinner, I didn't realize there would be guests!" She finished the sentence with a tinkling laugh that made me feel completely and utterly unwanted.

Queen Astrid's eyes crinkled as she smiled at Lady Katye. "My son loves to take in strays, but that will soon change."

I flinched at the insult obviously directed at me, but before I could think of a response, Wynn spoke up.

"Mother, Arianwen is my guest and should be treated with respect."

My heart fell as, once again, Wynn did not claim me as anything more than a visitor in his home. Maybe the incredible weeks we'd spent together sharing our bodies and dreaming of a possible future had meant more to me than they had to him.

The queen dismissed his statement with a wave of her hand. "Oh, Wynn, don't be so sensitive. I'm sure you will move your guest to the refugee housing now that Lady Katye has returned."

Wynn glared at his mother, a tiny muscle in his jaw twitching as he held himself back. Before he could cause more of a scene on my behalf, I placed my hand on his arm and said quietly, "Why don't we take our seats?" Every part of me wanted to run from the room as quickly as possible, but I wouldn't give them the satisfaction of feeling like they'd won.

He nodded tersely and escorted me to the table. I had to be missing something, considering how familiar Lady Katye was with the queen. Was she a cousin? But cousins don't look at each other the way she had looked at Wynn—as if he were something she wanted to devour.

As I sat down next to Wynn, the staff set a place setting in front of me. Another reminder that I had not been invited to this meal. Trying to be amicable, I looked across the table at Lady Katye and asked, "You mentioned this being a family dinner, how are you related to the royal family?"

Wynn stiffened beside me. He reached under the table, grabbing my hand and squeezing it as if to tell me something. I ignored him as I waited for Lady Katye's answer, praying to the stars that my suspicions were wrong.

"Wynn and I grew up together, our families are very close," she said, her face smug. "Not to mention, Wynn and I will be married, so I will be an official member of the royal family soon enough."

The room started spinning as my world tipped off its axis.

Married? How could he have kept this from me?

It took every single piece of my willpower to keep my emotions off my face, and even then, I wasn't sure I'd succeeded.

"Oh? Congratulations. Wynn had not mentioned he was betrothed."

The king muttered something under his breath, and the queen silenced him with a glare. Wynn's hand tightened on mine again, but I shook it off, grabbing my wine and taking a rather unladylike gulp.

Ignoring me, Queen Astrid said, "We will need to set the date immediately. It's been too long since the Court of Air has had such a great celebration. Preparations can begin as soon as tomorrow. We can discuss all the details."

As usual, she acted like I did not exist, and in this case, I was grateful to not be a part of the conversation. Wynn's hand squeezed my thigh under the table, and I looked up at him in surprise. His eyes pleaded with me for a chance to explain, but I didn't care. He had already shattered my heart. No explanation could fix it.

The courses came and went, and I felt utterly numb the whole time. The conversation flowed around me, but I had no idea what they were saying. Wynn sat next to me, his entire body tense, and said very little. I should have listened to my gut and stayed in my room, the dinner was unbearable.

When had Wynn planned to tell me he was betrothed to someone else? Surely, he should have thought to mention it before he took me to bed. My hurt turned to rage the longer I sat and simmered in silence.

The meal came to a close, and as our final course was cleared away, I rose from my seat and gave a quick curtsy to the king and queen. "Your Majesties, it has been, as always, an honor to dine with you. May I please be excused?"

The king waved his hand in dismissal, and I curtsied again, turning to leave.

"I'll walk you back," Wynn said as he stood to leave with me.

"No, please. Stay and catch up with your betrothed. I can find my way back to my room on my own. I insist."

His eyes pleaded with me to reconsider, but I shook my head and made my way out of the room, my head held high, ignoring the tinkling laugh that followed me out the door.

※

I made it to my room before I broke. Once I crossed the threshold, I dissolved into a heaving, sobbing mess. I hadn't thought it possible to feel such pain and wretched disappointment. Part of me had thought there might have been a scenario where I could have stayed with Wynn, but now I knew there was no hope for us.

I needed to be under water. I kicked off my shoes and ripped at my dress, crystals scattering across the floor as it tore in my haste. More tears fell as I recalled Wynn's comment about taking me out of it himself, and I let out a sob. The stars must have cursed me for turning away from my duty. The humiliation and pain had to be my punishment for abandoning my matri-ritus and falling in love with an Adamas male.

Not wanting to bother Mari to prepare a bath, I filled the tub with icy water I summoned from outside and I submersed myself. The peace I'd usually found eluded me and I continued crying under the water. I needed to leave—immediately. Perhaps there was still time to salvage my future. Yes, I'd been gone far longer than I was supposed to have been, but I would find an excuse. More than likely, my family would be so relieved that I had returned, they would not examine my story too closely.

Firm in my resolve, I climbed out of the tub and dried off using a fluffy towel and my magic to pull the water from my hair before putting on my robe. Glancing at myself in the mirror over the sink, I saw a broken creature staring back. I grabbed a cloth to wipe away the smudged makeup, then washed the rest of my face and braided my hair back in preparation for my journey.

I entered the bedroom and inhaled a quick breath when I spotted Wynn seated before the fireplace, his head in his hands.

Faex, I did not want to see him again. The stars must truly be against me.

"We really must stop meeting like this," I said, my voice dripping with bitter sarcasm. "How fitting that my last night here would end like my first: with you, an unwanted guest, in my room."

Wynn's tortured gaze met mine as he wrung his hands. "Arianwen, please let me explain."

"Explain? How could you possibly explain? You turned me into your whore while betrothed to another!" I yelled. "You made me think you loved me and wanted a future with me even though you're promised to someone else! She's *delightful* by the way."

"My star . . ." Wynn pleaded.

"Do *not* call me that again. I am not *your* anything anymore," I spat.

Wynn leaned back as if I had struck him across the face with my words, then his eyes filled with anger as he rose to his feet. "You are not innocent in all this. You are just as betrothed as I am!" he said, raising his voice.

My mouth dropped open. "How dare you use me as an excuse! You knew from the start that I was unwillingly betrothed, and the fact that I came with you and stayed here meant that I chose you, not him!"

"Chose me?" A humorless laugh erupted from him. "You haven't chosen me. Every moment of every day, I have wondered to myself when you were going to ask me to take you home. You never chose me."

"You never asked! If it mattered that much to you, why didn't you say something? You *lied* to me, making me think I was the only one in your life." My voice broke as I wrapped my arms around myself.

"Why would I have told you about Katye if I knew you had no intention of staying? My parents have talked about a betrothal to her for years, but nothing has ever been official . . . until now." He paced in front of me.

"How could you make love to me while your heart belongs to another?"

Wynn stopped pacing, the intensity in his eyes holding me in place. "Katye has *never* had my heart. This marriage would be one of convenience to protect our family line. I need to produce an Adamas heir to carry on my family's legacy."

"So you were always planning on marrying her and, what? Keeping me as your mistress on the side?" I asked, aghast, backing away from him.

"I thought I had more time to tell you and figure this all out with you," he said, running his hands back through his hair in frustration.

"You're unbelievable! I thought I knew you, but you are a stars-damned liar."

"It's my duty!" he roared. "I am now an only child and have a responsibility to my family and the Court of Air!"

"Don't talk to me about duty," I said bitterly. "I abandoned my duty to stay here with you, and the stars have cursed me for it. The fact that you thought I would be willing to share you with another, be your mistress, means you never knew me at all."

"You would have my heart . . . Wouldn't that be enough?" His gaze tore through me, breaking me as he cornered me against the wall.

I stared up at him, wondering how our beautiful time together had turned into a nightmare. "Wynn . . . I—"

He interrupted me with a kiss, pushing me against the wall, his body hard and unforgiving. I froze, my anger rising again, and I pushed him away, breaking the kiss. Wynn backed off, his eyes a mirror of my own devastation. I hated him. I loved him. I wanted nothing more than to erase the last hours of my life. Was there any hope? Could we salvage us somehow? Could he change his mind?

I cried out in frustration and fused my lips back to his, wanting to replace the pain with pleasure. All of my hurt and anger turned to heated passion as our kisses became frantic. Why did I want him? I needed to hate him.

Wynn picked me up and carried me to the bed, only breaking our kiss to strip off his clothes. Our joining wasn't tender and loving but wild and desperate. There were no sweet words uttered between us, only moans and cries. After, we collapsed next to each other, our chests heaving, exhaustion claiming us. As I drifted off to sleep, all I could think was, "*It's not enough.*"

Hours later, I awoke tangled in Wynn's arms. Staring at the ceiling, the pain crashed over me in waves. I had to leave. The longer I stayed, the harder it would be for me to say no to him. There was no way I could share him with someone else, even if he claimed not to care for her. So after carefully extricating myself from him and the bed, I slipped into some clothes and silently gathered the rest of my things.

Wynn stirred and turned his head toward the window, the light of the moon and stars shining on his peaceful, shimmering face. My heart ached at the thought of never seeing him again, but I had to leave to survive with any pieces of my heart intact. After one last glance to try to memorize his face, I fled the palatium.

I raced down the familiar streets of Zephyria. Most of the lights were out, and there was very little movement, save for the few guards patrolling the streets. I knew how to avoid being seen as I made my way to the aeries. Being stopped wasn't a concern, as I had come to know most of the guards and they had all been kind to me, but I wanted to get as much of a head start on Wynn as possible. I didn't know if I'd be strong enough to resist if he asked me to stay.

Guilt trickled through me when I realized that I was leaving without saying goodbye to anyone. I thought of Wynn's cabala and Liisa. My broken heart shattered even more knowing I was losing them as well. I felt especially guilty about not letting anyone at the hospitium know I wasn't returning. Working there had given me such purpose, I only hoped that I would be able to continue my work as a healer when I returned home.

The aeries came into view, and I headed toward Luminara. While I still wasn't completely comfortable flying and had never flown on my own, I felt fairly safe with her, as she and I had come to an understanding. I found her harness and approached her, hoping she would let me near without Wynn present. Luminara tilted her head, peering at me with curiosity, but did not object as I got her ready to fly.

"Thank you for cooperating, Luminara." I spoke softly as I climbed onto her back and strapped myself in. She chirped in excitement, and before I knew it, we took off into the sky, soaring through the mountain passes. Clinging to her, the wind merciless without Wynn's magic barrier shielding me, I closed my eyes, trusting that Luminara would take me where I needed to go.

CHAPTER 42

HANG ON

AELLA

There were only six of us left. Jara—the last of the Aurum fae. Ona and Ramalia—the two remaining Aereus fae. Lewenne, Viera, and myself—the final three Argenti fae.

All I could do was cling to the hope that they would not kill us all. But deep down, I knew they'd never let all six of us walk out of there alive. If we didn't win the Matri-Ludus or "accidentally" die in the final event, Himmel had explained, new roles would be given to us as consolation. I knew it wouldn't come without cost, though.

Whether or not the Nameless Key was real, what they had done to Enneli and Zaita was proof that they possessed some kind of power to make us forget ourselves.

The thought of being forced to give up my name had been horrifying at first, but the more I'd considered it, the more appealing it had started to sound. Considering all the trauma we'd been through, the ability to forget the horrors we'd seen might have been a small mercy. Maybe it would have been better to forget. Live a life without all the burdens of the past. Without all the nightmares.

But I couldn't bear the thought of letting go of the memories of my family and Viera. They were the rocks I held onto that gave me the strength to keep fighting. I had to get through this alive, my memory intact. I had no other choice.

The center of the arena had been transformed into a steep mountain of obstacles with a cairn at the top which held a wedding ring. Nephos explained that the first to reach the top and place the ring on their finger would be hailed the winner and earn the coveted position as bride to the prince.

I imagined myself winning the Matri-Ludus, marrying Kaleidos. We'd get to be together and it would all be over. I'd finally be safe, and there would be no more death. Well, no more death until the next draft, and the next, and so on. If I won, it wouldn't change anything. I'd be sitting up in that box beside the prince during the next Matri-Ludus, watching the contests right alongside the Iris until Kaleidos had gained enough power to replace his father. The thought made me sick—how the Iris thrived on chaos, and destruction, how they reveled in our demise.

Nephos announced the commencement of the race, and we were off.

This is it. All I have to do is get through this. Survive one last trial.

I have escaped shadows.

I have resisted illusion.

I am stronger than I think I am.

I will not give up.

At first, it was almost as though I was flying. I ran with everything I had, my arms and legs propelling me forward. I needed as much of a head start as possible. That was the easy part. Soon, I'd be climbing the steep slope, scaling rocks, and avoiding pitfalls.

Once I started the incline, there was a noticeable change. I no longer felt weightless and free. My legs started to burn, my out-of-shape muscles crying out in pain. The lack of daily swimming and the light diet they'd had us on had led to an atrophy of my muscles and a noticeable loss in strength. But I needed to power through and not think about how much my body was screaming at me to stop.

The mountain loomed overhead, appearing much larger than it had before I'd started, and when I looked behind me, it seemed as though I'd hardly made any progress.

I lost my position in the lead as Ona and Ramalia scaled the mountain with such grace. Their powers made the land shift under their feet to help them and left the earth jagged and cracked in their wake. Now the rest of us would have to find other ways up and around the deep, splintered pits.

Jara took her time, conserving her strength, but she was an excellent climber, probably from traversing the mountainous trees of the Easthen Forest. The rest of the Argenti seemed to be struggling in the way that I was. But I continued on, repeating my mantras over and over again as I climbed.

I am stronger than I think I am.

I can do this.

I will do this.

I have come too far to give up now.

Ahead of me was a steep rock face. Afraid of losing more time, I decided to go straight over it rather than trying to find a way around. I'd climbed similar formations plenty of times around Iveria, so I felt confident it wouldn't be too hard. If I could scale this rock as quickly as I'd been able to climb the ones back home, it might give me the opportunity to get ahead. *I might still have a chance at winning this thing.* The only difference with this rock face was that I wouldn't have a cushion of water beneath me if I fell. *I will not fall.*

At first, it was manageable and I climbed with speed . . . until the stone began cutting into the soft palms of my hands. I had not seen the razor-sharp edges of the rock face before I'd chosen my path.

Halfway up, I dared a glance behind me again and caught sight of the steep drop. It seemed to lengthen and stretch, giving me a sinking sensation—as if simply by looking, it might have pulled me down into a fall. If I were to lose my grip, I'd go tumbling down, and the thought made my hands sweat which made it even more difficult to hang on.

I wiped my hand on my leather bodice, leaving smears of blood. The sight made me dizzy with fear, and I had to remind myself that I had not lost that much. *It always looks like more than it is.* My throat tightened and my eyes burned with tears as I clung to the side of the rock, my hands slick with sweat and blood.

The cloudless sky stretched above, and in the darkness, I could not see any stars. They had abandoned us.

A whimper threatened to escape as I realized I was stuck, frozen in place. I could barely hold on, let alone climb higher, and I did not think I could survive the fall. I took quick, short breaths as I began to panic which only added to the tingling and nervous sensations in my arms and legs. My muscles quivered, and I knew within moments that they would give out and I would fall. I would not survive the fall.

To my right, Jara scaled one of the gashes in the mountain left by the earth fae. As she passed me, our eyes met. I couldn't expect sympathy from her. We were in direct competition. She should have been happy to see me fall. Cursing under her breath, she made her way over to the top of the rock face I was attempting to climb.

Wordlessly, she reached down to help me, gripping my hand in hers. She gave me a good pull, and with the rest of my strength, I heaved myself over the final edge of rock, collapsing at the top to rest and catch my breath. My arms were weak and unsteady, and I was not sure what I would do if I had to scale another section like that.

Jara gave me an expression that said, "*We're even,*" then continued on.

I rested there, lying on my back, breathing heavily. I turned my head to take in my surroundings, looking for the rest of the contestants, and I spotted the Aereus ladies, Ona and Ramalia, so far ahead of everyone else—this challenge was no obstacle for them. Unless someone stopped them, one of them would win. Lewenne was catching up, stronger than she appeared, her motivation for revenge fueling her. She took a lengthier path, avoiding the large rock formation I'd just climbed. Viera, even with the prince's favor, struggled in the back.

Thoughts of doubt stormed my mind like an unwelcome guest, making me want to give up. I would never catch up to Ona and Ramalia. I could never regain the strength needed to finish the race. I was never going to win the Matri-Ludus. What was the point in still trying? If I just waited for the competition to end, I might at least stand a chance at surviving.

I looked back again only to see Viera fighting to continue her climb. Even in last place, she continued. She would never give up.

I have come too far to give up now.

I blinked back tears and willed myself to continue on, immediately regretting my rest because it had made getting up and starting again that much harder. I wasn't even a third of the way up yet, but I forced myself to roll over and pushed myself back up to stand.

As my muscles strained to climb, my mind fought with almost as much fervor.

I can do this.

I will do this.

I have come too far to give up now.

This was bigger than me. I needed to remember that. I had to remember what I was fighting for, who I was fighting for. Images of my sister, Mila, flashed before me. My little sister could be drafted and end up with the fate of so many who had fallen in competitions.

I thought of Ulli and saw my sister in her place, being torn down and fed upon by the shadow fangs.

Enough.

I'd had enough.

I would never have a chance to do anything about it if I didn't keep fighting.

A scream drew my attention up ahead, but a spray of rocks and debris descended upon me, forcing me to curl up against the side of the mountain, protecting my head with my arms. I dared a peek, only to see a bronze body hurtling down toward us.

"Ramalia!" Ona screamed as her friend tumbled down the side of the mountain like a rag doll.

The roar of the crowd reverberated through the air, thousands of feet thundering against the stands. Their jeers and rallying cries rained down upon us like fuel for hounds in a race.

My eyes widened as I helplessly watched Viera try to maneuver herself out of the way, but with the steep terrain, she had few options. The moment stretched as if we were half-frozen in time, moving in slow motion.

I witnessed the moment Viera realized she was stuck. The fear and then the acceptance. It happened in the blink of an eye. She looked up to the heavens, then spread her arms out wide right before Ramalia barreled into her, and the two went crashing down.

I couldn't move as I stared, watching my best friend tumble down the hill, arms and legs a tangle of unnatural angles. Viera and Ramalia plummeted down the mountain, coming to a halt at the bottom. Their bloodied and broken bodies lay motionless at the base of the slope.

I wanted to scream, to cry, to throw myself down the mountain too, but I stared, frozen in disbelief. Waiting for a sign that she was okay. Waiting for her to move, to blink her eyes, to groan, anything. But deep down, I knew she could not have survived such a fall.

Blood pooled around them as they lay there, bodies twisted and destroyed. If they were to live, they would need immediate medical attention. Attention they would not receive.

My disbelief turned into rage. The sheer injustice of it—Viera, the one person among us who had unquestionably deserved to live, a radiant beacon of light, extinguished so abruptly. A well of emotion burned and writhed inside my chest, straining to be let out.

I would kill them all for what they had done.

A strong wind picked up overhead and storm clouds rolled in. Fierce and mighty, in contrast to my waning physical strength, the clouds crackled with power.

The arena went silent.

The back of my neck prickled, and I knew what I had to do. *It might be my only chance.* And if I did not act, more would die, of that I was certain. I could not stand by and let this continue if I had the power to intervene. I could end this. I had to at least try. *For Viera.*

I closed my eyes, remembering my friend, seeing her as she had been: full of life and light and strength. I thought of her as she'd encouraged me and challenged me those past weeks. How she'd never given up hope and always believed in me.

That was the last bit of strength I needed. Even in death, Viera gave me that final surge, filling me with resolute power. I stood tall.

Everyone—the crowd, the contestants, the king—seemed to stop what they were doing to watch as I reached one hand up to the sky. My hair floated up around me. Every nerve in my body tingled with a sort of fizzing, static sensation. The air swirled around me, picking up dirt and rock, spinning so fast that it concealed me from sight. Then, in an instant, it shot out, spraying into the stands, aimed directly for the Iris.

The hurtling swarm of jagged debris killed hundreds of Iris spectators upon impact. The rest screamed and scrambled over themselves to flee for the exits.

When the debris cleared, I was hovering six feet off the ground, holding a bolt of lightning. I scanned the box for Kal. My hope was in his hands. If he were to take the throne, he would stop the madness. He would put an end to the bloody and violent Matri-Ludus competitions. He'd have to. In my heart, I knew, given the opportunity, he would.

But he was gone.

I turned my attention to King Solanos who stared right back at me. For a moment, a flicker of fear flashed in his eyes, but then the twist of a smile curved the corner of his lips. His defiant grin pushed me over the edge, and I aimed the bolt of lightning right for his heart.

"For Viera!" I cried out and let loose.

The lightning shot through the air at blazing speed, straight for the king, and in a flash, there was a blinding and deafening explosion which blasted me off my feet in a wave. My vision tunneled into darkness.

Chapter 43

Aftershock

AELLA

I awoke to a kick in the stomach and muffled voices. My ears were ringing, and I couldn't understand what was happening around me. I blinked my eyes open. They burned—the feeling of tiny grains of sand swimming under my eyelids made it hard to keep them open. My mouth tasted like coins. I lifted my head slightly, but my body ached and forced me back down to the ground. It felt like I'd been trampled. I hissed in a breath as I forced myself to try again. I could make out that I was still in the arena and Iris guards were surrounding me. Crude laughter echoed around me, then another kick to my diaphragm left me gasping for air.

Rough hands picked me up and deposited me onto a stretcher. My body was stiff and achy, the tumultuous ride down the hill torturous as if I were a piece of seaweed being tossed against the rocks. All of my muscles were spent, leaving me unable to fight back.

It took me a moment to remember what had happened, but when I recalled the fear in the king's eyes before I'd thrown the lightning bolt, a smile stretched across my face. *He must be dead.* He had to be. *There is no way he could have stopped that lightning bolt.*

But why was I being handled so forcefully? Where was the prince?

"Kaleidos!" I gasped out. "I need . . . to see . . . the prince!"

The males handling me laughed and continued carrying me.

I fought to ask them again, but, in reply, I received a blow to the head, knocking me into unconsciousness.

△

I woke up again as I was being dropped onto the floor of a dark, windowless cell.

"I need to see Prince Kaleidos!" I said with as much strength as I could muster. Again I was ignored, and the heavy iron door slammed shut with a clang.

The floor was damp mud, and the air was thick and stifling. My breathing picked up in a panic as reality set in. *Surely the prince will come for me.* I just needed to wait. He would come and get me out of there. I tried calming myself down. I tried to tell myself everything was going to be okay. But my mind kept replaying Viera's face as she'd realized she could not escape her fate. Over and over again, I saw her mangled body at the bottom of the hill.

Nothing would ever be okay again.

Tears rolled down my cheeks. My throat ached, and I heaved as I sobbed. Curled up on my side, I held my knees to my chest. I cried because there was nothing I could do to bring her back. I'd failed her. My truest friend. The one person who had always had my back. I'd failed to protect her. And now she was gone. Nothing mattered without her. Nothing. Nothing. Nothing. Nothing. Nothing. And when the darkness closed in around me, I let myself fall into it.

△

"Wake up, girl!" came a familiar, cruel voice.

I blinked open my swollen eyes. Himmel stood at the entrance to the cell with a pinched expression. Two royal guards stood right outside the door.

"We can do this the easy way or the fun way. Tell me, girl, which will it be?"

I was too defeated to respond. I had lost all motivation. Nothing mattered anymore.

Himmel recognized the resigned expression on my face and frowned. "Very well. Remove your clothes."

I didn't move.

"The fun way it is." She smiled. "Guards!"

The two Iris guards stalked into the room. Grabbing me by the wrists, they hurled me off the floor, and each pinned an arm against the wall.

"If you don't cooperate, my dear, there are worse things you can endure than dying . . ." She strutted slowly toward me. "And these boys wouldn't mind inflicting them upon you." She forced my drooped head back with a rigid grip on my jaw to make me look at her.

I stared into her cold, soulless eyes. I wanted to tell her that I didn't care, that nothing they could do would compare to the pain of losing Viera. I almost welcomed the idea of torture as a means of distraction.

Himmel gave a signal and the two guards released me and stepped out of the cell. My wrists seared in pain from where they'd rammed them against the ragged stone wall.

"Remove your clothes," Himmel repeated, "or I'll have them skin you alive."

For lack of will, I almost took her up on her threat. But when a tortured scream echoed through the dungeons, I realized I wasn't as strong as I'd thought. There was still more they could take from me. A lot more. And that spurred me into action. So I untied my sandals, then methodically began removing the muddy layers of leather and fabric pasted onto my skin with sweat, dirt, and blood.

Once I was bare with nothing but my tangle of long, black hair left to cloak me, Himmel began inspecting every inch of my skin. It took me a moment to realize what she was doing.

As she pulled my hair back and inspected my neck, a small inhale alerted me that she had discovered my birthmark.

"There you are!" Himmel whispered, then she tsked. "And to think you've been hiding right under our noses all this time. The king will want to see this."

"Kaleidos?" I asked.

"Oh, you didn't think you actually killed King Solanos, did you? Foolish girl. We are not so *easy* to kill." Himmel marched out of my cell, and the door clanked shut behind her.

A roar came out of me unlike any I'd ever screamed before. I screamed and I screamed until I had nothing left in me. Until my throat was dry as bones and my vocal cords were so worn out that they could no longer make sound.

The king is still alive.

Chapter 22

The Plea

Arianwen

Full of trepidation, I approached the entrance to the palatium. Before I could talk myself out of it, I pounded as loud as I could on the doors, hoping I wouldn't be turned away. They opened soundlessly, and an aged Emil greeted me.

"Miss? Can I help you?" he asked in confusion. "Do you realize what time it is?"

"I'm sorry. I know it's late, but I have to speak with the prince," I pleaded.

His eyebrows rose up to his hairline as he stared at me incredulously. "The prince? Miss, you will need to come back tomorrow and request an audience with the royal family."

"Please," I begged. "I'm already running out of time. I have an urgent request for Prince Wynn. Don't you recognize me, Emil?"

His brow furrowed in confusion before a light of recognition filled his eyes. "Miss Arianwen?" he asked.

"Yes! Emil, please. I wouldn't have come if it wasn't a matter of life or death. I need to speak with the prince."

"He's the king now," Emil said, his eyes downcast. "This isn't a good time. King Volare recently passed, and the royal family is in mourning."

"I'm so sorry to hear that. May the stars bring him peace . . ." I wrung my hands together, unsure of what else to say.

Emil started to close the door, but I stuck a hand out to stop it, my eyes pleading. "I know you never cared much for me, but if you could please tell the king that I need to speak with him urgently, I would be forever in your debt."

Emil looked at me with pity. "I'm sorry, miss, try again tomorrow. I will let the king know you stopped by." The door closed with a resounding thud of finality.

"Faex!" I shouted as I slumped down against it.

He could have at least tried! What if I'm too late?

Thick tears started falling down my cheeks as I hugged my knees to my chest, trying to hold myself together.

It's going to be all right. I will try again tomorrow.

Where in the stars will I sleep tonight? Will anyone even be willing to see me after the way I left?

Get yourself together, Ari. You will figure this out.

Wiping my eyes, I stood to my feet and started walking in the direction of Liisa's apartment. Maybe the stars would save me and she wouldn't turn me away.

I'd made it a few paces when I heard my name uttered by a voice I had never thought I'd hear again. My eyes closed in relief, and I took a deep breath before turning around to face my past for the first time in twenty-five years.

"Wynn . . ." I whispered. Then, remembering myself and the news Emil had shared, I dropped into a curtsy and said a little louder, "Your Majesty."

He stared at me as if he were seeing a ghost. His fair skin was impossibly fairer, his eyes—the icy blue I remembered—filled with sadness. My heart started racing, memories of our brief time together rushing to the forefront of my mind. There in front of me was the source of my greatest heartbreak but also one of my greatest joys.

Wynn cleared his throat, his eyes glistening with unshed tears, and said, "What are you doing here, Arianwen?"

"Your Maj—"

"Stop. I'll always be Wynn to you."

Clutching my hands in front of me, I looked at him with pleading eyes. "Wynn, I came here to beg for your help. I can't lose her. Please. You must help her escape."

He took a step closer to me. "Help who?"

Reaching deep within to gather all my courage, I straightened my shoulders and replied, "Our daughter."

He stepped away from me, his face full of shock and hurt as if I had slapped him, reminding me of the night I had left. I flinched as the painful memories swept over me.

His voice deepened into a growl. "I don't have a daughter. Surely, if I did, you would have had the courtesy to tell me before now."

Tears sprung to my eyes. "I'm so sorry I never told you, but you chose *her*, and I wasn't going to be your mistress. I had no idea when I left—"

"You could have found a way to tell me! I had the right to know I was a father!"

Anger mixed with my regret as I raised my voice to match his. "She has a wonderful father—Verus has always treated her like his own blood."

"So why are you here asking for my help?" he sneered. "Let Verus help her."

"Don't you think he would if he could? The Iris have her! She was drafted, but I know in my heart that she is not safe. She carries your element but has never learned how to wield it, and if they discover her secret . . . I think it's her. She's the one the prophecy spoke of. She is marked by the stars."

Wynn's face blanched, his eyes full of fear. "No . . ."

"If they harm or kill her . . . I couldn't live with myself if I didn't at least try to save her somehow, but I can't do it without you. Please . . . help me."

Wynn shook his head in despair. "No one has ever attempted a rescue out of Prisma, it is far too dangerous."

My shoulders slumped in defeat. "I should have tried to send her away, but I never thought they'd choose her . . . Faex, what have I done?"

Wynn ran his fingers through his hair, the gesture so familiar, it hurt. Returning had been a mistake but one I'd had to make for the sake of my daughter.

"I cannot promise you anything, but I will gather my cabala and try to reach out to contacts I have near Prisma. Perhaps we can mount a rescue, but there is no guarantee."

I sucked in a breath, a glimmer of hope rising within me. "Thank you, Wynn. You have no idea how much this means to me." I wrapped my arms around myself. The adrenaline that had been coursing through my veins had dissipated and left me weak.

"Arianwen, you look exhausted. Please come and rest while I make arrangements." Wynn gestured toward the palatium. He closed his eyes, running his fingers through his hair again. "We are not done talking. I am *so* angry with you for keeping this from me! After everything—"

"I tried to do what was best for her," I interrupted. Raising my chin, I rolled my shoulders back and stared at him in defiance, holding my hand up, the mark visible. "You guaranteed that I could never tell her about you or where she came from."

His face was stricken with regret. He opened his mouth as if to speak but closed it instead, his lips forming a thin line. He offered me his arm, but as I stepped toward him to take it, I stumbled and almost fell to my knees.

Before I could protest, Wynn swept me up into his arms, a sad smile on his face. "There is much I regret about those days but never you. I just wish you would have gotten word to me. Everything would be different."

Unsure of how to respond, I stayed silent as he carried me in through the halls of the still-familiar palatium. I found myself relaxing despite myself, his hold familiar and safe, his scent a reminder of days past. When he set me on my feet in front of the door to my old chambers, he asked, "What is she like?" His eyes were full of unshed tears.

"She's beautiful, stubborn, and strong. Her eyes are a darker shade of blue than yours, but I can still see you looking at me when she smiles."

"What's her name?"

"Aella."

If you enjoyed this book, please leave us a review!
Thank you so much for reading.
We hope you join us for the conclusion of Aella and Arianwen's story in Book 2! Coming Fall 2024

Acknowledgements

First and foremost, we would like to thank God for the gifts of creativity and storytelling, and our families for all of their love, patience, and support.

To our children and husbands, you have been the unsung heroes of this journey, enduring subpar dinners when our creative streaks demanded more attention than our culinary skills. Our houses may have been a little messier, but this book wouldn't have been possible without you cheering us on as we stepped into something brand new.

To our incredible developmental/copy/line editor, Rachel. We were so incredibly nervous going into this process, and you have been nothing but amazing and supportive each and every step of the way. You're not just an editor, but you have also become a friend, and we're so grateful that Bookstagram brought us together. Your excitement and belief in this story encouraged us to keep moving forward during moments we felt like quitting. We salute you for putting up with two opinionated sisters and double the trouble of interpreting our distinct voices and writing styles.

To Justin and Holly, our very first readers, thank you so much for loving our story and cheering us on. Your helpful feedback and enthusiasm made us believe we could actually do this! Seeing and hearing your reactions was priceless.

To our incredible Beta Team, Christina Allen, Jaclyn McMillan, Karrie W., Sophie, and Suz, our book would not be where it is without all of your incredible feedback. Getting to experience your reactions and love for the book fueled us to keep going. Thanks also to Rachel for organizing and helping facilitate the entire beta reading process. Honorable mentions to the beta cats who helped with edits: Billy, Binx, Boogie, Marv, Obie, Rat, and Todd, to name a few.

To our friends who never shut up about the book, who have helped us work up the courage to believe in ourselves and put ourselves out there. We couldn't have done it without you all or, God forbid, the coffee!

To Vanessa, you have been such an incredible friend. You were one of the first authors to show us how welcoming and supportive the indie author community can be. Thank you for believing in us and cheering us on.

To Midnight Tide Publishing, thank you for bringing us in and making us feel like part of the family. We are so incredibly honored that our debut found its home with you. Being part of such a fun-loving, helpful community of writers has been invaluable.

To the Bookstagram community, thank you for opening your arms to us and celebrating our debut. We are so grateful for all the new friends and connections we have made.

To our readers, thank you for taking a chance on us. We hope you find as much magic within these pages as we did writing them.

Our acknowledgements wouldn't be complete without taking a moment to recognize each other. Our creative journey through this book has been filled with laughter, tears, and more cups of coffee than we ought to admit. Writing together has been an adventure that has brought us closer than ever, even while living states apart. While we have always shared our love for fantasy, we've now discovered the magic of storytelling and the limitless possibilities of our shared dreams. Without each other's faith, encouragement, and relentless commitment to our vision, this book would never have become a reality.

To the magic that is sisterhood!

About the Authors

Meet Stephanie Combs and Valerie Rivers, a dynamic sister duo who share an enthusiasm for writing and storytelling.

Stephanie's passion for literature ignited at a young age, shaping her into an insatiable reader. Her love for writing began with crafting short fictional tales and poetry during her childhood—a spark that only intensified as she delved into writing stories for her college newspaper while pursuing a degree in Broadcast Journalism. Stephanie's sense of humor shines through her writing, infusing her work with witty banter and endearing characters. She resides in Maryland with her musical husband and four rambunctious children. When she's not sneaking in a writing session, you can find her nose stuck in a book or baking goodies for the family.

Valerie resides in sunny South Florida with her pilot husband and three children. Not your typical fantasy author, she brings a fresh perspective to the genre due to her unique background as an artist and intensive care nurse. In her free time, when she isn't writing, she's either working on her next art project obsession or lost in the landscape of her imagination. Embracing her inherent creativity, she weaves fantasy worlds and crafts captivating narratives that transport readers to breathtaking realms of wonder.

You can find more on their website at:
silverflamebooks.com

Follow them on Instagram:
Stephanie - @stephdevourerofbooks
Valerie - @valerieriversauthor

More From Midnight Tide

Through the Wicked Wood by Kristen R. Moore

"What is more fearsome? The monster that stands before you? Or the one that lives within you."

Elora Leigh is in hiding.

As an Enchantress, she has spent the last several years running not only from a king that hunts magick, but from the guilt and grief of losing her mother.

Content in her solitude, Elora's life among the trees is disrupted when she crosses paths with the most unlikely of allies.

A thief determined to keep his village afloat, Sorin will do whatever it takes to provide for his people, especially now that the lands have been hit by Mother Gaia's fury. Fishing has ceased, crops won't grow, and the animals they've relied on for food have mostly disappeared leaving him desperate for a change.

When Elora and Sorin discover a common thirst for justice in the Kingdom of Valebridge, they set out on a journey to fend for those who cannot fend for themselves and take back power from the corrupt king.

But the deeper they go through the Wicked Woods, the more Elora realizes those she thought she could trust may not be who she thinks they are.

Family secrets, ancient magick, a kindling romance, and tangles of lies begin to reveal themselves. Elora must make a decision; trust this stranger to help defeat those harnessing magick in the Kingdom, or let the demons of her past push her back into hiding and away from who she was born to be.

Through the Wicked Wood is an adult fantasy romance and intended for readers over 18 years of age. Please check content warnings as some material may be sensitive for some readers.

Available Now

Made in the USA
Middletown, DE
06 April 2025